P9-BZS-308

**"I'm taking the midnight shift with Noah. If danger strikes, it will probably be then."**

So Seth would be with Noah. Rebecca had to admit that knowing this made her feel a little better. "Look, I don't mean to be a pain, Mr. Armstrong, but these are my children. I have a right to know that they are safe. Or at least as safe as you can make them."

He nodded. "I agree you do have that right. But you have to trust me to keep them as safe as I possibly can."

Did she trust him? No, why should she? Rebecca told herself she didn't really know the man at all. Still, Pony Express superintendent Mr. Bromley trusted him, so what other choice did she have? She'd have to try to trust Seth Armstrong to watch after her boys.

How did a mother release that kind of trust to a stranger? She reminded herself that to keep her family together, she'd have to try.

# Rhonda Gibson
## and

*USA TODAY* Bestselling Author

# Stacy Henrie

# Pony Express Courtship
# &
# The Express Rider's Lady

**LOVE INSPIRED**
INSPIRATIONAL ROMANCE

If you purchased this book without a cover you should be aware that this book is stolen property. It was reported as "unsold and destroyed" to the publisher, and neither the author nor the publisher has received any payment for this "stripped book."

# LOVE INSPIRED®
## INSPIRATIONAL ROMANCE

Recycling programs for this product may not exist in your area.

ISBN-13: 978-1-335-50316-9

Pony Express Courtship and The Express Rider's Lady

Copyright © 2022 by Harlequin Books S.A.

Pony Express Courtship
First published in 2016. This edition published in 2022.
Copyright © 2016 by Rhonda Gibson

The Express Rider's Lady
First published in 2016. This edition published in 2022.
Copyright © 2016 by Stacy Henrie

All rights reserved. No part of this book may be used or reproduced in any manner whatsoever without written permission except in the case of brief quotations embodied in critical articles and reviews.

This is a work of fiction. Names, characters, places and incidents are either the product of the author's imagination or are used fictitiously. Any resemblance to actual persons, living or dead, businesses, companies, events or locales is entirely coincidental.

This edition published by arrangement with Harlequin Books S.A.

For questions and comments about the quality of this book, please contact us at CustomerService@Harlequin.com.

Love Inspired
22 Adelaide St. West, 41st Floor
Toronto, Ontario M5H 4E3, Canada
www.LoveInspired.com

**Printed in U.S.A.**

# CONTENTS

**Rhonda Gibson** lives in Oklahoma with her husband, James. She has two children and four beautiful grandchildren. Reading is something Rhonda has enjoyed her whole life and writing stems from that love. When she isn't writing or reading, she enjoys gardening and making cards for her friends and family. Rhonda hopes her writing will entertain, encourage and bring others closer to God.

### Books by Rhonda Gibson

### Love Inspired Historical

*Pony Express Courtship*
*Pony Express Hero*
*Pony Express Christmas Bride*
*Pony Express Mail-Order Bride*
*Pony Express Special Delivery*
*Baby on Her Doorstep*
*Wagon Train Wedding*

Visit the Author Profile page at LoveInspired.com for more titles.

# PONY EXPRESS COURTSHIP

Rhonda Gibson

A man's heart deviseth his way:
but the Lord directeth his steps.
—*Proverbs* 16:9

This book is dedicated to the men
who rode the Pony Express routes.

To my husband, James Gibson,
my best friend and strongest supporter.

And to my Heavenly Father,
who helps me to reach my dreams.

# Chapter One

*Dove Creek, Wyoming*
*February 1860*

"What were you thinking?" Rebecca Young demanded of her youngest son, Benjamin. She tossed the water bucket to the side. Her body shook as fearful images built in her mind. "You could have been killed." The acrid smell of smoke in the early-morning air almost choked her as she fought for control. Benjamin might be adopted, but she loved him as much as she loved her daughter, Joy. The thought of losing him in a fire tore at her heart, leaving her feeling raw.

Black soot covered his young face and tears traced dirty tracks down his cheeks. He coughed, echoing coughs from others around them. The eight-year-old boy wrung his hands and shook his head from side to side. "I didn't mean for it to happen, Ma."

Fear and anger warred for control of her emotions. If Jacob hadn't seen the flames tearing through the barn and gotten Benjamin out, her youngest son would have died in the fire. She couldn't—she heaved a deep sigh—no, she *wouldn't* let her fear take the sting out of her scolding. "But it did happen, Benjamin. How many times have I told you not to take a lantern into the barn?"

The tears increased and dripped off his quivering chin. Big brandy-colored eyes met her gaze. Fear filled them. Was it fear of her, or the fact that he could have died in the fire? "I'm sorry, Ma." His voiced choked; he threw his arms around her waist and buried his head against her.

Rebecca ran her hands down his thin arms then embraced him tightly, unmindful of the black soot being smeared against the white of her apron.

Her gaze moved from one to the other of the six young men who stood in the yard. Her other adopted sons. Rebecca barely held back the tears, her heart winging a prayer of thanks that none of them were hurt putting out the flames.

Her oldest son, twenty-year-old Jacob, stared morosely at what used to be their barn.

The second oldest son, nineteen-year-old Andrew, kneeled on one knee at the edge of the clearing. He most likely desired privacy when he prayed, but that was a luxury big families couldn't afford. How she'd love to join him and thank the Lord for His protection. Each of the boys had learned early on from her deceased husband, John, to pray about everything. She couldn't help but be proud of Andrew for knowing where their help came from. Clayton, who'd just had his nineteenth birthday, dropped his water bucket, pure frustration lining his young face, and stomped back to the house. Rebecca knew he tried hard to hold in the pent-up fear and hopelessness that the burning barn caused and made a mental note to go to him as soon as she could.

Eighteen-year-old Thomas and eighteen-year-old Philip stood side by side, eyes darting back and forth, watching everything as it unfolded. The boys were best friends and had vowed to always stick together even before she and John adopted them.

Twelve-year-old Noah, the newest member of her family, looked ready to bolt. He stood frozen, motionless, waiting for what she would say or do next. He'd only been with her a couple of months and wasn't sure about anything yet. He reminded her of a hungry dog— ready to fight if needed, but hoping for love and a little food to fill his belly.

The morning sun shone brightly over all of them now. But when the fire had first been detected, it had still been dark. Her boys had rushed to put out the flames, but they'd been no match for the heat radiating from the inferno. A heap of smoking, blackened timber filled the spot where the barn once stood. Thankfully, her five-year-old daughter, Joy, hadn't come out to assist.

If John had been here, this never would have happened. Once more the loss of her husband struck home. How often in the past eight months had she wished that he was still alive? Too often.

After twelve years of marriage it was hard to believe he was gone. The boy sobbing into her apron drew her thoughts away from the past and her sorrow. She stroked Benjamin's light brown hair.

An unfamiliar cough sounded and then a man cleared his throat. "I hate to disturb you, ma'am."

She had all but forgotten the stranger who had raced into the yard and jumped in to help put out the blaze. Rebecca released Benjamin and turned toward the man. "I'm sorry, Mr...." She waited for him to fill in his name.

"Seth Armstrong."

Rebecca wiped her hands on her apron. "Thank you, Mr. Armstrong, for stopping by to help put out the fire." Thanks to his help, the fire had been subdued faster than it normally would have taken, but not before they'd lost the barn and everything in it.

"I was happy to help, Mrs. Young," Seth answered, pulling her from her musings.

How did he know her name?

Before she could ask, Jacob barked out orders to the other boys. "Andrew, you and Philip go gather up the horses that arrived yesterday, put them in the training corral and feed them. Thomas, milk the cow and go get Clayton, tell him I said to find Brownie and Snowball and hitch up the wagon. We're going to town for lumber." He watched as the boys scrambled to do as he said.

"What do you want me to do?" Noah asked quietly.

Jacob walked over to the twelve-year-old and bent down to eye level. In a softer voice he asked, "Would you take Beni into the house and give him a good washing?"

Noah nodded. He walked over to Benjamin. "Come on, Beni. Jacob says we have to get you cleaned up."

The two boys left the yard and Noah had planted his hand firmly on Benjamin's shoulder.

Jacob stood once more and came to stand beside Rebecca. She was very proud of her oldest son. John's death had hit him the hardest and he'd taken to heart her husband's last words—to take care of the family.

Her gaze returned to Seth Armstrong. He was a big man with deep green eyes and black hair. His shoulders were wide. And his hair touched his collar. Rebecca wondered if she was in some sort of shock. What did it matter what the stranger looked like? More important, how did he know her? Did her deceased husband owe him money? She prayed not. Even though John had left her secure, she didn't have room in her budget to pay out extra money.

As if sensing her confusion, Jacob asked, "What can we do for you, Mr. Armstrong?"

His green eyes met Jacob's. "Well, I suppose you could show me to my room." He turned his attention back on Rebecca. "I'm the Pony Express station keeper that Mr. Bromley told you would be arriving." He walked back to his horse and pulled down a carpetbag from the back of his saddle.

If John hadn't already signed the contract to use their farm as a home station, Rebecca would have been tempted to call the whole thing off. But the boys needed the extra income and she didn't want them to be forced to leave the farm to find other jobs. If it was in her power she'd keep them together as a family for as long as possible. Now she simply had to trust in the Lord and pray that everything worked out.

When John had told Rebecca of the Pony Express

and how Mr. Bromley, the Pony Express ramrod, would be by to tell them more about what their part in it entailed, Rebecca never dreamed she'd be singlehandedly dealing with this many changes. Now that Seth Armstrong was here, she felt even more alone. Her farm was to be the home station and her boys Pony Express riders.

The original plan had been for John to be the one running the station, not a stranger. But once Mr. Bromley learned of John's death, he had told her he'd be sending a station keeper to replace him. She'd suggested Jacob, but the route superintendent feared Jacob's brothers wouldn't listen and obey him like they would someone else, so he'd sent this new man.

"Mr. Bromley sent you?" Jacob's question was for Seth, but he looked to Rebecca for answers, not the man who had just claimed to be the new boss on the farm. Confusion and hurt laced the depths of his eyes.

Rebecca's heart sank knowing he wondered why she hadn't told him of this latest development. She nodded. "Yes. Mr. Bromley came out last week when you and the others were fixing fences in the back pasture. When he found out that John had passed, he insisted we needed a station keeper. I planned to tell you and the other boys soon." She hadn't expected the replacement to arrive a week later and had thought she'd have more time to break it gently to Jacob.

Jacob nodded, but a thin veil of hardness covered his eyes. He turned his gaze back to Seth. "I'll show you where you can put your things."

Rebecca watched them head to the bunkhouse. She heard Jacob ask, "You got any papers on you? Proving you are who you say you are?" His young voice held strength, a strength she'd leaned on too heavily in the past few months.

Seth Armstrong chuckled. "Sure have. Right here in my bag. I'll show them to you and Mrs. Young, once I get settled in." He pulled his horse behind him as Jacob led the way to the bunkhouse.

She turned and looked at the smoldering pile of embers that used to be her barn. Gone. In just a few minutes the barn had burned to the ground. What had Benjamin been doing out here? Especially in the early hours of the morning?

Rebecca stepped closer to the rubble. She sighed. It looked as if she would have to dip into her funds to rebuild the barn. Jacob would have to ask for credit from the lumber mill and she'd add the nails to her growing tab at the general store. Once they had the total cost of the barn and all the supplies they'd need, she'd get the money from the bank and pay both men. She'd learned shortly after John's death that if she didn't deal with the men in this manner, they'd take advantage of her and she ended up paying more than what she'd actually owed. That wasn't going to happen again.

As she walked back to the house, Rebecca called to the new Pony Express station keeper and Jacob. "Breakfast will be ready in half an hour. Don't make me wait."

The desire to call out to Mr. Armstrong to return to where he came from pulled at her vocal cords. She would like nothing more than to have the peace and quiet of her farm restored. But Rebecca knew that wasn't possible. If she wanted to keep her family together, then the Pony Express would have to be a big part of it, and that included Seth Armstrong.

Seth laid his bag on the bed. Jacob had taken him to the small room off to the left-hand side of the bunkhouse. It contained a bed, a side table and a chest with a washbasin on the top. A wooden box hung above the trunk and held a razor and hand mirror. An adjoining door led to the remainder of the bunkhouse, giving him two methods of entry.

"I'll get my things out of here after breakfast." Jacob stood with his hand on the doorknob.

Seth hoped his words rang true as he said, "I hate to put you out."

Jacob shook his head. "The other boys will be more comfortable with me than you in the other room with them."

"I'm sure they will." Seth took his Bible out of the bag and laid it down on the table.

Jacob studied the book as if it was a snake. "You read that often?"

"Every night."

The boy nodded. "I'll leave you to settle in and go check on the others." He didn't wait for an answer, but simply walked out the door.

Seth looked down at the worn brown leather of his Bible. It was the same one that his father had preached from and studied over for many hours. Jacob had acted as if it was poisonous, or might inflict harm, instead of being a balm that offered soothing words to a troubled soul. Had he been placed here to help the boy find his way to God? He doubted Jacob would welcome him in that area of his life any more than he welcomed him now as the new Pony Express station keeper.

He moved to the only window in the bunkhouse and looked out at the burned barn. Smoke still spiraled upward to the sky. Building a new barn would help him get to know the young men who were now his charges. Seth planned on staying just long enough to teach them how to survive the trail they were soon to be riding and then he'd continue on to search for Charlotte, his lost mail-order bride.

His thoughts went to the woman who had promised to be his bride. The last letter he'd received from her said she was taking the first stage out of California and should arrive in a few weeks, only she'd never showed. After his grandmother's death, Seth had left his home in St. Joseph, Missouri, and begun searching for Charlotte. He was a man of his word and he intended to keep his promise to his grandmother. He'd find Charlotte and marry her. He knew he wouldn't fall in love. His mother had taught him that to love someone meant getting hurt and he'd never go through what his father had. Never.

He doubted Charlotte had come to any harm. Her letters had indicated she didn't want to get married any more than he did, but the girl had no other choices at the time. She'd been up-front in her reasons for answering his advertisement—lack of money and nowhere else to turn. He'd been honest, too, telling her he was trying to keep his last promise to his now-deceased grandmother. He'd also told her he didn't believe in falling in love, as it only led to heartbreak and death. His own mother had deserted him and his father when he was a child. No, he wouldn't open himself up to that kind of hurt again. He'd keep his promise to get married. He'd assured his grandmother he wouldn't be alone after she died and he'd keep that promise, one way or another.

Unfortunately, shortly after leaving St. Joseph, a couple of road bandits had relieved him of his money. Thankfully, with some quick thinking and the fact that Sam, his horse, had been faster than the men, he'd gotten away.

Needing money, he'd returned to St. Joseph and signed on with the Pony Express. As the station keeper it was his job to swear in the boys and get them ready for the job ahead of them. But once he earned enough money, Seth planned on continuing his search for Charlotte. Taking a deep breath, he left the confines of his new room and walked outside just as Mrs. Young began to ring the dinner bell.

Its loud clang filled the yard and got the attention of all the boys. She looked to him and nodded. He returned the nod and headed toward the house. Rebecca Young looked as if she was in her early twenties, and from what he'd seen this morning, she seemed to rely on her oldest child to run the farm.

The boys were older than he'd thought they'd be. But from the looks of them, they would all make good riders. Mr. Bromley had told him they were just a bunch of farm boys and would need a lot of training. That was why Seth had arrived at the farm in early February instead of closer to his scheduled date of April third. He was happy to see the Pony Express horses had arrived safely. One of the boys closed the corral gate and headed up to the house.

Was he ready for all this responsibility? His gaze moved to the young men as they hurried to the house for breakfast. Mrs. Young stood on the porch hugging each of them before they went inside. She was a pretty little thing with a lot on her slender shoulders. He silently reminded himself not to get attached to any of the Young family, especially Rebecca Young.

He had to find Charlotte. Even though he had never met her, he still felt responsible for her and he wouldn't break his promise to his grandmother.

Rebecca wasn't sure she was up to the changes about to take place on her farm and in her home. Already things were different. Breakfast proved to be a quiet affair. Everyone seemed lost in their own thoughts or afraid to speak lest something worse occurred. Seth Armstrong made several attempts at polite conversation, but finally lapsed into an awkward silence when no one seemed inclined to answer with more than one word. Finally they each took their plates to the kitchen and then left single file. Rebecca cleared the rest of the table and washed the dishes. She wiped up the countertops and table, then poured the dishwater into the hog slop bucket.

Wagon wheels crunched near the front porch, reminding her that they were going to town for supplies. "Joy!" she called up the stairs. "Time to go!"

A smile parted Rebecca's lips as she watched her five-year-old daughter cross the room. Joy had changed from her nightgown into a simple brown dress and had pulled her fine blond hair into a blue ribbon. "I got my- self ready," she said, twirling in a circle.

"I can see that. You look very pretty." Rebecca grabbed her pale blue cloak and bonnet from the peg by the front door, then helped Joy into hers.

They stepped out onto the porch and Clayton jumped down from the driver's seat to help them up. Benjamin, Philip and Thomas ran from the bunkhouse and landed in the back of the wagon with loud thuds.

"Where are Andrew, Noah and Jacob?" Rebecca asked, looking back at her sons.

"Mr. Armstrong says Andrew and Noah need to stay here and take care of the place," Thomas answered, giving Philip a shove.

That accounted for Andrew and Noah, but not for Jacob and Seth. Rebecca looked toward the bunkhouse. "Where are Mr. Armstrong and Jacob?"

"Mr. Armstrong said we can call him Seth," Ben- jamin answered with a grin.

"That doesn't answer her question, Beni," Philip said. He turned to look at Rebecca. "They are inside talking about why Jacob thinks we should all go to town."

Thomas snickered. "If you call that talking."

Rebecca lowered herself from the wagon. It was bad enough that Seth Armstrong had announced he was their new boss, but to cause strife this soon...well that was unacceptable.

"Ma, I wouldn't interfere if I was you," Clayton warned from his seat. "Jacob is in kind of a foul mood."

"I can imagine." Rebecca turned to the bunkhouse. "You boys stay put. We'll be ready to go in a minute."

She heard raised voices before she got to the door. Rebecca pushed the heavy wooden door open and walked inside. Her sons turned expectantly. "What's the ruckus?" she asked, placing both hands on her hips and giving her children the "mother" look.

Jacob and Andrew each clamped their lips together. Noah studied the end of his muddy boot. It was obvious her boys had no intention of answering her.

Seth crossed his arms and met her gaze full-on. "We men are having a discussion."

"From what I heard—" she didn't bother telling him she heard it from Philip and Thomas "—you expect Andrew and Noah to stay here while the rest of us head to town." Rebecca held up a hand to stop him from answering. "And if I know Jacob, he's not happy with the arrangement and intends to stay with Andrew himself." Her gaze moved from her oldest son to Seth. "Do I have it right so far?" Her eyes locked with the station keeper's.

"I'd say that about sums it up," Seth responded.

"Mr. Armstrong, may I ask why you want the two boys to stay behind? We've always gone to town as a family before." His eyes were the prettiest shade of blue-green that she'd ever saw. Did they turn that color when he was angry? She mentally shook the thought away and focused on the problem at hand.

Seth sighed. "With the horses loose, Indians or bandits could come and steal them while we are gone."

"That's why I should stay," Jacob growled between clenched teeth.

Seth turned to Jacob. "I need you to help me bargain for supplies. The men in town don't know or trust me just yet. And since I don't know them, either, I need you to make sure the Pony Express doesn't get cheated."

Rebecca realized that what he said was true. She knew that even though the men in town knew her, they didn't want to bargain with a woman. They'd made that very clear shortly after John's death. Jacob had a wonderful working relationship with them and the chances of them accepting Seth Armstrong from the get-go were slim to none.

"I have funds that we can use to rebuild the barn," Seth said. "I'm sure Mr. Russell and Mr. Bromley will approve, considering they need the barn to house the Pony Express horses."

Rebecca looked to Noah. The boy hadn't looked up from his boots. He was so young. She didn't like the idea of leaving him and Andrew alone on the ranch any more than Jacob. "Why leave Noah? He's only twelve years old."

"Because Jacob says that Noah is the best at using a rifle." Seth's gaze never left Jacob's face, daring him to deny it.

That was true, too. Over the past few weeks, Noah had proven he could shoot the antennae off a grasshopper, if he had to. Rebecca walked between the men and looked her oldest son in the eyes. "Jacob, what he's asking isn't unreasonable. I'm sure that Andrew will see that Noah is kept safe."

Jacob's eyes held warmth and sadness in their depths. He nodded. "I'm sure he can, but it is my job to take care of this farm and my family."

Unaware of the sorrow and weight of the promise Jacob had made to John, Seth interrupted, "Not anymore—it's mine. Be in the wagon in five minutes." He turned on his boot heels and left them standing looking at each other.

Rebecca concealed her anger toward Seth. Who did he think he was, coming in here and demanding that these boys follow him blindly? He didn't know them. Or what they'd been through since John's death.

She thought about staying home with Andrew and Noah, but she needed to get supplies for the house, and if she stayed behind, who would keep Seth and Jacob from coming to blows? She sighed. "Come along, Jacob. We'll do as he asks today." But as soon as they returned from town, she thought to herself, she'd be having a word with Seth Armstrong.

## Chapter Two

The trip into town was frosty to say the least. Seth could feel the anger boiling over from both Rebecca and Jacob. He'd known coming into this job that it would be difficult. But he'd also thought that Rebecca and her boys knew what they were getting into.

As Dove Creek came into view, Seth stopped the wagon. After coming off the farm, the landscape had become flat and dusty. There were a few trees scattered about the town, but it didn't offer the peace and greenery of the Young farm.

"Is this the first time you've been to town?" Rebecca's soft voice drew him like bees to honey.

He nodded. "Yes. It's not quite what I expected. Dove Creek sounds so pretty."

A soft chuckle came from deep in her throat.

"Ma says that all the time," Benjamin said from the back of the wagon.

Seth glanced over his shoulder at the little boy. He was sitting beside Joy and they'd been looking at a picture book most of the way to town. "She's right."

Benjamin nodded as if they'd come to a profound agreement and then turned his attention back to his sister and the book. Of all the siblings, those two looked most like brother and sister.

Bromley hadn't told him anything about the family, other than their pa had died and that Mr. Russell and Mr. Young had made an agreement before the Pony Express had even been constructed. Seth's orders were to swear in the boys by having them say the Pony Express rider's oath and teach them what would be expected from them as Pony Express riders.

He flipped the reins over the horse's backs and continued down the hill. The sooner they got to town, the sooner they could get home. He didn't like leaving the other two boys at the house any more than Jacob did, but without a bar, the animals were out in the open and needed protection from not only Indians and bandits, but also other wild animals.

Seth felt the restrained movement as Rebecca shifted on the seat beside him. His gaze moved in her direction and caught the profile of Jacob, who sat beside his mother. The boy's jaw was clenched and his eyes directed straight ahead. Rebecca had rested a slender hand on her son's leg in silent comfort.

Returning his attention back to driving, Seth inwardly sighed. He and Jacob would have to sit down and talk about the boy's attitude. Seth was sure there was more to it than just not wanting to leave his brothers behind.

"Would you drop Joy and me off at the general store?" Rebecca asked.

His gaze moved over the town. There was just a dirt

road, and plain wooden-faced stores lined the streets. Smoke billowed from the top of each one and the smell of pine teased the air around them. At least they could warm up a bit before they started the long trek back. The church sat on the hill to the right side of them and he could tell by the children playing in the yard that it also served as the town school. Why weren't the smaller Young children in attendance?

Since it really wasn't any of his business, Seth chose to answer Rebecca's question instead of asking one of his own. "We can do that." He directed the horses down Main Street and continued to study the dusty town.

A saloon stood tall at the far end of the settlement. Not that he'd ever go there, but he knew the boys were of an age that they might be tempted. Seth mentally made a note to talk to the boys about such places, after they repeated the oath. As their boss he didn't want them coming to town and getting drunk. Best to nip that sort of behavior in the bud. It would not be allowed.

He pulled the wagon up in front of the general store and hopped down. Seth turned to help Rebecca down but Jacob assisted her, his gentleness evident in the way he held her hand until she got her balance. Clayton had climbed out of the wagon and helped Joy down, as well. Benjamin scrambled over the side.

"Whoa! Where do you think you're going?" Seth asked, moving to block the boy's descent.

Benjamin jerked away from him. "To help Ma."

"Not today. I need every man's help to load lumber and nails."

Benjamin's little chest puffed out. "I get to help?"

"You're one of the men," Seth said, walking back to the front of the wagon.

He grinned as Benjamin whispered, "Did ya hear that, Ma? I'm one of the men."

At least he'd made good points with one of the Young men.

Rebecca took Joy's small hand within hers and entered the general store. A bell rang out announcing their arrival. She inhaled the onslaught of scents that greeted her. Spices and leather fought the strongest for her attention. Colorful burlap flour bags lined the middle shelf, right at eye level, and she ran a hand over them, her mind zipping along with plans for Joy's next dress. The material proved soft to the touch and Joy loved to spin around, showing off the big flower design.

Joy's hand tightened on hers as if giving a warning and she looked up. The owner of the general store, a mountain of a man, approached them. She glanced down at her daughter, wondering if Joy felt the same sense of unease she herself did around him.

"Hello, Mrs. Young. What can I help you find today?" He kneeled down in front of Joy. "How are you today, Miss Joy."

As was her custom, Joy hid her face in Rebecca's skirt. She mumbled, "Good."

He held out his large hand. On top of his palm rested a lemon drop. "I'm glad to hear that." His big brown eyes looked up at Rebecca. "Cat got your tongue today?"

Rebecca felt her ire rising. The man never did or said anything out of place; but he constantly made her feel uneasy. She handed him her list. "Hello, Mr. Edwards." She patted Joy's back. "Go ahead and take the candy, Joy."

Joy tentatively took the candy and popped it into her mouth. Around the sweet she said, "Thank you."

Mr. Edwards laughed loudly and stood. "See, that wasn't so hard." His gaze moved to the list and he whistled. "I see the men running the Pony Express pay you well."

The list was longer than usual but Rebecca didn't really understand why he assumed that Mr. Russell gave her the money for the items. Still, she didn't correct him. She'd let him think what he wanted.

John had left his family in good financial stability. Thanks to his wisdom with money matters and his inheritance, she and Joy would never have to work a day of their lives. But it wasn't enough to give the boys money to start their lives. John had said the Pony Express would give them the money they needed and open doors for each of them. She prayed it would be so.

Once more Rebecca felt the store owner's brown eyes focused on her. "The church picnic is this Sunday. Would you like me to come out to the farm and escort you and the children to it?"

He'd never been so bold before. Rebecca's hand fluttered to her chest. What would her older boys think of Mr. Edwards calling them *children*? She focused on the best way to reject him. "Thank you, Mr. Edwards, but that won't be necessary."

Something flashed in his eyes before he turned away from her. "You might reconsider—I hear the road bandits are becoming bolder. I'm sure they wouldn't have a problem taking a single woman's wagon and any cash she carried from her and a passel of kids."

Did he think she and the boys were helpless? Heat filled her face and boiled through her blood. If so, was he threatening her?

She took a deep breath to calm herself. Experience had taught her to carefully consider her words before speaking. Her father-in-law, on the other hand, had often said plain talk was easily understood and that was just what the man in front of her would get.

"I don't need a man to take care of me, Mr. Edwards. The good Lord has protected us through many dangerous situations and I have no doubt He will continue to do so. I don't know if you've noticed, but my boys are no longer little boys, but men." As an afterthought she added, "But thanks so very much for your concern and for the invite."

Joy poked her head out. Her sweet young voice broke the awkward silence between the adults. Worry lined her words. "Mr. Armstrong and Jacob will be with us, won't they, Ma?"

She stroked her daughter's silky hair, wishing Joy hadn't broken her silence. "Yes, sweetie. There is nothing to fear."

The bell over the door jingled again. Rebecca turned to see Mrs. Little and her eldest daughter enter the store. She wondered if all the women in the area brought someone with them when they came to visit the general store.

Mr. Edwards paid no heed to the other two women. "Mr. Armstrong?" His eyes bore into Joy's as he waited for an answer. "Who is this Mr. Armstrong?"

Joy tucked her head behind Rebecca's skirt again. Rebecca stepped in front of her daughter, protecting her from questions she had no knowledge how to answer. "I'd like to get our supplies as soon as possible, Mr. Edwards. The men will be back shortly to pick us up."

Mrs. Little waited until the storekeeper went to retrieve the items on Rebecca's list. "So you have a new man working for you?" she asked.

Well, it sure hadn't taken long for that little tidbit to make its way around the gossip mill. She had learned one thing living in Dove Creek and that was people had very little to occupy their minds, so interest in the people around them bordered on harassment. However, Rebecca couldn't dismiss the older woman as easily as she had Mr. Edwards. She'd been raised to respect her elders, and Mrs. Little could easily have been her mother. "He doesn't exactly work for me."

Mr. Edwards moved closer to them. He continued to add items to the box he'd begun to fill, but seemed to linger ever so near.

"I see." The condemning sound in Mrs. Little's voice had Rebecca quickly explaining.

"Mr. Armstrong works for the Pony Express. He's been hired to be the station keeper by Mr. Bromley." Rebecca moved to the fabric, where she knew Mr. Edwards couldn't pretend to be gathering her supplies, since she hadn't added any sewing notions to her list.

Mrs. Little followed. "Is this a young man, dear?"

Joy followed her mother about the fabric table. She picked up an edge to a pink print and said, "This is pretty."

Rebecca touched the material. "I'm not sure his age, Mrs. Little. I only just met him this morning."

The daughter snorted, drawing a frown from her mother's face. "Catherine, that is very rude."

Catherine was a newly married woman, but still had enough respect for her parent to look contrite and say "Sorry, Ma."

Mrs. Little patted her daughter's hand and turned her attention back to Rebecca. "Is he older than your pa?"

Rebecca hated this line of questioning. She knew where the older woman was going and didn't like it. "No, but I don't know how much younger than Pa he is."

"Is he married?" Catherine asked, admiring a blue print.

Rebecca frowned. "I don't know that, either."

"Then what do you know?" Mr. Edwards asked.

"I know he showed up this morning, helped us put the fire out that burned our barn and announced that he is the new station keeper. That's all I know." Rebecca waved at the box in Mr. Edwards's hands. "One of the boys will be back shortly to get our supplies. Please add the total to my tab, Mr. Edwards. I will be in on the first of the month to settle up." She turned on her heels. "Come, Joy."

The sound of Joy's shoes tapping against the hardwood floor assured Rebecca that her daughter had followed her outside the store. Rebecca wasn't sure if she was angry with Mrs. Little and Mr. Edwards, or at herself.

She didn't know a thing about Mr. Armstrong other

than what she'd told them. Why had she been so quick to accept him at face value? He'd waltzed in, said he was the station keeper and proceeded to boss them all around.

"Ma! Slow down," Joy called behind her.

Rebecca stopped and looked at her daughter. "I'm sorry, Joy." She waited for the little girl to catch up with her, then continued on.

Her boys were with a virtual stranger. How had she been so careless? Rebecca planned on finding out just who Seth Armstrong was and she planned to do it now.

After all, once Mrs. Little realized that he was a nice young man, she'd have the whole town in an uproar. They'd be wondering what went on out at the Young farm. How could Mr. Bromley have put her in this situation? Could she continue with this business arrangement?

Seth handed Mr. Kaziah the remainder of the payment for the wood and nails. He knew it would be pricey, but hadn't expected it to be quite this expensive and wondered if the lumberman had overcharged him and the boys. Thankfully, Mr. Russell, one of the Pony Express founders, had supplied him with a hefty budget for turning the farm into a Pony Express station. Seth had been told by Mr. Bromley that since the buildings were already there, they hadn't done much work to the place and to spend what he needed to on the repairs. He'd have to send a full report to the older gentleman, explaining this added expense.

"Here comes Ma and Joy," Benjamin announced from his perch on the bench of the wagon.

He turned to see the boy's mother heading toward them. Her face was set, but it was her eyes that caught and held his attention. She glowered at him, the blue orbs piercing the distance between them.

"She looks mad." Benjamin turned to face his brother, confirming Seth's earlier thought. "I wonder why."

Philip answered, "Beni, mas don't get mad. Dogs get mad. Mas get angry." A teasing grin touched the young boy's lips but his eyes seemed weary.

Thomas slapped his brother on the back. "Good one, Phil."

"Jacob, Mr. Armstrong. I need to speak to you both, now please," Rebecca announced as she walked toward the lumberyard.

Seth turned back to Mr. Kaziah. "Thank you for helping us load the wagon. You'll be sending the rest out later today, right?"

The older man nodded and then leaned toward him. In a low, gruff voice he whispered, "I don't envy you. Taking on a passel of kids and that woman. She's a bit of a feisty one." He turned away and hurried back inside the lumber mill before Seth could answer.

What did he mean *take on*? Surely, Mr. Kaziah hadn't assumed that he and Mrs. Young were courting. He shook his head and then turned to face Rebecca. Jacob already stood by her side and was now holding Joy in his arms. The little girl rested her head in the neck of her big brother.

When he was within talking range, Seth asked, "What happened, Mrs. Young?"

She stopped as if his question took her by surprise.

"I just realized that I never got a look at that paper you said you carried from Mr. Bromley." She placed both hands on her hips and waited for him to speak.

Seth frowned and tilted his head to the side. "That's important now?" he asked. What had happened at the store to cause her to demand to see it now? Was that a speck of fear he saw in her eyes?

She nodded, brought up her arms and crossed them over her chest. Her eyes bore into Seth's.

Jacob set down Joy. "Everything is all right, Ma. I saw it. Mr. Armstrong is who he says he is." He tilted up the little girl's face and smiled down at her. "Joy, go ask Thomas to help you into the wagon."

The little girl nodded. "All right, Jacob." She turned and ran to her other brothers.

So that was it. Rebecca had been afraid she'd left her children's care in the hands of a dangerous stranger. Even though they were grown men, Rebecca still saw them as her babies. He softened his voice and offered her a smile. "I will be happy to show them to you, too, Mrs. Young, when we get back to the farm." Seth waited for her nod then turned back toward the wagon. Over his shoulder he asked, "Do we need to return to the store to pick up your purchases?" He was aware that she hadn't brought anything with her except Joy and her handbag.

"Yes, please." Her voice sounded tired, almost sad.

Seth turned to look at her. Her shoulders slumped and her eyes had changed from angry to simply drained. Was the excitement of the day turning out to be too much for the woman? One would think she'd be used to busy days with seven boys and a little girl to take care of. He noted that both Benjamin and Joy were seated on the wagon bench. In a loud voice, he said, "We're done here. Let's go."

Without hesitation the young men climbed in on top of the wood.

Jacob walked with his mother, but as soon as he'd helped her up onto the wagon, he shook his head at his brothers. "Off, guys. The horses have enough to pull without adding our weight to their load."

Just as quickly, the young men all climbed back down.

Seth nodded. Jacob was right. "Beni, do you know how to drive a wagon?" he asked.

The youngest Young boy grinned from ear to ear and nodded. He quickly picked up the reins. "Sure do, Seth. Want me to drive us home?"

Rebecca stood to disembark from the wagon also.

"Mrs. Young, why don't you stay seated?" He indicated with a tilt of his head that Benjamin needed a supervisor sitting beside him. The boy held the reins tightly, waiting for his reply.

She nodded her understanding and returned to her seat.

Seth answered the little boy. "I'd appreciate it if you would drive the wagon, Benjamin. Your brothers and I will follow behind making sure that the wood stays in place."

Seth looked down at his new brown boots. He had a sneaking suspicion that he would soon be wishing he had brought his horse to town before they got back to the farm. In his rush to prove his leadership, he'd decided to drive the wagon to town, never once considering that he'd more than likely end up walking back. *Lesson learned, Armstrong*, he thought as he followed the wagon toward the general store.

Other than the Pony Express horses and the two old mares, Brownie and Snow, Seth realized that the boys didn't have mounts of their own. Once they got back to the farm, he'd remedy that and give the boys each a Pony Express horse to take care of and bond with.

Jacob strolled along beside him. In a low voice he said, "We should have thought ahead and brought more horses."

Seth jerked his head around and looked at the young man. The twinkle in Jacob's eyes attested to the fact that he, too, saw the folly of their earlier disagreement. "Yep, won't let that happen again."

"Nope, I don't reckon we will," Jacob agreed.

A cold breeze stirred the hair on his neck. "I was thinking all you boys need a mount of your own to train with. What do you think?" Seth waited to see if the boy realized that he was being offered respect by his inclusion in the decision.

Jacob nodded. "We all know how to ride, you don't have to worry about that, but I'm a little concerned about the younger boys riding unfamiliar horses. All except Noah, who seems to be very talented with a horse as well as his gun."

Seth nodded and listened as the other boys joked and chatted behind them. "Well, that's one of the first things we'll do, then, as well as we rebuild the barn. I don't like that the animals are out in the open."

"Neither do I."

The wagon stopped in front of the general store. Rebecca turned on the seat. "Jacob, would you go in and get our supplies, please?"

"Yes, ma'am." Jacob stepped up on the boardwalk and entered the store. Rebecca turned back to her younger children.

Two women stood across the street and talked behind their fans, while a couple of well-dressed businessmen stood with their hands in their front pockets and Seth noticed that the sheriff leaned on the post in front of the jail. All eyes seemed to be trained on them.

Seth looked to the other boys. He wondered what the town must think of them all standing behind the wagon like a bunch of stray dogs. In two long strides he stood with the boys. "When we get back to the farm I'd like for you boys to go to the corral and pick out a mount. This is the last time we are leaving town on foot."

Excitement coursed through the boys at his words. The discussion of colors and gender filled the air. He grinned. So far his relationship with the Young family had been tense, but maybe now it would get smoother.

Seth turned back to the wagon in time to see Jacob exit the store. The young man's clenched jaw and burning eyes spoke volumes as to his anger. So whatever had set off Mrs. Young had just happened to Jacob.

His gaze moved to the store, where a big man now stood in the doorway. The man wore a shopkeeper's apron but something about him screamed he wasn't your typical salesman. No, this man meant trouble for the Young family and now with his eyes boring into Seth, Seth knew he meant trouble for him, too.

"Here you go, Ma." Jacob set the box on top of the lumber and then looked to Benjamin. "Lead the way home, Beni." He offered the boy a smile that didn't quite meet his eyes.

When Jacob fell into step beside Seth, Seth asked, "Want to talk about it?"

"Nope."

That was answer enough for Seth. "Fair 'nough, but if you change your mind…" He let the rest hang between them.

Jacob nodded his understanding. Glancing over his shoulder, he saw that his brothers were excited about something and asked, "What has them all in a dither?"

Seth grinned. "Just told them they can choose a horse when we get back."

Again Jacob nodded and then fell silent. His brow furrowed between his eyes. Seth realized that in a day, the Young family's lives had been changed.

He could relate to change; his life had also been altered in the past few months. On her deathbed, his grandmother had made him promise to marry. He'd ordered a mail-order bride and then his grandmother had died. His mail-order bride, Charlotte, had disappeared. He'd quit his job at the St. Joseph railroad and begun his mission to locate her. He'd been robbed by outlaws and it had been necessary to find a job. Thus the reason he now found himself an employee of the Pony Express as the station keeper on the Young farm. He would work and save his money so he could continue the search for Charlotte because he had to fulfill his promise to his grandmother.

The air seemed to match Jacob's mood and turned frosty. Seth sighed inwardly. He had a job to do and knew he couldn't do it alone, so silently he turned to his Maker. *Lord, this family's emotions are all over the place. Please, help me to bring some kind of peace to them while I'm here.*

## Chapter Three

$\smallsmile$

Anger radiated from her oldest son. She'd felt it all the way from town. As she climbed down from the wagon, Rebecca called to him, "Jacob, will you help me carry the supplies into the house?" Rebecca had a feeling she knew what was wrong with Jacob.

"Sure, Ma." Jacob took the box from the wagon and followed her up the porch steps.

"Boys, let's unload this wood," Seth ordered. His strong voice had her other sons hurrying to do his bidding.

Rebecca held the door open for Joy and Jacob. Once inside she said, "Joy, go change into your work clothes." Then she headed for the kitchen, where the real work awaited her.

She allowed Jacob to place the box on the kitchen counter and then asked, "What happened in the general store that upset you so?"

Jacob met her gaze. "Do you have any idea what they are saying about you and Seth?" He lowered his eyes as if realizing for the first time how personal this situation was for his mother.

"I have a good idea of what Mr. Edwards says." She began to unload the box.

Anguish filled the young boy's voice. "It isn't right."

Rebecca sighed. "No, son, it isn't, but I can't stop people from talking." She met his gaze. "We need the money the Pony Express pays to provide a future for you boys and the experience it offers could be useful later in life. You're going to make history, I just know it. Papa John thought so, too."

"Well, we may not be able to stop them from talking but I made the decision to move back into the house on the way home. You and the little kids need a grown man to watch over things." He put both hands on the back of the chair and leaned into it.

She turned her back on him to hide her grin. Her oldest son planned to protect her reputation. Rebecca nodded. "I like that idea. Why don't you take the room across from mine?"

His sigh warmed her heart. Day after day, Jacob proved to be a good man and, God willing, would make a good husband someday, too. "I'll go help unload the wood and then bring my things inside."

Rebecca turned from the spices she'd just taken from the box. "Jacob, wait."

He stopped and looked at her, his eyes sad. Things had changed a lot for the young man in just a matter of hours. Rebecca walked over to him and wrapped her arms around his narrow waist.

Jacob hugged her back. "It will be all right, Ma.

Seth seems like a good man. I'm sure he'll set folks straight soon enough."

Rebecca grinned. Once more the boy thought only of her. She pulled away. "I'm sure he will, son." She released him. "You better go on out and help with the lumber."

Jacob patted her shoulder, then turned to do as she said. Rebecca wanted to pull him back, offer him comfort, but Jacob wasn't twelve years old anymore. He'd work through whatever bothered him in his own time. She just prayed he'd share his troubles with her should they get too great for him to carry alone.

Seth looked around the barnyard. The lumber had been delivered from the general store. Each of the boys had chosen a mount to care for and Jacob had shared his concerns about his ma and younger siblings being in the house alone at night.

The horses moved quietly in the corral as the sun sank in the western sky. Weariness hung about Seth's shoulders like a dark thundercloud.

Rebecca stepped out on the front porch. He waved to her and watched as she walked across the yard to join him. A light blue shawl hung over her shoulders, and her hair, which he'd only seen up in a bun, now hung down her back in a braid that reminded him of a golden lasso.

When she got within speaking distance he said, "I'm about to swear the boys in as Pony Express men. Would you like to join us?"

"Yes, John and I had planned on doing that as a family, so I should be there, even if he can't be." Rebecca pulled the edges of her shawl tighter around her shoulders. Sorrow filled her pretty blue eyes. "Is it a ceremony-type swearing in or a simple handshake and 'welcome to the Pony Express'?"

"It's a solemn formality, so, yes, I guess it's a ceremony."

"Would you like to use the house? I could put on the tablecloth we use for special occasions. It's late but shouldn't take but a few minutes."

"No, that won't be necessary. In front of the fireplace will be fine. That way, Benjamin will see how we do things and learn what's ahead for him and perhaps even look forward to it."

Seth had thought about having her come to the bunkhouse, but at her suggestion he decided it might be better to have the boys go to her. Plus, she'd have to bundle up Joy and Beni, so it would be easier on her if he brought the boys to the house. "I'll get the boys and we'll be right in," he offered.

"Thank you." She turned and walked back to the house.

Ten minutes later, they assembled in the living room, Joy propped against Rebecca's legs, her cornsilk doll in her lap. There was an air of expectancy among them, an excitement about the unknown.

Seth cleared his throat. "This is an important day as you boys take your first step into manhood. When a boy can handle responsibility, can be depended on to carry out a job, then he is thought to be a man. I trust that each of you will with honesty and pride uphold your position in the United States Postal Service." He reached to pick up his Bible from the table. "If you young men will step forward we will commence with the swearing in." They walked forward, shyness preventing them from showing how eager and proud they were to be involved in something bigger than themselves.

When they stood in front of him, he paused a moment, his gaze moving from one to the other. "Lift your right hand and repeat after me. 'I—'" he waited until each boy had voiced his name, then continued "'—do hereby swear, before the Great and Living God, that during my engagement, and while I am an employee of Russell, Majors and Waddell, I will, under no circumstances, use profane language, that I will drink no intoxicating liquors, that I will not quarrel or fight with any other employee of the firm, and that in every respect I will conduct myself honestly, be faithful to my duties, and so direct all my acts as to win the confidence of my employers, so help me God.'"

The boys repeated the words with force and pride. Seth glanced at Rebecca and noticed Benjamin standing beside her, holding the same pose as the other boys. He walked over to him. "Benjamin, did you say the oath, also?"

Benjamin nodded his small head, his eyes down.

Rebecca dropped a hand onto the little boy's shoulder and gave it a gentle squeeze. Her eyes begged Seth to let the boy pretend to be a Pony Express rider.

Seth kneeled down in front of him. "Do you understand what you've agreed to?" he asked.

Benjamin bravely met his gaze. "Yes, sir."

Seth nodded. "Well, in that case, go get in line with the other men. You've pledged to be a Pony Express man." He stood and met Rebecca's gaze as the little boy darted around him and went to stand beside Jacob. Gratitude and moisture filled her eyes.

For a moment, Seth understood her burden. She had a houseful of children to care for and she did it on her own. His respect for her inched up a degree. Seth nodded at her then returned his attention to the young men now fully in his charge.

Seth picked up the stack of Bibles that he'd carried with him to the farm, now a full-fledged Pony Express station. He handed one to each of them. "You are now employees of the Pony Express. Jacob, I have decided that you will be the station's stock tender. Your job is to take care of all the horses and make sure that a horse is ready to ride at all times. Andrew, Clayton, Thomas, Philip and Noah, you will all be riders. Your job is to make sure that the mail goes through." Each young man nodded in turn.

Benjamin studied the tip of his brown boots. Seth knew the boy felt left out. He ran his small hand over the engraving on the front of his new Bible.

Seth fought the grin that threatened to break across his face. He steeled himself and then said, "Benjamin, you are too young to be a Pony Express rider, so I am making you the stock tender's assistant. It will be your job to help Jacob take care of the horses and barn. Whatever Jacob or I ask you to do, you will do it."

A smile split Benjamin's lips. "I'll be the best stock tender's 'sistant that anyone has ever met."

Seth wasn't sure there were other stock tender assistants in the Pony Express, but he nodded just the same. "I'm sure you will." He motioned for everyone to sit down, then pulled up a stool for himself and faced them. "I'm not sure what Mr. Bromley told you about your jobs, but let me assure you they are dangerous. You will face bad weather, robbers, outlaws and Indians. None of these should be taken lightly. You'll have to think on your feet, learn to outrun, outsmart, and you need to trust your gut. The main point is, stay alive but get the mail through. Do you have any questions?" Seth immediately looked to Benjamin, but the boy remained silent along with his brothers. "Since there are no questions, let me explain to you exactly what my job entails. I am called a station keeper for a home station—that's what the farm is called. I make sure that you men are ready to ride. That the station runs smoothly and that the horses are tended well. I also make sure that during your stay at the home station you aren't idle. You will follow my orders. If I say build a fence, you build a fence. If I say ride on out, you ride on out. Is that understood?"

"What about Ma?" Benjamin asked.

Seth looked at the boy. "What about your mother?"

"Does she have to take orders, too?" His eyes challenged Seth, something Seth hadn't expected. He smiled at the boy.

"No, your mother isn't a Pony Express employee."

"Oh."

Clayton asked, "What if Ma says to chop wood and you say to ride out, then what?"

"You ride out," Seth answered, aware they walked a tight line here. "But if you aren't working for me and your Ma says chop wood, you best chop wood."

Rebecca spoke for the first time since they'd all arrived in her living room. "Mr. Armstrong, I can understand the boys' confusion." She pushed a strand of hair behind her ear. "They simply want to know who has the most authority, you or me?"

Seth knew that. How many other station managers had to answer questions like these? He doubted any of them did. "It's really very simple. They work for me. Each boy will have time off and that is when they can do whatever you need or want them to."

Her eyes flashed but she simply nodded. He noted her growing quietness as he outlined the job. First the barn had to be rebuilt and second they'd need to work on their riding skills.

Did she disagree with him on what her sons would be doing? Or did she just not like the way he'd come in and replaced her deceased husband? Confrontation wasn't his strong suit when it came to women, but Seth had known from the start that he and Rebecca Young must have a heart-to-heart discussion about what might and would happen to her farm and children.

Rebecca finished making Jacob's bed then headed to the living room to wait for Seth and Jacob to return to the house. Joy and Benjamin were both tucked in for the night and the house seemed very quiet. Normally she relished this time, but tonight the stillness seemed to grate on her frayed nerves.

Earlier, as the boys had filed out to return to the bunkhouse, Seth had stood beside her and quietly asked if he could speak to her in private. She'd agreed. Not because he'd asked for the meeting, but because there were things she needed to say to him.

She'd have to be both blunt and gentle in her words to the man. Rebecca knew without him having to say so that he wasn't going to agree with her thoughts, but she had to speak them.

Would he fire the boys? Tell Mr. Bromley that the Young farm wouldn't make a good home station after all? What would she do if he did that? What would become of her boys?

If they worked for the Pony Express, each one of them could potentially earn enough to buy a parcel of land, or go to a college back east. They would have a foot up to a better life. John had left her well-off, financially, but the boys would need to earn their own way.

But at what cost? Their lives?

# *Chapter Four*

Rebecca heard them come through the door and stopped pacing. Jacob carried a box with his things in it. Cold air whipped about the room as Seth closed the door behind them. He, too, carried a box of Jacob's things.

"I'll take these to Jacob's room and then be back for our talk," he told her as he passed.

She had to get her thoughts together. How should she approach her concerns with him? Calmly and quietly. That was the way she always approached John— Seth would be no different.

He reentered the room alone. Rebecca sat down on the couch and motioned for him to take the chair across from her. She decided that since he asked to speak to her, she'd let him go first.

Seth sat down but leaned forward on the edge of the seat, placing his brown hat on his knee. "Mrs. Young, I get the impression that you don't care for the way I'm running things around here." He lifted his right eyebrow as if to accent his statement.

Rebecca chose her words carefully. "I have my concerns. You've been here one day and I can't say what you are doing is good or bad."

"But?"

She took a deep breath. "But I didn't think my two youngest boys would be working with the Pony Express."

He sat back. "So you are objecting to me swearing Noah and Benjamin in as employees of the Pony Express?"

"Yes." She knitted her fingers together and laid them in her lap. "Well, no." She shrugged to hide her confusion. "I know you included Beni so he could feel important. I'm grateful." To her annoyance she heard herself start to stammer. She forced her voice to steady and reined in her thoughts. "I just feel Noah is too young and small to be a rider and Beni shouldn't be burdened with such a heavy workload." She searched his eyes, looking for signs of anger.

Seth offered her a grin. "Benjamin is too young to ride. That's why I made him Jacob's assistant. The boy wants to prove himself and who would be a better teacher than his oldest brother?"

Rebecca recognized a spark of amusement in his gaze and relaxed a little. "Yes, Beni wants to do what his big brothers do."

"As for Noah, Jacob seems to think Noah is the best horseman on the farm and stated that he is good with his gun. Both are important skills I need in riders."

She clutched her hands tightly in her lap. "But he's twelve and I've only had him a few months. I don't know if he's ready for this responsibility." Rebecca searched Seth's face. Did he understand what she was saying?

Seth leaned forward again. "What do you mean you've only had him a few months?" His eyes searched hers, looking for what she could only assume was both confusion and truth.

"Noah is adopted, Mr. Armstrong. All of the boys are. I thought Mr. Bromley would have told you that." From the look on his face it was obvious Seth hadn't known.

"No, he didn't," Seth said. "I thought it odd that none of them look like you or each other. Well—" his voice broke in midsentence "—except Joy, she looks like you." He offered her a smile.

Rebecca couldn't help but smile. "Joy is my daughter by birth. She is the only child John and I have. But that doesn't change the fact that I love the boys just as much as I do Joy and I don't want to see them get hurt...or die."

Seth met her gaze and held it. Sincerity rang through his voice as he vowed, "I promise as long as I am the station keeper here, I will do everything in my power to keep the boys safe and alive. Safety is the reason I will teach them how to ride, shoot and avoid trouble while out on the trail."

She understood that the boys would be in danger and that she didn't consider them to really be men. The orphanage had called them men at the age of twelve, the same age as Noah, but to her they were still her little boys.

"I know you are still concerned and I can't blame you. Being a Pony Express employee is dangerous.

The only thing I can do is teach them how to survive and pray that God keeps them safe. It's either that or I fire them all and have Mr. Bromley send me a new set of men." He shook his head. "I really don't want to do that, Mrs. Young. I truly believe these young men have what it takes to be riders. I'll leave that decision up to you."

Rebecca didn't want him to fire the boys. She'd promised John that she wouldn't interfere when this time came. John had wanted his sons to become honorable, strong individuals who could take care of themselves and their families, should the Lord one day bless them with such. He firmly believed the Pony Express would provide the training that life had cheated these boys out of. "No, they would never forgive me if I asked you to fire them." She didn't tell him that the money the boys made would provide for their future well-being, establishing them in whatever careers they chose.

He exhaled as if he'd been holding his breath. "Thank you. I know this is hard for you and I want to make it easier on both of us. How about we have a nightly meeting? I can fill you in on what I'm doing with the boys in regard to their duties as Pony Express riders and you can tell me if you need them to assist you with something specific around the farm."

It was a reasonable request and far more than some men would have offered her if they had been in Seth's position. Rebecca nodded. "That would be nice, thank you."

They sat still for several moments. The sound of boots retreating down the hallway alerted Rebecca that one or more of her children had listened in on their conversation. A grin crossed Seth's lips. He'd heard it, too.

"Mr. Armstrong, I'd like to suggest that we have our conversations out on the porch if the weather permits. I'm sure there will be times when we don't want others hearing your reports." Rebecca unclasped her hands and then stood.

"That sounds like a good idea to me. If the boys think you need a chaperone, they can watch us through the window of the bunkhouse." He picked up his hat from his knee and stood also. He pulled a piece of paper from his hip pocket and handed it to her.

Rebecca looked down at the paper. "What's this?"

"The letter from Mr. Bromley. I should have shared it with you sooner. You can return it to me in the morning." Seth walked to the door and left.

She sank down onto the couch. Was she doing the right thing letting the boys continue working for the Pony Express? Sure, they each would need the money they'd make, but... Rebecca warred with her conscience—did they need the money so badly that she'd allow them to put their lives in danger? Wasn't her job as the adult and their mother to protect them until they were old enough to know what they were doing?

Not wanting to answer that question, Rebecca pressed on with her thoughts as she looked down at the letter. Without the money, the older boys would have to leave home and seek out work. Her family would swiftly break up.

So soon after losing John, Rebecca knew she wouldn't be able to cope with losing any of the boys. And there was always the likelihood that they'd find other work, maybe even more dangerous work. She shuddered at that thought.

She couldn't allow that to happen to her precious boys. No, to keep her family together Rebecca would allow the boys to continue working for the Pony Express.

Seth looked up at the framework of the barn. He stood amazed at how quickly he and the boys had gotten the structure up. Sawdust floated in the sun's rays and the pleasant smell of pine mingled with their sweat and filled the air around him.

He placed a hand on the pole closest to him and gave a shove. It didn't budge. Solid and stable. His smile broadened in approval. They'd worked hard and accomplished a lot in one morning. Could be that this little group of misfits would accomplish much more than he had hoped for. But one thing had been proven to him as they worked. The boys needed a firm hand to stay at the job; they worked as long as you kept your eye on them, but fun was uppermost in their minds.

His gaze moved to the boys now washing up for lunch. It wasn't hot outside, but all of them had cast off their coats while they worked. Even little Benjamin had worked hard alongside his brothers.

Seth had been aware of Rebecca watching them all morning. She'd frowned when he'd yelled at Philip for playing around instead of doing his work. It wasn't hard to figure out that the boys worked on their own time schedule. Seth wondered how long their adoptive father had been dead. Had he allowed them to play when they were supposed to do chores?

A good while later, Seth left the bunkhouse feeling refreshed. Thanks to his time alone with the Lord, he now had more direction. Clayton carried a sandwich and a glass of milk out to him. The rest of the boys followed.

"Ma said you need to eat something." The young man handed him the sandwich and milk.

He grinned his thanks and took a big bite. Thick ham and cheese coated his taste buds. The butter-flavored bread that surrounded them tasted wonderful. His stomach growled its appreciation. Seth swallowed. "Let's head to the corral." He waved the sandwich.

Feeling as if someone was watching them, Seth turned to the house and found Rebecca standing in the doorway. He waved to her and once more smiled his thanks before turning back to the corral, where the boys waited.

"I thought we were going to work on the barn," Jacob said as Seth approached.

"We are, but first I wanted to spend some time with the horses." He looked out at the ten horses. "Have you each chosen the horse you want to train with?" He knew they had but wanted to make sure that one of them hadn't changed his mind.

The six older boys nodded. Benjamin climbed up on the fence. He looked longingly out at the horses.

"Benjamin?"

The eight-year-old turned to look at him. "Yes, sir?"

"Sir?" Seth allowed a surprised, questioning note to enter his voice.

Benjamin nodded.

"Benjamin, looks like you and I need to get a few

things straight." Seth walked over and leaned against the fence beside the little boy. "The rest of you, go find some rope and then round up your horses."

The boys pushed and shoved as they went in search of rope. Jacob and Andrew followed at a slower pace, shaking their heads. When they were all out of earshot, Seth told Benjamin, "First, let's get this straight. I'm not sir, I'm Seth."

The boy nodded still, looking sad. Seth reached over and tousled his hair.

"Good. Now, how come you didn't pick a horse?"

Benjamin sighed and climbed a rung higher on the fence, watching the boys exit the stable and enter the corral. "I'm not going to be a rider. I heard you tell Ma last night."

Seth rubbed his chin. So it had been Benjamin eavesdropping the night before. "Yes, I did say that, but I think you should have a mount." He watched closely as Jacob returned and quietly singled out a rum-colored pinto, gently rubbing its mane, talking in a low voice. Thomas and Philip followed suit. For all their pushing and shoving, once they were within the corral, they became serious.

"You do?" Hope filled the little boy's voice.

"Yep, seems to me you'll need one if we all ride into town or if I need you to go out to the back pasture and get one of the other boys. There are all kinds of reasons a boy needs a horse." Seth lifted a brow in question, holding the boy's gaze. "Don't you think so?"

Benjamin nodded. His hair flopped down into his eyes. "Can I pick out one now?" he asked, already preparing to climb down from the fence.

"Yes, but go see if one of the older boys will help you find some rope."

"Yippee!" Benjamin ran to the barn, where Andrew and Noah stood cutting lengths of rope.

Each boy returned to the corral and began trying to catch the horses. They weren't all bad at roping. Jacob, Andrew and Noah were the best and as soon as each caught their own horse, they helped the four brothers. Seth coached from the sidelines.

"I want a horse, too, Ma." Joy's young voice sounded behind him.

He turned to face the little girl and Rebecca. Seth finished the milk in his glass and handed it to Rebecca.

"You don't need a horse, Joy," she answered her daughter, taking his glass but looking down at her little girl.

"Thanks for lunch," Seth said, even though he could tell her attention wasn't on him.

"What if I need to go get one of them out of the pasture? I'll need a horse then," Joy argued. Her lip protruded as she looked up at her mother.

Seth was no child expert but he could read the defiance on the cute little face. Her blue-green eyes demanded answers. He had to turn his head to hide his grin, but just as quickly he returned his attention to them. What would Rebecca's argument be with the child?

She shook her pretty head. "You won't be going to the pasture to get the boys. Now stop sassing." Rebecca looked back to Seth. "Are you sure it's wise to give Benjamin one of the horses?" She tugged her shawl tighter around her shoulders.

"I wouldn't do it if I didn't think so," Seth answered. "He needs to learn to ride just like the others." He called to the young men behind him, "Boys, bring the horses out here."

"Come along, Joy. We need to get back to the house and let the men work." Rebecca's voice seemed to hold frost. She took the little girl's hand and headed back to the house.

Seth sighed. He'd warned her that the boys would all have horses. Clayton opened the gate to the corral and waited until all his brothers had passed through before closing it again.

The animals tossed their heads in obvious dislike of the ropes. "Since we lost all our tack in the fire, we'll need to buy new harnesses and saddles next time we're in town," Seth told them as he walked about, inspecting each horse.

"Until then, I suppose we can use my horse's saddle and bridle. Wait here and get to know your horse." Seth walked back to the bunkhouse and retrieved his bridle and saddle.

"Since we only have one, you will have to take turns. Starting with the oldest. The rest of you will walk about the farm with your horse. Talk to it, sing to it, do whatever it takes for it to learn the sound of your voice." Seth carried the bridle and saddle over to Jacob.

Jacob grinned. "Seth, I've been saddling a horse since I was twelve."

"Not this horse," Seth pointed out. "I want you to saddle and ride him for about thirty minutes and then come back." He turned to address all the boys. "These horses will become your best friends. It is up to each of you to take care of these animals as if they were family. They will most likely save your life out there, so give them the respect they deserve."

Each of the boys nodded and petted their horse.

Seth grinned. "Now, I know this is going to sound silly, but if you have a girl horse, talk to her like she's your sweetheart. If you have a boy, talk to him as if he were your best friend. Animals can sense when they are liked and respected."

Benjamin kneeled down and looked under his horse. When he turned to Seth he announced, "I have a boy. Good thing, too, 'cause I don't know how to talk to a sweetheart."

Laughter and good-natured bantering followed.

"Don't worry, little brother. You'll learn soon enough." Noah grinned across at Benjamin as if he already knew how to talk to a sweetheart. This created more teasing and joking among them all.

Seth shook his head and laughed with them. Working with the boys would be anything but boring. He felt, more than saw, Rebecca watching from the porch. Tonight he'd have to tell her more about how he planned to train with the boys. He hoped that would put her mind at ease. But from the way she paced on the porch, he somehow doubted it would.

## Chapter Five

Rebecca tucked her daughter into bed.

"Ma, I want a horse, too."

She put Joy's favorite doll under her arm, then smoothed the quilt over them both. "I know, dear. I heard you asking the Lord to change my mind."

A big smile split the little girl's mouth and brightened eyes. "Did He?"

Rebecca chuckled. "No, He did not." She picked up her daughter's dress and hung it in the closet. "He hasn't said a word to me about it, but if the good Lord sees fit to tell me to change my mind, I will. Until then, you put the thought out of your head and get some sleep." She leaned over and kissed Joy's forehead.

"I love you, Ma." Joy's soft whisper touched Rebecca deeply.

"I love you, too, my Joy." Rebecca blew out the candle and carried it from the room.

Benjamin's room was beside his sister's. Rebecca opened the door a crack. "All tucked in, Benjamin?" she asked. A soft snore was her only answer. Rebecca tiptoed into his room and looked down at him. His hair fell over his small forehead. He was just a little boy.

Memories of earlier in the day caused her heart to quicken in her chest. She'd about swallowed her tongue when she'd seen him leading the big black gelding about the yard. Benjamin looked so much smaller than the other boys and his horse appeared twice as big.

She brushed the hair off his forehead and planted a soft kiss in its place. A smile twitched at his lips. Rebecca stood. Seth worked the little boy too hard—she'd have a word with him tonight. Rebecca blew the candle out beside Benjamin's bed and left the room.

Jacob leaned against the wall outside Benjamin's bedroom. "How's the little guy doing?"

Rebecca smiled at her oldest son. "He's plum tuckered out."

Pride filled his voice as he answered, "He put in a full day's work."

"I know. I'm going to have a word with Mr. Armstrong about pushing him too hard. He's just a little boy." Rebecca set both of the candles on the table in the hall.

"Ma, Seth didn't drive Beni to work hard. The little guy is trying to prove that he can do anything us older boys can do." Jacob pushed away from the wall. "Seth seems like a good man. I don't think he'd do anything to harm Beni or any of the boys."

Rebecca studied Jacob. "You like him?" she asked, a little surprised. So far, Jacob seemed to buck every decision or action the station keeper suggested, but here he stood now, defending him.

Jacob looked down at his boots. "He's not Papa John

but unless I've read him wrong, he is a good man." He turned to enter his room. "'Night, Ma."

"Good night, Jacob."

Rebecca walked down the hall and into the living room. Seth Armstrong might be a good man but she still thought he might be a bit too hard on the younger boys. After all, the man wasn't a parent, had never dealt with little legs that hurt in the night from cramps or muscle spasms.

She'd seen how he'd pushed Noah hard all day while they worked on the barn. Noah wasn't like the other boys. Building things and working with wood wasn't something he enjoyed. Now, give the boy a rifle or a fishing pole and he'd do anything you asked with either of them and he'd do it joyfully. She'd have to explain that to Seth so he'd ease up on the boy. After all, it seemed as if that should be something he'd want to know.

She walked to the kitchen and set the coffeepot onto the back warmer. Rebecca inhaled the hearty aroma and decided one more cup wouldn't hurt her.

Seth's voice stilled her hand as she poured hot liquid into her favorite mug. "I'd like a cup of that, if you have plenty."

Rebecca turned and handed him her mug. "Here you go." Then she reached for another cup.

"You might want to grab your coat—it's getting colder and colder out there," Seth said, leading the way to the front porch.

Rebecca grabbed her blue cloak off the hook by the front door and followed him. He walked to the porch swing and sat down.

"I hope you don't mind sharing the swing. I'm a mite tired." Seth yawned as if to prove his point.

Rebecca eased down beside him. "Not at all." Her gaze moved out to the horse corral. Several horses could be seen, their hooves clopping against the hard ground. She noticed that one of the boys stood by the fence, but she couldn't make out which of her sons it was.

As if he could read her mind, Seth offered, "That's Andrew—he pulled first watch."

She turned to look at him. "What do you mean 'pulled first watch'?"

"Until the barn is finished, the boys have to take turns keeping watch over the animals. Indians or bandits could attempt to steal them." He took a cautious sip of his coffee.

Rebecca frowned. "Why aren't you guarding them? You are the station keeper after all." She heard the accusation in her voice and flinched inwardly.

As expected, he came back with a bit of harshness of his own. "Because I've assigned Andrew to do it."

"But he's just a boy." Rebecca wished she could take the spoken thought back as soon as it hit the night air.

His voice softened. "No, he's a man." Seth blew into his cup to cool the coffee.

Rebecca didn't see him that way. She still remembered the day she and John had brought Andrew home with them. He was twelve and scared. Andrew had clung to John and didn't want to let him go, even though it was way past bedtime. Andrew had reminded her so much of her brother, Mark, that she'd begged John to sleep in the little boy's room. John had, leaving her to dwell on the past and her brother's fear and eventual death.

It was Mark's death from exposure to the weather when he'd been forced to leave the orphanage at the age of twelve that had prompted Rebecca and John to adopt the boys on their twelfth birthdays. Rebecca wanted to save as many of the boys as she could.

"Rebecca, you are going to have to let them grow up," Seth said quietly.

It was the first time he'd used her Christian name and she enjoyed the way it sounded. Rebecca looked at him. The light from the moon shone across his face. His eyes held hers. There was no anger in their depths and for that she was thankful.

"You don't know them like I do. They all have pasts, pasts that you will never understand," Rebecca told him.

Seth nodded. His eyes searched out Andrew as he said, "You are right there. But I do know he's willing to protect you from all harm and that's what he's doing right now. He's being a man and he's protecting what he believes is his to protect."

Rebecca turned her attention to the corral also. Was Andrew really protecting her and not just the horses? "I still don't know why he has to take the first watch."

"He asked for it," Seth answered.

"Why?" Rebecca turned her attention back to the station keeper.

Seth laughed. "He said he's less likely to fall asleep now than later in the night or early in the morning. Made sense to me, so I agreed."

"So all the boys have a time to watch?" she asked, not happy with the idea.

"Yep, even Benjamin."

Did his shoulders just straighten? Was he anticipating her negative reaction? Well, she wasn't about to disappoint him. "I won't have Benjamin sitting out there in the cold alone while the rest of us sleep." She turned on the seat to face him. "I can't believe even you would do that to an eight-year-old boy."

"Well, that's nice to know. And I didn't say the boy would be alone." Seth pushed up from the seat and went to stand by the porch rail.

Rebecca felt heat fill her cheeks. She'd misjudged him. "Oh, good. I'm glad you are going to be with him."

"I didn't say that, either." Seth watched her over the top of his cup.

"Then who will be with him?" Rebecca was beginning to feel exasperated with him.

"Jacob. They are taking the last hour of the morning," Seth answered. "Before you ask, I'm taking the midnight shift with Noah. If danger strikes, it will probably be then."

So he would be with Noah. Rebecca had to admit that knowing this made her feel a little better. "Look, I don't mean to be a pain, Mr. Armstrong, but these are my children. I have a right to know that they are safe. Or at least as safe as you can make them."

He nodded. "I agree you do have that right. But you have to trust me to keep them as safe as I possibly can."

Did she trust him? No, why should she? Rebecca told herself she didn't really know the man at all. Still,

Mr. Bromley trusted him, so what other choice did she have? She'd have to try to trust Seth Armstrong to watch after her boys. How did a mother release that kind of trust to a stranger? She reminded herself that to keep her family together, she'd have to try.

Seth watched the emotions war across her delicate features. He knew what he asked wasn't easy for her. She'd irritated him as well as made him feel empathy for her all in the past few minutes.

He tossed the remainder of his coffee off the porch. "Look, Rebecca. Over the next few days the boys and I are going to finish the barn and work with the horses—"

"That's another thing," she interrupted. "I don't think Benjamin is old enough to work with the horses."

Exasperation filled him. Why couldn't she just accept that he knew what he was doing? "Benjamin is eight years old. By the time I was six, I was riding and caring for my own horse. He's more than old enough."

Rebecca studied his face. "Why do you want him to ride a horse?" Suspicion filled her voice. "He's too small and you know it. Why, his feet barely reach the stirrups."

"Because he may need to do so. Being a Pony Express station makes this farm vulnerable to all kinds of enemies. Benjamin is small, he can ride fast and get help should we need it." Seth took off his hat and rested it on the railing.

"It's dangerous."

He nodded. "Yes, you're right, it is. But it's also why we train them the proper way to act and treat horses.

If you don't trust me, then at least trust Jacob. He's in charge of Benjamin's learning." Seth had seen how she relied on her oldest son. The boy seemed dependable and for that Seth was grateful.

"All right, but please don't put them in unnecessary danger." Rebecca stood and pulled her shawl closer around her slender body.

Seth handed her his coffee mug. "I better get some shut-eye. Tomorrow is going to be a long day." He paused to look at her. "Do you need anything from town?"

"I don't believe so. Why?" She stopped in front of the closed door.

Seth hurried to help her open it. "We need saddles and bridles for the horses. The ones we had burned in the fire."

She turned to face him. "Do you need me to go with you?"

Her eyes searched his face.

"No. I just figured if you needed anything you might like to go." Seth enjoyed the way her eyes sparkled in the evening light. The moon hung in such a way as to shine in her eyes.

"I see. I don't believe I need anything but if I change my mind I'll let you know over breakfast." Rebecca moved into the house. "Thank you for keeping me informed." She smiled a tired grin and then shut the wooden door behind her.

She really was a beautiful woman. Her weary grin had caused his heart to do a little dance. For the first time, he had noticed twin dimples in her cheeks. He'd always been a sucker for dimples. Seth shook his head to clear it of those unwanted thoughts and feelings. He had a fiancée out there somewhere and had no room for such thoughts.

He walked to where Andrew sat on a stump keeping watch over the horses. His eyes looked heavenward. "Looks like we might get some cold weather soon," Andrew said in way of greeting.

Seth followed his line of vision. The moon now played hide-and-seek with the dark clouds. A soft ring circled the moon.

"Rain or snow?" he asked.

"Probably rain," Andrew answered, meeting Seth's gaze. "I don't think it is cold enough for snow, but I could be wrong." The young man shrugged.

A nippy breeze lifted the hair on Seth's neck. "I believe you are right, but it for sure is getting colder."

Andrew pulled up his collar. "Yep."

Seth leaned against the fence rail facing the horses. The night's silence offered comfort. The horses snorted from time to time and their feet shuffled against the hard-packed dirt. If he closed his eyes he could almost smell their musky scents.

"It's peaceful out here," Andrew said. He'd moved to stand beside Seth at the railing. He laid his rifle on the top bar and sighed. "Did Ma give you a hard time about Beni taking a watch?" he asked.

"Not after she learned that Jacob would be with him," Seth answered truthfully. He'd expected her to put up a better argument. He glanced in Andrew's direction.

Andrew seemed ever watchful. "That's good. Ma's very protective of Beni, and now Noah."

"How long has Noah been on the farm?" Seth asked, deliberately focusing his attention on the horses.

Andrew heaved a sigh. "About three months, give or take a day. Beni has been here since he was three. The rest of us arrived shortly after our twelfth birthdays."

Seth could understand Rebecca's concern. Beni probably still seemed like a baby to her. Noah hadn't been here long and with the changes going on at the farm and in his life, Rebecca must be worried about his reactions to those changes.

"Are you an orphan, too?" Andrew stared at Seth.

"I guess that depends on how you look at it. I didn't grow up in an orphanage but I no longer have any family left." He held the boy's gaze, waiting for the next question that was sure to follow.

It didn't take long for Andrew. He asked, "Is that why you signed on with the Pony Express?"

"No, I signed on because I'd been robbed by bandits and needed the money." Seth didn't add that he'd been searching for his mail-order bride when he was attacked.

"What was that like?" Andrew picked up his gun and cradled it in his arms. Whether he was angling for company on his watch or was simply curious, Seth couldn't tell, but decided to answer him honestly.

"Well, I was traveling alone and had decided to bed down in a small grove of trees just outside of town. Normally, my horse lets me know if anyone is around, but on this night, the horse didn't alert me. Or if he did, I simply didn't hear him. Anyway, the next thing I knew three men surrounded me with guns."

"Did you try to fight them?" Andrew propped his

leg on the fence and turned from looking at the horses. His face filled with excitement. Seth made a note of his lack of attention to what might be happening around them.

"No, I chose to live instead."

Andrew sighed in disappointment. "So you just gave them your money." He turned away and studied the house.

"Yes, I gave them my money and all my supplies, too."

"Why didn't you fight them?" Andrew faced him once more. The accusation in his voice caused Seth to pause. It seemed there was more to the question than just curiosity.

"Andrew, there is a time to fight and a time to surrender. Knowing the difference can mean life or death."

"But they took all your money and supplies."

Seth nodded. "Yes, but they left me with my life. There is no shame in not fighting when the odds are against you." He laid a hand on the young man's shoulder. It was obvious that Andrew had either backed down from a fight or had fought and lost.

"Maybe, but I will never let a man take what is mine away." Andrew straightened his shoulders and stepped away from Seth.

It was obvious that the boy was hurting, but Seth didn't think now was the time to confront that hurt. He decided to pray about it instead. "Well, I think I'll turn in now. Do you need me to spot you for a few minutes? Or will you be all right until Philip relieves you?"

Andrew's shoulders drooped. "I'll be all right. I don't have much longer to wait now."

"Good night." Seth walked away, leaving the young man to his guard duty and his own thoughts. Each boy had a story to tell. He couldn't help but wonder about Andrew's.

In his room, Seth kneeled down beside his bed and prayed. "Lord, please help me as I work with these young men. I know Andrew is hurting. Please help him to overcome his past and look toward a bright new future. And, Lord, if I can be of service to You or him, please show me how. Amen." He pulled himself up on the side of the bed.

Working on the Young farm could possibly be more challenging than he'd expected. Seth couldn't deny that he found Rebecca Young attractive and that made him cautious to even explore thoughts on the matter. How could a man, in such a short time, feel so strong a connection to another person? He could almost guess her next words and he read the expressions on her face and in her eyes so easily. Yet, when it came to the workings of her mind, she seemed to guard herself carefully. And that made him want to keep himself separated from Rebecca and the rest of her family, but, on the other hand, he also felt as if he wanted to jump in with both feet and help them in any way he could. But in doing so, would he regret the outcome?

## Chapter Six

Rebecca peered out the window, tongue-tied in surprise as the stage sloshed through the rain puddles in her front yard. What on earth was it doing here? The stage never passed this way. She stepped out onto the front porch.

Seth dashed from the bunkhouse, trying to avoid the tracks made from the wheels. He pulled off his hat and arched a brow at her as he bounded up onto the porch. "I didn't think the stage stopped here," he said in way of greeting.

"It doesn't," Rebecca answered, watching as the stage came to a complete stop.

The driver jumped from his seat up top. Water and mud splashed around his already soaked pant legs as he hurried to open the door in the pouring rain.

Rebecca watched as a tall, thin, mustached man with graying hair descended the coach steps. He carried a briefcase and his boots shone like oiled lanterns. Rebecca almost cringed as he stepped from the last rung directly into the mud. Mr. James Bromley, one of the

Pony Express division superintendents, had graced them with his presence.

She whispered to Seth, "Were you expecting him today?"

"No, I was not," he said with quiet emphasis. "I can only assume he's here to check on my progress with the boys."

Mr. Bromley stepped up onto the porch. "Mrs. Young, Seth."

Seth stepped forward and shook the older man's hand. "Mr. Bromley, you chose a dreary day to come for a visit."

The other man laughed. "It's pleasant here. In other places along the route they're still getting snow."

Rebecca stepped forward. "Please, come inside out of the rain. I've made a fresh pot of coffee and you can conduct your business out of the weather." She held the door open.

"Thank you, Mrs. Young, that would be most appreciated." Mr. Bromley wiped his feet on the rag rug she'd placed in front of the door and then swept past her. The smell of cigar smoke wafted from him to her sensitive nose.

Seth took the door and held it open for her. He offered an encouraging grin. She passed him in the doorway and immediately noted that Mr. Bromley had made himself at home.

Joy sat on the floor beside the window playing with blocks the boys had given her from the scraps they'd used in rebuilding the barn. She looked up in surprise to find a stranger sitting on her mother's couch.

"Joy, come with me to the kitchen. We'll leave the

men to discuss their business in private." Rebecca didn't wait for the little girl to respond but turned toward her comfortable kitchen. The hearty scent of fresh-brewed coffee filled the sweet-smelling kitchen.

When they were out of earshot of the men, Joy asked, "Ma, can we give Seth some of the cookies we made?"

The two of them had spent the morning making sugar cookies. "I'm sure he would like that. Why don't you get a plate and put some on it. Make sure the plate isn't chipped. We want to present our best to Mr. Bromley, don't we?"

"Yes, Ma." Joy hurried to the cupboard and reached for one of the special plates used for company. "I hope he likes them."

"Who? Mr. Bromley?" Rebecca asked. She suspected her daughter was talking about Seth. The little girl followed him around like a puppy. Thankfully, he didn't seem to mind.

"Yes, but also Seth." The little girl moved to the big platter of cookies that sat on the counter and picked out several bigger ones. "I think these are the prettiest, don't you?" she asked.

Rebecca glanced over her shoulder and looked at the cookies. "They sure are," she agreed.

The smile that graced her daughter's sweet face pushed away some of the concern Rebecca felt at Mr. Bromley's arrival. She prayed he'd approve of Seth's methods and progress with the boys. She told herself it had nothing to do with liking Seth, it had to do with the boys having to adjust to a new station keeper, if Mr. Bromley didn't approve of Seth and his methods.

A few minutes later, she and Joy were back in the sitting room passing out coffee and cookies. Seth smiled his thanks. He appeared relaxed so Rebecca assumed all had gone well in the men's discussion.

"I hope you like sugar cookies, Mr. Bromley," Rebecca said as she handed him his cup.

He selected a cookie from the plate Joy held out to him and smiled. "As a matter of fact, I do." Mr. Bromley took a bite, closed his eyes and sighed.

Joy smiled at Seth. "I made them. Do you like them, too, Seth?" she asked.

Seth met Rebecca's gaze over the little girl's head. He took a bite of the cookie and chewed slowly. A teasing glint entered his eyes as he asked Joy, "Did you dip your finger in the batter?"

Joy shook her head. "No. Ma says that's yucky and not to do it."

Seth laughed. "Well, these are the sweetest and best cookies I've ever tasted."

"Mrs. Young, have you considered selling your coffee and cookies?" Mr. Bromley asked in a serious voice.

She set down the coffee tray and frowned. "No. Besides, who would I sell them to?" Rebecca doubted she could sell them at the general store and she didn't want to deal with Mr. Edwards to try.

He sat forward. "I'm glad you asked. Part of the reason I'm here today is to tell you that we'd like to use your farm as a stagecoach stop as well as a Pony Express home station." The older man stopped speaking and let his words sink in.

Rebecca looked to Seth, who simply shrugged his

shoulders. She turned her attention back to Mr. Bromley and asked, "Do you need my permission to have it stop here?" She wasn't sure if having her home become the stagecoach stop was a good idea. How would it affect the boys?

"Since the farm belongs to you, yes. We've discovered that the stage riders need a break and your place is in the middle of the two stops it already makes," he explained.

Rebecca nodded. She knew the stage passed about a mile away from the house. It made sense that if they were going to add an additional stop they make it at her farm. She hesitated, though. Would the benefits of allowing it to stop here outweigh the drawbacks?

"If you wanted to sell refreshments to the passengers, we would have no problem with that and I'm sure they would be most appreciative," he added, as if trying to persuade her to allow it. "The stop would only be for about thirty minutes—enough time to allow the tired travelers to stretch their legs, and the coach driver time to water and rest the horses before pressing on."

Rebecca picked up a cookie and nibbled its crispy edge. If she could sell food to the travelers it would mean a little extra income. It would also mean she could have supplies delivered right to her front door, not to mention get to see people more often. She liked the thought of that. Even with all the kids it became very lonesome during the winter when they didn't go to town but once every few months. "How often would it pass through?"

"A couple of times a week. I'll be able to give you a schedule as soon as I have your permission to use the farm," he answered, reaching in his pocket and pulling out a slip of paper.

Deciding to give it a try, Rebecca asked, "The refreshments wouldn't need to be large meals, would they?"

"No, something simple, like these cookies or a sandwich." He unfolded the paper and studied it. "It looks like the stage would run on Mondays from east to west and Thursdays from west to east—they should both arrive around ten thirty in the morning." Mr. Bromley looked up at her. "So what do you think? Can we make this a regular stop?"

Rebecca nodded. "I think that will be fine as long as the stage rider will take care of his horses himself."

"That he will, Mrs. Young." Mr. Bromley finished his coffee and stood. "Thank you for the cookies and coffee. Now I need to be on my way." He pulled his hat back on his head and walked to the door.

Rebecca followed him. "When will the stage start stopping here?" she asked as her mind began to do a mental inventory of her supplies.

"We'll need to check the route, make sure there are no ruts or trees down. Plan for next Monday to be the first time it stops." He smiled at her. "Thank you for agreeing."

She returned his smile. "You're welcome."

The driver of the stage hurried to open the door for the businessman. Mr. Bromley dashed out into the rain and Seth ran toward the bunkhouse, where the rest of the boys waited. The stage pulled away and Seth disappeared into the bunkhouse. Disappointment ate at her. She would have liked to talk to him about her new business venture. When had she started thinking of Seth as a sounding board? He'd only been there a week and she realized she'd begun to look forward to their chats in the evening. That was only natural, wasn't it?

Seth felt as if a weight had been taken off his shoulders. He hadn't expected Mr. Bromley today, but his encouraging words had come at a much-needed time. His boss seemed happy the boys were doing well in their preparations for the many rides they would be completing in the days to come. The fact that his boss had arrived by stage at first had puzzled him, since the stage normally passed about a mile to the north of the farm. As their conversation continued Mr. Bromley had asked a few pointed questions about Rebecca, and Seth became a little uncomfortable, wondering why his boss needed to know if Seth thought Rebecca had a good business head. When he asked if she cooperated with Seth with regard to his training of the boys, Seth took the bull by the horns and asked him why all the questions. Once satisfied that the questions were for her good, he answered with honesty and told his boss that over the past few days he'd come to admire Mrs. Young and her family.

Then, just before Rebecca and Joy had returned, Mr. Bromley had given Seth more money to buy needed supplies for the barn, such as bridles, saddles and feed. All in all it turned out to be a good visit.

Seth shook the water from his hat and then entered the bunkhouse. Philip and Thomas were playing checkers beside the black potbellied stove. Andrew lay on his bunk with a book resting over his face. Noah sat on his bunk sharpening his knife. Jacob patiently schooled Beni on the different types of knots. They held a rope between them and Jacob watched Benjamin closely, only guiding when necessary.

"Jacob, can I have a word with you?" Seth asked, opening the door to his room.

"Sure, Seth." Jacob nodded to Benjamin. "Keep practicing, I'll be right back to see how you're doing."

Seth waited for the young man to walk to him then proceeded into his bedroom. He sat down on his bed and indicated that Jacob should take the rocker that sat in the corner. Once Jacob was seated, Seth said, "Now that the barn is built, I'd like for you to move into the tack room."

Jacob studied the tips of his muddy boots. "I'd like to, Seth, but someone needs to stay with Ma in the house."

"Why? When I got here you were all staying out here in the bunkhouse," Seth reminded him, aware that this was important to Jacob.

Still looking down, Jacob answered, "Yes, but you weren't here then." He looked up with challenging eyes.

Seth sat up a little straighter. "Jacob, I know you are trying to tell me something, but for the life of me I can't figure out what. Why don't you just spit out whatever is bothering you?"

"Ma needs a chaperone."

"A chaperone?"

Jacob nodded. "Yep, people in town are talking."

"About your mother and me?"

"Yes, sir."

Seth breathed in deeply. "Was that what had you and

your mother tied in knots when we all went to town together that first day?"

Jacob nodded.

He should have seen this coming. Seth exhaled and said, "I see. But how do the townsfolk know you are staying in the house?"

Jacob rubbed the dark stubble on his chin. "I guess they don't."

"So, if we moved Andrew into the house, no one would know that you moved out?" Seth asked, easing into a more comfortable position.

"No, I suppose not," Jacob answered, looking as if he might argue further.

Seth spoke quickly, not giving him a chance. "As the stock tender you need to stay in the tack room so that you are closer to the horses. We will need the horses ready to go at a moment's notice. Riders will arrive in the middle of the night as well as during the day. You have to be prepared. Do you want to have to tiptoe out of the house every time you hear a rider come in?"

"I'm not sure Andrew will want to move into the house," Jacob answered. He stood slowly. "I'll ask him—if he's agreeable then I'll move out to the barn."

He watched Jacob shut the door behind him. The sound of thunder shook the house. The storm reminded Seth of the Youngs. Just when he thought things were going well and they were all working together, lightning seemed to strike and was always followed by thunder.

There was no doubt in his mind that if Andrew didn't want to move into the main house, Jacob wouldn't be moving into the tack room in the barn. He laid down on his bed and listened to the rain hit the tin roof.

And if that wasn't enough, now the townspeople were talking about Rebecca and him. As far as he knew, neither of them had given them reason to talk. Seth sighed. Jacob felt as if he needed to protect his mother's reputation but really wasn't able to.

Frustration gnawed at his gut. If he didn't need the money to find Charlotte, Seth would move on. He didn't need this family's problems and he certainly never intended to cause them more. Drawing on the only source that had sustained him the past couple of years, Seth closed his eyes and prayed that God would provide a way to keep Rebecca's reputation free of harm and that God would help him find Charlotte so that he could return home to St. Joseph.

# Chapter Seven

After dinner, Seth walked out to the front porch. The rain had stopped but it had brought a chilling wind. He wrapped his coat tighter around his body and sat down on the porch swing. The sound of kids laughing and talking loudly caused him to grin. Even though the Young kids weren't related, they behaved very much like brothers and sister.

Over the meal, Rebecca had told them all that not only was the farm a Pony Express station, but now it was also a stage stop. She explained that twice a week the stage would stop there and she and Joy would sell things like sandwiches, cookies and beverages to the passengers. The boys had asked questions and Rebecca had answered each of them with more patience than Seth thought he could ever exhibit. Joy excitedly told her brothers how much Mr. Bromley had enjoyed her cookies. Seth had to admit that he'd felt a bit like an outsider.

Even now, sitting on the porch, he longed to join in but felt he had nothing to contribute. After he found and married Charlotte, would he then feel like part of a family? With no brothers or sisters, Seth had grown up an only child. His mother had abandoned him and his father when he was very young. Grandmother always said his pa had died of a broken heart. Seth gleaned from the retelling that women couldn't be trusted and loving one would break your heart and kill you. As an adult, he didn't believe that his dad literally died of a broken heart, but Seth did know that women couldn't be trusted. If it wasn't for his grandmother, he'd not be on this wild-goose chase looking for a woman who'd probably simply changed her mind about marriage.

"So this is where you got off to," Rebecca said, coming through the front door. She wore a light brown dress and her blue cloak covered most of it.

The swing rocked gently under her slight weight as she sat. He grinned over at her. "Yes, it's a little quieter out here."

At that moment, Joy let out a loud squeal and Rebecca laughed. "Yes, they are a mite keyed up tonight. It's probably from being cooped up most of the day."

If she hadn't said it, he would have. "Joy is very excited about the stage stopping here," he said as the little girl's voice drifted through the window.

"Yes, she wants to make all the cookies we sell." Rebecca pulled her cloak tighter about her middle.

"She told me she'd read a recipe that had nuts in it that I wanted to try. I didn't know she could read," he said, looking over at his pretty companion.

"Oh, she can a little, but mostly she calls looking at pictures reading." Rebecca smiled proudly. "But she'll be reading real books in no time."

Seth cocked his head to one side and studied her profile. She pushed back a wayward strand of dark hair, her fingers strong and slim, her face a perfect oval. She had a strength that did not lessen her femininity one bit and she carried herself confidently. The wind lifted one of her curls and his eyes followed the movement, making it difficult to concentrate on her words. No woman had affected him like Rebecca seemed to.

She looked at him expectantly and he reined in his thoughts to their conversation. After a moment he said, "I'm sure she will be reading soon. Joy's a very bright child. She's old enough to go to school now, isn't she?" As casually as possible, he stood and walked to the porch rail.

The smile slipped from her face and sadness filled her voice. "John and I had talked about letting her start this fall." She sighed heavily. "I think I'll continue with our plans and let her attend. Even though I hate letting my baby go."

Seth didn't know what to say. He hadn't meant to make her sad.

As if she realized her mood had changed the atmosphere around them, Rebecca offered him a bright smile that didn't quite meet her eyes. "So, did you and Mr. Bromley have a nice visit this afternoon?"

"We did. He gave us extra money to buy the barn supplies and seemed pleased with the boys' progress. Not a bad visit at all." Seth knew his words echoed his thoughts from earlier in the day.

"I'm glad." She paused then asked, "What do you think about the stage stopping here? You didn't say a word during dinner about it." She worried her bottom lip with her pretty white teeth.

"I think it's a great idea," he answered. He'd had a thought earlier and maybe now was the time to ask Rebecca for a favor. Before he could mention it, she spoke.

"If the offer still stands, I need to go into town tomorrow after all. I don't have enough ingredients to make cookies and I'd like to pick up some tea. Ladies seem to like tea more than coffee, I think."

Seth remembered Jacob's words about the townsfolk talking about them. He'd planned on going for the needed supplies but now thought he'd send Jacob instead. "The offer still stands. I'll ask Jacob to hitch up the wagon in the morning."

"Thank you." She started to get up.

"Before you go inside, I'd like to ask a favor of you," Seth blurted out, afraid she'd leave and he'd lose his nerve.

Rebecca eased back into the swing. "All right."

He took a deep breath. "I know you don't know me very well and I probably shouldn't even ask, but since the stage is coming through here, it might be a good opportunity." Why did he feel so breathless?

Caution filled her voice as she asked, "What might be a good opportunity?"

Seth rolled his shoulders and started again. "Let me start at the beginning. A few months ago my grandmother asked me to find a nice girl and get married." He saw the shock on her face and held up his hand. "Hold on, let me finish."

At her nod, he continued, "So I placed an ad for a mail-order bride." Seth watched her relax and pressed on. "My grandmother's dying wish was that I get married."

Rebecca asked, "Why would she ask you to get married, if she was dying?"

"She didn't want to leave me without anyone to take care of me…love me, I guess you could say. Anyway, now that my grandmother has passed on, I have no other relatives that I know of." Seth glanced at her face to see if she understood.

Rebecca nodded. "That makes sense. Did you get a mail-order bride?" she asked, looking up at him.

"Yes and no."

A frown creased the center of her brow. "I don't understand."

Seth grinned. "Maybe I should just tell you everything and then let you ask questions." He hoped she heard the teasing in his voice and didn't think him rude.

Rebecca smoothed out her skirt and nodded. "That might work best." A tiny smile tilted up one corner of her mouth and she shook her head. "Although, men are not always the best at storytelling."

"Agreed." He wondered if she knew how easy she was to talk to. He'd never told his story to anyone, yet here he stood eager for her input. "Yes, a young woman answered my ad. Her name is Charlotte Fisher. She wrote and said she'd be on the first stage to St. Joseph, only she never arrived. Grandmother died but not before she made me promise to find Charlotte." He stopped and inhaled the cold night air. "I have been looking for Charlotte ever since." His gaze searched Rebecca's. Sadness filled her sweet face, only this time he could see that she wasn't sad for herself, but for him and his loss.

He pressed on with his story. "A few weeks ago while traveling alone, three men held me up and took all my money. When I filed a report with the town sheriff, I told him I needed work that would let me travel and keep me close to the stage route at the same time. He mentioned the Pony Express that had just started up. I found Mr. Bromley and he hired me. The rest you know. That's why I work for the Pony Express—to make money so I can continue my search for Charlotte." He eased back against the porch rail. Seth couldn't remember the last time he'd talked this much.

"So, no honorable intentions to see that the mail gets through?"

He stiffened at the challenge in her voice, but boldly lifted his chin and met her gaze. Only to stare tongue-tied. She had a hand pressed to her mouth to stifle the giggles threatening to escape. In spite of himself he chuckled.

"If you could only have seen your face when I said that."

"I thought you were judging my intentions."

"How could I judge your intentions when I'm doing the same thing?"

He quirked a brow at her. "How so?"

"My reasons for accepting the stage stop have nothing to do with the mail. It serves several purposes and all of them are personal." Her expression stilled and grew serious. "So, how can I help you?"

Seth had difficulty pulling his gaze away from hers. "Well, the stage runs both east and west, which means that Charlotte is probably somewhere along the line. Last I heard from her she was coming from California. What I'd like to ask you to do is each time the stage stops here to inquire if anyone knows her and, if so, where I can find her?"

Rebecca nodded. "I'm not sure that will work but I'm more than happy to help you any way I can." She stood and stretched. "I'm tired and if we're going to town, I'd like to leave right after breakfast."

"Oh, and one more thing before you go." Seth pushed away from the porch railing. When she turned to face him, he asked, "Did Jacob tell you I want him to move into the barn's tack room?"

"No, but that's understandable," she offered.

Seth was pleased that Rebecca wasn't going to fight him on this move. "I'm glad you don't object."

"I'll talk to him. There really is no reason for him to stay in the house with me and the younger kids." She reached for the door and then stopped and turned to face him once more. "Is there anything else?"

He shook his head. "Not tonight. Thank you, Rebecca. For everything." Seth realized he'd used her Christian name and quickly bounded off the porch. What had possessed him to become so personal with her? He couldn't slip up like that again. Even though he did enjoy the way her name tripped off his lips, with ease and satisfaction. No, it wouldn't—or rather, it couldn't—happen again.

Rebecca hadn't slept well. She'd wrestled with the fact that Seth had used her given name and she certainly hadn't minded. If anything, she'd liked the way

her name sounded when he said it. All night she'd
fought with herself. Should she ask him not to use her
Christian name? Or pretend it wasn't a big deal?

"Ma, is everything all right?" Jacob asked. He
guided the horses over the muddy road, careful to avoid
all potholes. Concern filled his face.

"Everything's fine. I was just thinking about my
supply list," she answered, attempting to smile at him.

They rode in silence for a few moments. Then Jacob
spoke. "Seth wants me to move into the barn's tack
room. I planned on asking Andrew to move into the
house with you and the little ones." He grinned over
his shoulder at Benjamin and Joy.

She knew her son thought himself her chaperone,
but regardless of what he said, the townsfolk would
continue to talk. Silently she prayed that the Lord
would send an answer to this problem. "That's not necessary, Jacob. I can take care of things in the house,"
Rebecca answered.

Jacob started to argue but then clamped his lips shut.
He focused on the road ahead.

"If he's moving out, does that mean I get to move
out, too?" Benjamin asked, pulling himself up on his
knees and clutching the wooden seat Rebecca and
Jacob sat upon.

Rebecca frowned. "No, you stay in the house. We
need at least one man watching over us, don't you
think?" she asked, eyeing her eight-year-old son, hoping that he'd not realize she stroked his ego to get him
to do what she wanted.

Benjamin puffed out his chest. "Oh, I hadn't thought
of that. I suppose you're right."

The rest of the trip passed quietly. Jacob and Rebecca were each lost in their own thoughts. Benjamin and Joy played school in the bed of the wagon. He took his role as big brother seriously as he read to her out of one of her picture books.

Their stops at the leather and lumberyard were pretty uneventful. Jacob had no trouble acquiring the needed bridles and saddles. He'd learned from the lumberman that one of his neighbors may have extra hay for sale, at least enough for them until the Pony Express supply wagon came out to the farm.

Rebecca dreaded stopping in at the general store. If there were any other stores in town that supplied household items, she would very easily switch her business to them. But there wasn't. She stood to climb down from the wagon but Jacob placed a hand on her arm. "Ma, I'll go get what you need." He jumped from the wagon and looked up at her expectantly.

She handed him her list. "You sure you don't mind, son?"

He took the list and grinned. "Nope, if these two behave I might use some of my Pony Express wages and get them each a penny candy."

Benjamin beamed at his little sister. "We'll be good, won't we, Joy?"

She bobbed her head and smiled back.

Jacob stepped onto the boardwalk and entered the store. Rebecca heard the bell announce her son's arrival. She really should have gone herself, but the thought of facing Mr. Edwards left her feeling cold. Her gaze moved to her younger children, who were once more absorbed in the picture book.

Maybe now with the extra income, she could order a few more books for them. When John died, she'd stopped the one-book-a-month shipment she'd intended to use for educating the kids. She alone was responsible for the money John left her and she'd had to learn over the past couple of months how to manage, and though it wasn't necessary to be frugal, John had taught them the Bible's teachings on being a good steward. She needed the money to last so she would never have to seek work and leave Joy alone with strangers.

The sound of the bell ringing over the door to the general store drew her attention away from the children. Fay Miller wiped at her eyes as she closed the door behind her. When she turned to face the street, Rebecca could see that tears ran down her chubby cheeks. Rebecca climbed down the wagon at a fast pace.

"Mrs. Miller, are you all right?" she asked, feeling foolish. If the woman was all right, she wouldn't be crying.

The older woman sniffed loudly and looked up at her. "Oh, hello, Rebecca dear."

Fay Miller always had a smile on her face and her sparkling gray eyes usually held a teasing glint, but not today. Something had to be terribly wrong to dissolve the sweet woman into tears. Rebecca hugged her about the shoulders. "What's wrong?"

"I'm old and useless, that's what's wrong," she wailed.

Rebecca's heart broke for the woman. "Nonsense, why would you say such a thing?" she asked, leading her toward the bench that sat outside the store.

Once seated, Mrs. Miller wiped her face with a big floral handkerchief. She sighed heavily and said, "Rebecca, I have outlived my usefulness."

"Why don't you start at the beginning and tell me what is going on," Rebecca suggested, patting the older woman's arm.

She nodded. "This morning Mr. Welsh, the man who owns my house, said he's going to sell it so that they can put up something called a telegraph pole and use my home for a telegraph office. He told me I had twenty-four hours to move out. Twenty-four hours!" Mrs. Miller cried.

Mrs. Miller was a widower. As far as Rebecca knew she and Mr. Miller had never had any children. The late Mr. Miller had been gone for ten years and Mrs. Miller had lived in that house for as long as Rebecca could remember. How could Mr. Welsh just kick her out like that?

She moaned into her handkerchief. "What am I going to do?"

Rebecca stared at her wagon for several long moments. Did everyone have problems? It would appear so, even sweet Mrs. Miller. She silently prayed for an answer to help her old friend. As Rebecca prayed, a thought began to build in her mind. Maybe they could help each other. Would the older woman be willing to move out to the farm? Or would she balk and say she'd rather stay in town?

# *Chapter Eight*

Rebecca turned to face her. She took the older woman's hands away from her face and looked into her tear-filled eyes. "Mrs. Miller, how would you like to move out to the farm with me and my boys?"

Mrs. Miller sniffled. "What?"

"Well, it occurs to me that the Lord may be answering both our prayers. I need a chaperone and you need a new home."

The older woman pulled one of her trembling hands free and wiped at her face again. "You want me to chaperone you?" Her voice quivered.

Rebecca explained, "Yes. I'm not sure if you've heard but the Pony Express sent out a man to be the station keeper at the farm. He stays out in the bunkhouse with the boys but last time I was in town, Mr. Edwards found out and he acted as if I was doing something wrong by letting the station keeper stay out at my place." Rebecca shook her head in disgust. "He is a Pony Express employee. It's his job, he has to live there. If you came to live with me, you'd be supplying me with a chaperone and I'd supply you with a roof over your head for the rest of your days." She smiled brightly at the woman. "Which, by the looks of things, will be for many, many years."

For the first time since she'd left the store, Mrs. Miller's mouth wobbled into a smile. "Are you sure you wouldn't mind an old woman rattling around in your house?" she asked.

"The only thing I mind is that you keep referring to yourself as an old woman," Rebecca assured her.

"Then I'll do it. But I don't want you thinking it's forever. We don't even know if we'll enjoy living together," Mrs. Miller said, but her actions belied her words. She eagerly reached for Rebecca's hand. "Oh, thank you, thank you."

Rebecca gathered her into a close hug. "I'll send Jacob and the little ones back to the house to unload the wagon and they can return for us in the morning. We'll get you packed up tonight." Excitement coursed through her at the thought of Mrs. Miller living on the ranch. She hadn't realized how much she'd missed another woman's presence. Her mother-in-law had died shortly after Rebecca's eighteenth birthday. That had been several years ago.

"Mrs. Miller, I am excited." Rebecca clapped her hands in glee.

"Now, now, Rebecca. If we are going to live together, you must stop calling me Mrs. Miller. Fay will do nicely." Fay's words chided, but her voice simmered with barely checked relief and joy.

Jacob came out of the store with a large box full

of supplies. He looked from his mother to the older woman, but respect for his elders kept him from asking the questions she felt sure were on the tip of his tongue.

"Jacob, Fay is moving in with us," Rebecca announced, sliding an arm around the older woman's shoulders.

To her son's credit he acted as if things like this were an everyday occurrence at their house. "Well, Mrs. Miller, all orphans are welcome at our place, even older ones."

Rebecca saw at once that Jacob could not have said anything that would please Fay more. She beamed with pride at her son.

The woman's eyes widened and she clasped her hands together and placed them over her heart. Her voice seemed to have lodged in her throat because all she said was "Aw."

"Jacob, I need you to take the supplies and the younger children back to the farm, while I help her pack."

He carried the box to the wagon. "Yes, Ma." He set it in the back with the little kids and then turned to face her once more. "Would you like a ride back to her house?"

"Did you get us candy?" Benjamin asked. The picture book had been forgotten.

"I think we'll walk," Fay answered, smiling happily. She turned to look at Rebecca. "If that's all right with you?"

Jacob answered Benjamin by handing each of them a peppermint stick. "Here you go, buddy."

"That is fine with me," Rebecca answered. She looped her arm inside the older woman's and started to walk toward Fay's house. "I can use the exercise."

Jacob pulled himself onto the wagon and then called after them, "Ma, what about supper?"

Rebecca stopped and grinned at him. "I guess it's a sandwich night for you all. There is ham in the larder and fresh bread. For dessert you can open a few jars of peaches. Joy will help you. Won't you, Joy?"

The little girl licked the sticky candy from her fingers and nodded.

"Oh, and Jacob, go ahead and move your things out to the barn. Mrs. Miller will be staying in your room."

"If this is too much trouble—" Fay began but Rebecca cut her off.

"Why, it's no trouble at all. We will be helping each other out of troublesome situations and as for my family…they will be fine for one day." She turned back to the wagon. "You all be good and mind Jacob."

Both of her youngest children answered, "Yes, Ma."

Jacob nodded. "I'll pick you up tomorrow at Mrs. Miller's."

Rebecca waved at them as he turned the horses around and then headed home. It had been a long time since she had been childless. And she'd never asked them to fend for their own dinner. For a moment Rebecca wondered if she was doing the right thing, then shook off the slight feeling of guilt. Mrs. Miller needed her and she needed the older woman. For the first time in a while, Rebecca felt as if she had a companion, maybe even someone she could confide in.

* * *

Seth looked up as the wagon rumbled into the yard. He immediately noticed that Rebecca wasn't with Jacob and the two youngest children. He hurried to the wagon. "Where is your mother?"

Jacob jumped down from the wagon and then helped Joy over the side. "She stayed in town to help Mrs. Miller pack her things. I'm to go back for them tomorrow."

"Who is Mrs. Miller?" Seth asked.

Jacob picked up the box of kitchen supplies and handed them to Benjamin. "Beni, take these to the kitchen and set them on the table." He turned to face Seth. "Mrs. Miller is a widow woman from town. Her husband passed away a few years ago and she has no children. I heard while I was in the store that the man who owns her house kicked her out this morning. I imagine Ma felt sorry for her and invited her to live out here."

"That was mighty nice of her," Seth said thoughtfully. Had Rebecca seen Mrs. Miller as a chaperone of sorts? Would her presence keep the townsfolk from gossiping about them? He hoped it would.

Andrew and Clayton walked out of the barn. Clayton laid the pitchfork he'd had in his hands against the wall. "Where's Ma?" Andrew asked, looking around as if he thought something terrible had happened to their mother.

"In town," Jacob answered.

Seth motioned for the boys to come closer. "Grab a saddle and take it to the barn." He turned his attention back to Jacob. "There are only three saddles here."

Jacob nodded. "Yep, that's all Mr. Grey had that we could buy today. I figured three would do until we got supplies from the Pony Express."

Seth picked up a bridle and examined the leather. "They won't be sending saddles and bridles. I'll go pick up the women and stop by Mr. Grey's tomorrow. Hopefully, we'll be able to order a couple more of each. What did you find out about hay?"

Jacob sat down on the bed of the wagon. "Mr. Browning has extra hay he can sell to us."

Seth nodded. He tried to focus on what Jacob was saying about the hay, but couldn't take his mind off Rebecca. What was she doing? Was she packing up Mrs. Miller and laughing? He loved her laugh. Sometimes she laughed softly and brought her hand up to quiet the giggles. Other times she burst out laughing, the sound floating up from her throat, most often at something one of the kids said or did. But her joy was always infectious, bringing a ready smile to others. With the widow coming to live with Rebecca, would their nightly chats on the porch end? Deep down Seth hoped not; he hated to admit it, but he'd miss those chats if they did. Then again, he'd begun to care about Rebecca and that was dangerous.

The next morning, Seth hitched up the wagon. His stomach growled and he grinned. Joy had decided to make breakfast for everyone and had served burned eggs, bacon and toast. He'd tried not to hurt the little girl's feelings but couldn't quite eat what she served.

It had been fun, though, watching her brothers distract her. While one pretended to eat the breakfast, another would rake theirs onto a plate below the table and pass it to the next one.

Clayton had rustled the plate outside. Seth had no idea what the boy had done with the burned mess once he was out of the house, but was glad that he hadn't had to choke it down. Little Joy had been thrilled to see all their cleaned plates.

Jacob had scolded his sister for cooking without supervision all while trying not to grin. They really were a unique and fun family to be around.

Once the wagon was hitched, he checked in on the boys and Joy. Jacob had taken both Joy and Benjamin under his wing. He had Beni mucking out one of the stalls and Joy rubbing oil into the leather on one of the saddles. Jacob himself forked fresh straw into each of the stalls. The other five boys each had a chore and were busy doing them. Seth sniffed appreciatively. New wood and new leather. What a combination.

"Jacob, I need you to make sure everything runs smoothly while I'm gone." Seth leaned against the barn door and met the young man's eyes.

Jacob laughed. There was no anger or animosity in his voice when he said, "I was doing that before you came along. I think I can do it again for one day."

Seth chuckled. "See that you do."

An hour later, he arrived in town. The streets teemed with people coming and going. He pulled the wagon beside the livery yard. Seth leaped down and walked to the general store. In most towns the general store was the meeting place for everyone. Seth hoped to get a bite to eat and then find out where Mrs. Miller lived.

He pushed the door open and the little bell sounded off, announcing his arrival.

The storekeeper came out from behind the counter. "How can I help you, stranger?" he asked.

The place was empty of customers, which surprised Seth. He walked over to the apple bin and pulled out a handful of dried apple. "I mainly came in for directions," he answered, taking a big bite from the fruit.

"As soon as you pay for the apples, I'll be happy to give you directions," the big man answered.

Seth looked at the marked price and pulled money from his pocket. "That should cover this handful." Seth handed it to the storekeeper. "Sorry about that. I forgot myself."

The big man took the money and walked back to his counter and the register. "Where do you need directions to?" he asked, dropping the coins in the drawer.

"Mrs. Miller's house," he answered, studying the man while he chewed. The store owner was tall and big-bellied, and his eyes were hard. Nothing about the man appealed to Seth. He seemed like a bully, which might explain why there were no customers in his store.

"Now, what business do you have with that sweet old woman?"

Seth could tell that the man didn't care about the woman but was simply being nosy. "It's a private matter and my own."

The man nodded. "I see." He stepped from around the counter and puffed up his chest, all the while tapping the side of his head and squinting as if he'd forgotten something. "You know, my memory isn't as good as it used to be."

"Then I won't waste any more of your time." Seth turned on his heels and left the store. He stood on the boardwalk and looked up and down Main Street. The last time he'd been in town he hadn't really taken the time to look around. He figured he had a few minutes and decided to do just that. His eyes scanned each building.

Dove Creek wasn't a very big town. Next to the general store was a small house—he assumed the general-store owner lived in it—and next to it was the doctor's home and office. On the next block sat the bank. It seemed to fill the whole block.

Seth walked toward the bank. Surely the banker would know where Mrs. Miller lived.

He entered the bank and looked about. Dark panel covered the walls and floor. A big desk sat in the middle of the room. He noted offices off to the sides and a staircase that led to the second floor.

Several people stood around the room. A line had formed in front of the bank-teller cage. He noticed that a checkerboard had been set up in one corner of the bank and two elderly gentlemen sat playing the game.

It dawned on Seth that this had become the meeting place of the townspeople instead of the general store. How odd, he thought.

"May I help you?" asked the man sitting at the desk.

Seth walked over to him. "Yes, I am looking for a Mrs. Miller."

"I'm sorry, no one works here by that name," the man said, looking down at the pile of papers in front of him.

He realized his mistake and tried again. "No, I don't

expect she does. I was wondering if you could direct me to her house."

Once more the man looked up. "No, I'm not sure that I could and even if I could, I'm not sure that I would or should." His eyes moved up and down Seth as if assessing his appearance.

"Is there someone here that can tell me?" Seth asked, beginning to feel flustered and realizing that he was drawing quite a bit of attention from the others.

The man sighed and stood. "Wait right here."

Seth nodded. The man walked toward one of the offices. He knocked on the door and entered shortly afterward. Maybe the bank wasn't the best place to ask for directions, he thought as he waited.

It felt as if everyone watched him, but Seth knew that was ridiculous. The line continued to move where the two bank tellers were working. He looked down at the chair in front of the desk and thought about sitting down to wait, but at that moment the man reappeared.

When he was within hearing distance, he said. "I'm sorry, sir. Bank policy is to not give out personal information on our depositors."

Well, that was good to know. Seth nodded his understanding and then turned to leave. The man laid a hand on his arm. He looked at him. With a nod of his head toward the old-timers playing checkers, the man said in a low voice, "But there is nothing to stop you from asking around."

Seth grinned. "Thank you. I think I will see how the game is going."

The man nodded once and dropped his hand.

"Thank you for coming in. If you ever need help opening an account, come on back in."

The two men looked up when Seth approached their table. "Good morning, gentlemen. I was wondering if either of you could tell me where Mrs. Miller lives. My name is Seth Armstrong and I'm supposed to pick up her and Mrs. Young this morning, but I forgot to get the address from Jacob."

One of the men held out his hand. "Nice to meet you, Mr. Armstrong. I'm Caleb Smith and this is my brother-in-law, Marcus Boyd." He returned to his game.

Seth leaned against the wall and waited. Sometimes older fellas wanted time to think about their next move both in life and while playing a game. Mr. Boyd jumped two of Mr. Smith's pieces.

With a grin, he looked up at Seth. "She lives behind the bank here. Her house is the one with the windows boarded up. I saw that landlord of hers boarding them up this morning. Just go to the end of the block and turn left. You won't miss it." He returned his focus to the game.

"Much obliged." Seth walked out of the bank.

The bright sunshine felt good on his face. He hurried to the livery and climbed aboard the wagon. If all went well, he'd have the ladies out to the farm by dinnertime.

As the horses rounded the corner, he saw Rebecca carrying a box to the edge of the street. He waved at her as he set the brake.

"Good morning, Mr. Armstrong."

Mr. Armstrong? Seth didn't like that. "Good morning, Mrs. Young." He frowned, not liking how that sounded any better.

"We're just about done packing," she said as she turned to walk back to the house. "I thought Jacob or Andrew would be coming for us."

Seth jumped down from the wagon and caught up with her. "I had Pony Express business to take care of."

"Are you finished with your business?" she asked, turning to face him.

"No, I wanted to find you first." Seth looked down into her pretty blue eyes. He should have taken care of ordering the saddles and tack before searching for her. Confusion filled his mind as he questioned his own motives for coming to her first.

"Why?"

That was the question of the moment, wasn't it? His gaze moved to the wagon. "I thought you might like to have the wagon to start loading up Mrs. Miller's things."

"Oh. Well. That was very sweet of you," she answered, though her expression made him think she doubted that was what he'd intended.

"I'll go take care of my business and then come back and help you finish loading," he offered.

Mrs. Miller came out of the kitchen. She smiled at Seth.

"Hello."

He nodded at her, tipping his hat. She was a plump little woman with graying brown hair and sparkling blue eyes. Seth fought the urge to stare. She reminded him of his grandmother. A lump the size of river bedrock clogged his throat and he quickly turned away from the women. "I'll be back shortly." He was surprised that his vocal chords worked at all. He hurried away and couldn't get away from them fast enough. His heart felt as if someone had plunged a knife through it. He'd thought he was done grieving for the woman who raised him, but he was wrong.

He walked to the livery with a heavy heart. Seeing Mrs. Miller made him realize that he needed to finish his job with the Pony Express so he could find the mail-order bride he'd promised his grandmother he'd marry. He had to get away from the family that made him long to be a part of them.

## Chapter Nine

A few days later, Rebecca happily baked sugar cookies in the kitchen while Joy played on the rug in the living room. The little girl had helped to make the batter and shape the sweet treats, but for the actual baking process, Rebecca insisted that she do it alone.

Fay sat at the table reading her Bible. Every so often the older woman would say "Amen." Or "Yes, yes, Lord." Rebecca knew she wasn't talking to her, but to her Bible and God. It hadn't taken Rebecca long to learn that Fay had a true love for their Lord. She prayed that someday she'd have the same strong convictions as Fay. Oh, Rebecca loved the Lord, but knew she failed Him in many ways.

Having Fay around the house had turned into a wonderful blessing. The older woman pitched in with the chores and meal preparation. She helped the boys if they needed something done, such as mending a sock or washing a shirt. And could the woman ever cook! What a blessing that was to Rebecca. She thanked the

Lord she no longer had to eat her own cooking all the time.

At first, she'd been worried about how the kids would adapt to Fay moving in, but they all welcomed her with open arms. Fay said she enjoyed having them around and helping out around the house.

"What time will the stage arrive?" Fay asked, looking up from her Bible.

Rebecca glanced at the clock that sat beside the stove. "In about thirty minutes. Mr. Bromley sent a new schedule and it said around one." She looked at the plates of cookies and the sandwiches. "Do you think I should offer hot tea for the ladies?"

Fay shrugged. "If you have it, it can't hurt." A grin split her face. "I wouldn't mind having a cup myself."

"Then I'll make a pot." Rebecca pulled her other coffeepot from under the cabinet and poured fresh water into it. John had spoiled her years ago by purchasing the extra pot. Every day she found some way to remember him.

As she made the tea, Rebecca allowed her thoughts to linger on her deceased husband. When she'd taken the job here on the farm as his mother's helper, she'd never dreamed they'd end up married. John's father had wanted his son married before he passed on and since Rebecca was the only gal around who was close to his age, John had offered to marry her when his mother died. By doing so, he'd fulfilled his father's wish and made sure that Rebecca would always be cared for. They had been good friends, and even though they weren't in love, he'd made sure she was happy. Somewhere along the way she supposed it might have turned into a deep love, the valuable kind, because how could you not love someone that forever put your happiness above his own. And he'd done that with everyone connected to him—the boys, Rebecca and most certainly the child of his heart, Joy.

Coffee wasn't a beverage Rebecca enjoyed, but, tea? She could drink her weight in tea. As the water heated, Rebecca realized that somewhere in the past few months, she'd given up her favorite beverage. Was it because making it reminded her of all that she'd lost? Or was it simply that until now, she'd had precious little time to think about her own likes and desires? Raising seven boys and a little girl left no time for oneself. In fact, it took all her time and energy.

She turned her attention back to Fay. The older woman had gone back to reading the Bible. "What passage are you reading today?"

Fay looked up. "The Book of Job." Her eyes took on a faraway look as she stared out the kitchen window. "That man has always fascinated me. He lost everything but his faith." She looked to Rebecca once more. "Faith is the strongest thing we have in our possession. Man can take everything else, but he can never take our faith in God. Never lose faith, Rebecca, and God will restore what has been taken from you."

The sound of the stagecoach pulling up in front of the house had both women jumping to their feet.

"It's early," Rebecca gasped. Grabbing the platter of sandwiches and cookies, she hurried to the sitting room and placed them on the sideboard she'd arranged for just that purpose.

Fay joined her a moment later, with serving plates and several cups.

"Thank you, Fay," Rebecca said as she hurried back to the kitchen for the coffee and tea. Silently she prayed, *Lord, please let this go well.*

Joy stood on the rug now, wringing her little hands together. She looked at her mother with concern etched on her sweet features.

Rebecca stopped and reassured her daughter. "Joy, there is no reason you can't stay in here and play if that's what you want to do."

Joy smiled. "Thank you, Ma." She slipped back down onto the rug.

What had caused Joy to become so tense at the arrival of the stage? Rebecca picked up both the tea and the coffeepot and hurried back to the sitting room. She made a mental note that after things settled down, she would ask her daughter about her reaction.

"Would you like for me to open the door?" Fay asked.

Rebecca set down the pots. She glanced up at the sign she'd created earlier in the day that had the prices of the food and beverages posted—sandwiches, five cents; two cookies, one cent; a cup of coffee, two cents. Fay had assured her that the prices were reasonable.

She turned around and smoothed out her apron over her dress. "Yes, please." Rebecca held her breath as icy air entered the room.

"Please, come on inside and warm up," Fay called to the passengers.

Two women and a man hurried into the warm room. They stopped just inside the doorway.

"Come on inside." Rebecca motioned for them to come sit down on the sofa and chairs.

She looked around the room, trying to see it as they would for the first time. The fireplace had a hearty fire roaring in it. The plush couch and chairs sat on each side of the fire, creating a rectangle. In between them was a small table that sat upon a light-colored rug. To her it felt cozy; what did it feel and look like to them?

The women hurried into the room, each taking a spot on the couch. They pulled their cloaks tightly about their bodies. They looked as if they were mother and daughter. Both had light blond hair and blue eyes. They were thin with pinched lips. "Thank you," the eldest said.

The gentleman moved closer to the fireplace and stood beside it. "That coffee smells wonderful."

Rebecca wasn't sure how to say that it was for sale. She glanced at Fay, who seemed to understand.

"Mrs. Young makes the best coffee in the whole territory," Fay proclaimed. "And she offers the fairest prices for the cup, too." She walked over to the sideboard and pointed up to the sign.

After reading it, the gentleman moved forward. He dropped several coins into the tin cup she'd placed on the sideboard for money and picked up a plate. "What kind of sandwiches are these, Mrs. Young?" he asked, placing one on his plate and then taking a cup of freshly poured coffee from Fay.

"Egg salad. The dressing is fresh. I made it just this morning," she answered.

The eldest woman stood. She dug in her purse and pulled out several coins.

Rebecca smiled. "What can I get for you?" she asked as the woman dropped her money into the cup.

"I'd like a sandwich. I've never acquired a taste for coffee." She wrinkled her nose as if the smell displeased her.

"We also have hot tea," Fay said, waving her hand to indicate the second pot.

A smile broke out over the woman's face. "Now, tea I could drink all day." She dropped more coins into the cup.

Soon all three of the passengers were munching on sandwiches and drinking from Rebecca's best china. She felt a moment of pride that the ladies and gentleman were enjoying her small serving of food.

Cold air filled the room as the stagecoach driver entered the house. "I think the weather's getting worse, folks. We need to get back on the road."

He was a skinny man who didn't appear to be over five foot three inches tall. Did stagecoach drivers have to be of small stature, like Pony Express riders? She hurried toward him. "Why don't you come in for a quick cup of coffee and a sandwich?" she asked, directing him toward the sideboard.

A worried expression covered his face. Maybe he didn't have the extra money for such things. If she wanted him to linger, she'd have to make it worth his while. "For the coach drivers, the coffee and meal are on the house, Mr...."

"Alexander, ma'am." He hurried to the food and scooped up a sandwich.

Fay poured him a cup of the coffee.

In two bites the sandwich was gone and the coffee

gulped down. "Thanks for the grub, ma'am." He motioned to the passengers. "Time to load up. We leave in two minutes." Mr. Alexander stomped across the floor and jerked open the door. Cold air rushed inside.

Fay chuckled. "Well, he's in a mighty big hurry."

The male passenger put his cup in the washtub that Rebecca had supplied and grinned. "I'd like to buy a couple of those cookies, Mrs. Young. If they are nearly as good as the sandwich, I'll be a very happy man."

Rebecca smiled her thanks, then quickly placed two of the biggest cookies into a cloth bag. She heard his coins hit the others in the cup.

He took the bag with a nod and then proceeded toward the door.

The two women, who had spoken quietly to each other during their short meal, hurriedly stood. The older one ordered, "Mr. James, wait just a moment and we'll go out with you. There is no reason to open that door more than we have to." She placed her dishes into the tub and also dropped money into the tin. "I'm sure Mrs. Young doesn't enjoy the cold air that comes in every time it's opened." She looked pointedly at the man then turned back to Rebecca. "I'd like two more sandwiches, to go. Me and my daughter still have a long journey ahead of us and I'm sure we'll find no better meals than the one you've provided today."

"Thank you." Rebecca reached for another bag and placed one sandwich inside. "Do you want them together or separate?" she asked, reaching for another bag.

"One bag is plenty."

She nodded, put the second sandwich with the first

and handed the bag to the woman, who took it and then walked toward the other two passengers.

Just as the man started to open the door, Rebecca remembered her promise to Seth. "Oh!"

They all three turned and looked at her startled.

"I'm sorry, I just remembered I promised to ask if any of you ever met a woman named Charlotte Fisher," Rebecca blurted out.

The two women shook their heads and the man answered, "Can't say that I have."

"Well, thank you." Rebecca walked toward them and closed the door as they left.

She turned to find Fay standing behind her. "I'll have to say, that went well." Fay patted her on the arm.

As Rebecca cleared the sideboard, she had to agree with Fay. They'd sold four cookies, one cup of coffee, two teas and five sandwiches. She added the money up in her head—that was thirty-three cents.

Fay picked up the dirty dishpan and headed to the kitchen. "You did good, Rebecca. But you have to get braver in telling them your prices." A teasing glint filled the older woman's eyes just before she disappeared into the kitchen.

Rebecca decided to split the money with Fay. The woman had helped her make the food and created the prices. Plus, at this rate, Rebecca felt she could be generous.

She scooped up the two plates of leftovers and headed back to the kitchen. Rebecca dreaded telling Seth that the passengers hadn't heard of Charlotte. Would he be terribly disappointed? Earlier he'd reminded her to ask. She cared about Seth—what would his reaction be should a passenger know her or her whereabouts? Would he leave them quickly? Or would he hesitate? After all, he'd never met Charlotte. A part of Rebecca dreaded that day. She told herself it was because she liked Seth and didn't want to see him hurt. Not because she was getting used to having him around and would miss him when he left.

Seth pointed the rifle at Clayton as he passed on his horse. The boy leaned across the side of the horse as if dodging a bullet. "Pkew!" Seth made the sound of a shooting gun and lowered the weapon.

Rebecca yelled behind him, "Have you lost your mind?" She came running across the pasture looking madder than a hornet. Her blue eyes blazed and her cloak flew around her.

When she came even with him, Seth answered, "No." Then he turned his attention to the thundering hooves that were fast approaching.

Noah came across his path. Once more Seth raised the gun.

Rebecca screamed and made a grab for the rifle. "Seth, stop!"

He lowered the weapon and faced her. "Rebecca, we are training here."

"You could kill him."

He shook his head. Didn't she trust him yet? Each night for over two weeks he told her what he'd done during the day and what he was planning for the next day. Fay would listen at the window and every once in a while they'd hear the older lady chuckle at Rebecca's many questions. He'd been patient but she had to let him do his job.

Trying to conceal his aggravation, Seth answered, "Not likely, Rebecca. The gun's not loaded, but don't tell them that—they need to believe the threat is real. I am teaching them how to avoid getting shot using their horses as shields."

Rebecca turned on her heels and marched back toward the house. Seth watched her go. Would she ever trust him with her boys? He'd hoped she'd realized that he wouldn't intentionally allow harm to come to them. Maybe she needed more than a couple of weeks.

The thought came to him, could he ever fall in love? Would he ever trust a woman not to leave him? Seth shook his head. That was nonsense thinking. Or was it?

His fondness for Rebecca was like a wild plant that was growing every day. Leaving her and the boys would probably be the hardest thing he'd ever have to do but he'd do it. He had made a promise to his grandmother and no matter how badly he might want to stay with the Young family, he couldn't.

# *Chapter Ten*

Seth watched as Noah and Clayton worked with their horses. He stood by the corral gate. It had been a couple of hours since Rebecca had come out and found him pretend shooting at her boys.

He'd since sent the boys off to do chores, except for Noah and Clayton. He pulled the two boys so that he could see where they were with their riding skills. Seth's plan was to spend a little time each day with separate boys so that he could assess their strengths and weaknesses.

Noah rode as if he'd been born on a horse. His body moved with the animal and he instinctively seemed to know what it would do next. He paid close attention to the horse and made sure to use his softest voice when speaking to her.

Clayton, on the other hand, acted as if he'd never seen a horse, let alone rode one. He mounted like a young girl, clung to the saddle horn and looked as skittish as a rat around a snake. He never spoke to his horse or directed it in any manner.

Seth called to Noah, "Noah, take your mount to the barn and cool her down. You've done a good job today."

"Thanks, Seth." The boy smiled broadly as he rode past.

He nodded to Noah and then called to Clayton, "Clayton, bring your horse here."

Clayton dismounted and then walked the horse to the railing, where Seth stood watching. "Yes, Seth?" Weariness filled the boy's voice.

"Why did you walk him over?" Seth asked, reaching out to pat the horse's velvety nose.

The boy shrugged. His head was down and his shoulders slumped under his coat.

"Do you like the horse?" Seth asked.

Clayton looked up and grinned. "It's a horse."

"Yes, but do you like him?" Seth ran his hand over the animal's neck.

"I suppose. Never been around horses before. The other guys like them, so I guess I'll grow to like them, too." Clayton twisted the lead rope in his gloved hands.

"How would you like to go out with me into the west pasture?" Seth asked, opening the gate and motioning for Clayton to lead the horse out.

"Sure. What are we going to do out there?" Clayton asked.

Seth fell into step beside him. He nudged the boy with his shoulder. "Honestly, I just want to take ol' Sam out for a ride."

"You named your horse ol' Sam?"

He chuckled at the boy's shock. "Well, just Sam. What have you named your mount?"

They entered the warmth of the barn, where Jacob

and Benjamin sat playing a game of checkers on a bale of hay. Seth walked back to the stall that held Sam. He listened as the boys talked.

"You beating him, Beni?" Clayton asked.

"Nope. Second game and I still haven't won," Benjamin answered Clayton. "But I ain't gonna quit tryin'."

"What would Ma say if she heard you talking like that, Benjamin?" Jacob scolded.

"Like what?" The boy's voice sounded defensive.

Seth thoroughly cinched the saddle under Sam's belly, grinning.

*"Ain't? Gonna? Tryin'?"* Jacob repeated.

Clayton laughed. "He sounds like a hickabilly to me."

"Ma would say he's uneducated and probably make him come inside for grammar lessons if she heard," Jacob replied with seriousness.

Benjamin whined, "You aren't going to tell her, are you?"

Seth pulled Sam from the stall. He watched Jacob ruffle the little boy's hair and laugh. "Not this time, but you really should watch how you talk. If Ma hears you talking like that, she'll have you in the house instead of out here in this nice warm barn. And you wouldn't be playing checkers, either, but reading from that grammar book she's so fond of."

"What about you, Clayton? Gonna tell on me?" Benjamin asked, looking up at his older brother.

"Not me. Be my misfortunate she'd make me practice with you. You're safe." Clayton grinned down at Benjamin.

Benjamin and Clayton seemed to have a special relationship. The boys' closeness made Seth wish he had brothers. It was too bad he was an only child. He pulled his horse up beside Clayton's. "Ready?"

Clayton nodded. "Ready as I'll ever be." Most eighteen-year-old boys would be thrilled to go out riding, but Clayton's tone sounded anything but thrilled.

Seth looked to Jacob. "Clayton and I are going to go check the fence along the west side of the border. We should be back in time for supper."

"I'll have Ma keep a plate warm for you both if you're late." Jacob turned his focus back on the game.

Once out of the barn, Seth pulled himself up into the saddle. He watched as Clayton did the same. Then he proceeded toward the west pasture.

After a few minutes, Clayton said, "I'm not sure I'm going to be a very good Pony Express rider."

Seth slowed Sam down so that he could talk to the boy. "No?"

Clayton shook his head.

"Why not?" Seth tilted his head to look the boy in the eyes.

"Riding horses has never been of any interest to me," Clayton answered, hanging on to the saddle horn as if he feared falling off.

Seth couldn't hide his surprise at the boy's words. He let them go for several moments before asking, "Then what does interest you?"

Clayton swallowed hard. "You'll just laugh."

"Maybe, but I promise I won't laugh out of meanness."

"All right. I like to doctor stuff."

There was nothing funny about that. Why would the

boy think he'd laugh? He'd never understand the work-ings of a young boy's mind. "Man or beast?"

"You aren't going to laugh?"

Seth frowned. "I don't understand why you would think I'd laugh. Doctoring is an honorable profession. There is nothing to laugh about." He led his horse down to the stream and dismounted.

Clayton followed. When he was on the ground, too, he answered, "All the guys laugh at me. Ma's the only one who doesn't. She's bought me a couple of books about doctoring people and told me I can do anything I put my mind to."

"She's right." Seth admired Rebecca for her wis-dom in not discouraging the boy like his brothers had.

"You really believe that?" Clayton asked, rubbing his horse's shoulder as it drank from the cold stream water.

"Yes, I believe that you can do anything you put your mind to. I also believe that God gives us our dreams and desires. So, if you want to be a doctor, who am I to question that?"

Seth pulled his horse back up the stream's bank. When on solid ground, he swung up into the saddle.

Clayton followed. He seemed in deep thought.

Seth led the way to the west pasture. His gaze fol-lowed the fence line, checking to see if there were any holes in the fence. Not finding any, he glanced back at Clayton.

The boy sat tall in the saddle. His hand no longer rested on the saddle horn. His head was back and he looked up into the sky. He'd been quiet for at least half an hour.

Not sure what more to say to the boy, Seth turned Sam back in the direction of home. They rode another ten minutes and Clayton galloped up beside him.

"Seth?"

"Yes."

"Do you think Ma will let me keep a little of the money I make with the Pony Express?"

Answering honestly, Seth said, "I don't know. You'll have to ask her." He watched the boy study the workings of the horse's neck. "What do you want the money for?"

"Well, I been thinking about what you said down by the stream and I think you are right. God did give me this dream to doctor animals, but I need to learn more about how to do it. So if Ma will let me have some of the money, I can buy books and learn more about doctoring," he answered with a faraway look in his eyes.

Seth wondered if doctoring people and doctoring animals were similar. Would studying books on how to take care of people also help Clayton learn to take care of animals? They weren't exactly the same thing. He almost laughed at his line of thinking, but then decided that Clayton might think he was laughing at him. Instead he decided to bring the subject back around to the reason he'd brought Clayton out to the pasture.

He looked over at the boy, whose thoughts seemed miles away. "You know, Clayton, you need to learn how to take care of your horse and how to ride him really well so that you can earn the money you need from the Pony Express."

The boy nodded. "I'll work really hard, Seth."

"Have you thought up a name for your horse?" Seth asked, patting Sam on the neck.

"Bones."

"Bones?"

Clayton smiled broadly. "Yep, he's going to be a doctor's horse. I once heard Papa John call the doctor in town Bones. He's going to help me earn the money to become a doctor. So I'm going to call him Bones."

Seth chuckled. "I like it."

They rode back to the farm with Seth giving Clayton pointers and teaching him how to control the horse with his knees. Seth couldn't help wondering what Rebecca would think when she learned from her son that Seth had encouraged him to become a doctor, an animal doctor at that. Would she be pleased? Or would it be another thing that he'd done she didn't approve of? Why did her approval matter to him? Seth didn't know why it mattered; he just realized that it did.

"Can you believe he was pretending to shoot them out of the saddle?" Rebecca asked Fay as she sewed a new button on one of the boy's shirts. She didn't give Fay a chance to answer. "He said he was teaching them how to use their horses as shields. Shields from what? Who would want to shoot at them?" She sighed in exasperation.

"Indians and robbers," Fay suggested, knotting off her thread. Using her teeth, she broke the thread from the sock she'd just mended.

Rebecca frowned. The thought of her boys being shot at frightened the daylights out of her. But in the world they lived in and with the talk of war in the air, it might become a reality. She shuddered at the thought of war and her boys forced to fight. "Yes, you're right. What Seth teaches them is important, but still I worry."

Fay stood up and stretched. "You wouldn't be much of a mother if you didn't worry," she told Rebecca, rubbing her back. "You know, I'm tempted to go take a nap like Joy."

"There is nothing stopping you from doing just that." Rebecca smiled up at her. "You've earned it. You've worked since sunup this morning."

"I'm not the only one who's worked hard today." Fay covered a yawn then continued, "I'm looking forward to having that beef stew you tossed together this morning."

Rebecca inhaled the aroma of thick beef-and-vegetable stew that filled the house. The wind blew against the house, making her shiver. "I hope it tastes as good as it smells," she said, picking up another shirt. This one had a tear in the sleeve.

"I'm sure it will taste even better."

Rebecca laughed and said, "Don't count on it. I've been known to make things that smelled wonderful but tasted like there might be skunk in it." She threaded her needle and began patching the shirt.

Fay stood by the fireplace for a moment, yawned once more and then said, "Yes, I believe I will lay down for a few minutes. If you are sure you don't mind."

"Not at all. I may close my eyes for a few, too," she said to make the older woman feel better about needing a rest.

Fay left the room. Rebecca heard the bedroom door shut. She leaned her head back and closed her eyes.

How many times would the prayer come to her mind? *Lord, am I doing right by my boys?* Watching Seth point that rifle at Clayton had taken her breath away. What if he'd forgotten and had a bullet in the chamber? Then what?

Rebecca kept her eyes closed as she thought about the days ahead. She knew now that the Pony Express wasn't safe. John had warned her that the boys would be alone on the trail. He'd told her he'd need to teach them how to survive while delivering the mail. It hadn't seemed real not that long ago. But now she had a better understanding of what the job entailed and the reality stated danger in more ways than one.

Since her husband was deceased, Rebecca knew that if the boys were to continue working for the Pony Express, she'd have to trust Seth. They seemed so young, but the orphanage had declared them men at the age of twelve.

Rebecca reminded herself that they were all just a few years younger than herself, except Noah and Beni. At the age of twenty-eight she felt very old. Weariness seeped from her in the form of a heavy sigh.

Seth Armstrong seemed to be doing all he could to teach the boys how to survive the Pony Express. Every evening, he reported to her the day's events and how well they were learning. Even Jacob seemed to be coming around. Her oldest son had told her that he trusted Seth's decisions.

Could she trust the Pony Express man? How far was he willing to go to make the boys into men? Had it entered his mind to start out with an unloaded gun and then move on to a loaded one? Rebecca's eyes snapped open. That was the first question she intended to ask him this evening. She'd most certainly not have him pointing loaded rifles at her boys. That was where she'd draw the line and dare him to cross it.

# Chapter Eleven

Seth thought she was joking but the seriousness reflected in her eyes told him otherwise. "You think I'd point a loaded gun at them?"

She crossed her arms over her chest. "How should I know what to think? When I came out to check on them this afternoon, you sure enough had a rifle pointed at their heads. I had no clue at the moment whether it was loaded or not."

He inhaled deeply and slowly released the air in his lungs. "What do I have to do to get you to understand that I would never put your boys in unneeded danger?" He heard the creaking of Fay's rocker that sat across the room from them. Her Bible lay on her lap and she seemed to be absorbed in its words.

They'd moved their nightly discussion into the house. It was nice to have the older woman in the house. Seth felt thankful that Rebecca had another woman to talk to. Had she discussed her fears with Fay? Did Fay trust him to take care of the boys?

"I don't know how you can make me understand,

but I do know that I thought I'd faint when I saw you pointing the gun at them."

Seth turned to face her. "Would it have made you feel better if I'd told you last night exactly what my plans were in teaching them to avoid bullets?"

"Perhaps—at least I would have known you weren't going to shoot them. All you said last night was that you were going to teach them how to avoid bullets on horseback." Rebecca walked to the fireplace. "I know you think I'm being difficult but I'm the only parent these boys have."

Interfering parents was probably the biggest reason why the owners of the Pony Express had asked for orphans. Seth kept the thought to himself. "I understand your concerns and I'm willing to help you put them aside. I just need to know how."

"Maybe you could let me know what you plan to do with the boys the night before you actually do it," she suggested.

Half an hour later, Seth dashed across the yard to the bunkhouse. He was no closer to gaining Rebecca's trust than he'd been when he'd entered the house earlier. Hopefully, telling her his plans for the boys tomorrow had made her feel better.

Andrew looked up when Seth entered the bunkhouse. A quick glance around told Seth the other boys had gone off to their beds. He asked in a soft voice, "What are you still doing up, Andrew?"

The young man stood. "I was waiting for you."

Seth motioned for Andrew to follow him into his room. Once they were both inside, he shut the door. "What can I do for you?"

"Clayton told me that Ma wasn't happy with you earlier today."

Seth walked over to his bed and sat down. "He did, did he?"

"Yes, sir. I wanted to tell you not to get upset with Ma. She means well."

Seth motioned for Andrew to sit down. When the boy had done so he answered, "I know she does, but your Ma has to let me run the Pony Express the way I see fit."

"Yes, sir, but Ma is just afraid we'll get hurt or quit and she wouldn't be able to stand that." Andrew looked down at his hands.

"Andrew, I am not going to hurt any of you boys. Everything I try to teach you is because I want to keep you from harm." Seth felt as if he was having the same conversation with Andrew that he'd had with Rebecca moments earlier.

"Not physical hurt, Seth."

Seth sat up straighter. "What kind of hurt?"

Andrew licked his dry lips. "In an orphanage there are many ways a child can be hurt. We all came from the orphanage and most of us wear the scars inside, where no one will see them. Ma doesn't want us to be hurt like that ever again." Determination filled his eyes as he met Seth's. A harshness, whether from anger or bitterness, filled his voice. "Ma and I are those kinds of orphans and we will not allow the other boys or ourselves to ever be hurt like that again."

Seth reached for his Bible, which rested on his nightstand beside the lamp.

"Don't tell me what that Good Book says or that

you are a Christian and will never hurt us. I've met Christians before and I have scars to prove it." Andrew jerked to his feet. He walked to the door with his head held high and his shoulders back. Just before he opened the door he said, "Seth, I'll ask you again not to be upset with Ma. She means well."

The new information that Rebecca had been an orphan, too, explained why she was so protective of the boys and why she didn't trust him to keep his word, and also accounted for her need to have the boys close. Aware that Andrew waited for a reaction from him, Seth nodded.

It seemed to be what the young man was waiting for. Andrew gently shut the door behind him, leaving Seth to question God on how he could help this family. Especially since he had a promise to keep to his grandmother.

The next morning, Seth chose Thomas to spend time with. He wanted to know what the boy knew and understood about the Pony Express and he also wanted to know the boy better.

The mount Thomas had chosen was a spirited mustang. Thomas could only ride him a few minutes before he ended up on the ground.

A jagged scar marked the right side of his youthful face and Seth figured the eighteen-year-old had a story to tell. Blond hair seemed to constantly hang in the boy's laughing green eyes.

"Well, how am I doing?" Thomas asked. His dancing eyes looked up at Seth from where he sat on the ground.

Seth laughed. "Well, considering your horse just threw you and you can still smile about it, I'd say pretty good." He reached down and offered the boy a hand up.

"Yeah, that's what I thought, too."

Thomas seemed to enjoy everything life tossed at him, from getting thrown off of his horse, to mucking out stalls. The boy really seemed to take life one event at a time. "I should have chosen a more agreeable horse, I suppose." He picked up his horse's reins and limped to the railing.

"Why did you choose this one?" Seth asked, following.

The boy looked over his shoulder at the compact black horse he'd chosen. "I suppose I liked his spirit. No matter how many times I get up on him to ride, he always proves that he might be little, but there is a lot of power in him."

Seth thought about the boy's words for a moment as Thomas dusted off his pants. He watched Thomas rub the horse's nose as if to tell him he was forgiven for throwing him to the ground. "So what you are telling me is that you like that he is small, but has lots of energy and you want to give him a chance to prove himself?"

Thomas nodded. "Everyone needs a chance to prove themselves, even horses." He reached up and rubbed the horse's velvety ears. "Isn't that right, boy?"

"You know, there is an easier way to let him get his energy out besides him flinging you to the ground like a sack of flour." Seth leaned against the fence and smiled.

"How's that?" Thomas asked, looking interested.

Seth pushed away from the rails. "You could start by taking him on a fast ride. Wouldn't it be better to have wind in your hair instead of dirt in your drawers?"

Thomas laughed. "Sure would. I didn't think we were allowed to take them out without permission," he admitted.

"Spirit is yours to do with as you see fit, to make him a good Pony Express horse. Just be courteous and let one of us know when you are going out."

Thomas studied him. "You named him Spirit?"

Seth shrugged. "It seemed to fit at the moment, but he's your horse and you can name him whatever you want."

"I thought more on the name Diablo, but Spirit works better." Thomas grinned. "Can we take Spirit for a run now?"

"Let me get Sam and we'll go for a long hard ride." Seth walked toward the barn, his thoughts filled with Thomas and what he'd learned from the boy. If he related to a spirited horse that he felt only wanted to prove himself, did that mean Thomas felt he had to prove himself to everyone around him, too?

Once more Seth felt the need to pray for the Young boys. They were orphans. Even though they were adopted by Rebecca and her deceased husband, in their hearts and minds they still felt like orphans and had many hurts to get through.

A few moments later, he and Thomas raced across the pasture. "Watch out for gopher holes," Seth called to the rushing boy and horse.

Thomas nodded. His hat hung down his back, his

blond hair waved in the wind. The scar down his face looked white against his tan skin.

How had Thomas obtained the scar? Had he been in a knife fight? Fallen on something sharp? There were so many unanswered questions about each of the boys. Someday, when they were better acquainted, he might start asking. An unwelcome tension entered Seth, right between the shoulder blades. He stretched in the saddle, seeking relief. Bit by bit, this family wormed their way into his thoughts and heart.

They rode on for several minutes. Seth slowed and allowed Thomas to speed ahead. The weather wasn't as cold as it had been the day before. He looked up into the sky and saw dark clouds coming in from the west.

Thomas pulled up beside him. "Looks like the weather might take a turn for the worse. Would it be all right with you if we stopped by the family cemetery before heading back?"

Seth glanced over at the boy. "Of course." He followed Thomas across the meadow to a small wooded area.

They crossed the stream and continued through the woods to a quiet open area. Thomas stopped his horse and dismounted. "Papa John always said to walk in from here. He said it showed respect to those who have gone home before us."

Sam came to a halt and Seth dismounted also. Seth followed Thomas the rest of the way. It would seem that at least one of the Young boys had learned respect from their adoptive father.

As they continued a short piece through the trees, silence surrounded them, although an occasional bird-call interrupted the peace of the woods. They came out of the trees into a small meadow. Three graves rested under a grove of cottonwood trees on a hill.

When they reached the top of the knoll, Seth could see the road that led to the farm. So this was where Rebecca's family had been laid to rest.

Thomas kneeled down on one knee beside the grave marked John Percival Young. He brushed sticks from the grave and sighed. "He was a great man."

"I'm sure he was," Seth replied, taking his hat off and holding it respectfully in his hands.

"In the five years I knew him, he never raised a hand to me or any of the boys." Thomas stood and brushed his hands against his pant legs. "Someday, I want to build a fence around the graves to keep wild animals out of here." He wiped the hair off his forehead.

Seth stood beside him and placed a hand on his shoulder. "I'd be happy to help you build it."

The two of them stood silently looking down on the graves. Seth read the names on the other two head-stones and realized that these must be John's parents. They were older, the names and dates wearing off the wooden crosses. "We could also freshen up the crosses," he suggested.

"I think Ma would like that," Thomas agreed.

A big drop of water hit Seth on the bridge of his nose. "We better head back before the storm hits." He touched his forehead slightly in a salute then slapped his hat back on his head.

Thomas nodded and turned to walk his horse down to the road. Seth kept a shoulder beneath his horse's neck, sheltering as best he could, but more drops of rain hit them both. Within minutes they were soaked through. The wind had turned cold while they'd been out riding and right now Seth wished he was back in his room, where warmth and dry clothes waited for him.

Once they were at the road, Thomas mounted his horse. "I'll race you back," he challenged.

Seth climbed aboard Sam and nodded. "Ready."

Together the two of them raced toward the barn. The horses' hooves beat a rapid rhythm against the wet ground. Seth lay close to his mount's back, urging him on to the barn. Rain pelted them, soaking both man and beast. Seth couldn't remember ever being so wet. When they got to the barn, Jacob met them in the doorway.

Both Seth and Thomas slid from their horses' backs. Thomas had won and the grin on his face spoke volumes of the pride he felt. Seth slapped him on the back. "Keep riding like that and you'll be a top-notch Pony Express rider," he assured him.

Thomas's grin spread even farther across his scarred face. "Thanks."

"I'll take care of Sam for you," Jacob offered, reaching for the reins. "Ma would like to see you in the house."

"Did she say what she wanted to see me about?" Seth asked, handing the reins over.

Jacob shook his head. "Nope. Just said to ask you to come inside when you and Thomas got back."

Seth looked out into the pouring rain. Within the past few minutes, it had created what looked like a small river through the middle of the front yard. He didn't look forward to getting even wetter, but the sooner he spoke to Rebecca, the sooner he could go to his room and get dry.

He looked at Thomas, who already held a towel and was drying his mount. "Thomas, do that quickly and get into some dry clothes. I don't want you getting sick."

The boy nodded and continued talking softly to the horse.

"Thanks for taking care of Sam," Seth said to Jacob, then took a deep breath and dashed into the freezing rain. Surely the temperature had dropped—the rain hadn't felt this cold earlier. His boots slid in the mud and water. He'd be glad when the early spring rains stopped and summer started.

Rebecca met him on the porch. "You didn't have to run in the rain," she scolded, offering him a towel to dry off with.

He ran the cloth over his arms and neck, not appreciating her annoying tone. "What did you need to see me about?"

"I wondered if you could take one of the boys out hunting tomorrow or the next day," she answered, not bothering to hide her irritation at his gruff attitude.

Fay stepped out onto the porch. "You two stop snapping at each other and get in here where it's warmer."

Like two obedient children, they did as she said. Seth followed Rebecca inside, wishing he hadn't been impatient with her. Fay closed the door behind them. "Why don't you go into the sitting room and stand by the fire," she said to Seth.

"Thanks, I believe I will." He pulled his hat from his head and walked across the hardwood floor. His boots made squishing noises as Seth marched past Rebecca toward the sound of crackling wood and the promise of warmth. Knowing he would have to apologize for his rude behavior had him pricklier than a wide-awake black bear in the wintertime.

What was it about Rebecca Young that sent a tickle of irritation up his neck? Not all the time, just when she spoke abruptly or accusingly. Could it simply be that the rain had put him in a bad mood? Or the fact that she'd summoned him to the house like a hired hand? Seth wasn't sure, but he knew he didn't like this feeling, not one little bit.

He wished at times like this that he could just be on his way. Let the Young family live their lives and he'd carry on with his. The thought sobered him.

Did he really want to leave them? Didn't the boys need him now more than ever? His gaze moved to Rebecca. Her hair hung down her back and her cheeks were rosy. Pretty blue eyes studied him and he wished he could take back the harshness of his words.

*Just don't allow yourself to get too close to any of them,* he thought. Seth prayed that he hadn't already.

## *Chapter Twelve*

Rebecca sat down on her favorite chair and picked up her sewing. The weather had turned nasty and so had her temper. She silently asked the Lord to forgive her. What was it about Seth Armstrong that had her emotions all in a knot?

He stood with his back to her. Wide shoulders stretched the wet material of his shirt. The edges of his hair curled around his collar. Seth braced his hands against the fireplace mantel.

Very aware of the creaking sound of Fay's rocker, Rebecca tried to focus on her mending. She didn't know what to say to him. He'd snapped at her like an old turtle. All she'd wanted to do was ask him to go hunting. They needed fresh meat.

Tears stung her eyes, making Rebecca angry. She had no intention of crying. Rebecca told herself she had nothing to cry about.

His warm voice washed over her like a healing balm. "I'm sorry, Rebecca. I'll be happy to take the boys out hunting tomorrow. It will also give me the opportunity to see how well they can shoot a gun."

Her voice cracked as she said, "Thank you."

The rocking stopped. Seth spun around to look at her. Rebecca focused on her mending. She didn't want to face either Fay or Seth with tears in her eyes. What was she going to do? She couldn't wipe the moisture away; they'd know for sure she was on the verge of crying like a baby.

"Ma, can I have a cookie?" Joy asked as she entered the room.

Rebecca practically jumped to her feet. "Yes, I'll help you get one." She hurried out of the room, very aware that both Seth and Fay still watched her.

Once in the kitchen, she wiped her eyes, then pulled down the cookie jar and handed Joy a cookie. "Here you go, sweetie."

"Ma, are you crying?" Joy asked, taking the cookie but not eating it. Her eyes studied her mother's face for an explanation.

Rebecca kneeled down to her daughter's level. "No, but I could use a hug."

Joy immediately went into her mother's arms. Rebecca held her tightly and enjoyed the sweet smell of her little girl. Joy liked the smell of vanilla and often put some behind her little ears. Rebecca grinned and then released her. "You smell nice," she said.

"I smell like nilla."

"Vanilla," Rebecca said, correcting her.

Joy nodded. "That's what I said. Nilla."

Rebecca leaned away from her daughter. "I know you can say it correctly. Why don't you?"

The little girl smiled. "That's the way Pa used to say it. Remember? I don't want to forget him so I use his words."

"I remember." The bittersweet memories flooded her mind. Rebecca gave Joy another quick hug and then stood. John was also the one who used to dab vanilla behind Joy's ears and then pretend to "eat her up." Funny that she hadn't thought about that in a long time.

She took Joy's hand and walked back to the sitting room, where Seth and Fay waited. Her gaze moved to where he stood by the fireplace.

He looked up as she entered the room. She ignored the question in his eyes. Instead Rebecca asked one. "What are you planning to do with the boys tomorrow?"

Seth turned his back to the fire. "Well, Noah, Philip, Andrew and I will go hunting. I'm assuming you want to replenish your meat supply, so I'll have Jacob, Clayton, Thomas and Benjamin go fishing. Then when we get back I want them to work with their horses. Sometime tomorrow evening I plan to have them practice passing the postage bag to each other."

Rebecca watched Joy nibble on her cookie, aware that she looked from one adult to the other. Did she feel the tension between Seth and Rebecca? Rebecca wondered if she shouldn't speak to Seth in private from now on.

Joy scrunched up her cute little nose. "What's a postage bag?" she asked Seth.

"It's the bag that will have the mail inside."

"Oh. Can I practice, too?" she asked.

Rebecca shook her head. "No, you are not a Pony Express rider like the boys."

Joy placed her small hand on her hip and announced, "When I grow up, I'm going to be a Pony Express rider, too."

Seth chuckled. "I don't doubt that you will."

Rebecca enjoyed the warm sound that seemed to bubble up from his chest. He really was a good man. His patience with the kids, especially Joy, gave her renewed confidence in the man. Yes, his methods scared her, but she'd have to learn to trust him to keep his word.

Joy looked up at her mother. "Ma, can I go fishing with Beni tomorrow?" She stuck a thumb into her parted lips.

Picking up her sewing, Rebecca sat down before answering. "I don't know. Babies don't go fishing." She hated that Joy still sucked on her thumb. She'd tried everything to break the habit, but nothing worked.

A light pink filled the little girl's cheeks as she jerked her thumb out of her mouth. "I'm not a baby," Joy protested.

Rebecca smiled at her daughter. "No, you are not. We'll have to see how the weather is tomorrow. If it's raining out there like it is now, we don't want you catching your death from cold."

As if on cue, Seth sneezed.

Fay, who had been silent so far, looked up and said, "Speaking of catching your death, Seth, you should probably get into some warm, dry clothes."

He nodded. "I believe you are right." Seth turned to face Rebecca once more. "Is there anything else we need to discuss before I go?" Seth quirked an eyebrow at her.

"No, I think that will be all. Thank you for coming in and easing my mind a mite." She offered him her most sincere smile. The last thing she needed was to offend the station keeper. He didn't have to share his plans with her and she really did appreciate his willingness to do so.

Seth put on his soggy hat and walked to the front door. "Have a good evening, ladies."

"Aren't you coming back in for supper?" Joy asked as she followed him.

He kneeled down in front of Joy. "Not tonight. I'm wet and cold. I think I'll stay in my room and get warmed up."

Rebecca's breath caught in her throat as his green eyes collided with hers over Joy's head. Tenderness filled the beautiful orbs as he continued talking to her daughter.

"Maybe your ma will send a plate out to the bunkhouse. I wouldn't mind eating in my room tonight." He turned his attention back to the little girl.

Joy smiled at him. "She will. Won't you, Ma?"

"Of course."

Seth stood. "Thank you." He brushed the top of Joy's head with his hand. "I'll see you in the morning," he said and then he was gone.

"He really is a nice man, Rebecca," Fay said as she closed her Bible.

Rebecca nodded. "He seems to be." She turned her head and watched out the window as he jogged across the rain-soaked front yard.

His boots slipped and for a moment, Rebecca held her breath, afraid he'd fall. When he'd managed to right himself, she released a huge sigh.

"He's a handsome young man, too," Fay said. She now stood beside Rebecca's chair and also watched Seth dash into the bunkhouse.

Rebecca ignored Fay's last comment.

"How old do you think he is?" Fay asked.

"Don't start matchmaking, Fay." Rebecca laid her sewing to the side.

"What's matchmaking?" Joy asked, reminding the two women that they weren't alone.

Rebecca turned her daughter away from the window. "You never mind what matchmaking is. Go straighten your room." She gave Joy a gentle push in the direction of her bedroom.

"All right, Ma." Joy skipped off.

Rebecca headed to the kitchen, where her beef stew and corn bread were cooking. Her thoughts returned to Seth. Fay was right, he was a handsome man. Mentally she answered Fay's last question—she figured Seth was probably a little older than her. She stirred the stew and then pulled the hot corn bread out of the oven.

Raindrops hit the pipe on the stove, spitting and spewing and sending a shiver down her spine. Poor Seth, he'd been soaked to the skin. She wondered if Thomas was as wet.

In the coming months, Rebecca expected the boys to be both wet and cold. She hated that they would be exposed to the weather and wondered if there was anything she could do to give them comfort. Would Seth ride the Pony Express, too?

Why was he in her thoughts so much today? Was it because he'd made her angry? Or was it because Fay had hinted at matchmaking between the two of them?

Seth was handsome but Rebecca couldn't allow him into her heart. She had a farm to run, children to take care of, and she had to preserve the memory of John for her daughter's sake. And she also needed to keep her family together. If she became interested in Seth as a future husband, then he might uproot her from the farm.

No, it was better not to think along those lines. Even if he did have lovely green eyes and a smile that melted her anger.

The horse flew past Seth. He tossed the flour sack up at Philip on the horse's back. It hit the young man squarely in the chest, knocking him from his horse and into the mud.

The others hooted and hollered from the sidelines. Seth shook his head. So far, none of the boys had been able to catch the pretend saddlebag.

Noah climbed aboard his small mustang. Seth doubted that Noah would fare any better than the other boys had, but he had to give him a chance to try.

Benjamin sloshed through the mud and scooped up the flour sack. He handed it up to Seth with a grin. "They ain't doin' so good, are they, Seth?"

"No, they aren't," Seth agreed, turning his horse back to the starting line.

Noah went to the opposite side of the pasture and rounded his mount. The boy laid low over his horse's neck and then at the yelp from Jacob kicked his horse into action. The little mustang ate the ground between them with super speed.

Seth met him halfway and tossed the flour bag. He was shocked to see Noah grab it in midair and loop it over his saddle horn.

More hoots and yells came from the sidelines. This time no laughter filled the air, only praise and questions. Seth wheeled his horse around and observed the boys.

How was it that Noah, the youngest at the age of twelve, was so much better at practically everything than the other boys? He rode his horse with more confidence than the others, shot a gun better and had a wicked way with his knife.

While hunting earlier in the morning, Seth noted that Noah seemed to be tracking the deer, unlike the others, who were simply hunting. When they'd finally come upon their prey, Noah had been the one to kill the first deer. Andrew had shot the second deer. Noah had also killed three rabbits with a flick of his wrist and a knife. He'd quickly shown Philip how he'd thrown the knife and together they killed two more rabbits. Noah had skills, but how had he acquired them? Seth doubted that they were taught such things in an orphanage.

Rebecca had been pleased with the two deer and five rabbits. Thankfully, the other boys had brought in a load of fish that would have made anyone proud. She praised them all on their hunting and fishing skills.

The boys were covered in mud, all except Jacob. He hadn't participated with the activity as he was the stock tender and more than likely wouldn't need to ride the trail. Then again...

Seth called out, "Jacob, saddle up. You might need to learn this, too."

Noah handed the bag to Jacob and then continued his conversation with his other brothers. Carrying the sack, Jacob walked back to the barn to get his horse. If the slump of his shoulders was any indication, Jacob wasn't happy with this new turn of events.

Seth rode over to where the other boys were still standing. "Come on, fellas. Team up into twos and practice running your horses toward each other. I want you to get as close as you can without touching your horses together. When you are coming in from a hard ride, you are going to need to be fast and accurate in your tossing of the mailbag." He watched as they hurried off to do his bidding.

A smile touched his lips as he thought of what Rebecca's reaction might have been if she'd seen the boys catapult from the backs of their horses. Would she have laughed, like he had? Or would she protest that her babies were treated too roughly?

A giggle behind him answered his question. Seth turned to see Rebecca cup a hand over her mouth. Her gaze was trained on Thomas and a smile lit up her eyes. "They are all covered in mud," she said between her fingers.

"Not yet, but they soon will be," Seth answered, pointing to a scowling Jacob. The young man had just swung into his saddle and slowly walked his horse toward them.

"Jacob is going to ride, too?"

Seth shrugged. "In an emergency, he might. I want

him to be able to catch the mailbag if he has to." He winked down at Joy, who clung to her mama's skirts.

When Jacob came within distance, Seth asked, "Ready?"

"As I'll ever be," Jacob responded. He continued to walk his horse to the far end of the pasture.

Rebecca giggled. "He doesn't look very happy about this, does he?"

Seth shook his head. "Nope. Should be fun." He instinctively winked at Rebecca before turning Sam away.

Why had he done that? He shouldn't be trifling with the mother of eight. Seth glanced over his shoulder and saw that she wasn't watching him at all, but had her eyes locked on the boys as they practiced. Maybe she hadn't noticed his slip.

His gaze moved to Joy. The little girl's mouth was slit into the biggest grin he'd ever seen. Her little eyes sparkled with hope and Seth felt dread ease into his heart.

He didn't want to build Joy's hopes that he might be interested in her mother. No, Seth needed to get a grip on himself. The last thing he needed was for the Young women to set their sights on him as a potential husband and father.

## Chapter Thirteen

Seth hit the ground with a swoosh. Jacob had nailed him with the flour bag. Cold mud seeped into his pants and made a sucking noise as he attempted to push out of it. His boots slipped and there was another whooshing sound.

With his thoughts on Rebecca and Joy, Seth had forgotten that Jacob had the sack. He frowned up at Jacob.

The twenty-year-old had the gall to grin down at him. "Looks like I'm not the only one who needs practice." He reached down a hand to pull up Seth.

Seth had the satisfaction of slapping cold mud into the other man's hand. He grinned when Jacob didn't flinch. With the strength of youth, Jacob pulled him to his feet.

"Don't forget our mud-covered saddlebag," Jacob said, whirling his mount around and waving cheekily to his mother and sister as he passed them.

Shaking the mud off his hands, Seth bent over and collected the sack. He looked to Sam, who stood to the right of him, seemingly ashamed of his master. He hung the bag on the horse's saddle horn and murmured into his ear, "You would have fallen off, too, if we had been in different positions."

The horse snorted and shook his massive head.

For the next hour, they practiced passing the saddlebag. Soon all of them were spending more time in the saddle and less in the mire. In a way, Seth was glad that the rain had created them a nice soft spot to land, but now they were all covered in mud. He didn't relish the idea of washing in the cold stream, but the idea of hauling water to the house and heating it appealed even less.

"Dinner will be in an hour," Rebecca called from the sidelines. She lifted Joy off the fence rail, where the little girl had been perched, laughing at her brothers.

"You heard her, men. Let's get some clean clothes and head to the stream." Seth didn't have to tell them twice. The boys dashed away on their horses straight toward the bunkhouse.

Jacob called after them, "Whatever mess you carry into the bunkhouse, you have to clean up." He continued on to the barn and his tack room.

Sometimes Seth envied Jacob. The boy had a building all to himself. Peace reigned in the barn. Not so in the bunkhouse. Brotherly rivalry and boyish jostling seemed to be the norm.

Noah trailed behind his brothers. Seth rode up beside him. "Why aren't you in a hurry to get to the bunkhouse?"

"You heard Jacob."

Seth looked to the retreating back of Jacob. "Yes."

A sly grin crossed Noah's lips. "If I'm the last one there, I can't be accused of making the mess."

Seth felt a laugh grow in his gut and then burst forth. Once he'd gotten his mirth under control, he said, "Noah, you are wiser than your years."

"Not really—they are just foolish for their advanced ages." He gently touched his boots to his mount's sides, leaving Seth to ponder the boy's words.

Long after everyone else was supposed to be in bed, Rebecca felt as if a pot full of water rested between her shoulder blades. She finished wiping down the counter and looked to Fay. The older woman leaned a mop against the wall and pushed the hair away from her face.

"Is it just me or was this the longest day of the year?" Fay slipped into one of the kitchen chairs.

Rebecca joined her at the table. "I don't know about it being the longest, but it was one of the hardest."

"Next time you send the men out for fresh meat, make sure they bring it in a little at a time." Fay yawned, proving she was exhausted beyond her normal tiredness.

"Why don't you head on to bed, Fay? I can take care of this." Rebecca indicated the piles of meat that filled trays on the kitchen table.

Fay shook her head. "No, four hands are better than two. I'll help you. I know you're tired, too."

Seth came into the kitchen through the back door. When he saw them staring at him, he grinned. "I thought I might help you put this meat away." Andrew, Clayton, Thomas and Philip followed him inside. "And I brought help."

Fay chuckled. "You are a blessing. We dreaded hauling all this out to the icehouse."

"Then dread no more," Philip said, grabbing a large tray and heading back out the door.

"Ladies, we'll take care of this. You can call it a day, if you want to." Seth picked another tray of meat and headed back outside.

Fay took off her apron and hung it on the nail beside the door. "Thank you, boys. I'm going to retire." She smiled at Rebecca. "You might as well let them take care of it and get some rest yourself." Then she walked out of the kitchen, barely hiding her yawn.

Rebecca couldn't let them do all of it. She knew they were tired, too. She'd seen the boys as they'd done their day of work and it hadn't been easy on them, either. Besides, she wanted it put away where she'd know what was what. She grabbed one of the smaller trays and hurried after Andrew and Clayton.

The icehouse wasn't far from the back door. Rebecca loved the small building and enjoyed going out. John's mother had taught her how to place the meat so that she'd never have to search for the part she wanted. Roasts, steaks, ground meats and delicacy meats all had their places in the small structure. She wasn't about to let the men simply toss it inside.

"I told you she'd follow us," Philip said, still holding his tray of meat. "Ma likes things put away orderly." He smiled broadly at Rebecca, assumably to take the sting out of his words.

Rebecca continued into the building. She set down

her load on the small table to the right of the door. "Just set it here and I'll put it where it belongs," she instructed needlessly as Philip and Seth had already joined her by the table.

The boys continued going back and forth between the icehouse and the kitchen, until they'd delivered all the meat. "That's the last of it, Ma," Jacob said as he set down the last tray.

"Thank you, son." She looked up to see the retreating back of Andrew. Jacob stood smiling at her. His eyes looked tired. "Go on to bed and tell the other boys thank you, too. It would have taken Fay and us forever to get all that meat out here."

He nodded and left. Rebecca wondered if Seth had, like the boys, already returned to the bunkhouse. They hadn't had time to discuss tomorrow, but she was beginning to trust Seth, so didn't feel the need to fuss about it. Although she did miss him. She pushed the thought away and went back to her work.

Rebecca took her time placing everything where she wanted it. A sense of satisfaction filled her as she pushed straw about the last few packages of meat, even though her shoulders ached and her fingers felt frozen to the bone.

Thinking herself alone, Rebecca jumped when she straightened up and saw Seth leaning against the frame studying her.

She gasped and placed a hand over her heart. "You scared the life out of me," she protested. "I thought you'd gone to the bunkhouse with the boys."

Seth pushed away from the frame and held the door open for her to exit. "I thought about it but realized you'd be half-frozen by the time you finished up in here." He followed her out. "So I took the liberty of making a fresh pot of tea in the kitchen to warm you up. I hope you don't mind."

He'd made tea for her? She knew he favored strong coffee. Rebecca turned to look at him. "That was very thoughtful of you. Thanks." It had been a long time since someone other than Fay had done something so nice for her.

"It was no trouble."

Rebecca realized that he'd not followed her. She stopped and turned to look at him. He stood by the icehouse with his hands tucked into his coat pockets. "You must be cold, too. Would you like to join me for a cup of that tea?"

He looked as if he might refuse. The notion hit Rebecca hard and she realized that she truly would enjoy his company if he accepted her invitation. To sweeten the idea for him she added, "I have apple pie warming on the back of the stove."

"Who am I to refuse apple pie?" He walked toward her with a teasing grin. A tingling she tried her best to ignore started in the pit of Rebecca's stomach.

She opened the kitchen door and slipped inside, the warmth enveloping her like a blanket. She'd reserved two slices of the pie for herself and Fay as a special treat after all the hard work they'd done that day. But since Fay was unaware of the gesture and Seth had been thoughtful in both getting the boys to help her and making the tea, she felt it only fair to share it with him.

"Please, have a seat at the table and I'll get the pie,"

she said, indicating that he should sit down at the small table.

He ignored her and walked to the coffeepot. "That's very kind, but I think I'll pour the tea. The sooner we have both on the table, the sooner I'll get to savor the pie." Seth carried the pot to the cabinet that housed the dishes and set it down, then reached for the cups.

How long had it been since a man had considered her feelings and overrode them for her benefit? Rebecca's emotions took a nosedive. Or maybe they soared out the top of her head. She couldn't be quite sure, but tears burned the backs of her eyelids and she fought a strong impulse to give in to them. She felt uncertain if her melancholy stemmed from his kindness or her overly tired body.

Taking a deep breath, she carried the pie plate to the table and grabbed two forks from the ceramic crock.

Seth set down the two steaming cups and together they slipped into chairs and sighed. He laughed. "Long day for the both of us, I'd wager."

"I hadn't considered the amount of work it takes to cure meat for storage." She offered him a tired smile.

He nodded. "Next time, we'll space out how much we bring back and the boys and I will do more of the work." Seth forked a bite of apple pie from his slice and slipped it into his mouth.

Rebecca followed the fork's action and realized that his top lip was thin, but the bottom one was full. His tongue snaked out and cleaned up the syrup left behind by the pie. She looked away, realizing that she'd been staring at his mouth.

Heat filled her face. She looked down at the pie

plate, realizing she should probably say something. "Thank you. That would be nice."

"Your apple pie tastes like my grandmother's," Seth said, closing his eyes and savoring the sweetness.

She took a tiny bite and let the cinnamon flavor coat her tongue. Apple pie was something else John's mother had taught her to make. Her own mother had left her and her brother at the orphanage when Rebecca was eight years old and her brother ten. Meals in the orphanage weren't fancy and the children were kept out of the kitchen. It wasn't until she came to help John's mother that she learned how to cook.

He chuckled. "That was a compliment. No need to look so sad."

Rebecca smiled. "I'm sorry. I was just remembering John's mother. She taught me how to cook. I miss her." It was all true, just not the complete reason for her look of sorrow.

"I imagine you do miss her," Seth said, taking a sip of the fresh tea.

She nodded. "Yes, like you miss your grandmother."

He set down his fork and cupped the mug in his hands. "I do miss her."

They sat in silence for several moments, each lost in their thoughts.

Rebecca glanced at him. Had he suffered a lot of loss in his life? She wondered what had happened to his parents and other family members. Had Seth had a brother or sister at some point in his life?

Her brother, Daniel, had been made to leave the orphanage at age twelve. Without a parent who truly loved him and prepared him for the world, he'd been totally clueless as to how to fend for himself. He should never have been on the streets trying to survive during winter. He'd failed, and she blamed the orphanage for his loss of life.

It was the next summer before Rebecca found out her brother had died. Grief such as she'd never known had cracked the fragile shell she'd built around herself when Daniel left the orphanage. Unaware even that she'd formed a wall of protection, when it came crashing down, despair became her daily companion. She'd had nightmares, and the staff had her treated for depression. Later, she'd suffered from a sense of hopelessness. If she couldn't help Daniel, the outcome of her own life appeared bleak.

But God had a plan. She learned early on to trust in Him and He had become her mainstay. Her life had taken a series of turns quite different from the ones Daniel had suffered.

Rebecca had vowed she would never pass up a chance to help those less fortunate. Thankfully, John had understood her need to keep as many boys off the streets as she could and had allowed her to adopt her boys. Those boys were her life now and she loved them all deeply.

"You have a very pretty smile," Seth said, pulling her back to the present.

Unaware she'd been smiling, Rebecca ducked her head in embarrassment. "Thank you." He must think her insane—in the past few minutes he'd seen her go from exhausted to tired and then to smiling.

"Does it bother you when I compliment you?" She glanced up to find him regarding her inquisitively.

Rebecca thought about it for a moment before answering. "No, it doesn't bother me. It just feels surprising to know that someone even considers my smile." She shrugged. "It's been a long time."

"You're a great lady, Rebecca. Someone should compliment you every day of your life." He pushed back his chair. "I'll see what I can do about that."

A tumble of confused thoughts and feelings assailed her. She let out a long, audible breath, but her voice deserted her. She could only stare at him. Crimson color slipped up the sides of his face and ears.

Seth walked to the door. "Umm, thanks for the tea and pie. I really should turn in now."

She picked up the pie plate and cups as she followed him. "Me, too."

"Right after breakfast, I'm taking the boys on a long ride. We'll cover the trail they'll be riding in a few weeks." He ran his hand over the back of his neck. "Just thought you'd like to know."

She nodded. "Would you like for me to pack some sandwiches?"

"If you don't mind. I'm only taking three of the boys tomorrow and then three the following day." Seth stood with his hand on the door.

"You're taking Jacob, too?"

Seth nodded. "Yep, he may have to be a relief rider. But more than likely he won't actually go out very often. Plus, as the stock tender I want him to learn the trail so that he'll know which horse to send out." The red color seeped from his face. Now that they were talking normally, he seemed to no longer feel embarrassed.

Rebecca spoke her thoughts aloud. "Which in turn will decide which boy will travel which trail."

"Sounds right."

She tilted her head to look at him better. "Wouldn't it be best to take all the boys at the same time, just in case they need to ride in both directions?"

He nodded approvingly. "Yes. And I will take them out again and go in the opposite direction than what they'll be traveling over the next couple of days."

Why didn't he just take them all tomorrow and again the next day? Rebecca didn't understand his job, but to her that made more sense.

As if he could read her thoughts, Seth yawned and said, "I'm taking them a few at a time to keep the focus on the job at hand. I want to make sure that they understand the trail and the dangers on it. All together they turn into a bunch of cutups."

His yawn had her mimicking the action. Rebecca covered her mouth. A warm chuckle drew her gaze to him once more.

"Good night, Rebecca."

"Seth?" Rebecca's courage almost failed when he turned to look at her. "Thanks for tonight."

"No thanks needed. Next time we won't bring back as much meat."

She took a deep breath and smiled. "No, I meant the other. It does a woman's heart good to have nice things said to her occasionally. And the tea, well, that was a sweet gesture, too."

They stared at each other, a spark of some indefinable emotion in his eyes. Did he feel the attraction, too?

Or was she simply overtired and seeing too much in him and his actions?

"Good night, Rebecca." He pushed open the door and disappeared into the night.

It seemed silly but Rebecca missed him already. She whispered, "Sweet dreams, Seth." Then she picked up the lantern and walked to her bedroom.

As she prepared for bed, Rebecca continued to focus on Seth and the work he was doing. He'd been working hard with her boys and she could already see that their self-confidence had grown. Even little Benjamin walked with straighter shoulders.

As she'd tucked him into bed, he'd told her that Seth and Jacob had taught him how to check the horse's legs to make sure they were straight and strong. His eyes shone and his cheeks puffed in pride at his newfound knowledge. How could she not love the new excitement her boys showed each time she talked to them? And it was due to Seth's way of treating them and the confidence he instilled.

The stage was due in the morning. Would Seth's mail-order bride be on it? Or would someone on the stage know who Charlotte was or where to locate her? She pulled back the covers on her bed and climbed inside.

Blowing out the lamp, Rebecca relaxed and sank into the cushioning softness. A thought niggled at her tired mind. Did she want Seth to find his fiancée?

Over the past couple of weeks she'd grown to like Seth Armstrong. He cared about her boys. She smiled into the darkness. They weren't boys anymore; they were men. Still, another man might break their spirits, not understand them like Seth did. His gentleness was one of the things she liked most about him.

In the stillness of the dark night, Rebecca faced her real fear. Did she have feelings for Seth? Feelings that went beyond friendship? No? Then why had her heart flip-flopped when he'd told her she had a pretty smile? Why did the pulse at the base of her throat jump every time their eyes met? And last but not least, why had it felt so good to have him compliment her?

She tossed over to her side.

These feelings were caused by tiredness, that was all. But that little voice just wouldn't keep quiet in her mind. She'd felt all that before today, so it stood to reason that tiredness played no part in her feelings.

Rebecca thumped her pillow in frustration. Why, why, why did she have to complicate matters with feelings? He'd complimented her, making her feel special. So what? He probably did that to anyone that cooked and cleaned for him. Yes, that had to be it.

She turned over to the other side and tucked her hand under her pillow. She wasn't acquiring feelings for Seth. She wouldn't allow it. Falling in love wasn't a part of her future, not with Seth, not with any man. Her children were her whole focus.

Her hand snaked across the bed and touched John's pillow. Besides, she wouldn't betray John's memory. The children had already faced many changes. Adding another man in their lives, well, to her way of thinking that just wouldn't be wise.

# *Chapter Fourteen*

❧

Seth didn't want to admit it, but his stomach felt as twisted as that apron. April had arrived with clear skies and anticipation in the air. He'd had two months to work with the boys and he felt they were as ready as they'd ever be. Since Noah was still his best horseman Seth decided to give him the first run. The uncertainty had plagued him all through the night.

Rebecca stood on the porch watching as they waited for the Pony Express rider from the east to arrive. Noah sat on his horse looking relaxed and ready to go. Rebecca twisted her apron in her hands, the only indicator that she was nervous.

Finally, unable to stand the tension, Seth sprinted up to the porch. Before he changed his mind he blurted out, "I'm going with him." Rebecca clasped her hands against her heart and pure relief washed over her features. She nodded.

It felt good. It was the right thing to do. Seth then turned and ran to the barn for his horse, Sam.

He couldn't let her fuss over the youngest rider and

Seth felt certain it would drive him insane not knowing if the boy had made his run without mishap. No matter how hard he tried, Seth couldn't help but care for the Young family.

Jacob met him halfway with Sam. "I thought you might need him," he said, handing the reins to Seth, an expression of satisfaction showing in his eyes.

"Thanks." Seth clapped a hand on his shoulder in appreciation. The boy had the makings of a great leader, discernment being one of the most important gifts to have been blessed with. It was for sure he'd gotten this situation sized correctly. "I'll be back as quick as I can. You're in charge. Be sure and write down the time that the rider coming in arrives." Seth jumped into the saddle.

He moved into position a few feet behind Noah. The boy turned in his saddle. Noah lifted an eyebrow in question then asked, "What's going on?"

"Change of plans. I'm going with you," Seth called to him, just as a bugle rang out, announcing the arrival of the other Pony Express rider.

With pride, Seth watched them exchange the saddlebag. Noah caught it in midair, whooped loudly and then put his heels to his pony's sides. The young boy shot off and Seth followed.

He paced Sam and allowed Noah his lead. As far as he knew none of the other Pony Express station keepers had two riders going at the same time, meaning a fresh mount would be waiting for Noah, but not for him.

Noah turned in his saddle, seeing that Seth rode farther and farther behind, and spun his horse and returned. "You're gonna have to ride faster than that if we are to make our time," he called.

When Noah was within hearing distance, Seth called to him, "Go on and ride like thunder. I'll follow more slowly and will catch up with you. Don't wait for me."

Noah didn't have to be told twice. The mail had to go through and it had to go through fast. They were on a timeline. They had ten days to get the mail from St. Joseph, Missouri, to Sacramento, California. Noah and the other boys had vowed to do a good job for the founders of the Pony Express and they all intended to see to it that they kept their word.

Four relay stations later, Seth caught up with Noah at the home station in Willow Springs. Noah sat on the front porch waiting for him. His feet were propped up on the porch rail. He had a satisfied grin on his face.

Seth climbed down off Sam. He patted his horse and then turned toward the home-station house.

"I made my time, Seth," he stated as Seth walked up the steps.

Seth nodded. "I'm proud of you."

Noah stood. "Now that you are here, I'm going to hit a bunk. Didn't get much sleep last night."

"Me, either," Seth confessed, following Noah off the porch and taking Sam by the reins and heading to the barn. "Soon as I get Sam tucked in, I may join you for some shut-eye."

Noah walked the short distance to a small bunkhouse. It wasn't nearly as big as the one at Dove Creek. Of course, Seth doubted there were as many boys here who called Willow Springs their home station, either.

The stock tender greeted him as he entered the barn. "I'm almost done with this one, Mr. Armstrong. If you want me to take care of your horse I'll be a couple of minutes."

When Seth couldn't remember the man's name, he realized he was tired. More so than he'd first thought. After crossing streams and being in the saddle for about seventy-five miles, he realized why they wanted to hire younger men. "I'll take care of him."

As he groomed Sam, his thoughts went to Rebecca. Over the past few weeks, she'd put distance between them. He missed her coming out to see what her boys were doing. She hadn't been rude during their nightly meetings, but kept to the point as to what she needed done.

The stagecoach hadn't produced the results he'd hoped for in finding Charlotte. Maybe it was time to try something else, but what? He yawned.

"I think you've brushed his coat enough, Mr. Armstrong," the stock tender said, bringing a bag of oats for Sam.

The sweet smell caused Seth's stomach to rumble. "Thank you." He nodded toward the oats.

"Cook has beans and corn bread on the stove, if you'd like," the man offered, patting Sam on the neck.

Seth had the feeling the stock tender would like nothing better than for him to leave and let him get on with his work. He realized that he'd have to make some form of reimbursement for the care of the extra horse if he teamed up his boys to travel the trail. They couldn't expect the other home stations to feed their animals and extra mouths.

He thanked the man once more and then headed back to the house. The station keeper, Joe Cantrell, sat on the porch. Good, Seth needed to talk to the man and now was the perfect time.

"Come on up and have a seat, Seth," Joe insisted. Grey hair topped the man's head and curled on his neck. Seth would guess his age to be about sixty. He held a piece of straw between his teeth and had the look of a man who wanted to talk.

"I believe I will." Seth climbed the stairs for a second time. He sank into the rocker that Noah had sat in earlier.

They rocked in silence for a couple of minutes. Then Joe spoke. "Your boy did good. Came in like a pro." He took the straw out of his mouth and studied the end of it. "I was a bit surprised when he told me you weren't far behind. What brings you my way?"

Seth liked Joe. He was a straight talker and didn't mince his words. "Well," he said, leaning his arms on his knees, "his ma was worried about him and I felt compelled to come along and make sure this first ride went smoothly."

"Yep, that's what I figured." Joe leaned back in the rocker and closed his eyes.

Seth didn't dare close his eyes. He'd be asleep in no time. Even though Joe's eyes were closed, Seth knew the station keeper wasn't sleeping. There was more to be said, so he waited to hear what it was.

Joe cleared his throat. "Wondered if having the boys' ma around would cause trouble."

"Naw, she isn't any trouble. Just worried about her boys." Seth wasn't about to tell Joe or anyone else how

Rebecca had clucked about the boys like a mother hen when he'd first arrived.

Joe stopped the rocking of the chair. "That's good."

"I do need to compensate you for the care of my horse and if it isn't too much trouble for a meal." Seth's stomach rumbled again, reminding him it had been a long time since he'd eaten.

"Is this going to become a habit? You riding along with the boys?" Joe asked, opening his eyes and searching Seth's face.

Seth stood. "No, I won't be coming, but one of the other men might. It really depends on you," he admitted.

"How so?"

He didn't want to tell Joe that Rebecca would be a nervous Nellie as long as her boys were out alone, but if they had someone to go with them on their rides, could team up, so to speak, Seth felt sure she'd feel much better. "I'm thinking of having my boys travel in teams of two. But if I do that I'll have horses eating here and an extra boy eating and sleeping here. You'll need some kind of payment for the extra mouths you'll be feeding."

Joe nodded and rubbed his chin, as if thinking about it. "Well, do you have any good hunters in your group?"

Seth grinned. "The best in the bunch is sleeping in your bunkhouse right now."

Disbelief filled the station keeper's eyes. "That slip of a boy is a good hunter?"

"The best I've seen in a long time."

Joe stood and stretched out his back. "Well, fresh meat is what we need. If your boy is as good as you think he is, I believe that will take care of the boy's meals. As for the horses, do you reckon you can spare the supplies to feed them?"

Seth nodded. "Yep, when they deliver Pony Express hay to Dove Creek, I'll just have them send part of the supplies here to you."

The older man slapped Seth on the back. "Go grab some grub and some sleep and tomorrow we'll take that boy of yours out to see if he can hunt."

Seth did as he was told, all the while wishing there was some way he could let Rebecca know that Noah had made it safe and sound. He already missed her and the other boys.

Rebecca hurried to the Young family cemetery just as the sun set. She wanted to clean off the graves and admire the new fence the boys and Seth had placed around it.

It had been two weeks since the Pony Express started running. A few days earlier the country had celebrated the fact that the boys who rode the trail were able to do so in ten days. She felt so proud and still a bit amazed that her boys were part of the event that made mail travel so much faster. Nowadays Rebecca hardly saw the boys since they came and went as they did.

Happily surprised when she found Andrew standing within the fence of the cemetery, Rebecca waved to him. She finished climbing the small hill just as Andrew hurried to open the little gate for her. "Hi, Ma. What are you doing up here so late?" he asked as she walked past him.

Her gaze moved to John's grave. There was no need

to worry about it being cluttered with leaves; someone had already cleaned it up. She looked to John's parents' graves and saw them clean, as well. "I came to take care of the family plots but I see someone has already done so." For a moment she allowed sadness to fill her. Without the excuse of cleaning, she really had no reason to linger up here with her son.

Sensing her sorrow, Andrew said, "I'm sorry. I took care of it this afternoon. If I had known you wanted to do it, I wouldn't have done so." He slapped his hat against his leg.

"Oh, Andrew, I'm not upset that you took care of them." She gave him a quick hug. "Thank you for taking care of Papa John's grave." She extended her hand. "And the others, too."

"I still miss him." Andrew kept his arm around her shoulders.

Rebecca nodded. "Me, too."

"But you know, Ma, Papa John wouldn't want you pining after him. He'd want you to start fresh."

She took a step back and looked up into her son's handsome face. "No, I'm sure he wouldn't, but what are you getting at, Andrew?"

A pink flush filled his ears. "Oh, nothing." He held up his hands as he studied her face. "Really."

"Then why did you say that?" she asked as she bent down to pick up a small stick and toss it over the fence.

Andrew put his hat on his head and dug his hands into his front pockets. "Well, I've been thinking about my own future as well as yours."

Fear clutched her throat. *Please, Lord, don't let him say he is leaving.* The silent prayer flew from her mind and she prayed it would reach heaven's gates before Andrew spoke again. "I see. And what have you been thinking?"

"Well, even though we are all orphans, Seth says we can still have a bright future, even you." He rocked on his boot heels.

"Seth said this, about me?" What else had Seth said about her? It dawned on her that Andrew said, *we can still have a bright future, even you.* "How does Seth know I was an orphan?"

Seemingly unaware of her building anger, Andrew answered, "We were talking one day and I mentioned it."

Trying hard not to let her frustration at being talked about come through in her voice, she asked, "Do you often speak of me?"

"Sure we do." A big grin crossed his face. "We're all very proud of you. You're a great ma."

His sweet words filled her heart but she still wanted to know if they were just talking and mentioned her, or if Seth had been putting his nose where it didn't belong, which was in her business. "Thanks, son. I'm proud of you, too."

"Every evening, after your visit with Seth, he comes to the bunkhouse and those of us that are there, except Jacob, read a little of the Bible and discuss what we've read." He opened the gate to leave.

Rebecca followed him out. She had no idea they were having a nightly Bible study. And the fact that Andrew was willing to participate surprised her, too. He and Jacob had quit reading with her and the younger ones after John's death.

"Did you know that there is a Scripture that talks about orphans and widows?"

Absentmindedly, Rebecca nodded.

"Seth says that since you are both, we need to take especially good care of you." He latched the gate behind them.

Rebecca stood in his path. "Andrew, has he been asking questions about me?"

Andrew shrugged. "Sometimes, but he asks questions about all of us. He even wanted to know about Papa John and his parents."

"I see." She glanced up at the sky. Stars were beginning to shine even though the sun wasn't completely down.

"Ma, I need to go. It's my turn to take the mail and the other rider will be here soon. Will you be all right walking back to the house?" Andrew looked in the direction of the woods.

Rebecca noticed that his horse stood there, munching on the new spring grass as if he and Andrew came here often. "Go on, son. I'll be fine. I'll take the road back to the house." She smiled at him.

"Walk off to the side. I'd hate for the pony rider to accidentally hit you." He sprinted to his horse and grabbed his reins.

"I'll be careful," she called to him. Rebecca watched him walk his horse to the road then spring into the saddle. Man and horse disappeared as they raced to the house.

Rebecca followed slowly. How dare Seth Armstrong discuss her with her boys! What had he thought? That he'd learn something new about her? And if so, what did he plan to do with this new knowledge? The speed of her footsteps increased. She'd have a few choice words for him this evening. She'd set him straight and since he didn't know her boundaries, Rebecca had every intention of sharing them.

## Chapter Fifteen

Seth both looked forward to his discussion with Rebecca tonight and dreaded it. He wanted to tell her how wonderfully the boys were doing and that he'd noticed that the south fence needed repairing. But over dinner he'd felt a deep tension coming from her direction. She'd refused to look him straight in the eye while eating, and that didn't bode well for his peace of mind. When his grandmother behaved this way, she usually had a burr under her saddle.

He walked up the steps and found Rebecca sitting on the porch. "Oh, I didn't realize we were meeting out here tonight." In two strides he was beside the swing she sat in. "It's nice enough. I'm enjoying this warmer weather."

Still she silently rocked. Yep, there was a burr somewhere. He leaned against the porch rail and waited for her to speak. When it was obvious she didn't have anything to add to his comments, he asked, "Is there something wrong?"

In a crisp, cold tone, she answered, "Depends."

Yep, definitely something ate at her. "Care to share?"

Her head snapped up and her blue eyes reminded him of blue ice. "I don't appreciate you talking to my boys about me, Seth Armstrong. You have no business asking them questions about me. If you want to know something, ask me yourself. Do not worry my boys with questions. And that goes for questions about John, too." She blew the hair off her forehead.

He studied her red cheeks. What had he asked that would have offended her? Come to think of it, Seth couldn't recall asking personal questions about her or John. He and the boys often discussed family, especially during Bible study, but as far as he could remember, Seth had never pried into her personal life.

"Well, what do you have to say for yourself?" she demanded in a soft yet dangerous voice.

Seth rubbed his jaw. "Well, for starters, I apologize. I wasn't aware I had pried. But evidently I have. For that I am sorry." And he truly meant the words.

Rebecca nodded, still looking as if she wanted to argue with him. "And another thing, I appreciate you starting up nightly Bible study with the boys. You've reminded me that this family goes to church on Sundays. Now, I know—" she held up her hand to stop his protest "—I've been negligent in that since you've been here, but starting this Sunday we are *all* going to church." She put great emphasis on the word *all*.

"Rebecca, I appreciate the sentiment behind your statement. It's a good thing to be faithful to church. But even you can see that at least one of the boys will need to ride." He stood a little taller. What would she say to that?

She inhaled and stood. "Then I suggest you start looking for a relief rider on Sundays because me and my boys are going to church and that's final. Since their father is gone, the responsibility for their spiritual raising is now mine and it's time I started taking it seriously." Rebecca pulled her shawl closer to her body and lifted her head. When he didn't immediately respond, she left him standing on the porch.

A chuckle sounded off to his right. Seth squinted his eyes and looked into the shadows. "Think that's funny, do you, Jacob?"

Jacob moved into the light that streamed from the window. "Sure do. You really ruffled Ma's feathers."

"Any idea how that happened?" Seth wondered if Jacob had been the one to tell Rebecca of the nightly Bible studies.

"Nope. I knew she was in a mood so I was going to come talk to her when I saw you walk up. Glad you got to her first. Now I know to stay away for a while." Jacob turned and walked in the direction of the barn.

Seth followed him. He wanted to ask if Rebecca held on to her anger long, but decided that asking probably wasn't the best thing. To his reckoning, that might be what she considered prying. As he entered the barn Seth settled it in his mind that those types of questions had been what had gotten him into trouble tonight. "Any idea who we can get to ride on Sunday?" He walked over to Sam's stall.

"You can always ask Bill tomorrow if he'll stay a couple of extra days and take Clayton's place. Or you can make the ride yourself." With that Jacob walked into the tack room and shut the door.

Seth rubbed Sam's nose. It would be nice to attend the Sunday service. He'd ask Bill if he'd take the ride, but if Bill refused Seth knew he'd ride in place of Clayton.

Rebecca Young was one stubborn woman. He knew she wouldn't back down and now he had to find a rider to take his boys' place every Sunday. His job just got a little harder.

He stepped out into the night and looked to the house, where Rebecca could be seen through the sitting room window. His grandmother had been stubborn and now Rebecca acted the same way. Both women intended to get what they wanted. Seth shook his head and muttered, "Lord, deliver me from stubborn women."

A star twinkled off in the distance. Would the Lord answer his prayer? And would Charlotte be just as stubborn as Rebecca and his grandmother? Seth frowned. He hadn't thought of his mail-order bride in a long time.

His gaze returned to the window. Rebecca sat in her chair rocking. It looked as if she was working on something in her lap. There was a stubborn tilt to her chin. Stubbornness was part of the reason Seth liked Rebecca. That and the fact that she stood up for what she believed in.

He shook his head. "Get a grip, ol' boy. One moment you like her, the next you want to wring her neck. Can't have it both ways. You can't like her too much anyway 'cause you're promised to another and don't you forget it." The thought came to him that Rebecca was the type of woman who would insist that love would be the only reason to get involved with a man. And love was not something he wanted or needed.

Sunday morning, Rebecca gathered her things and led her children out the church doors. She heard Seth's voice behind her as he shook the preacher's hand and thanked him for the sermon. He'd surprised her by attending. Not that she didn't believe him a God-fearing man, but she'd expected him to stay behind and take Clayton's place on the Pony Express trail.

Fay stayed behind. Said her rheumatism was acting up. She also promised to make sure that Bill had a big lunch before he took off for his ride.

It really was too bad that the Pony Express didn't take off Sundays. From what Rebecca had seen of Bill, he could have used a morning in church. The young man seemed rough around the edges, but most of the young men that came through Dove Creek's home station looked as if they could use a mother's care.

"What did you pack for lunch?" Philip asked, reaching toward the two baskets that Rebecca had shoved under the wagon seat.

She slapped at his hands. "Get out of there. You'll find out as soon as we get to the meadow." She scooted over and let Jacob take the reins.

Philip laughed and hopped onto his horse. "Then let's go. I'm starving."

"Ma, can I ride with Seth?" Joy asked, pulling at her skirt.

Rebecca turned to look at her daughter. Joy looked

pretty with a light blue bow in her long blond hair. Seth sat on top of Sam not more than a foot away from them.

"It's up to Seth, sweetheart."

Joy squealed. She jumped up and Rebecca grabbed the back of her dress to keep her from falling out of the wagon.

"If you keep jumping around like that, I'm going to change my mind," Rebecca warned. She wished she hadn't agreed, when Seth bent over and scooped up the little girl.

He winked at Joy. "Too late."

Rebecca couldn't get over how nice he looked with his hair combed into place, wearing a light green shirt covered by a tan jacket with what looked like leather patches on the elbows. His jeans looked new and his black boots shined. The black hat he wore on his head was pushed back and he gave her a playful grin.

"It's never too late for me to change my mind, Seth Armstrong, and don't you forget it," she teased back.

The wagon lurched as it took off. Her other boys all mounted their horses and surrounded the wagon as it pulled out of the churchyard.

A smile touched her lips as she heard Benjamin tell Seth, "Yep, she changes her mind if you make her mad. You and Joy better be nice."

She cut her eyes and looked at Seth and Joy. Joy looked happier than a girl with two playful kittens. Her blue-green eyes stared up at Seth adoringly.

The boys laughed and talked as they drove to the meadow. Only Jacob rode in silence. Rebecca looped her arm in his and laid her head on his shoulder. In a quiet voice she asked, "What did you think of the service this morning, Jacob?"

He shrugged. "It was fine."

Rebecca knew of all the young men in her care that Jacob was the only one who either didn't believe in God or had simply given up on Him. She didn't know how to reach the boy. Since John's death he'd been quiet and reserved, especially when it came to talking about his Maker.

"Ma, can I put the blanket out?" Benjamin asked.

She lifted her head. "Sure you can, but I get to pick the spot."

"Is this meadow much farther?" Seth asked.

Thomas answered. "Just over that rise. I'll race you."

"You're on!" Seth replied.

Rebecca watched them shoot off in front of the wagon. Seth's arms wrapped around the little girl's waist protectively.

Joy's blond hair flew out behind them. Her giggles filled the air as she hung on to the saddle horn.

Was her daughter getting too close to the station keeper? Rebecca watched them top the rise and go over the other side. As soon as Seth could find his mail-order bride, he'd be gone; she knew this to be true. Maybe she should limit Joy's time with the handsome man. Rebecca stopped herself. Had she just thought of Seth as a handsome man?

He was, but Rebecca didn't think it wise to think of him that way. She made a mental note to stop thinking about him altogether. The wagon topped the hill and she looked down into the meadow to find Seth tossing Joy into the air as if she was a sack of flour. Her joyful laughter couldn't be ignored. Joy was falling in love with Seth. Not in the way a woman fell in love with a man, but as a friend she was going to miss terribly when he left.

Jacob spoke. "Everyone likes him."

Had she said her thoughts aloud? No, Rebecca was pretty sure she hadn't. "True. He's a nice man."

"Yes, he is." He stopped the wagon, set the brake and hopped down to help Rebecca unload the food.

The boys were all tying their horses up to keep them from wandering too far. Rebecca lowered her voice and asked Jacob, "Do you think Joy is getting too attached to him?"

He looked to where Seth swung Joy around and around in a circle. "Possibly. All the boys are. I don't think it can be helped."

Jacob was probably right. Rebecca handed him the last box and then climbed down from the wagon. She looked at the meadow and smiled. "I love it here."

Benjamin hurried to her side. "Ma, can I put the blanket down now?" His eager eyes met hers. He clutched the old quilt close to his heart.

Rebecca laughed. The boy only wanted to spread the cover so that they could start lunch. He'd grown a full two inches in the past few weeks and eating had become a favorite pastime for him. "Yes, over by that small grove of trees." She pointed to where a group of cottonwood trees stood proudly.

Her gaze moved to Seth once more. Was she becoming too attached to him, too? If so, how could she put more distance between them?

\* \* \*

Seth clutched his stomach and groaned. "Rebecca, I think that was the best lunch I've had in a very long time."

Benjamin nodded his agreement. "Ma makes the best fried chicken around."

"I agree." Seth closed his eyes and leaned his back against the tree. "But I believe I ate too much."

"Seth, come play with me." Joy grabbed his hand and pulled.

He cracked an eye and said, "Oh, Joy, girl. My tummy is too full to play right now."

Thomas stood and stretched. "I'll play with you, Joy."

"Can we play duck, duck, goose?" Joy jumped up and down.

Seth listened as first Philip, then Noah and Benjamin, agreed to play duck, duck, goose. They walked a short ways from the picnic area and began to form a circle for the game.

He watched as the boys slowed their running speed so that their sister could outrun them and take their place in the grass. All except young Benjamin. He always beat his little sister and crowed to the others that he was the fastest one there. Seth chuckled.

The three older boys stood beside the wagon. He couldn't make out their conversation but knew it was friendly by the way one or the other would laugh from time to time. This was the most relaxed he'd seen the family and to tell the truth, Seth enjoyed it.

Rebecca began to gather up the food and place it in the boxes. He was amazed at how well she'd packed their meal and had even packed tin cups for them to drink cold cider out of.

Seth sat up to help her. He handed her a jar that had once held pickles. His hand brushed hers and warmth traveled up his arm where their skin connected.

"Thank you, Seth, but I can do this." She looked down at her hand where it had touched his.

Had she felt the warmth also? He wasn't ready to leave just yet and from the looks of the happy kids, Seth didn't think they would be ready to go, either. "Can't you sit a while and enjoy the sun on your face? You work hard all the time. Surely you can spare an hour or so to relax and have some thinking time."

She put the lid and ring on the pickle jar and placed it in the basket. Gathering her skirt in one hand, she sat beside Seth with her back pressed against the same tree.

"What's this thinking time you're talking about, Seth?" Her voice sounded a little shaky to his ears. So perhaps she had felt the warmth they'd just shared.

"My grandmother used to make me take a nap every Sunday afternoon. But after I turned ten and no longer wanted to take naps, she said for me to get out away from the house so I wouldn't wake up her. She told me to go think on things."

"And did you?"

He nodded. "That became my favorite time of the week."

She drew an invisible pattern between them on the quilt. "What did you think on?"

"Oh, the things that had happened in the past. Things I wanted to do in the future." He chewed on a piece of grass. "I'd map out a plan in my head how to accomplish more."

"Is that all?"

He turned his head to face her, allowing a teasing expression to enter his eyes. "What? You don't think that was enough?"

"No," she said, bumping his shoulder lightly with her own. "I'm sure you thought on lots of things and I think that's one of the best suggestions I've heard. But you misunderstood. I wanted to know all that you accomplished."

He stretched his legs out in front of him, crossed his arms on his chest and put his head back against the tree. "I guess the main thing I thought about was how to make myself into the type of person I wanted to be. I already had a strong opinion as to what I didn't want, but at ten had a hard time figuring out what I did want."

"Deep thoughts for a ten-year-old."

"Maybe. But I see myself in Beni. He tries so hard to be good all the time, but occasionally the mischievousness sneaks out. I try to convince him that's normal, but each time you punish him, he thinks it's a direct hit against his character."

She chuckled and he turned to study her profile. Wisps of hair framed her oval face. Her face showed a strength that did not lessen her femininity. The beginnings of a smile tipped the corners of her mouth. One dimple winked in his direction. "I'm thinking he already has you wrapped around his little finger."

"No," he growled, turning her smile into an infectious grin. "Why would you think that?"

"Because that little rascal kept playing John and me

against each other. John would make him stand in the corner and he would look at me with those big eyes and say, 'I'm a bad boy, Ma. You need to pray for me.' Then I would tell John that we were wounding his spirit. I became upset and John would dismiss the punishment."

"Oh, no, that's not good. How did it turn out?"

"Well, one day we heard Beni bragging to Philip. 'I just pucker my lips like I'm gonna cry and tell Ma I'm a bad boy. She doesn't ever want me to think I'm a bad boy. She makes Pa let me go.'"

Seth couldn't help it. He guffawed. "That little faker. Then what happened?"

"Next time John put him in the corner, I agreed that he was a bad boy and that he would stand even longer in the corner because that's what happened to bad boys. He knew we were onto him. He never tried it again, but he did go overboard trying to be good to prove he wasn't bad."

"That explains a lot. I bet you have stories like this on all the boys, don't you?"

She looked at him, her expression suddenly somber. The silence lengthened between them, making him uncomfortable. What had he said wrong? He studied her face. "Why are you looking at me like that?"

"Are you asking because you care about the boys or so you can use the stories against them?"

Seth breathed in shallow gasps. The tension between them increased with frightening speed. He glowered at her then turned away, jumping up to gather their things. He'd been so stupid.

For a second it had felt as if they were courting, but the look on her face said that wasn't the case and probably never would be. "Thank you for letting me tag along with your family today, Rebecca. I thoroughly enjoyed myself."

Regret filled her voice. "Seth, wait."

"Let it alone, Rebecca. I understand." Seth felt an acute sense of loss. She would never trust him, that was evident, so how could they continue working together? How would he make it without the boys he'd come to love?

He looked to where the kids were now playing freeze tag. Joy squealed as Benjamin tagged her. She froze into place and yelled for Philip to unfreeze her. They really were a great bunch of kids. He was glad he got to see them so relaxed and acting like kids.

"Come on, kids! Time to pack up and head home," Rebecca called to them. She looked at Seth. "I'm sorry I spoiled our fun."

Seth swallowed with difficulty but found his voice. "It was time to leave anyway. The boys need to feed the livestock." Seth watched the older boys walk over and take the boxes back to the wagon. Jacob shook the blanket out and then folded it.

"Aw, Ma, do we have to go?" Benjamin protested. He dragged his boots across the grass and looked dejected.

"Yes."

The boys all headed for their horses, but Joy came running to Seth. "Can I ride home with you, Seth?"

Rebecca answered before he could. "Not this time, Joy. I want you to ride with me."

"But, Ma. I don't get to ride all the time like the boys do," she protested.

Seth wondered why Rebecca didn't want the little girl to ride with him. He waited to see what Rebecca would say.

"No buts, Joy. Go to Jacob. He'll help you into the wagon." Rebecca didn't meet Seth's inquisitive look. She simply followed her daughter.

How did women do that? He was the one offended, but she acted as if he'd hurt her. He shook his head in disbelief and mounted his horse.

On the ride back to the farm, Seth took the time to think. He'd thought they were getting on well together. But a relationship without trust could never survive, even one that wasn't romantic.

# Chapter Sixteen

Rebecca kept watch over the road that led past her house. The stagecoach should be rolling in any minute and she was also expecting Thomas and Philip's return. She hung the last of the boys' shirts on the line to dry, placed the empty basket on her hip and headed back to the house.

Fay met her at the door. "I put the sweetbread and sandwiches out on the sideboard."

"Thank you, Fay. I'll make a fresh pot of coffee..."

"That's already been done, too." Fay wiped her hands on her apron. A light coating of flour dusted the smock that covered her house dress. "I hope you don't mind, but I thought I'd get a start on the dough for tonight's biscuits."

Rebecca smiled. "Mind? I don't know what I would have done without you over the last few weeks. I'm so glad you decided to stay out here with us."

"Me, too," Joy said from her place on the rug.

Her daughter was surrounded by doll clothes that Fay had made for Joy's baby. It was amazing how much one woman could do to change the dynamics of the family. Rebecca couldn't imagine life without her.

"Me three." Fay grinned down at Joy then she looked back up at Rebecca. "You and your family have given me new life and a new purpose."

The sound of the stage pulling into the yard alerted the women it was time to get to work. Rebecca pulled her wet apron from her waist and tied on a clean one. She patted her hair into place and then pushed through the door that separated the kitchen from the main living space. Fay followed.

A quick glance around confirmed that the room was in order and ready to receive their guests. Earlier in the week she and Fay had set up the small table that had been in the kitchen for their guests to eat. Fay had already set out the food and fluffed the pillows that rested on the settee. All that was left was to answer the door.

Two ladies entered the room. Neither looked very happy. The youngest one said to the other, "I thought they were going to overtake us. Didn't you?"

"I already told you, yes, Grace. I'd really rather not think about it for a few minutes."

"Winifred, how can we not think about it? We have to get back into that contraption and pray they don't give chase again," Grace answered in a huffy voice.

Rebecca cleared her throat. "Ladies, if you would like refreshments, the sideboard is this way." She motioned toward where the food sat waiting.

"Thank you," Winifred answered. She walked to the sideboard and began loading a plate with sandwiches and sweetbread.

Had she seen the sign? Rebecca started to point

it out, but then Winifred dug into her handbag and dropped the money into the crock.

Fay waited until they sat down and then asked, "Who was chasing you, dear?"

Grace looked as if she were about to explode with the news. "Road bandits. They chased us for a long time. I felt sure they would catch up with us." She shoved a bite of sweetbread into her mouth. Around the treat, Grace continued, "They would have taken all our money."

Winifred shook her head, seemingly annoyed at her companion.

"Well, they would have," Grace said.

A huge sigh whooshed from Winifred. "They could have killed us or worse," the older woman said.

"How many were there?" Rebecca asked. She poured herself a cup of coffee and sat down on the couch. Would they chase her boys? Thomas and Philip still hadn't returned. *Lord, please keep my boys safe.*

"Just two," Grace answered. "But they looked big and mean."

The stagecoach driver opened the door. "Ladies, we'll be leaving in five minutes."

Rebecca got the ladies a piece of cheesecloth to wrap up their leftovers.

Winifred took it. "Thank you. This was very nice and has settled my nerves somewhat." She stood to leave.

"You're welcome." Rebecca walked them to the door. "Oh, before you go, do either of you know a Charlotte Fisher?"

Both women shook their heads. Grace answered,

"No, but if we meet her we'll tell her you inquired about her."

Rebecca felt both disappointed and a little glad. She wasn't ready for Seth to take off. Her boys respected him and she didn't know who Mr. Bromley might send as his replacement. At least that was what she told herself. "Thank you. Safe traveling, ladies."

When they left, Rebecca closed the door. "What do you think of that?" she asked Fay.

The older woman shook her head. "The bandits are getting braver. The men on the last stage said they'd not chased them once they realized they had guns at the ready. Most likely they thought the women were no threat to them."

Rebecca looked at her. "I didn't realize that you'd talked to the men about road bandits."

"You stepped out of the room to help Joy with something," Fay explained as she picked up the plate of sandwiches and sweetbread. "I think I'll run these outside to the boys, if that's all right with you."

"Sure, I know they will enjoy them." Rebecca carried the coffeepot back to the kitchen.

Road bandits were a concern for everyone. They seemed to be getting braver or maybe she'd just not heard about them much since the station hadn't been on the stagecoach route. Either way, she wasn't happy with knowing they were out there.

As Rebecca cooked and cleaned the rest of the evening, she prayed for her boys and the people on the stagecoach. Her nerves were stretched taut when Seth and the boys came to the house for dinner.

"It smells good, Ma," Andrew said enthusiastically as he took his seat at the table.

Rebecca grinned at him. "It should—it's your favorite." She set a platter of steaks on the table.

Fay added baked potatoes and hot rolls. She turned and took a bowl of hot green beans from Joy's small hands.

Andrew laughed. "This is everyone's favorite meal." He poured milk into his glass.

Rebecca patted him on the shoulder. "True."

A few minutes later, Seth said the blessing and they passed around the plates of food. Rebecca looked to Jacob's, Thomas's and Philip's empty chairs.

"They should be back any minute now," Seth said, taking a potato and putting it on his plate.

She swallowed as the urge to cry almost overtook her. "I know." Rebecca wished her voice didn't sound so weak.

Fay reached over and patted her hand. "The boys are fine, Rebecca. Don't borrow trouble."

To prove Fay's words, the door banged open and both Thomas and Philip entered the house. Excitement flowed from them in invisible waves.

Jacob followed behind them and shut the door. "Sorry we're late, Ma." He slid into his chair.

The other two boys were already in their chairs and reaching for the plates of food. "Us, too," Thomas said around a mouthful of bread.

"We ran into a little trouble," Philip said, sharing a grin with Thomas.

Benjamin looked up from his plate. His brandy-colored eyes sparkled with excitement. "What kind of trouble?"

Thomas leaned forward for dramatic effect. "Indians."

"Really? You saw Indians?" Benjamin all but bounced in his chair.

Philip answered, "Sure did. We had to outrun them."

Thomas waved his fork in the air. "They were easy to outrun."

Rebecca's gaze met Seth's across the table. Was he thinking the same thing she was? Did the boys seem to be enjoying this adventure just a little too much? Hadn't Seth taught them that Indians were a real threat? She wanted to scream at him to say something. Scold them. Anything but just sit there.

When he didn't obey her silent orders, Rebecca decided she'd need to talk to him about emphasizing the real dangers of riding the Pony Express. Because from the way Thomas and Philip were going on now, he obviously had not done his job with them.

Seth could almost hear her thoughts. She was angry and scared. Her eyes screamed at him, but he refused to reprimand the boys at the dinner table.

He cleared his throat to get their attention. Everyone looked to him except Rebecca—suddenly she was very interested in the pattern on the edge of her plate. "Boys, let your vittles fill your mouth." Seth looked pointedly to Rebecca.

Understanding crossed their features. Both boys took great interest in their supper. The rest of the family found other things to talk about.

Everyone but Benjamin. "But I want to hear about the Indians," he protested.

Seth caught his eye. Keeping his voice calm but firm he said, "The dinner table is no place for such talk."

Benjamin dropped his gaze. "All right, Seth." Under his voice he mumbled, "But I'm going to the bunkhouse with the men tonight and learn about them Indians."

Grins split Thomas's and Philip's faces as they chewed. When Benjamin looked up at them with awe in his eyes, Philip winked at him.

Yes, they needed a talking-to. Indians weren't to be taken lightly and yes, Benjamin needed to hear what Seth had to say, too. Between the Indians and the road bandits, the Pony Express trail was becoming more and more dangerous.

Rebecca pushed her food around on her plate. It didn't take an educated man to know that she was upset and rightly so. Seth dreaded tonight's meeting. The way she shot sharp looks in his direction told him that she had a lot on her mind and that he was going to get the brunt of it.

Fay kept Joy entertained with talk about needlework. The two discussed an alphabet sampler that Joy was working on. "We'll have to see about getting some new colors of thread," Fay said.

Joy grinned. "Blue? Can we get blue?"

"No, I think you should get your favorite color," Clayton said around a mouth full of potatoes.

"But blue is my favorite color," Joy protested.

Clayton hid a smile. "Oh, well then maybe you should get my favorite color. Can you guess what it is?"

"Red?" Joy asked.

He shook his head. "Try again."

She tapped her bottom lip with her fork. Her gaze moved across the table to Andrew, who mouthed *yellow*. "Yellow." She beamed at Clayton.

"Very good."

Joy giggled. "I will look for yellow, too."

Dinner continued with small talk of the day and then everyone was leaving the table. The boys all thanked their mother for the meal, took their plates to the kitchen and then made their way back to the bunkhouse.

Seth stopped Thomas and Philip as they hurried to the door. In a soft voice he said, "Hold all Indian talk until I get out there. I want to hear all the details. So wait for me."

"Sure, Seth," Thomas said and then the boys walked a little slower out of the house.

Seth turned to the table. Fay and Rebecca were already clearing the remaining dirty dishes. "Let me give you ladies a hand," he offered, picking up the food bowls and carrying them to the kitchen.

Fay grinned at him. "There's no need for that."

"I think there is. You two work hard all day. A little help from me will give you a little more time to relax." He returned to the dining room to pick up dirty glasses.

His gaze moved to Joy, who now sat in the parlor with her needlework. She looked up and he grinned at her. "My favorite color is blue-green," he said winking at her.

"Hey, Ma says my eyes are blue-green."

He laughed. "So they are." Seth carried the glasses into the kitchen.

Rebecca was pouring hot water into the washtub. She scraped soap off into the water and swished it around. It didn't create many bubbles but would clean the dishes well enough.

He picked up a dish towel and stood beside her. "I'll rinse and dry if you'll wash."

Rebecca looked at him. "All right. Thanks."

"I'll scrub down the table and chairs," Fay said, grabbing a cloth and wetting it in Rebecca's dishwater. She then returned to the dining room.

As soon as she was out of the room, Rebecca demanded, "Didn't you teach those boys that Indians could be dangerous?"

He rinsed and dried the glass she handed him. "Yes, but obviously, I didn't do a very good job. Tonight I'll have a good talking-to with them about both the Indians and the road bandits. Then tomorrow I plan on having all the boys practice using their guns and rifles." He put the glass to the side and reached for another.

"Thank you. I hate that they have to learn to point a gun at another human being."

"So do I. But both the Indians and the bandits have guns and know how to use them. God never intended for us to shoot each other with them, but sometimes for our own safety, we have to."

When he finished talking, Rebecca answered, "I know. John taught me how to use a Colt but I never really wanted to."

Seth dried another plate. "I promise, I will emphasize to them that taking another person's life is not the purpose of carrying the gun. It's to be used only if necessary."

They continued working in silence. Fay entered the room and got the broom, then returned to the dining room. Seth wanted to talk to Rebecca, assure her he had the boys' best intentions at heart, but didn't know how to do so. Talking to women was often hard, especially when their emotions were involved.

Would he be able to talk to Charlotte should he find her? Did he want to? Part of him wanted to give up the search for his fiancée, but Seth knew he had to keep his promise to his grandmother.

When the last dish was dried, Seth hung his wet towel on a hook by the basin area. "Well, I need to get out there where the boys are." He walked to the back door.

"Seth?"

He turned at her questioning voice. "Yes."

"Today when the stage came, two women were on it. They talked about road bandits. Would you caution the boys about them, as well?"

"I will." She looked so lost and scared that he wanted to walk across the room and hug her fears away.

But Fay chose that moment to come back into the kitchen. "Seth, we asked about Miss Charlotte but the two women on the stage had never heard of her." She set the broom back against the wall by the kitchen door.

"Thank you for asking. I'm not sure I'll find her this way." He leaned his hip against the doorjamb.

Fay shook her head. "It's a long shot for sure."

"We'll keep asking," Rebecca assured him.

Seth nodded and then pushed away from the door frame. "Good night, ladies."

Both echoed back. "Good night."

He stepped out into the cool night air. Maybe he should start thinking about moving on so that he could find Charlotte. If Fay hadn't come back in when she had, Seth was pretty sure he would have acted on his feelings and hugged Rebecca.

His thoughts went to the excitement and joy that the boys had gotten from running into the Indians, and he knew he still had work to do here at Dove Creek. He couldn't leave knowing the Young men weren't well trained. It was his job to keep them safe.

His inner voice taunted him, *Are you sure it's because you want to keep them safe, or have you allowed yourself to become attached to the Young family? Especially Rebecca Young?*

## Chapter Seventeen

Seth watched as the boys took turns racing past a fence post and trying to shoot a can off it. They all were able to knock it off on their first run-through.

Jacob stood beside him. "The target needs to be moving."

"Any suggestions on how to make that happen? We can't have them shooting at each other." His frustration was showing but Seth didn't care.

"I think so."

Seth turned to face him. "Let's hear it."

"Well, you could tie a rope around a can, toss it over a limb of a tree. Get behind the tree, so they don't shoot you, and then pull on the rope to make the can go up and down. They ride their horses past and try to shoot the can." He grinned.

It wasn't a bad idea, as long as he stayed behind the tree. "I noticed you said *I* could hold the rope and hide behind the tree."

Jacob tried to look serious, but his eyes danced with merriment. "Well, you wouldn't want them to have to live with killing their oldest brother if they were to miss, would you?"

Seth laughed. "I might be willing to risk it." He slapped Jacob on the back. "Go get the rope."

By the end of the day, Seth's nerves were shot. The young men were great at shooting nonmoving objects, but terrible at shooting moving ones. Earlier in the day he'd made the mistake of stepping out from behind the tree and a bullet had whizzed past his right ear. The poor tree had more holes in it than one of Rebecca's colanders.

It hadn't helped that Jacob had stood by the barn door and laughed. Seth didn't really see what was so funny and was beginning to lose his sense of humor. He'd noticed Rebecca had come out and stood on the porch for a few minutes watching. Her pretty face had confusion written all over it. What she had to be confused about, he had no idea.

Still standing behind the tree, Seth called the boys to a stop. He waited a couple of minutes before stepping out. Jacob walked across the yard to join him.

"Want me to wave the can for a bit?" Jacob asked. When Seth didn't answer immediately, he suggested, "You might be able to tell the boys what they are doing wrong."

Why not let Jacob stand behind the tree and have bullets whiz around him for a few minutes? Who knew, Jacob might realize how serious this was. Jacob might even feel bad for laughing at him. "All right."

Jacob looked to his brothers and raised his chin as if to say "take your best shot, boys." He went behind the tree and began pulling on the rope.

Seth watched as the young men lined up to practice again. He rubbed his hands together gleefully at the lesson Jacob was about to learn. They'd already decided they'd go in order of oldest to youngest.

Andrew raced toward the can and swerved just as he came within a few feet of it. He fired off his shot and the sound of metal hitting metal pinged in the afternoon air.

He'd hit it! Seth couldn't believe it. Andrew tipped his hat at him as he rode past and went to the end of the line.

Clayton took off at a dead run. His horse was surefooted and, using both hands, Clayton sighted his rifle at the moving can. He fired his rifle and within seconds the sound of the bullet hitting the can echoed in the yard.

He'd hit it, too! Seth stared at the moving can that now had two bullet holes in it. Clayton also tipped his hat at Seth as he rode past.

Thomas and Philip decided to go together. Their argument earlier in the day was that since they always rode the trail together, they should train together, too. Their horses raced toward the tree and at the last minute both boys fired on the moving can. Thomas hit it high, Philip hit it low. They passed him, eyes dancing and lips twitching.

He'd been had. Seth didn't know whether to be angry or amused. All afternoon he'd heard their bullets whiz over his head and around the tree. Not once had any of them hit the can.

As Noah raced past, Seth knew he would hit the can. Noah was the best shot of all. Using his Colt, he emptied it into the can. Why hadn't he realized sooner that the boys had been playing with him? He should have known that Noah could hit a moving target. Just weeks before the boy had brought down a running elk.

Benjamin grinned as he passed Seth. Seth spread his legs and waited for the boy to miss. Beni was only eight years old. Seth fully expected the youngster to miss. Metal hitting metal brought the realization that he was wrong again. The boy whooped as he raced back to his brothers.

Jacob came out from behind the tree. He rubbed his chin. "I don't know how they got so good so fast."

The other boys rode over to them.

Seth looked from one to the other. He tried to keep his face stern as he met each of their laughing eyes. "I guess they've had a lot of practice."

Jacob and all the boys howled their merriment.

Seth tucked his hands in his back pockets and waited them out. He was proud of them. Each would be able to hold their own on the trail, even Beni. But he didn't enjoy the fact that they'd let him believe they were horrible shots all afternoon.

When he quit laughing, Jacob said, "Aw, Seth. You taught them all well."

Seth shook his head. "Not me. I believe your Papa John taught you all well."

It was Andrew who spoke for all of them this time. "With guns and rifles, yes. But not about safety. We all listened last night and realized we haven't been taking the dangers of the trail serious enough."

He didn't understand what that had to do with them

tricking him all day. They'd been able to shoot the can, so why hadn't they?

As if to answer his question, Andrew continued, "Don't be angry, Seth. If we had all hit the can earlier, would you feel as confident about our shooting abilities then as you do now? We wanted to show you that given the choice, we can hit the target or we can hit close enough to the target to scare it. Like you said, never take a life if you don't have to."

The dinner bell began clanging. Each boy—no, each man—looked at him, waiting to be dismissed. They were good men and they could do their job. He was proud of them.

"Go on. Enjoy your dinner."

They didn't have to be told twice. Six of the boys took off for the porch. They each tied off their horses and hurried to the washbasin outside the back door.

Jacob stood beside him. "Are you angry with us?" Weariness filled his eyes.

Seth grinned. "No, I'm proud of you."

The young man continued to study his face. "Don't think we don't need you anymore. We do." He turned to join his brothers at the house.

Seth called after him, "Jacob, would you mind asking your ma if she'll fix me a plate and bring it to me after you all are done with supper?"

Jacob nodded. "Be happy to."

Seth walked to his room in the bunkhouse. He wanted to believe that the Young men needed him, but was beginning to think he'd been fooling himself. His legs felt like lead as he walked. He had some powerful praying to do. Maybe it was time for him to go.

Time to fulfill his promise to his grandmother. Time to leave the Young farm. He'd ask the Lord. If he felt God release him to go search for Charlotte, he'd leave.

Over the next few days, Rebecca noticed that Seth was quieter than usual. Their nightly visits were all business, and half the time he took his meals in his room. She missed him.

Today he and the four of the boys were mending fences. Noah was hunting and Benjamin was in his room with a cold. Andrew was on the trail.

Fay stepped out on the porch with her. "The stage is late."

"Yes. Do you think we should send for Seth?" Rebecca asked. Her gaze scanned the direction in which she'd seen the boys leave.

Joy came out on the porch carrying her dolly. "I'll go get him," she offered.

"Oh, no, you won't." Rebecca ran her hand over the little girl's silky blond hair.

"Want me to wake Beni up? He can go get Seth," Joy said, not the least bit upset that her mother had told her no.

"No, he's too sick to be going out to the pasture." Rebecca looked at Fay. "Will you watch the kids for me? I'll go see what Seth and Jacob think about the stage being almost an hour late."

"Be happy to," Fay answered. She looked down at Joy. "Let's go sample those sugar cookies. We can take a couple up to Beni, too."

Joy ran to the door and yanked it open. "All right."

Fay laughed. "I wish I still had that kind of energy or knew a good store where they sold it."

Rebecca grinned. She knew just how the older woman felt. "I'll be right back."

It had been a while since Rebecca had ridden a horse and she wasn't sure she wanted to take the time to saddle one now. She looked down the road again. An uneasy feeling crept up her spine and into her hair, causing goose bumps to run up and down her arms. The need to hurry had her jogging across the yard and heading toward the north pasture. Saddling a horse would be time wasted.

Her thoughts went to Andrew as she ran. The long grass pulled at her shoes and skirt. Rebecca slowed to a fast walk. It wouldn't do for her to step into a gopher hole and twist her ankle.

She didn't know how long she'd been searching, but Rebecca was glad when she heard a horse whinny a greeting. Turning in the direction of the sound, Rebecca began to jog.

Seth saw her first and stopped hammering. He said something to Jacob, who had been holding the log in place. Both men dropped what they were doing and got on their horses to meet her.

Jacob got to her first. "Ma, is everything all right? Is it Beni?"

Seth joined them.

"Everything is fine at the house but the stage is over an hour late." She looked up at Seth. "I thought I'd better tell you. I have an uneasy feeling about it."

"I'm glad you did." Seth looked to Jacob. "Go tell the others to finish up here and then head to the house.

You and I are going to go ahead and check on the stage."

Jacob nodded and then returned to his brothers.

Seth kicked his foot out of the stirrup and leaned over with his hand extended to Rebecca. "You can ride with me back to the house."

She eyed the big horse. "I don't know, Seth. It's not really proper."

"Jacob's horse is a Pony Express horse." He wiggled his fingers at her as an invitation to take his hand.

Rebecca didn't know what the significance was of Jacob's horse being a Pony Express horse. But her feet were aching from walking across the uneven pasture and she decided no one was going to see her on Seth's horse anyway. She put her hand in his, put one foot in the stirrup and then swung up behind him.

Jacob joined them as Rebecca was tucking her skirt modestly under her legs. "Done." His gaze moved to Rebecca and he grinned.

Seth nodded. "Good." He touched his heels to the big horse's sides and took off back to the house at a gallop.

Rebecca wrapped her arms around Seth's waist and hung on. She hadn't expected him to run the horse back. Did he sense, like her, that the stage was in trouble? Could road bandits or Indians have attacked them? She rested her cheek against his warm back and silently prayed for the people aboard the stage.

# Chapter Eighteen

Seth enjoyed the feel of Rebecca's arms wound tightly around his waist. He almost hated to see the house come into view, but also felt an urgency to find the stagecoach. Since it wasn't sitting in front of the house, he assumed it hadn't arrived.

He kicked his boot out of the stirrup once more and helped Rebecca swing down from Sam's back. He missed her closeness immediately.

Fay stepped out onto the porch.

"Any sign of them?" Seth asked.

She shook her head and answered with a worried frown. "No, and now they are really late."

"Jacob and I will see if we can find them." Seth spun Sam around without waiting to see if Jacob was in agreement with him or not. He headed in the direction that the stage should have arrived from.

"What do you think happened to them?" Jacob asked, pulling along beside him.

Seth looked in his direction. "I'm not sure. Perhaps they broke a wheel."

They rounded a bend about a mile and a half from the farm and there stood the stagecoach. The driver sat on the seat of the coach in just his pants. No hat, shirt or boots. No horses, either.

Seth recognized him as Ty Walker. He reached the stage first. "What happened, Ty?"

"Bandits." The poor driver sounded downtrodden. "Three of them, came in hard and fast. Hit us before we knew what had happened."

"Is anyone hurt?" Seth asked.

"Just our pride," Ty answered. He kept his gaze focused on the horizon.

"Why didn't you walk the rest of the way to the farm?" Jacob asked. His gaze was on the alert in case the bandits were still about.

"Can't get the womenfolk to budge." He continued to look straight ahead as if looking back at the carriage might scald his eyeballs.

Seth got down and started to walk to the coach. He had a feeling he understood the coachman's strange behavior when he heard a woman's voice call out from inside the wagon. "Stay there. Don't come any closer."

Jacob frowned. "What is going on here?"

"I gather the bandits took everything?" Seth asked as he walked back to Sam and began to remove his saddle.

"Just about."

"Jacob, I believe we are going to need your saddle blanket." He laid his own saddle on the ground and pulled the blanket that it rested on from the horse.

Giving the blanket a good shake, he waited for Jacob to finish unsaddling his horse. Jacob looked confused but did as Seth asked him to. Within a matter of minutes Seth had both blankets and was walking back to the wagon.

"I've got a couple of blankets you ladies can wrap up in. Do you want me to hand them to you through the door?" Seth asked.

"Yes, please." A hand snaked out the door and a woman's fingers wiggled as if to say "give it here."

Seth placed the blankets in her hand and then walked back to the other two men. Jacob's ears had turned a soft pink and the stagecoach driver tried not to smile. The man now wore Jacob's jacket for a shirt.

Jacob dropped his saddle back on his horse's back and tied the cinch. "What now?" he asked Seth. "We can't ride them back without saddle blankets."

"It's not that far—we'll walk," Seth answered.

They could hear the women in the carriage fussing.

"I don't think this is much better," one complained.

The other answered, "Would you like to try this one instead?"

"No, yours is smaller and I need the bigger one. Make sure it covers me completely." After a couple of seconds she demanded, "Well?"

"You are decently covered."

Seth picked up his saddle and put it on Sam's back. He called over his shoulder, "Ladies, we need to get going. Those bandits might decide to return."

They shot out of the coach like two cats in a room full of rocking chairs. Like the coachman, they wore no shoes or hats. Wrapped in the blankets they were decent enough, but their dispositions were not to be trifled with.

"If you ladies are ready, Jacob and I will lead the way." Seth led Sam back down the road they had just traveled. He didn't look back and he tried not to chuckle as the ladies followed the two horses and three men back to the farm.

Sam's blanket barely covered the robust woman behind him. She was short and fat with a double chin and black ringlets that hung about her shoulders. The other woman was tall and slender and looked to be about Jacob's age. She was pretty with light brown hair and blue eyes the color of a clear riverbed.

Seth glanced to Jacob. If the young man had noticed the young woman, he showed no sign of it. He walked beside his horse and looked forward.

"We sure are blessed you came along, Seth," Ty said, hobbling along beside him. "Not sure what I would have done, if the sun had set on us."

Seth nodded. "It still gets chilly here at night. You would have been cold, that's for sure."

Jacob glanced over his shoulder. Then turned back around.

"How they doing?" the driver asked in a low voice.

"Seem to be doin' just fine," Jacob answered. "I don't think they're very happy about the way things have turned out."

"None of us are," the driver answered. "If only I could have gotten to my gun faster."

Seth shook his head. "If you had, you might be dead right now. Didn't you say there were three of them?"

"Yep, and nasty, too. Could have killed us. They had no trouble stripping us down to our unmentionables and taking everything." He glanced over his shoulder, then turned around. In a low voice he continued, "But that big one, she gave them what for. Said she'd have her husband hunt them down like a couple of foxes and skin them alive." He chuckled. "You should have seen their faces."

Jacob looked to Seth, who shrugged. Like Jacob, he couldn't see the humor in it, but then again, he hadn't faced death and lived to tell about it, either.

Rebecca, Fay and Joy stood on the front porch waiting for them. Seth focused on Rebecca's sweet smile. Her twin dimples winked in her cheeks. She said something to Joy and the little girl ran into the house.

Both women hurried off the porch and came out to meet them. Rebecca spoke first. "Is everyone all right?" she asked, rushing to the older woman's side and wrapping a supportive arm around her thick waist.

"We're much better now," the older woman said.

"I'm Rebecca Young and this is Fay Miller. I sent my little girl to get you both clean blankets to wrap up in. I'm so sorry to see you've had trouble."

"Thank you, Mrs. Young. I'm Martha Ranger and this is Emma Jordan. A clean blanket will be nice. Not that I'm complaining, mind you. It was nice of the men to loan us their saddle blankets in our time of need." Martha sneezed.

"Please, call me Rebecca." The women walked past the men as if unaware that they'd stopped walking and let them pass.

"Then you must call us Martha and Emma. I hope we aren't too much trouble. Those scoundrels took all our dresses and shoes. It might be a while before we can replace them." She pulled the blanket up to her chin.

Rebecca helped her up the porch just as Joy burst through the door.

"Here are the clean blankets, Ma." She stopped and stared up at the newcomers.

"Thank you, Joy." Rebecca took the blankets and draped them over her arm. She looked to Seth. "Would you take Mr. Walker to the bunkhouse and see if he can wear any of the boys' extra boots?"

Seth felt like one of her children. "I'll be happy to," he answered.

"Jacob, I'll send Joy out to the barn in a couple of minutes with your horse blankets." Rebecca held the door open for the women, who hurried inside. She turned to look over her shoulder at Seth.

He didn't know what to make of her glance. Her gaze connected with his and she offered a soft smile. Was she simply grateful they had found the passengers? Or had she been concerned for him? Seth didn't know and he didn't want to read too much into that expression.

As the women told her and Fay what happened when the bandits attacked them, Rebecca worried more and more about Andrew. He was out there alone. Her gaze moved to the window, praying that her son would arrive soon.

The sound of a bugle filled the air. Rebecca ran to the window and watched as Andrew raced into the yard. His horse stopped in front of the barn, where another rider was prepared to take the mailbag.

Andrew jumped from the horse and tossed the bag to the other rider. He turned to the house and waved to his mother. Relief washed over her even as she prayed for the other young man, who now was alone on the Pony Express trail. She bowed her head. "Thank You, Lord, for bringing my boy home."

She felt a hand on her shoulder. Rebecca turned to look at the young woman beside her. "Praying was the only thing that kept me calm during the robbery. I'm glad God brought your son home."

"Thank you, Emma." Rebecca patted her hand and then turned to face her. "That dress looks pretty on you."

Emma twirled about. "It fits me nicely. Thank you for sharing it."

Pretty pink material swirled about Emma's slim ankles. It brought the color out in her cheeks, giving her a fresh, happy appearance. Rebecca smiled. "I'm not sharing it, Emma. I'm giving it to you."

The girl stopped turning. Her face sobered. "You are? Why?"

"Because it gives you pleasure and I want you to have it." Rebecca watched as the girl studied her face. It was as if Emma was looking for an alternative reason to be given the gift.

Emma ran her hands down the soft fabric. "Thank you. This is the nicest gift I've ever received."

Martha stepped out of Rebecca's bedroom. Rebecca had given the older woman one of her mother-in-law's dresses. It had to be taken out a little on the sides, but with Fay's swift needle, they had altered the dress to fit the older woman.

"You look lovely," Rebecca said.

The older woman huffed. "Well, it isn't as nice as what I'm accustomed to, but it will do." She looked at Emma. "It's nice to see you wearing something appropriate for your station."

Did the woman realize how rude she sounded? Or was it just her social position that caused her to speak in such an impolite manner?

Emma looked away. Her joy from a moment earlier now seemed clouded. "Thank you." She walked to the window and looked out across the yard.

"What are you looking at?" Martha demanded, coming to stand beside her.

Rebecca's gaze moved past the women. The boys were returning from mending the fence. It was obvious that they'd raced back to the house.

Joy stood between Jacob and Andrew. Her little face lit up at the sight of her brothers.

Martha huffed. "Rebecca, I don't believe I'd let my little girl socialize with the help. It's not the proper way to raise a young lady." She turned from the window.

It took all Rebecca could do to smile. "The hired help, as you call them, are her brothers. I guess we need to get something straight."

Martha raised her chin. "Yes?"

"As long as you are staying here, under my roof, I expect you to treat everyone as equals, including Emma. This is first and foremost my home and I will have peace and politeness at all times." Rebecca crossed her arms over her chest and held the woman's gaze.

Fay stepped through the bedroom door behind Martha and nodded her approval.

"I can treat her any way I please." Martha mimicked Rebecca's stance.

Rebecca nodded. "But this is my home and Emma is my guest, just as you are. Now, if you want one of the boys to take you to town, I'll be happy to make the arrangements." Martha started to interrupt but Rebecca held up her hand. "But there is only one place to stay in town and they don't accept credit."

Anger filled Martha's eyes. "So what you are telling me is that I really have no choice. Abide by your rules or find myself out in the cold." Martha dropped onto the couch. Her lips were pinched into a pucker.

Behind Martha's back, a small grin twitched at Emma's lips. She covered her mouth with her hand to hide her pleasure at seeing Martha made to show respect for others.

"I think you'll find it easier to do than what you think. And it may only be for one night," Rebecca added. She turned to walk into the kitchen. "Emma, would you mind helping me peel potatoes for dinner?"

Emma followed her. "No, I don't mind."

Rebecca told the young woman where the root cellar was and asked her to gather twenty-six potatoes. She figured two potatoes per person would be enough. While the girl was gone, Rebecca wondered if she'd been too hard on Martha.

A few months ago she'd been living quietly with her boys and Joy. Then Seth had arrived and they'd all adjusted, to the point where it felt as if he belonged with them. Fay had joined them shortly after Seth and she, too, now felt like a member of the family.

Instinctively, Rebecca knew that once more everything was about to change. How long would Martha, Emma and Mr. Walker be her guests? Would Martha make things harder than they needed to be? Once the boys saw how pretty Emma was, Rebecca knew she could be facing a whole other set of problems. Even Seth might find the girl attractive.

Something in her heart ached at the thought. Would he be interested in Emma? If so, would he give up his search for Charlotte? Rebecca took a deep breath. She'd allowed herself to care for Seth and now she wasn't so sure she wanted to see him become involved with another woman.

Perhaps Emma was too young for Seth. Still, he had his heart set on marrying Charlotte. Plus, John's memory was too important to the kids for her to even think that she might have feelings for the station keeper.

But a part of her ached at the thought that he would be moving on as soon as he found out where Charlotte might be. If only she hadn't promised to help him search for her. Rebecca knew she wouldn't go back on her word, even if her word broke her heart.

# *Chapter Nineteen*

Over dinner Seth and Ty made plans to ride into town the following morning to tell the sheriff about the holdup. It was also decided that after dinner, the boys would go get the stagecoach and bring it to the farm. Seth asked them to all go, because he felt there was safety in numbers.

The stage would be moving on after they returned from town the following day with fresh horses to pull it. Mr. Walker seemed happy at the idea of getting a good night's sleep and a couple of hot meals before he continued on with his job.

Martha and Emma also seemed content to enjoy the food and beds that Rebecca supplied. It had been established that Martha would be staying in Fay's room with her and Emma would be sleeping in Rebecca's room. Martha didn't say much to anyone, just simply ate her food and avoided eye contact with the rest of the women.

Benjamin sat at the table looking tired, but the fever had left his cheeks and the sparkle was back in his eyes.

His voice sounded as if a small bullfrog had crawled into his throat. Joy laughed every time Beni spoke.

Seth noticed that Rebecca seemed quiet and wondered if she was feeling the strain of having added guests. Her attention seemed focused on Beni and Joy. None of the older boys seemed to notice their mother's silence. They were too interested in Emma.

The young woman smiled shyly at them as they passed her plates of food. Thomas and Philip seemed to compete for her attention. Although, Seth couldn't help but notice that Emma appeared to be more interested in Andrew.

He turned his attention back to Rebecca. Her gaze told him she'd caught him staring at Emma and the boys. What must she think? Seth realized his attention had been on the younger woman for too long. Rebecca's cheeks were a soft pink. She broke away from his gaze.

Had he seen jealousy in her expression? Surely not. Rebecca hadn't conveyed any interest in him. Why would she start now? And how would he feel if she was attracted to him?

He wasn't looking for love. And he had a mail-order bride to find. Seth panicked and pushed away from the table. He had to get out of the house. There was too much going on around him and he felt trapped in the thoughts that were threatening him.

Everyone turned to look at him. "I just realized I need to go check on something in the barn."

Jacob moved to go with him.

Seth stopped him. "No, Jacob. Stay and finish your dinner." He left his half-eaten dinner and hurried out of the house and into the fresh night air.

He walked to the barn and opened the heavy door. Warmth and the scents of hay and horse welcomed him. What was wrong with him? Was he so afraid of Rebecca's feelings that he'd run from the house like a scared mouse?

He was and he had. The realization hit him in the gut. Seth knew without a shadow of a doubt that he cared for Rebecca.

Rebecca yawned and crawled into bed. Emma was already there. "Thank you for letting me stay with you tonight. It's been a long time since I've slept in a soft bed like this one," the young woman said, also yawning.

"You're welcome." The sheets felt cool and welcoming.

Rebecca blew out the lamp and listened to Emma's breathing. She liked the girl and was glad to see that she hadn't egged on the boys tonight. But Rebecca hadn't liked the fact that Seth had studied the girl so intently at dinner. He hadn't come to the house for their nightly chat, but she supposed that was because he'd already told everyone that he and Mr. Walker would be running to town the following morning.

"Rebecca?"

She tried to make her voice sound sleepy. "Uh-huh?"

"Thank you for making Mrs. Ranger be nice to me." Her voice sounded sad in the darkness. "She doesn't like it, but it's nice for a change."

Curiosity ate at her. "Why do you work for Martha, Emma?"

Emma sighed. "My pa sold me to her. So I don't exactly work for her. She owns me."

Rebecca knew that people had slaves, but since Emma was white, she hadn't expected her to be a slave. Her heart went out to the young girl. "I'm sorry. I guess my making her be nice to you isn't going to help you later, is it?"

"No, but for now I don't care," Emma admitted. "She bought me when I was thirteen years old and most of the time she's kind, but sometimes, well…" Her words trailed off into the thick darkness.

To Rebecca's way of thinking it wasn't right for anyone to own another person, no matter what color their skin. It wasn't right. She tried to keep the conviction out of her voice as she asked, "How long have you been with her?"

"Five years."

Rebecca couldn't imagine being a slave for five years. When she'd come to work for the Young family at the age of sixteen, they had treated her like family. Taught her how to cook and clean, but not as a slave. At the orphanage she'd been treated harshly, but that was the way everyone was treated. It was just the way things were.

Emma's soft breathing told Rebecca the girl had gone to sleep. It broke her heart to think that Emma had no freedom to call her own.

Rebecca woke very early with the same thoughts running through her mind. The sun was nowhere on the horizon, but she couldn't go back to sleep. Emma needed to be free. But how? She got up and let the girl sleep.

Fay sat at the kitchen table nursing a cup of coffee. A frown marred her features and she stared out the dark window.

"You're up early," Rebecca said, helping herself to the fresh-brewed coffee.

"I've a lot on my mind this morning," Fay answered, rocking the cup back and forth between her hands. "Why are you up so early?"

Rebecca slid into the chair across from Fay. "Same reason. Couldn't sleep."

Fay leaned forward and whispered, "Is it our house-guests that are keeping you awake?"

She took a sip from her coffee. "Yes. I learned something last night that has me concerned."

"I bet it's the same thing I learned." Fay sighed and took a sip from her cup. "It always amazes me how we humans can be so cruel to one another."

Rebecca sat her cup down. "Did Martha tell you that she owns Emma?"

Fay nodded. "Oh, yes. She plans on selling her in Missouri."

The news shocked Rebecca. "I wonder if Emma knows."

Fay shook her head. "No, I don't believe she does. Martha is pretty angry with her right now and I think she made the decision last night. At least that's the impression I got."

A plan began to form in Rebecca's mind. She couldn't stand the idea of Martha selling off Emma like a piece of livestock. "How much does a slave cost?"

"I heard that they were running about eight hundred dollars." Fay set down her cup. "Are you thinking about buying one?"

Rebecca nodded. "Yes, but that's a bit high. Did Martha say how much she wanted for Emma?"

"Can't say that she did." Fay ran her finger over the rim of the coffee mug. "You know, I think I'll talk to her and see what she might be asking for the girl. It would be easy for me to play the old-lady card and say I needed the girl's help. Do you think you could come up with the money?"

Rebecca licked her bottom lip. "I'm not sure. The boys might be willing to help. The Pony Express pays them fifty dollars each, every two weeks, to be riders." She knew they'd gotten paid a few days earlier and hated to ask them for their money, but to save Emma, she'd do it.

Fay's gaze moved out the window again. "The light just came on in the bunkhouse."

Rebecca stood. "I'll ask them and come right back." She grabbed her shawl off the hook by the door and quietly left the house.

The mornings were still cool, but the air felt nice on her hot cheeks. Would the boys be willing to help her? She wouldn't demand their help but hoped they'd offer it. Raising her fist, she knocked quietly on the door.

Andrew opened it a crack and looked out. "Ma? Is everything all right?"

She pushed past him. The scent of unwashed clothes assaulted her senses. Rebecca had more pressing matters to discuss, so she tried to ignore the odor. "Yes and no. Are all the boys awake?"

He shook his head. "No, but I can wake them." He

pulled on his shirt as he went to each bunk and woke his brothers.

Rebecca sat down by the woodstove and waited for them. Hair tousled, clothes half-on and rubbing sleep from their eyes, they slowly came to sit around her. "Noah, would you go get Jacob, please? And be as quiet as you can in doing so. Don't wake Mr. Walker, if you can help it."

With a nod, Noah slipped out the door.

Andrew looked at Rebecca. "What's this about?"

"When Noah and Jacob get back, I'll tell everyone at once. I'm sorry to get you all up so early and I wouldn't have done so if it wasn't necessary." Rebecca folded her hands in her lap and waited. She thought about mentioning the smell in the room and then decided against it. It wouldn't do to put them on the offensive before asking for a favor.

Her gaze moved to the closed door that led to Seth's quarters. Was he awake? If so, would he join them? She couldn't ask him to help so she prayed he'd stay in his room, at least until her business with the boys was finished.

Jacob and Noah slipped into the bunkhouse. The concern on her oldest son's face caused her to feel guilty.

"Come on in, boys." She motioned for them to sit down.

Noah sat down on the floor at her feet. Jacob pulled a chair from the table that sat against the wall.

As soon as they were seated, Rebecca began. "Last night, I learned something that really bothered me."

She looked at each boy in turn to make sure she had their total attention. "Emma is a slave."

"What?" Thomas and Philip looked at each other, as they both had the same reaction.

"Martha and her husband own her," Rebecca answered.

Thomas jumped to his feet. "What can we do to free her?"

"We could kidnap her and take her away from here," Philip answered.

Jacob growled from his chair, "Shut up and let Ma talk."

Rebecca shook her head. "No, they'd just have the sheriff find you and both of you would be in trouble with the law."

Philip clamped his mouth shut. Rebecca knew the boy hadn't given up on his idea.

"Fay and I have another idea. Fay is going to offer to buy Emma from Martha." Rebecca watched their faces go from furious indignation to surprise. She smiled. "Once Martha leaves, we will give Emma her freedom."

The boys all began to talk and ask questions at once. The room buzzed with their excited voices. Andrew's topped the others.

He asked, "What can we do to help?"

Silence filled the room as they all looked to her expectantly. "We need the money to buy her."

Jacob stood up and walked to the stove. "How much?"

Rebecca knew this was the moment of truth. Her boys would either give her the money or tell her she asked too much. She met each boy's eyes before answering. "Whatever you want to give us. I'm not telling you how much—you all have worked hard for your money. If you don't want to give it to me, I understand." Rebecca knew she was asking a lot from the boys.

The boys looked at each other and then slowly each rose from their sitting places. Thomas dug into his front pocket and handed Rebecca his pay. Philip moved to his bunk and pulled out a small box, then returned to hand her his money. Jacob slipped out the door.

Rebecca hadn't thought that Jacob would refuse to help, but she couldn't bring herself to be upset with him. She knew he was saving his money—he'd never said so but she was sure Jacob planned on someday going in search of his real mother.

Andrew and Clayton each gave her their wages. Noah handed her his money, as well.

"Thank you, boys. I know how much this means to you." She held the money out in front of her. "It may not be enough. Fay said that slaves are sold for about eight hundred dollars each. I'm going to add money to this and we'll all need to pray that it's enough. If Martha refuses, I'll make sure you get your money back."

Jacob slipped back into the bunkhouse. He walked up to his mother and gave her his money. She knew he got paid more than his brothers as a stock tender. She didn't look at the amount of money he handed her, simply tucked it with the rest. His eyes met hers and he said, "No one should be held a slave."

"Thank you, son." She met each boy's eyes. Her boys were no longer children, but grown men. "Thank you, all."

They looked away, embarrassed by the look of pride Rebecca was sure shone on her face. "Before I go I have to tell you what Fay and I have in mind."

The young men all sat back down. They leaned forward to hear her better. Each face told her that whatever she said, they would accept.

"Fay is going to offer to buy Emma. She's going to pretend that she's getting too old to take care of herself and needs a slave to help her." Rebecca looked at them.

Clayton asked, "Why don't you just buy her?"

Rebecca shook her head. "Martha doesn't like me. I've made her treat Emma with respect while they are here. I think she would refuse out of spite."

Thomas grinned. "What if one of us offered to marry her?"

Philip punched him in the arm. "She's not going to let me marry Emma. She wants the money."

"I wasn't talking about you, chicken head." Thomas punched him back.

"Knock it off, you two," Jacob growled at them. "No one is going to marry her."

"You just want her for yourself," Philip mumbled.

Rebecca spoke sharply. "Boys. We're going to stick to the plan of Fay offering to buy her. But I don't want you boys acting like you know anything about it. Not that Emma is a slave. Not that Martha is planning on selling her. And most important, not that Fay is interested in buying her. Don't even mention this to Mr. Walker or Seth. Let's keep it in the family. If we want things to go smoothly, we are going to have to trust Fay to make it happen. Do you understand?"

They nodded in turn. Rebecca stood and tucked

the money into her dress pocket. "Good. I need to get back in the house before I'm missed." She walked to the door. But before she slipped out, Rebecca turned to look at them. In a stern voice she said, "You need to air this place out and bring your filthy clothes to the house. It reeks in here."

The young men looked surprised and even a little embarrassed. Noah sniffed the air. "Told you so," he said to the room at large.

Rebecca hurried back to the house. She decided to go through the kitchen. Since the boys were up, they'd be wanting breakfast soon.

As Rebecca walked her mind worked. Had Martha woken yet? Would she be willing to sell Emma to Fay? Even thinking about buying another human being felt odd. She knew she'd have to heed her own words and not show her true emotions and knowledge that Fay was offering to buy Emma. Rebecca silently prayed that they had enough money to purchase the girl's freedom.

# *Chapter Twenty*

Seth stood on his side of the door, listening as Rebecca told her boys what she wanted and needed from them. His admiration for the woman went up as she explained that Emma was a slave and Fay was going to use their money to buy her. Since he couldn't see them, Seth could only assume that each of the young men had handed over their hard-earned wages.

The sound of the bunkhouse door closing again told him Rebecca had left. Her parting shot about the smell had him chuckling. Women noticed such things, where men didn't. Thanks to her, he now had more jobs to keep the young men busy while he and the coach driver were in town.

As he dressed, Seth decided to give to the fund to buy Emma's freedom. Slavery was an ugly thing. He pulled on his boots and went to his Bible, where he'd tucked his earnings.

As he took out a hundred dollars, Seth wondered how he was going to get the money to Rebecca. He couldn't just hand it to her—she'd think one of the boys had told him and he'd heard her telling them not to let on to him about what was going on. He had to admit that it had stung when she'd said it. It was true that he wasn't a part of their family and he'd do well to remember that. Even if at times he felt as if he was.

Rebecca Young was a private person—hadn't she been upset when she'd thought he'd been snooping into her life? If she figured out that he'd been eavesdropping on her conversation with her sons, that might cause more trust issues between them. He sighed and sat down on the edge of his cot.

The money rested in his hands, money he'd intended to use to help him find Charlotte. So far there had been no leads on his mail-order bride through the stagecoach line…maybe there never would be. Seth knew that soon he'd need to move on, keep looking for her. He'd promised his grandmother he'd find Charlotte, but he also felt drawn to help free Emma.

Seth bowed his head and silently prayed. Only the Lord could give his mind peace as to what to do with the money. After several long minutes, he felt the urge to help Emma outweigh the need to go in search for Charlotte. He took that as an answer to his unspoken prayer.

He tucked the money into his pants pocket and laid the Bible back down on the table. He put on his jacket and prepared to leave the room.

Seth opened the adjourning door in the bunkhouse and stepped into the boys' living quarters. They looked up at him as he entered. "Good morning." He walked over to the coffeepot and poured himself a cup. "You fellas are up awful early."

No one responded to his comment.

Seth tipped the cup to his lips and grimaced as the thick brew coated his tongue. He swallowed and frowned. "Who had coffee duty? This stuff tastes like blackened mud."

Thomas chuckled. "We found something Noah isn't good at."

Noah ducked his head. The back of his neck turned red.

Seth chuckled. "Good to know he's human." He put down his cup.

They all chuckled. When they'd quieted down again, Seth continued, "Ty and I will be heading to town after breakfast. Be on the lookout for Indians and road bandits. I want you to team up if you decide to leave the farmhouse. Also, don't leave the women without at least one of you here."

Phillip asked, "Do you think they'll cause trouble here at the station?"

"Only time will tell but it's better to be safe than sorry," Seth answered. He waited to see if there were more questions. When it didn't seem that there were, he said, "Jacob will be in charge today. We're not expecting a rider but if one comes in, I believe it's Clayton's turn to head out."

Clayton nodded his agreement. "I'll be ready."

"Good." Seth walked toward the door. While he'd been talking he'd decided to give the money to Fay, not Rebecca. It would probably be easier to slip the money to the older woman than to explain to Rebecca how he knew they needed it.

Jacob stood. "Last night I noticed that one of the

carriage wheels is cracking. You might want to take a look before you leave." He pulled his jacket off a hook by the door and slipped his arms inside.

"Why don't you show me now and I'll give you the list of chores for the day." Seth pulled the door open. He stopped and looked at each young man. "Why don't you boys air this place out today. It's beginning to smell like something died in here." He stepped outside with Jacob right behind him.

He half expected Jacob to say his ma had said the same thing, but the young man kept quiet. Seth followed Jacob to where the boys had unhitched the coach beside the barn. Ty stood beside it, looking at the wheel.

"I was just about to show Seth that wheel," Jacob said.

Ty rubbed the back of his neck. "It's cracked. Can't take the chance of it busting on the trail."

"Looks like we'll need to haul it to town in our wagon," Seth said, looking to Jacob.

Jacob nodded. "I'll see that we get the wheel off and the wagon hitched up."

"Don't go bothering yourself with taking it off, son. It's my coach. I'll take it off." Ty rolled up his sleeves and kneeled beside the wagon.

Jacob nodded. "I'll hitch up the wagon. I assume you'll want to leave right after breakfast," he said, looking to Seth for the answer to the unasked question.

Seth realized the trip to town was going to take longer than he'd first anticipated. He nodded.

Rebecca stepped out on the porch and began clanging the dinner bell. The boys tumbled out of the bunkhouse, reminding Seth of a gangly bunch of puppies. He watched as they hurried to the farmhouse.

She looked pretty this morning with her light brown hair pulled back in a ponytail. The brown dress with a white apron covering her middle hugged her shape. The smile on her face as she watched her sons warmed his heart. Seth didn't want to admit it, but her kindness and generosity for Emma had melted another section of his heart toward her.

He shook off the thought. "Men, let's go grab some breakfast before that pack eats it all," Seth said to Jacob and Ty. He walked to the house.

Jacob fell into step beside him. Seth knew Jacob knew what to do to keep the boys busy, but began telling him what he expected, just in case Jacob decided to take it easy on his brothers. "Have the boys feed and exercise the horses today. Especially the Pony Express horses. Also, have them clean the barn, muck the stalls, make sure the hay is stacked and dry. We should be getting another supply of feed this week— have them clear out a spot to put it in. Have them haul up fresh water and make sure they air out the bunkhouse. If that's not enough, have them rub oil into the saddles and bridles."

Ty chuckled behind them. "And I thought my job was hard."

Seth glanced over his shoulder. "Just wait until you try to convince the men in town to give you credit for fixing your wheel and two new horses. You'll think we have it easy out here."

The older man groaned. "Don't remind me."

They all washed their hands in the basin and proceeded into the house. Seth looked for Fay but didn't see her at the table. Martha and Emma were there and like the night before Thomas and Philip sat on each side of the young woman, hoping to get her attention.

Beni looked much better. The little boy smiled at him and said, "Seth, tell Ma I'm well enough to go back to work."

Rebecca gave the little boy a stern look. She handed him a bowl filled with what looked like oatmeal.

Seth laughed. "Sorry, partner. You have to get permission from your doctor before you can come back to work. If she says you are up to it, then I'm sure Jacob can find you something to do."

Rebecca looked over the little boy's head and smiled her thanks. Her twin dimples brightened his day.

He didn't see Fay at the table. Seth hoped he'd find her in the kitchen. Everyone was filling their plates and chatting among themselves. He slipped out of the dining room and was relieved to see Fay dishing up biscuits at the stove.

Seth pulled the money from his pocket. He hurried to her side and tucked it into her apron pocket. "That's for Emma," he whispered.

She looked at him with wise eyes. "Thank you, Seth, that's very kind of you."

He shook his head. "Kindness has nothing to do with it. I want her free—everyone deserves to be free."

Fay nodded. "That they do." She thrust a plate full of buttered biscuits in his hands.

"Um, Fay. Would you keep this between us? I don't want Rebecca to know I know what you two are up to." He stared down at the bread, praying she wouldn't ask him how he knew in the first place, if Rebecca hadn't told him.

She patted his arm. "Your thoughtfulness is safe with me."

Seth glanced up to find her looking at him with warmth in her eyes. He nodded, happy to know she wouldn't say anything about the money. "Thanks."

"Now take that bread out before it gets cold," she ordered, returning to the pan of biscuits and butter.

He did as he was told, feeling much like a little boy again. His grandmother often had him toting plates of food to the table. Sorrow cut into his chest. He missed his grandmother, but Fay was swiftly filling that empty spot in his heart. Oh, she could never replace his grandmother, but she did make missing her a little easier.

When he reentered the dining room, Rebecca looked up. She was slowly filling an empty space in his heart, too. Seth handed the plate to Jacob. He silently prayed, *Lord, please don't let me get any more attached to this family.*

Rebecca dried the last breakfast dish and then began to wash a pot of beans. Chili beans sounded good for dinner, with corn bread. She smiled as she looked to the table, where Beni and Joy were looking at a picture book.

"We're done, Ma. Can I go help Jacob now?" Beni asked.

She set her beans to the side and went to the little boy. Rebecca gave him a hug. "Yes, but only until lunchtime. I know you think you are all well, but I think you will need a rest time this afternoon."

He pulled out of her embrace. "All right." Beni ran for the door and yanked it open.

"Wait!" Rebecca called after him.

He stopped and came back. "You said I could go."

"Yes, I did, but not without your coat."

"But, Ma, it's not cold outside."

"Benjamin Theo Young, you will wear your coat or you can go back to bed." She pointed at the coat hanging by the door.

He pulled it off the hook and slipped his arms into it. "It's on," Benjamin said, his voice a croak.

"I want to go, too." Joy reached for her cloak.

Rebecca shook her head. "Not today, Joy. You have a bedroom to clean."

The little girl frowned. "I don't want to clean my room."

Fay came into the room laughing. "I don't want to clean mine, either, but it needs to be done. Why don't I help you clean yours and then you can help me clean mine?"

Joy smiled broadly. "All right."

As soon as they were gone, Rebecca noticed Martha sitting on the couch. She walked over to her and asked, "Would you like to come into the kitchen with me?"

"Why? So you can put me to work, too?"

Rebecca forced a smile. The woman was almost impossible to get along with but she'd try. "No, I thought you might like some company and I know I would."

"Well, if you insist." Martha stood. "Where is Emma?"

Rebecca grimaced. "I sent her out to collect the

eggs." She walked toward the kitchen, waiting for a mean comment.

Martha followed. "Good, that girl needs to be working."

"Do you know her very well?" Rebecca asked, swishing the beans about in the water.

Martha sat down at the kitchen table. She picked up the kids' picture book and leafed through the pages. "Well enough."

Rebecca worked in silence, thinking about what she could say that wouldn't get her head taken off. "That's good." She wondered how Seth and Mr. Walker were getting along. Had they made it to town yet? Bought the wheel? Horses?

"She makes a good traveling companion," Martha said out of the blue.

"Where are you headed?" Rebecca asked, pouring the dirty water off the beans.

"Missouri. My husband went there a few months ago on a business trip. We're joining him there."

Rebecca looked over her shoulder at the older woman. Could she be selling Emma because the girl was getting older and more attractive? Could she be afraid the younger woman might attract her husband's attentions?

"This is a cute book," Martha said.

"Yes, I enjoy reading it to the kids and they love the colorful pictures." Rebecca poured fresh water over the pot of beans and set it on the back of the stove to start boiling.

She poured herself a cup of coffee and one for Martha. Then she put several cookies on a plate and carried them to the table. "Care to join me in a snack?"

The older woman looked up and grinned. "Thank you." She took one of the coffee cups and a cookie.

Rebecca pulled out a chair and sat down. "Emma mentioned earlier that you came from California."

Martha nodded. "Yes, my husband sells mining equipment. With the gold rush, we ended up in Sacramento." She broke her cookie in half.

"Sounds interesting."

She shook her head. "Not really. There aren't a lot of women there and those that are work from sunup to sundown, unless they have husbands who can work for them." Martha laughed.

Rebecca wasn't sure why the older woman laughed, but decided that since she was in such a good mood she'd ask about Charlotte. "By any chance do you know a woman named Charlotte Fisher?"

Martha studied her for a few minutes. "Charlotte isn't in my social circle but I have seen her working at one of the eating establishments there."

"You've met her?" Rebecca asked, unable to keep the excitement out of her voice.

The older woman set down her cup. "Yes, a couple of times. Emma probably knows her better. How do you know Charlotte?"

"She's…"

Emma came through the back door humming a soft tune. She looked to the two women, who had stopped talking and were staring at her. "Is something wrong?"

Rebecca jumped to her feet. "No, everything is great!" She took the egg basket out of Emma's hands.

"Do you know Charlotte Fisher?" She set the basket on the counter and pulled Emma to a kitchen chair.

The young girl's eyes widened and she looked to Martha.

"Answer her," Martha barked.

"Y-yes."

Rebecca tried to calm herself. She reached over and patted Emma's hands. "You aren't in any trouble, Emma. I've been helping Seth look for Charlotte. You are the first people who know her. I'm just excited. Not angry."

Emma grinned and her shoulders relaxed. "Oh, Charlotte is a very nice person. She can't remember anything about her life before she arrived in Sacramento. I'm not sure why she can't remember. We never really discussed that. I only know her from short trips to get Martha lunch. How do you know her?"

Rebecca explained that she really didn't know the young woman but that she'd been asking passengers of the stagecoach about Charlotte for Seth. She didn't say that Charlotte was his mail-order bride or that he'd been searching for her for months. Instead she patted Emma's hand again and then got up to get the girl a cup of coffee.

Dread and excitement filled Rebecca at the thought of telling Seth that they'd found his Charlotte. His Charlotte. The words echoed in her mind like the hammering of nails in a coffin.

What was life going to be like after he was gone? Deep sorrow melted the excitement of a few minutes ago. Seth would probably be leaving them soon. Rebecca couldn't explain it, but her heart ached.

## Chapter Twenty-One

Seth felt as if someone had punched him. The trip to town had been a total waste of time. As he'd predicted the businessmen in town refused to give Ty credit for a new wheel and horses. He and the ladies would have to stay put until the stagecoach line sent fresh horses and money to fix the wheel.

If that wasn't bad enough, the sheriff didn't seem too interested in catching the road bandits. He'd promised to keep a lookout for them, but had no intentions of calling together a posse, his excuse being that it was planting season and too many farmers were preparing their fields for future crops and didn't have time to enforce the law.

Ty sighed as he climbed down from the wagon. "Thanks for loaning me the wagon, Seth. It's a shame the men in town are so untrusting."

Seth nodded. He looked to the house longingly. Had Rebecca saved him and Ty dinner trays? Or would it be a miss-a-meal night, as his grandmother used to call it when he'd returned after supper and dishes had been washed and put away?

Jacob walked out of the barn. "How'd it go in town?" he asked as he helped unhitch the horses from the wagon.

"Can't say it went well," Ty answered.

The young man shook his head. "That's too bad. Ma saved you both a plate. She said for you to go on up to the house when you got back." He pulled one of the horses into the barn. Ty followed him with the second.

Seth knew Sam had to be taken care of before he filled his belly with fine cooking. He wondered how Rebecca was going to feel with the extra women in the house for a few days. At least with them having more time, maybe Fay could talk Martha into selling Emma to her at a reasonable price.

His thoughts moved to the young men in his care as he unsaddled his horse. It didn't take much for him to realize he'd come to care for them and that to ensure their safety they needed a plan. There was no doubt in his mind that the road bandits would strike again.

Jacob came to stand beside him. "Why don't you go on up to the house and eat, and I'll take care of Sam. Ma seemed excited to see you as soon as you got back."

Rebecca missed him? Seth handed him the horse comb. "Thanks." He turned to Ty. "Come on with me. You can finish that later."

Ty yawned. "Would you mind asking the missus if you can bring my plate out here? I'm mighty tired and not fit for female companionship." He made a point of covering his mouth as if to stifle another big yawn.

Was it all an act? Ty hadn't seemed that tired a few

minutes earlier. Was the older man trying to give him some privacy with Rebecca? Or avoid his passengers and their many questions? "Be happy to."

He walked to the house and entered it through the kitchen. The warm smell of buttery corn bread greeted his hungry belly. He moved to the stove, where a plate sat on the back and there was a big pot beside it. Seth lifted the lid of the pot and inhaled the scent of chili beans. His stomach growled its appreciation.

Rebecca entered the kitchen from the dining area. Her hair was down and hung about her shoulders in soft waves. Big blue eyes searched his. "Did you get everything done in town?" she asked, pulling two bowls and plates out from under the cabinet.

"No, I'm afraid the stagecoach passengers will need to stay on with us for a few more days." Seth leaned a hip against the counter and simply looked at her. Her hair looked silky soft. How upset would she be if he reached out and touched it? He stuck his hands in his pockets to keep them from acting on their own.

"Oh." Her blue eyes met his. "Sit down and I'll get your supper ready," she ordered, gently nudging him to the side so that she could get to the beans and corn bread.

Seth did as she asked and sat down at the table. "Ty would like to eat out in the barn. Says he's too tired to eat in the house. I'll run it out to him real quick if you'll pack it up."

"Benjamin can take it out to him. I have something important I want to tell you." She dished up two bowls of chili beans and put corn bread on two plates. Rebecca sat one in front of him and then said, "I'll get

Benjamin to take this out and then I need to talk to you." Rebecca left to get her son.

She'd already said that she needed to talk to him. Her serious face and low voice alerted him to the fact that whatever Rebecca had to say was important.

Jacob had said she was excited but she didn't seem excited to him. She almost seemed depressed. Had something happened with Emma? Had Martha refused to sell her slave to Fay?

He said a quick prayer over his supper and then nibbled at the bread. Rebecca and Benjamin entered the kitchen.

"Hi, Seth. Ma let me work with Jacob this morning." His little throat still sounded scratchy but it was obvious that Benjamin was on the mend.

"I'm glad to hear that." His thoughts went to the story Rebecca had told him about the little boy on the day of their picnic and he smiled.

Rebecca handed the boy a tray with a covered plate and bowl on it. "Take this to Mr. Walker in the barn."

"Can you give him some cookies, too?" the boy asked, looking longingly at the cookie jar.

She walked over and took out one cookie. Rebecca wrapped it in cheesecloth and laid it beside the plate. "There, I'll have to ask him in the morning if he enjoyed his cookie as much as you enjoyed yours."

Benjamin twisted his face up in thought. "You know, I could have him eat it first and then I can tell you how he liked it." He licked his lips in anticipation.

Seth hid his grin behind a spoonful of chili.

"That won't be necessary." Rebecca planted both

hands on her hips. "I expect you back in this house and in bed before he has time to eat his cookie. Now scoot."

Benjamin frowned. "Yes, Ma." The back door closed with a bang behind him.

Seth chuckled. "He really is a little scamp, isn't he?"

Rebecca finally released her pent-up grin. "That he is."

She came to the table and sat down.

He picked up his spoon and sampled the chili. It really was very good. Seth continued to eat while Rebecca drew imaginary circles on the table. After several long minutes of this, he couldn't remain quiet a moment longer. "I believe you said you have something to tell me." He tore his bread apart and took a big bite.

She straightened in her chair. "I do. Today I asked Martha if she'd ever met Charlotte."

His hand stopped halfway to his mouth. "And?"

"And both she and Emma know Charlotte. She's living in Sacramento and is a server at one of the restaurants there." Rebecca studied his face. What was she looking for?

Seth put down his spoon.

Benjamin banged back into the house. "I'm back," he announced breathlessly.

"Good. Thank you. Now go get back into bed. I'll tuck you in again in a few minutes." Rebecca motioned for Benjamin to leave the room.

He stopped by the table. "You all right, Seth?"

Seth looked at the little boy. Was his shock that plain on his face? "I'm fine, Benjamin. See you in the morning." He really hadn't expected Rebecca to find Charlotte. At first it had seemed like a good idea, but after so many people had said they hadn't heard of her, he'd begun to think of it as a long shot.

"'Night." Benjamin left the kitchen slowly.

As soon as the little boy was gone, Seth turned his attention back on Rebecca. "So what did they say?" Did he sound excited or worried? Seth didn't know.

"Just that she's living in Sacramento and that she only knows her name. Charlotte told Emma she can't remember anything before she arrived." Rebecca wiped at imaginary crumbs on the table.

"If she couldn't remember where she was going, that would explain why she didn't show up in St. Joseph," Seth said absently. He pushed his plate away, no longer hungry. His emotions were torn. "What I need is more answers. Are the ladies already retired for the night?"

"Yes, but I'm sure they will be happy to answer any questions you have for them in the morning." She picked up his dishes.

Seth stood. "I think I'll turn in myself." This was crazy. He'd been looking for Charlotte. Wanted to find her to fulfill his promise to his grandmother. Now he wasn't sure what he wanted to do.

The Young family had become very dear to him. He couldn't leave now. Not with bandits robbing people and Indians chasing the boys on the trail.

"Seth?"

He looked to Rebecca. She stood before him, holding out a cookie. "Don't forget your dessert." Her soft smile only made his decision harder.

Without thinking, Seth pulled her to him and kissed her lips. His hands moved to hold her head close to his. Her hair felt silky soft and smelled like lavender soap.

He gently messaged her scalp and savored the taste of sugar cookie on her lips.

He didn't rush the action. It might be the only time in his life that he would get to kiss her. Moving his lips softly against hers, he felt her arms travel around his waist and her hands press against his back. Seth didn't care if Fay or anyone else walked in. He wanted to enjoy knowing that for a few moments he could express his feelings for her.

It happened so fast that Rebecca was caught off guard. The last thing she'd expected was for Seth to kiss her. And the second-to-last thing she'd expected was that she'd relish his kiss.

She'd always enjoyed kissing John, but kissing Seth took her breath away. Rebecca stepped deeper into his embrace. His hands in her hair felt wonderful.

When he released her she felt dazed. Her fingers moved up to the tingling in her lips. Rebecca looked into his face and saw a tenderness there that she'd never seen on anyone's face before. Then he spun on his booted heels and headed for the door.

Seth stopped and turned to face her again. With one hand on the door he said, "I'm sorry. I shouldn't have done that." And then he was gone.

Rebecca couldn't sleep after being thoroughly kissed. She tossed and turned all night. How could he kiss her like that and then go find Charlotte? Did the kiss mean anything? Was he really sorry that he'd kissed her?

Those questions and more troubled her all night. She continued to replay the kiss in her mind. It had felt so right, but was it? What if one of the boys had walked in? Or Fay?

When morning finally arrived, Rebecca still hadn't found sleep. She pulled on her housecoat and went to the kitchen to start the coffee and breakfast.

The smells of scrambled eggs, coffee and bacon soon filled the kitchen. She could hear her houseguests coming into the dining room and stepped out on the porch to ring the dinner bell.

Fay and Emma entered the kitchen. "Can we help you get this on the table?" Fay asked, picking up a platter of eggs.

"Yes, thank you. If you can set the table, I'll go get dressed." At their nods of agreement, Rebecca hurried to her room to change into a day dress and pull her hair into a braid.

By the time she returned to the dining room everyone was seated. Jacob said the blessing and then the plates were being passed around. She tried to avoid Seth's gaze by focusing on helping Joy with her plate.

She noticed that the little girl's hair was braided and had a pretty pink ribbon in it. "You look very pretty this morning."

"Emma helped me fix my hair." Joy beamed across at her new friend.

Rebecca smiled. "Thank you, Emma. That was very nice of you."

Emma winked at Joy. "It was fun. Wasn't it, Joy?"

"Yep. I like the way she braided my hair," Joy answered. "She made it look like yours."

Rebecca hugged Joy to her. "Yes, she did."

The rest of breakfast was a noisy time. Everyone

talked and ate. The boys were getting ready to go do their chores when Seth's strong voice stopped them.

"Before everyone leaves the table I have an announcement to make."

Rebecca held her breath. Was he leaving? Her heart broke and Rebecca knew she'd fallen in love with Seth. She'd known it for some time now, but hadn't faced the fact. How could she? She still loved John. Was she betraying his love and memory? What if Seth loved her back? Would he break his promise to his grandmother and not marry Charlotte? No, Seth was a man of his word.

"This concerns you all. Until the road bandits are captured, I want you all to stick close to the farm. If you need to go to town, I think instead of taking the main road you should take one that's less traveled. According to the sheriff the bandits seem to be sticking close to the main road. Also, go in twos or more. No one should travel alone. It's not safe. Is this agreeable to everyone?" Seth met each person's gaze and waited for their nod of consent before moving on to the next person.

Rebecca felt as if the oxygen had been sucked out of the room when he looked to her. His gaze bored into hers and he waited for her to nod. She did so and tore her eyes from his.

"Does anyone have any questions or want to add anything more?" Seth asked, looking about the table.

When no one answered he smiled. "Good, then I guess we can start our day."

The boys all shoved back their chairs, picked up

their dirty dishes, carried them to the kitchen and then filed out of the house.

Seth waited until they were all gone and then turned back to the table. "Mrs. Ranger and Miss Jordan, yesterday we learned that you will need to stay here until the stage company sends more horses and money to fix the wheel on your coach. I hope you don't mind."

"We don't mind," Martha answered for both of them.

Joy clapped her hands with happiness. "Emma, you get to stay longer." She jumped from her chair and hurried to stand by the young woman. "Want to go look at my picture books?"

Emma ran her hand over the little girl's head. "Sure."

"Miss Jordan, would you wait just a few more minutes? I need to ask you and Mrs. Ranger a couple of questions about Charlotte Fisher." Seth rested his hands on the back of the chair.

Rebecca stood. "If you will excuse me, I'll clean the dishes." She quickly began to gather up the remaining dirty dishes.

"I'll help you." Fay stood also and picked up hers and Joy's plates.

Once in the kitchen Rebecca realized her hands were shaking. She prepared the dishwater and scraped the food from the plates the boys had left.

Fay added her plates to them and then stepped back to look at her. "What's wrong with you this morning? Are you feeling bad?"

"No, I'm just a little tired. I had trouble sleeping last night." It was the truth.

Fay nodded. "That explains the dark circles under your eyes." She began washing the cups.

Rebecca touched the skin under her eyes. Did she really have dark circles? She grabbed a pot and tried to see her reflection in it.

In a low voice Fay said, "I spoke to Martha last night about buying Emma."

She lowered the pot and walked closer to Fay. "What did she say?"

"Said she wants five hundred for her," Fay answered.

Rebecca sighed. "We only have four. What are we going to do?"

"I already paid her the five hundred." Fay smiled over her shoulder at Rebecca. "I had a hundred you didn't know about."

"Did you get papers?" Rebecca asked, trying to hide the excitement in her voice.

"Yep, and to keep them safe I hid them in your room. But she made me promise not to tell Emma."

"Why not?" Rebecca didn't like the sound of that. What games was the other woman playing?

Fay passed her a clean plate to dry. "Said she wants to tell her just before she leaves so the girl won't carry on."

"Do you believe her?" Rebecca put the plate in the cupboard.

Fay shrugged. "I have papers that say Emma Kate Jordan is legally mine. And I have a bill of sale to prove it."

Rebecca nodded. Something didn't feel right. She thought Martha would have either fought to keep Emma from Fay, or she would have gloated to the girl that she sold her. The desire to talk to Seth about it pulled at her. But she knew he had other things on his mind. Like finding his lost mail-order bride. His conversation with Martha and Emma now proved he'd decided to go look for his future bride. Would she be able to forget him after he left? Or would she forever have a hole in her heart?

## Chapter Twenty-Two

Seth was disappointed that Emma and Martha didn't know any more about Charlotte than what they'd shared with Rebecca. All day he'd tossed their words around in his head. It seemed Charlotte couldn't remember her life before arriving in Sacramento. Emma said she was a sweet woman and very pretty with auburn-colored hair and green eyes.

He knew he couldn't leave the Pony Express station until the road bandits had been captured and his friends were no long in danger. Also, before he left he'd need to contact Mr. Bromley and let him know that he was quitting and why. Then he'd need to wait for his replacement.

The thought of leaving the farm, Rebecca and the boys made him sad. He'd learned to care deeply for the family and wasn't looking forward to saying goodbye, especially to Rebecca. Seth knew he'd fallen in love with the pretty lady.

But he had no intention of telling her. He'd made a promise to his grandmother and he intended to keep it. If he left now, he'd not have to worry about Rebecca breaking his heart or leaving him, like his mother had his father.

Not that she'd given him any indication that she cared or loved him. As a matter of fact, she'd acted as if he didn't exist today. How could she do that? He was aware of her presence even when they weren't in the same room. *Because she doesn't love you.* The thought hurt more than he cared to admit.

He stepped up on the front porch. Deep in thought, he was surprised when the porch swing squeaked. Seth looked to where Rebecca sat waiting for him. "I thought you'd be inside," he said, walking over to her.

"I needed fresh air. It's a little crowded in there," she answered, gently swinging.

Through the window he could see Martha sat on the sofa reading a book. Emma, Benjamin and Joy were working on what looked like a puzzle at the table and Fay sat in her rocker by the window sewing what looked like a quilt block. "It does look a mite crowded in there," he said, leaning against the porch rail.

"Did you learn anything new from Martha and Emma about Charlotte?" Rebecca asked.

He shook his head. "No, other than what they told you, they don't seem to know her."

Her voice sounded husky when she asked, "Are you going to be leaving soon to find her now that you know she's in Sacramento?"

Did she care about him after all? Or was she coming down with Benjamin's cold? "No, I'm not going until after the sheriff catches those road bandits."

"What if he doesn't catch them? Are you never going to find her?" Rebecca asked. She sniffled.

"Are you coming down with Benjamin's cold?" Seth asked, moving closer to her so that he could see her face better.

Rebecca touched her cheeks as if checking for a fever. "I don't think so."

He wanted to reach out and feel her face. Not only to check for a fever, but just to feel her warmth. Seth stared into her beautiful blue eyes. He was going to miss her when he left.

"Seth?"

Mentally he shook himself. "Yes?"

"What if the sheriff doesn't catch the bandits? Then what?"

She dropped her hands back into her lap and searched his face.

He straightened. "They will make a mistake and he'll catch them. Bad guys always make a mistake." Seth offered her a grin to lighten the mood.

Rebecca stood and pulled her shawl closer to her body. She looked him in the eyes and said, "I hope so." She reached out and touched his arm, then pulled her hand away quickly. "I think I'll go in now. I'm not feeling very well."

Seth watched her hurry back into the house. She stopped by Fay's chair, said something in a low voice and then disappeared from sight. Did she really feel bad? Or was she just tired of being with him? Why had she cared so much whether or not he was going to go look for Charlotte? Did she want him to leave? Or stay?

His emotions felt as ragged as frayed rope. Seth turned to go to his room. What he needed was time with the Lord.

The next morning, Seth was still no closer to knowing what to do. Just when he thought that the Lord had assured him that all would be well, he'd worry again about what to do about Charlotte and Rebecca.

He was rubbing oil into his saddle when Jacob sat down on the hay bale beside him. Dust puffed up and Seth sneezed.

In his normal straight-to-the-point way, Jacob said, "You know, Seth, you could always send Miss Charlotte a letter using the Pony Express boys."

Seth cut his eyes at Jacob. Why hadn't he thought of that? He couldn't send it in the mailbag, but maybe the boys could pass it off to one another until it reached Sacramento. The last rider could hand deliver it to Charlotte. "That's a good idea."

"Next rider's expected in an hour." Jacob got up and went to saddle up Clayton's horse. "I'm sure Clayton would be happy to start the letter on its way."

He set the oil and saddle to the side. "I'll be in my room, if anyone needs me." Seth walked out of the barn even though he felt like running. The sooner he got the letter on its way, the sooner he'd know what to do about Charlotte, the Pony Express job and, most important, Rebecca. If Charlotte set him free from his commitment, he'd be able to tell Rebecca how he felt about her.

Even as he found paper and a pencil, Seth couldn't shake the fear that if he told Rebecca he loved her she would break his heart. Would she stay with him or, like his mother, would she desert him?

Rebecca spent the next three days avoiding Seth and fighting Benjamin's cold. She felt worn to a frazzle. Since she'd sold Emma to Fay, Martha hadn't changed much. She still spent her days in the sitting room, reading or complaining. Emma seemed happier than ever. Now that Fay had given her her papers and told Emma she was free, the young woman had blossomed even more. Rebecca had offered Emma a home for as long as she wanted. Even though it wasn't expected, Emma tried to help out as much as possible. She and Fay made sure that Rebecca didn't overexert herself.

Her chest ached but she couldn't decide if it was from the cold or if it was simply her heart breaking knowing that Seth would be leaving soon. Rebecca found herself reliving their one and only kiss and wishing for more time with him.

She stretched and yawned. Thanks to Fay's thoughtfulness, Rebecca had enjoyed a long afternoon nap. She pulled on her shoes and walked into the sitting room. It was empty. The house was quieter than usual. She'd gotten used to lots of talking and laughter.

Rebecca headed to the kitchen, where she found a note propped up next to the cookie jar.

Rebecca,
The stage horses finally arrived and Martha and Mr. Walker left shortly afterward. Clayton agreed to take myself, Emma and Joy into town. Emma is happy to be free and we are going to

buy fabric to make her a new dress to celebrate.
We'll be home in time for dinner.
Love, Fay

A relieved sigh eased through her dry lips. Martha
Ranger had been a thorn in her side ever since she'd
arrived. Rebecca was glad to see that she was gone.
The house felt warmer than usual so Rebecca opened
the back door to let in a cool breeze.

She'd not eaten much for lunch and decided to make
herself a fried egg and potato. It wasn't often that Rebecca fixed a meal for herself alone, but today she
wanted to celebrate Martha's departure with her favorite meal, breakfast.

Her face and neck felt as if they were on fire and
she wondered if perhaps she had a fever. Then she decided that it was probably just the afternoon heat that
was making her feel feverish.

Pulling a potato from the bin, Rebecca found her
sharpest knife and began to peel it. It wasn't a large potato, but would be the perfect size for one person. She'd
just about finished when a hacking cough squeezed
through her lungs. The knife slipped and cut a long,
deep line through the center of her palm.

Blood poured from the wound. It burned like wild-
fire and brought tears to Rebecca's eyes. She grabbed
a tea towel and pressed it to the wound. Within a few
moments the cloth was saturated. She pulled the cloth
away but couldn't see how deep the wound was because blood continued to pour from it.

She needed a doctor to look at it. Rebecca grabbed
a clean towel and wrapped it tightly around her palm.

Without being told, she knew that her hand would need stitches. She walked out to the barn to see if one of the boys could ride with her to town.

Jacob looked up and grinned when she came into the barn. "Hey, Ma, how are you feeling?"

"Better but I cut my hand and need to go let the doctor have a look at it." Rebecca kept her palm closed so that Jacob couldn't see how bad the cut was. "Is Andrew or Clayton around so they can go with me?"

He shook his head. "No, Clayton took the women into town and Andrew and the rest of the men, except for me and Noah, are out in the back pasture trying to round up calves." Jacob looked down at her hand. "How bad is it?"

Rebecca put more pressure on her palm. She knew Clayton was with Fay; she'd simply forgotten. "Oh, not too bad. Noah, saddle Brownie for me." She turned her attention back to Jacob. "I'll just take Brownie and the back road to town."

Worry etched his young features. "Ma, if you would wait I could go with you. The other rider should be here in a few minutes and then I'll be free to go."

Noah pulled Brownie toward her. His dark eyes studied her face and Rebecca had the feeling that he understood her urgency to get to town. He held Brownie still while she pulled herself up into the saddle with her good hand. "When you get finished here, you can catch up with me, Jacob. If it's just a few minutes, I won't be in any danger."

She didn't give him time to argue. Rebecca could feel blood seeping through the thick towel. Her head felt fuzzy. She hated being sick and hoped that the doctor could give her some medicine for her cold, too. "I'll see you soon, son," she called over her shoulder as Brownie headed to town.

Half a mile down the back road, Rebecca looked down at the cloth. Blood darkened the fabric until she could no longer see the pattern. She felt light-headed and sleepy. A yawn forced its way past her dry lips. With her free hand she felt her forehead. It was hot. Feverish and bleeding, Rebecca welcomed the sound of horse's hooves coming up behind her.

She turned, expecting to see Jacob.

Instead two men with cloth across their faces were whipping their horses to catch up with her. Rebecca put her heels into the little mare's side, prompting her to run. But Brownie was no match for the two younger horses.

One of the men leaned over and grabbed the reins from Rebecca's good hand. "Whoa!" he yelled and pulled on Brownie's bit until she came to a stop.

"Give us your money," the other barked as he pointed a gun at Rebecca.

She swayed in the saddle. "I don't have any money."

"That's what they all say, lady," the second man growled.

His voice sounded familiar. Rebecca squinted at him. "Do I know you?"

The other bandit laughed. "Nope, but we know you. Now give us your money and get down from that horse." He waved the gun at her.

Rebecca felt foolish. Why hadn't she followed Seth's orders and waited for Jacob to come with her? She swayed in the saddle, but hung on to the horn.

Would she see Seth or the boys again? What would these men do to her? She wished she'd told Seth she loved him. Rebecca had been so concerned about John and the boys' feelings that she hadn't expressed her own. Now it might be too late.

Seth arrived back at the farm just as Noah and his horse shot off down the road carrying the Pony Express mailbag. The thrill of the ride flashed across the boy's face as he passed him. He raised a hand and prayed for Noah's safety before heading to the barn.

Jacob came running to him and slid to a stop to the side of Sam. His eyes held worry and frustration.

Seth could sense that something was wrong, dreadfully wrong. His gaze moved to the house. Was Rebecca feeling worse?

Fear filled Jacob's voice as he said, "Seth, Ma took off for town alone. She hurt her hand and wouldn't wait for me to go with her to the doctor."

"How long has she been gone?" Seth asked, trying to control the pounding of his heart.

Jacob's answer sounded clipped and frantic. "About a half hour. The rider was late and I couldn't leave Noah here alone. Someone had to document the time of the rider's arrival. I've already saddled a horse to go after her."

"No, you stay here. I'll find her, Jacob." He put his heels in Sam's side. The horse took off like a bullet from a smoking gun. Seth leaned low over Sam's neck and prayed. What had the woman been thinking? He'd warned them all to stay in groups when leaving the ranch.

Seth pushed Sam harder than ever before. He felt that still small voice telling him to hurry. Deep down, Seth knew Rebecca was in trouble. If anything happened to her, he'd be heartbroken. The thought seemed ironic. He'd kept his distance from her to keep his heart safe and now the threat of separation from her caused it to ache anyway.

When he topped the small rise and saw Rebecca trapped between two masked men, Seth pulled his Colt from its holster and aimed for the sky. If he didn't have to kill the men, but could scare them off, he would. He pulled the trigger and pushed Sam to race faster toward the woman he knew that he loved.

The men turned. One ran at the sight of Seth barreling down toward them. The other pointed his gun at Seth and fired.

Seth pressed his body close to Sam's and continued racing forward. He watched in horror as Rebecca went limp and slipped off Brownie's back.

The big man fired again at Seth. Anger seeped from the man's eyes. His stance said that as soon as Seth was in range, he'd kill him.

Seth aimed for the man's shooting arm and returned fire. He hated shooting but had to get to Rebecca. Had the man shot her? Or had she fainted?

His bullet hit true—the bandit grabbed his shoulder and turned his horse to follow his fellow outlaw. They disappeared over the next hill just as Seth jumped from Sam's back to Rebecca's side.

Rebecca groaned as he kneeled beside her and lifted her up into his arms. He cradled her hot body against his chest and arms. She was burning up with a fever. Smears of blood covered the front of her dress.

She opened her eyes, and her dimples winked at him. "Seth? You came for me?" Her glazed eyes told him that she was no longer aware of pain or heat from the fever.

"Yes, I came for you. Where are you hurt?" he asked, feeling her arms and torso for gunshot wounds.

She waved a bloody hand in front of his face. "I cut myself."

Satisfied she hadn't been shot, Seth picked up the bloody rag she'd used to cover the cut. He wrapped her hand and said, "I can see that."

She closed her eyes and he gently laid her back down on the ground. Gathering Brownie's reins and keeping a close watch out for the road bandits, he tied the little mare to the back of Sam's saddle, then hurried back to Rebecca.

Rebecca opened her eyes and looked at him. Her eyes had turned from their clear exquisiteness to that of a beautiful storm, dark but filled with a haze that only a summer storm could produce, or in this case pain and fever. "Are you taking me home, Seth?" she asked in a drowsy voice.

"No, I'm taking you to the doctor, but first we need to get you up on Sam. Can you stand up?" He leaned over and helped her stand. She closed her eyes and swayed against him. "Stay with me, Rebecca."

She opened her eyes and reached up and touched his jaw. "Always." Once more she slumped against him.

With more strength than he knew he possessed, Seth scooped her up against him and walked over to Sam.

How was he going to get her on? *Lord, I need Your help here.* He looked up into the clear blue sky and quietly pleaded with God to help him get her on the horse.

Sam snorted and then buckled his front legs, then his back. He turned his big head and stared at Seth as if to say, *Well, what are you waiting for?*

Seth put Rebecca into the saddle and while holding her upright climbed on behind her. Sam stood. "Thank You, Lord!" Seth shouted and then grabbed the reins while holding on to Rebecca.

The trip into town felt as if it was taking forever. Seth continued to pray over Rebecca. She'd lost a lot of blood and the fever wasn't helping her. He rode in as fast as Sam could go and still tow her horse behind them.

The doctor stood on the sidewalk in front of his home and office. He hurried to help Seth get Rebecca off the horse. "What happened?"

"Jacob says she cut her hand."

"With what, a rusty knife? She's burning up with fever." The doctor allowed Seth to sweep Rebecca into his arms. He held the door to let them inside.

"She's been sick for a couple of days. I had no idea she was running a fever until I found her on the trail and brought her here." Seth laid her down on the cot that the doctor pointed to.

"You'll have to wait outside, young man." The doctor was already peeling the cloth from Rebecca's hand.

Seth walked to the door, but before exiting, he turned to look at Rebecca's pale face. Dark brown eyelashes fanned out under her eyes. He wished those eyes were open now, but she seemed to be sleeping.

Her cheeks sported two red spots, making the rest of her face look powdery white.

Her hair had fallen down in his hurry to get her to town and now rested around her head on the pillow. His mind went to the silky softness of the strands. He'd only touched them once and that had been while kissing her.

The doctor cleared his throat and pointedly looked at the door. "I can't help her until you leave."

Seth left. He stepped out onto the porch. A rocker invited him to sit down but he couldn't. Sam and Brownie needed to be taken care of. He called through the door, "I'll be at the livery. If not there, the sheriff's office."

He heard the doctor grunt and took that as an indication that the man had heard him. Seth walked Sam to the livery, and Brownie followed, still tied to Sam's saddle.

*Thank You, Lord for helping me get her here. And, Lord, please make her well. Her sons need her.* He paused, lowered his head and confessed in a quiet voice, "I need her."

Even as he said the words, Seth knew that he didn't have a future with Rebecca. He really didn't want to confess, even to himself, that he loved her, but deep down he knew he did. Was it wrong to resent the promise he'd made to his grandmother? To Charlotte? Would he be able to live with the fact that he was marrying one woman but in love with another?

## Chapter Twenty-Three

The next day, Rebecca woke up at the doctor's office. She knew she'd suffered from fever throughout the night and that her hand burned as if someone had branded her palm. A white bandage covered the cut.

During her fever-induced sleep, she recalled Seth coming over a hill with his gun blazing in the air.

The doctor came into the room. "Oh, good, you're awake." He smiled kindly at her and touched the back of his hand to her forehead. "And the fever is gone. That's a good sign."

She pushed up on her elbows. "Where's Seth? Did he make it through the gunfight all right?"

"There was a gunfight?" The doctor grinned at her. "Honey, I think you dreamed that."

"No, he shot at the road bandits who were trying to rob me." She fell back against the pillow. Had she dreamed it?

The doctor unwrapped her hand and inspected his handiwork.

The soft sound of the door clicking into place told

her someone else had entered the room. "She's right, Doc. I did shoot at the men trying to hold her up." He came around and grinned at Rebecca. "I'm glad to see you awake. How do you feel?"

The tenderness in his eyes touched her heart. "Well, my hand feels as if someone stuck a branding iron to it, but other than that, I feel better."

The doctor shook his head. "Someday, when we both have a little time, you'll have to tell me all about that gunfight, Seth."

Seth laughed. "It really wasn't much of a gunfight, but I'll be happy to tell you all about it."

"As for you, young lady, if Seth here wants to take you home, you have to promise to keep those stitches clean and let them heal. I'll come out in a few days and see if we can take them out." He rewrapped her hand and gave her a gentle pat on the arm.

"It would be my pleasure to take her home," Seth answered. "I'll just leave you to get ready." He stepped back out the door.

The doctor handed Rebecca a small pouch. "This has some herbs in it. I want you to take a teaspoon a day out, soak them in water and then use the water to wash that hand. They'll speed along the healing." At her nod, he continued, "Your dress is hanging over there. The missus tried to get the blood out for you, but I'm afraid it might still be stained."

"Thank you for the herbs. I'd like to thank her before I leave," Rebecca said, looking at her dress. She didn't see any stains.

"Good. I'm sending her in to help you with those buttons, so you'll have your chance." The doctor left her alone. Rebecca pushed off the sheet and stood slowly. Her hand throbbed so she held it up.

The door opened again. The doctor's wife, a plump woman with a sweet face, entered the room. "Doc says you are ready to go home. How do you feel?"

Rebecca wondered how often she'd have to answer that question before the day was over. "Better, Mrs. Bridges. We're blessed to have a good doctor in town."

The other woman walked over and pulled down Rebecca's dress. "You're blessed to have such a handsome young man who worries about you." She helped her step into the dress. "He stayed all night, sat in that chair."

Seth had stayed all night with her? She smiled. "That was sweet of him." Why would he do such a thing? Why hadn't he just had Fay come sit with her? Rebecca didn't want to think too much of the situation. So she pushed those thoughts to the back of her mind and focused on getting dressed.

After the dress was buttoned, Mrs. Bridges helped Rebecca with her shoes. "Thank you for getting the stains out of my dress," Rebecca said. It felt odd to have someone else button her shoes for her.

"It was no trouble at all. I was glad to help." She stepped back and looked Rebecca over. "Would you like me to brush your hair for you? It's a little wild-looking."

Rebecca looked down at her hand and nodded. She'd not realized how much help she was going to need over the next few days, but she couldn't even comb her own hair.

Mrs. Bridges chattered about the church bake sale

that was coming up while she combed Rebecca's hair out and then pulled it up into a bun on top of her head. "I'll be making my spice cake this year." She stepped back and looked at her handiwork. "All done." The doctor's wife smiled at her.

"Thank you."

Seth called through the door, "About ready?"

Mrs. Bridges opened the door. "She's ready." She beamed at Rebecca

Rebecca walked slowly to Seth. Her head still felt a little light, but she didn't say anything because she wanted to go home. "Thank you for everything." Tears stung her eyes as she realized just how much this woman had done for her.

"It was my pleasure."

Rebecca followed Seth out onto the porch. She expected to see Brownie and Sam standing in the road, but instead she saw that both of them were hooked up to a wagon. "You didn't have to get a wagon, Seth. I could have ridden Brownie home."

"Um, no, you couldn't. I want to make sure I get you back to the farm in one piece. Those boys of yours would skin me alive if you fell off and broke your neck." He held his hand out to help her up.

As soon as she was seated, Seth pulled himself up onto the wagon and took the reins in his hands. Rebecca didn't know what to say. She clutched the herb pouch in her hands and enjoyed the cool breeze on her face.

"You look pretty," Seth said once they'd passed the town's border.

Rebecca rubbed her lips together. "Thank you. I'm

sure I look like death warmed over." She studied her hands.

"No, that's how you looked yesterday when I brought you to town. Now with a little color in your cheeks you are as pretty as those pink evening primroses over there." He pointed off to his right and grinned at her.

She felt heat fill her face and ducked her chin. Was that sweet talk? Or was he just trying to be kind? Rebecca turned her head to look at the field of flowers. They were pretty.

Unsure what to say but knowing that she wanted to tell him how much he meant to her, Rebecca decided not to say anything at all. He had a mail-order bride that he'd soon be going to see and possibly wed. Sorrow filled her at the thought, but she decided to ignore it and enjoy the beautiful flowers that were blooming all around her. Her telling Seth that she was in love with him wouldn't change anything.

Seth pulled into the yard just as the sun was setting. Everyone had been watching for them and within minutes the wagon was surrounded.

Jacob reached up and helped his mother down. He hugged her close and growled, "If you ever do that again, I will…"

Whatever he was going to threaten was lost among the others pushing him away and taking their turn hugging her. Each boy greeted Rebecca with hugs and pats. Little Benjamin hugged her about the waist and Joy clung to one leg.

Fay called from the door, "Come on, everyone. Let's get her inside."

Andrew scooped up Joy, and Benjamin released her waist. Seth gently took Rebecca's elbow and walked with her to the house.

Fay and Emma met her at the door. The two women hugged her and fussed over her injured hand. Seth guided her to the sofa.

Benjamin rushed to her side. "Tell us about the bad men, Ma."

She pulled him closer to her side with her good hand. "Well, Benjamin, I learned a lesson from those bad men." Rebecca looked down into his brandy-colored eyes.

Awe filled his voice and he said, "You did?"

"Uh-huh."

"What did you learn?" he asked, never breaking eye contact.

Rebecca looked to Seth. "Well, first off, I learned never disobey Seth. If I hadn't taken off by myself, I might never have had to face those two men."

"Yeah, Jacob said that was foolish of you." Benjamin looked to his older brother.

"Oh, he did, did he?" Rebecca also looked to her oldest son.

Happy to be the center of attention, Benjamin continued, "Yep, he said even mas can do foolish things sometimes."

Rebecca smiled at Jacob. "He's right, Benjamin. It was foolish of me to take off on my own. I put myself in danger, and Seth. He could have been shot."

Joy wasn't going to be left out. She pushed out of Andrew's arms and crawled into Rebecca's lap. Her thumb went into her mouth and she laid her head on her mother's chest.

"I'm sorry I worried everyone. I promise from now on I won't leave the farm without a companion. Those men were mean and could have done a lot of harm to me. I should have listened to Seth and Jacob." She looked around the room at each person.

They were her family, even Emma and Fay. And the care she saw in their eyes touched her heart. Rebecca recognized that the boys would eventually leave the farm, but knowing they loved her so much made the realization a little more bearable.

Clayton drew everyone's attention off his mother. "What did the sheriff say, Seth?"

Seth leaned against the fireplace. "He said they'd keep a lookout for the road bandits."

"That's it?" Thomas demanded. "After what they tried to do to Ma, that's all he's going to do about it?"

The rest of the boys began to grumble, too.

Fay broke in to their complaining. "Now, see here, boys. The sheriff will do what he can to find them. That's all we can ask."

Philip grunted. "No, he could round up some men and go find those low-down…"

"Philip!" Rebecca wasn't sure what her son was going to call them, but she felt sure it wasn't nice or appropriate in a room full of children and women.

Jacob spoke up. "Listen, we stick to the rules. Don't go anywhere without someone with you. Don't leave the farm unless you have to. And let the sheriff do his job the way he sees fit." He eyed each of his younger brothers. "We are not the law or above the law."

Seth nodded. "Jacob is right. We have a job to do for the Pony Express. What is that job?"

"The mail must go through!" seven young voices boomed all at once.

The room burst into laughter. Rebecca smiled at her family. They began visiting and playing around. It felt good to be home. She yawned.

Fay leaned down over the back of the couch and asked, "Are you ready to retire?"

"Not yet." Rebecca patted the hand that rested on her shoulder. "I want to enjoy my family for a little longer."

Emma sat on the arm of the chair. "Are you hungry, Rebecca? I made corned beef and cabbage for dinner. I'll be happy to dish you up a plate." She stood, waiting for Rebecca's consent.

"That sounds wonderful, Emma. Thank you."

The young girl beamed and hurried off to the kitchen.

Fay called after her, "Grab her a hot biscuit, too."

As soon as Emma left the room, Fay complimented her. "That girl can cook. Just wait until you taste her biscuits."

Rebecca watched her boys. Thomas and Philip were obvious in their admiration for Emma, but it was Andrew who caught her attention. He watched the young woman prance from the room and a small smile teased his lips before Andrew pulled his facial features back into serious lines. Was he interested in Emma? Or did she simply amuse him?

The next day, Rebecca felt useless as Fay and Emma prepared for the incoming stagecoach. Her hand felt stiff, but other than that Rebecca didn't feel any different. She wanted to make cookies, wipe down the tables and do her job. But Fay was having no part of it.

"You work too hard. Just relax and let us take care of you for a change." The older woman fussed as she pulled out the tray of sweetbreads she'd made.

"All right, I'm going to the sitting room." Rebecca used her good hand and pushed through the door that joined the two rooms.

Joy sat by the fireplace playing with her doll. She looked up when her mother came in and smiled. "Look, Ma, Emma fixed my doll's hair like mine."

Rebecca grinned. "She sure did. It is very pretty."

The little girl nodded and went back to changing the doll's dress. Rebecca moved to the window and watched as several of the boys applied whitewash to the corral fence. She couldn't hear what they were saying, but their laughter drifted on the breeze toward the house.

Noah was standing in front of the barn with his horse. He seemed to be examining one of the horse's front hooves. His pant legs looked a little short on his boots. Had the boy had a growth spurt? When he stood up and flexed his shoulders she saw that the material appeared tight across his back. Yes, it was time to take him shopping again.

The stagecoach pulled in and all the boys looked toward it. Seth came out of the barn. He saw her standing in the window and waved before going into the bunkhouse. Rebecca turned her attention to the stage.

A beautiful young woman came out first. Her auburn hair shone in the sunlight. She was dressed in a simple green traveling dress and black shoes showed under her skirt. Next came a man. He wore a black business suit and his hat was smaller than the hats her boys and Seth wore.

Rebecca tried to remember what it was called but the name escaped her mind.

Fay and Emma hurried into the room. Each had a plate and were carrying them to the sideboard. Coffee and tea were ready, along with cups and saucers for serving. Emma took Joy's hand and returned to the kitchen.

Rebecca moved to the door and opened it just as the pair stepped onto the front porch. "Welcome. I hope you've had a safe trip so far."

The woman smiled sweetly at her. Rebecca was taken aback by the pure beauty of her emerald-green eyes. "Thank you. We've been blessed with no mishaps," she said as she passed.

The gentleman smiled at her, too, as he walked past. "This is the Dove Creek Pony Express station. Is that correct?" he asked.

Rebecca shut the door. "Yes, it is. Would either of you like a refreshment before you continue on your journey?"

"That would be lovely," the woman said as she walked toward Fay and the table. The light scent of rose water traveled with her.

Seth walked up behind Rebecca. "I see our guests are helping themselves to your fine cooking," he whispered against her ear.

She shivered and looked to the ground. "Not mine. Fay wouldn't let me help in the kitchen," Rebecca whispered back. She found herself wanting to lean into him.

He chuckled. "Good for her."

Rebecca felt someone watching them. She looked up to find the woman staring at Seth with interested eyes.

"Do you think Fay would slap my hand if I snatched a sandwich and maybe a slice of that sweetbread?" he asked, glancing at the table.

"Are you kidding? She'd let you take both plates if you wanted to," Rebecca answered. It was true. Fay thought that Seth could do no wrong, especially after he told how he'd rescued Rebecca from the outlaws.

He grinned. "I'll settle for one sandwich and a slice of bread." Seth walked over to Fay.

Rebecca turned her attention to the passengers. They both sat at the table. The woman's gaze continued to follow Seth. Why was she so interested in him? He was a handsome man, but so was her companion. So what did she find so intriguing about Seth?

Rebecca felt uncomfortable and she knew why. This woman was beautiful and she was interested in Seth. And for the first time in her life, Rebecca experienced jealousy.

# Chapter Twenty-Four

Seth felt the woman's gaze upon him, but decided to ignore her. The thought that she was trying to make her companion jealous bothered him and he decided that as soon as he finished his sandwich he'd head back out to the barn.

Fay handed him a glass with tea in it. "Here, this should help wash that bread down."

He smiled his thanks, took a sip and then asked, "How is she doing today?"

Fay glanced over at Rebecca. She'd moved to the rocker by the window and picked up Fay's Bible. "Good. She wants to help but I told her she has to let her hand rest a few days before she starts using it."

"I'm glad she has you watching over her," Seth said, taking a big bite out of the sandwich.

Fay frowned at him. "If you keep gulping your food, you're going to choke."

He chewed and swallowed. "I'm just in a hurry to get back to the barn," Seth explained. He took a swallow of the tea.

Fay teased him in a quiet voice. "Why? Because our guests are making you uncomfortable?"

"You feel it, too?" he whispered.

She laughed softly. "No, I don't feel anything but I can see that you have drawn some attention from the woman. I think she likes you," Fay whispered back.

Seth stuffed the last of the sandwich in his mouth. He already had two women to worry about; he didn't want or need to add another. As soon as he could swallow, he drank the last of his tea and handed Fay back the glass. "Thanks for the sandwich." He turned to leave but her voice stopped him.

"Aren't you going to take a slice of sweetbread with you?"

He turned back to her. She'd wrapped it in a soft piece of cloth and handed it to him. From the corner of his eye, Seth could see that the passengers were finishing up their meal and were standing to leave. "Thank you, Fay." He thought to go back out the kitchen.

A male voice stopped him. "Excuse me, but are you Seth Armstrong?" he asked.

Seth inhaled through his nose and released the air through his mouth. Then he turned to face the man with a smile. At least he hoped it was a smile and not a grimace. "Yes, I am."

The man walked toward him with an outstretched hand. "I'm Ben Wheeler. May we speak to you outside?"

Seth shook the man's hand. "Of course." His gaze moved to the woman and for the first time he really looked at her. Emma's words about Charlotte came back to him. *She's a sweet woman with auburn hair and green eyes.* Seth realized he was looking in the face of his mail-order bride.

She extended her hand also. "Seth, I'm Charlotte. Charlotte Fisher."

He took her delicate hand in his. His gaze moved to Rebecca, who stared back at him with big blue eyes. Seth felt the air leave his lungs.

Mr. Wheeler cleared his throat. "Is there someplace private we can talk?" he asked.

Seth released Charlotte's hand. "Yes, yes, there is." He opened the front door and inhaled the scent of roses as Charlotte passed him.

Once outside, Seth looked around for a place to take them. He knew that if they stayed on the porch, Rebecca would be able to hear every word they said.

Charlotte motioned toward the stage. "We could sit inside the coach and talk."

"That's an excellent idea," Mr. Wheeler agreed, leading the way.

Mr. Wheeler helped Charlotte into the stage and then motioned for Seth to follow her. "This is between the two of you." He made eye contact with Seth and said, "I hope you make the right decision." Mr. Wheeler nodded his head and closed the door on the coach.

Charlotte folded her hands in her lap and searched Seth's face. "I can't believe we are finally meeting."

He looked around the carriage. "Me, either. This wasn't exactly how I thought it would happen." Seth studied her face. "I'm sorry I didn't find you as fast as I'd planned."

Charlotte shook her head. "No, it was my fault. Let me explain."

Seth nodded, happy to finally find out what had happened to her.

"I left on the day I sent you that last letter but to get to the station I had to walk through a cold rainstorm. When the stage left I was soaked and already starting to feel bad. We got about halfway to St. Joseph and I was very sick. Fever and chills shook my body. The ladies on the coach were afraid I was going to make them sick, too. So they talked the driver into leaving me behind." Her green eyes took on a faraway look as if she was reliving those moments.

"Why didn't you take the next stage and continue on? I would have taken care of you." He leaned forward and took her hands in his.

Charlotte smiled. "I'm sure you would have, but I didn't have any more money and the next stage wouldn't arrive for another two days. The lady at the stagecoach stop said I could sleep in the barn. So I stumbled to the barn and tried to get better. When the stagecoach arrived I was weak from lack of food and the fever that had consumed me. But I was determined to get to you." Her green eyes searched his.

Seth couldn't believe how cruel the women had treated Charlotte. She was beautiful and jealousy was a cruel beast that some women fought. Of course, jealousy may have had nothing to do with their treatment of Charlotte; it could have been their fear of getting sick. "I'm sorry I didn't get to you first," he confessed. "You don't have to tell me this, if it is too painful. You are here now and that's what is important."

"No, I have to tell you the whole story." She pulled her hands from his. "I made it out of the barn but tripped when I took a step to get into the coach." Her hand went to her head. "The fall knocked me out and when I awoke, I had no idea who I was or where I'd been going." She dropped her hand back in her lap. "But thankfully, Mr. Wheeler was on that stage. He's a doctor. He found out from the woman at the station that my name was Charlotte Fisher." A gentle smile touched her lips. "Ben says he fell in love with me the moment he saw me. Can you believe that?"

Seth sat back in his seat. So the man outside the door was in love with Charlotte. He smiled at her. "Yes, I can. You are a very beautiful woman."

She giggled. "Well, that day I was anything but beautiful. Anyway, he nursed me back to health, took me back to Sacramento and helped me find a job at the restaurant."

Seth was confused. It was obvious that Charlotte was in love with Ben also, so why was she here? He knew she hadn't had time to get his letter. How did she know where he was? If she didn't know he was here and it was a complete accident, how had they known he was Seth Armstrong?

"I'm almost done, I promise." Charlotte sat up straighter. "I was working one day when I heard a conversation between two men who had just arrived on the afternoon stage. One of the men asked the other if he thought they might run into Charlotte Fisher, that gal that Seth Armstrong was looking for in Dove Creek. I don't know why it happened but hearing both our names in the same sentence had my memories flooding back to me. I remembered why I was on the stage.

That night I told Ben and explained to him that I had to come find you." She inhaled deeply.

Seth searched her face. "But you love Ben, so why did you come here looking for me?"

"I came to ask you to release me from my promise. I know I said I'd marry you and I will, if you won't release me, but please, Seth. Ben wants to marry me, and my heart will shatter into a million pieces if I can't marry him. He's the first man who hasn't looked at me and only seen outside beauty. He saw me when I was sick, dirty and starving, and he loved me on sight." Her hands shook in her lap. Tears filled her eyes and spilled down her cheeks.

Seth leaned forward and placed his hands on hers once more. "It's all right. I release you, Charlotte."

She grabbed him and hugged him, then leaned back. "But what about your promise to your grandmother?"

He shifted on the hard seat. "She made me promise to get married. She didn't say it had to be to you."

A smile tipped her lips once more. "You're happy I'm releasing you, aren't you?"

Seth nodded. His heart was about to explode out of his chest with happiness. Now that he knew what had happened to Charlotte and she'd asked him to release her, he was free to tell Rebecca how he felt about her.

"It's the woman from the house, isn't it? The one with the bandaged hand." She wisely crossed her arms over her chest and gave him a stern look.

Seth laughed. "Yes, but she doesn't know how I feel, so I'm a little unsure what the future holds now. Thank you for coming and telling me what had happened to you. I wish you and Mr. Wheeler the best." Seth stood to exit the coach.

"I wish you the best, too, Seth. If you tell her that you love her, I'm sure your future will be bright."

How could Charlotte be so sure? Would Rebecca believe that he loved her? Would she say yes if he asked her to marry him?

*Lord, let Your will be done.* He silently prayed that his will and God's will were in alignment.

Rebecca watched from the window as Seth climbed out of the coach. Charlotte followed, looking happier now that they'd had their talk. What had she said to him? They'd been in the coach so long.

"What do you think they talked about?" Emma asked, standing beside her.

Fay answered from the sofa. "It's none of our business, ladies."

Rebecca ignored Fay. "I don't know but look how happy she is now."

Emma nodded. "But she's getting back in the coach and so is the man. Are they leaving?"

The coach pulled away from the house and continued on its route, carrying Charlotte and Mr. Wheeler with it. Rebecca watched as Seth hurried to the bunkhouse. "He never even looked back." She turned from the window. "I'm tired. I think I'll go lie down for a little while." Rebecca started to walk out of the room but stopped. "Thank you both for taking care of the passengers today."

Emma asked, "Rebecca, are you feeling all right?"

"I'm fine. I just need to rest." She didn't tell them

that her heart was breaking. Seth seemed happy, Charlotte seemed happy and Rebecca couldn't help but feel miserable.

She went to her room and shut the door. The desire to throw herself across the bed and weep pulled strongly at her. Was Charlotte going on to St. Joseph to wait for Seth? Were they still planning on getting married?

Deep down Rebecca felt sure that they hadn't broken off their marriage since they both looked so happy. Even Charlotte's companion had looked pleased.

Rebecca avoided the bed and moved to the stuffed chair that sat beside the window. She picked up her Bible off the side table and opened it to Proverbs.

To her, Proverbs was the book of wisdom—at least that was what she liked to think. She read Proverbs, chapter sixteen, verse nine, out loud. "'A man's heart deviseth his way: but the Lord directeth his steps.'"

Peace washed over her. God was in control. Seth may have been in her life for a little while and if he left, she'd be fine because God would never leave her.

She closed the Bible and lay across her bed. "Lord, I trust You to direct my steps." Rebecca closed her eyes, sadly wishing that her steps and Seth's walked side by side.

Seth paced the bunkhouse. He knew that God had brought him to the Young farm to teach him about love. When he'd arrived he'd sworn never to fall in love, to never let anyone hurt him like his mother had hurt him and his father. But all that had changed.

He loved Rebecca. He wanted to marry her. He also respected her sons enough to ask their permission.

Philip entered the bunkhouse first. When he saw Seth, he frowned. "Is everything all right?" he asked.

"Better than all right. Go tell the other boys to come here. I'd like to have a meeting with them."

Philip nodded. "Let me change out of these wet socks and I'll go get them."

It seemed to take forever for Philip to do the simple task of changing socks. And it took even longer for all the boys to make their way into the bunkhouse.

"This is everyone," Philip announced unnecessarily.

Seth walked to the stove and stood in front of it, facing them. "Today my mail-order bride came to the farm."

"What?"

"Where is she?"

"I didn't see her."

"Are you going to marry her here?"

"Does Ma like her?"

Jacob stopped the questions. "Shut up, and let him talk."

"She released me from marrying her. It would seem Charlotte has met someone more to her liking and so have I." Seth took a breath and was immediately interrupted again with questions and outrage.

"Who did she meet?"

"What does more to her liking mean?"

"Who have you met?"

"Enough!" Jacob yelled.

All the boys looked to him.

"If you interrupt Seth one more time, I am going to thrash you."

They seemed to take their older brother at his word and quieted down again. All eyes turned to Seth.

Seth answered their questions. "She met a doctor and they are going to get married. That's what I meant by more to her liking. As for who I have met." He paused. For the first time he worried the Young men might reject him and his idea to marry their mother.

Jacob grinned. "Go on, tell them who you have met."

Seth swallowed and then rushed on. "I met your mother and I want to marry her."

Andrew stood. In a tense voice he asked, "Why?"

The two men locked gazes. "Because I love her," Seth answered.

Jacob stood, too. He stepped between Andrew and Seth as if he thought Andrew would start a fight. Jacob said, "Then you should marry her."

Andrew nodded his approval.

Clayton, Thomas and Philip grinned up at him.

Noah shrugged. "If you love her, then you should marry her."

Benjamin stood and looked up at Seth. He didn't say anything and he didn't nod. Seth kneeled down in front of him. This little boy meant the world to him and he needed his approval as much, or more, than the others'. "Beni, I can't marry her unless all the Young men approve. It wouldn't be right."

"Would I have to call you Papa Seth?"

The seriousness in Benjamin's voice reminded Seth that in Beni's eyes he was trying to take John's place in their lives. He shook his head. "No, you don't. I'll always be Seth to you. I can't take Papa John's place in your heart, Beni. No one can."

He looked to his other brothers, who nodded their heads at him. Benjamin looked back to Seth. "Then I reckon it's all right with me, if you want to marry Ma."

Seth stood and faced them once more. He swallowed. "Thanks."

They laughed and clapped him on the back. Andrew stood off to the side with his arms crossed over his chest. Seth turned to him. "Andrew, are you sure you're all right with me asking her to marry me?"

"Yep, I was just thinking. Now you have to actually ask her. These guys are acting like she's already said yes. She might say no." He turned and walked out of the bunkhouse.

Seth's heart sank. Andrew was right. What if she did say no? What if she did reject him? Would she feel like Beni, that no man could take her late husband's place?

# Chapter Twenty-Five

The next morning, Seth was still worrying about Rebecca's answer. The sound of a rider coming in fast drew his attention. There weren't any Pony Express riders scheduled. He stepped out his side door and watched as the sheriff entered the yard.

He walked over to him. "What brings you out this morning, Sheriff?"

The sheriff leaned on his horse's saddle horn. "Just thought you'd like to know we caught our road bandits. It was thanks to your quick shooting."

"Who are they?" Jacob asked, coming to stand beside Seth. The other boys crowded around them, too.

The sheriff tipped his hat back. "Jake Edwards."

"Mr. Edwards that owns the general store?" Clayton asked.

"One and the same. Seems he and a couple of his old buddies were making extra money on the side by robbing stagecoach passengers. Seth here put a bullet in Edwards." He grinned. "Those things smart when they get infected. Bring a man to tears and to the doctor."

"How'd you catch the other two?" Seth asked.

"Seems the pain was pretty bad and he told Doc everything while the bullet was being removed." He rubbed his chin. "Who knew Doc could get information like that just by taking out a bullet?"

Seth was glad the men were behind bars. "Thanks for letting us know, Sheriff. We'll breathe a little easier around here."

The sheriff nodded. "Well, I best be getting back to town. I have prisoners waiting for breakfast this morning." He spun around and headed back to town.

All the way into the house, the boys talked about Mr. Edwards and the fact that they knew he was no good all along. Seth listened but didn't add to the conversation. His thoughts were on Rebecca and how she was going to answer his marriage proposal.

Rebecca listened to the boys repeat what the sheriff had said. She watched Seth's reaction to the news. He seemed distracted and she couldn't help but wonder if he was thinking of Charlotte.

They hadn't had their nightly meeting the evening before. Seth hadn't bothered to come in for dinner. Had he been packing a bag? Even now, was he planning on leaving after breakfast?

The boys lingered over breakfast longer than normal. She noticed that they watched Seth, too. Were they concerned that he would be leaving soon?

It was Andrew who finally said, "Seth, are you doing this today or should we go on and do our chores?"

Seth looked startled for a moment and then he swallowed hard and stood to his feet. He walked to Rebecca's end of the table and offered her his hand.

Unsure what was going on, Rebecca allowed him to pull her up. She opened her mouth to ask what he was doing when he laid a finger over her lips.

"Rebecca Young, I have known for a while now that I love you, but because of Charlotte and my promise to marry her, I haven't been able to tell you. Until today." He stopped and searched her eyes.

Had he just told her he loved her? In front of her kids, Fay and Emma? She looked around the room. The boys all just sat watching expectantly. Fay covered her mouth with her hand and Emma and Joy sat staring with big eyes. She looked back to Seth. "I…"

Seth kneeled down on one knee in front of her. "I love you, Rebecca Young. Will you marry me?" His warm eyes held all the love that was within his heart.

"I do love you, Seth, but I can't agree to marry you."

He stood. Pain reflected in his eyes. "Why not?"

She looked to her children. "I need their permission."

Smiles broke out over the boys' faces.

Jacob laughed. "Ma, we've already given Seth our approval."

A smile began to touch her lips. Seth had respected her and her boys enough to ask their permission. "What about you, Joy?"

She felt Seth's arm snake around her waist.

"I like Seth. I want to keep him."

Rebecca turned to face Seth. His eyes now held understanding, but uncertainty at what her answer was going to be. "I want to keep you, too. Yes, I'll marry you."

Seth didn't give her a chance to change her mind. He pulled her close and kissed her lips. The boys hooted, the women laughed and Rebecca relaxed in his arms.

When he pulled away from her, she whispered against his lips, "I love you, too, Seth. I have for a while now."

He hugged her close. Rebecca savored the warmth of his arms as she thanked the Lord for bringing Seth into their lives. And for helping her to realize that God was in control and it was all right to love again.

# Epilogue

Rebecca looked at her reflection. The full-length mirror had been a wedding present from the boys. She admired the soft cream-colored dress Fay had presented her with the day before. It was much prettier than the blue Sunday dress she'd intended to wear. Tiny pearl-like beads lined the sleeves and the train of the gown.

"You are beautiful, Ma."

She smiled over her shoulder at her eldest son, Jacob. He was to walk her the short distance to her groom. He wore a blue suit that looked snug about his wide shoulders. No longer was he the twelve-year-old boy she'd adopted. Jacob was a man.

"Thank you, son." She looked back at her reflection. Like her, Jacob had a right to start his life again. He needed to know about his mother.

He placed both hands on her shoulders. "Ready?" Their gazes met in the glass.

"Almost." She turned and gave him a hug, then pulled away. "But first I have to tell you about your real mother."

His back straightened. "Today's not the day for that, Ma. We can talk about her another time." Jacob held his arm out for her to take.

Rebecca placed a gloved hand in the crook of his elbow. "I know where she is and I want you to go to her. If for no other reason than to find out why she abandoned you."

Jacob led them to the door. He pulled it open and nodded. "All right. Where is she?"

She swallowed hard. As soon as he knew, Jacob would leave. Rebecca was sure of it. "In California. A few years ago, she married. I'm not sure where in California they live, but she was last known to be somewhere in the vicinity of the Pony Express station called Twelve Mile Station."

He patted her hand. "Thank you for telling me, Ma."

Rebecca pulled him to a stop. "Aren't you going to go find her?" She studied her son's face, wanting to know and yet not wanting to know if he was leaving.

Jacob turned her to face him squarely. "Yes, I am, but I will come back. This is my home. You are my true mother. Nothing will change that." He used his thumb to wipe away a tear that had slipped down her cheek at his words. A smile touched his lips. "But first we have a wedding to attend. And I can't take you in there with tears on your face. Seth would have my guts for garters."

His words caused her to chuckle. Rebecca nodded. "Promise you'll say goodbye before you head out?"

"Promise." He kissed her cheek. "Now let's get you married." Jacob turned and offered her his elbow once more.

Rebecca took it. She pushed all thoughts of Jacob and his future aside and focused on her own future. A future filled with Seth and the rest of the boys and little Joy.

Jacob walked her to Seth, who stood in front of the fireplace looking handsome in his dark pants, light blue shirt and cowboy boots. His smile was for her alone.

She couldn't pull her gaze from his. He was all she'd ever wanted in a husband. They shared friendship, as she and John had, but they also shared so much more. His touch made her feel warm and safe. His smile brightened her day and his voice sent shivers down her spine like no other man's ever had. She'd loved John and nothing and no one could take from that. But now she shared a special love with Seth.

Rebecca thanked the Lord that she could love both men without taking from either of them. They were both special to her in their own ways. Loving Seth would be a new chapter in her life, one she intended to savor.

As she repeated her vows and looked into Seth's strong face, she remembered the day he'd come racing into the yard to help put out a barn fire. Unbeknownst to him, he'd ignited her heart with flames of love. She silently thanked the Lord above for bringing such a wonderful man into her life.

"You may kiss your bride."

Seth pulled her close and gently kissed her lips. She ignored the wedding party and focused solely on her new husband. He was all she'd ever hoped for and so much more.

* * * * *

**Stacy Henrie** has always had a love for history, fiction and chocolate. She earned her BA in public relations before turning her attention to raising a family and writing inspirational historical romances. The wife of an entrepreneur husband and a mother of three, Stacy loves to live out history through her fictional characters. In addition to being an author, she is also a reader, a road-trip enthusiast and a novice interior decorator.

### Books by Stacy Henrie

### Love Inspired Historical

Visit the Author Profile page
at LoveInspired.com for more titles.

# THE EXPRESS RIDER'S
# LADY

Stacy Henrie

Be strong and of a good courage; be not afraid,
neither be thou dismayed: for the Lord thy God
is with thee whithersoever thou goest.
—*Joshua* 1:9

For my three families—the one I call my own, the one I grew up in and the one I married into. Love you all.

Thank you to my agent, Jessica Alvarez, the best advocate an author could ask for, and to my editor, Elizabeth Mazer, who was as excited as me to see Myles and Delsie's story come together. Thanks also to Giselle Regus for her excellent editorial help and suggestions. A final thanks to my readers, especially those of you who've traveled with me from the Old West to the battlefronts of WWI and back again.

# Chapter One

❧

*Saint Joseph, Missouri, June 1860*

"Can I help you, miss?" The horseman cocked an eyebrow at Delsie, his surprise evident in each line of his weathered face. Clearly he wasn't used to finding ladies standing around the Pony Express Stables. Especially at this early hour.

Delsie forced her lips into a smile, despite the nervousness making her stomach roil. Good thing she hadn't eaten any breakfast at the hotel. "I'd like to speak to your fastest Express rider."

The man rubbed his stubbled chin. "I suppose that'd be Myles Patton, miss. But if you need a letter delivered right quick, you ought to take it to the office at the Patee House hotel."

"This concerns more than a letter." She drew herself up to full height, although the top of her rounded hat still didn't reach the man's shoulder. "May I speak with him please?"

The man shrugged. "I think he's inside the stables.

His run begins in less than an hour. If you'll wait here, I'll get him."

"Thank you." She exhaled with relief. One obstacle down. Now if she could only convince this Mr. Patton to go along with her plan.

Delsie turned her back on the open stable doors and brought her handkerchief to her nose. The smell of manure, permeating the morning air, made her nausea worse.

*Hold on, Lillie.* Delsie clutched her leather valise tighter in her hand as she thought of her sister. *I'm coming.*

Her luggage held a change of clothes, a nightgown, a few toiletries, money she'd received in exchange for selling nearly all of her inherited jewelry and the most recent letter from her older sister. One of many unopened letters Delsie had just discovered inside her father's desk back home in Pennsylvania.

A man strode toward her, his face shadowed beneath his hat. He wore an elaborate riding uniform, complete with silver decorations and a scabbard hanging at his side. Delsie blinked in surprise; she'd been expecting a ruffian in a rawhide jacket and trousers.

"Mr. Patton?" She tucked her handkerchief into the sleeve of her blue riding habit.

He tipped up his hat, revealing black eyes and a dark beard that accentuated his strong jaw and bronzed skin. Delsie gulped. He was rather handsome, in a rough sort of way, minus the scowl on his face and the way he sized her up as if she were a pampered child.

"Who are you?" he asked in a tone bordering on rudeness. "And what do you want?"

He certainly wasn't taken in by the beauty of her dark hair or her midnight-blue eyes like her would-be beau Flynn Coppell always claimed to be. But perhaps that was a good thing. If this Mr. Patton agreed to help her they'd be spending a great deal of time in each other's company.

"My name is Delsie Radford," she said with feigned cheerfulness. "I'm here to request a ride."

"Livery stable's down the street." He turned away.

"Wait. You don't understand." She hazarded a step toward his retreating figure. "I need a ride to California."

He spun back, his eyes traveling the length of her again. Delsie tried not to squirm under his scrutiny. "I'm guessing that fancy getup you're wearing means you can read."

She frowned. "Of course I can read."

"Good. Then you'll notice the sign above the building here says Pony Express Stables and not the Overland Stagecoach. Good day, Miss Radford." He twisted on his spurred heel once more.

Throwing propriety to the wind, Delsie rushed after him. "I can't take the stage, Mr. Patton. That's a three-week journey and I must be in California in eighteen days. Not a day later."

"Can't be done," he barked over his shoulder.

Delsie finally caught up with him, close enough to reach out and grip his sleeve. He froze immediately at her touch. An almost panicked expression flickered across his shadowed face, but at least he'd stopped.

"I read about the incredible feat the Express riders performed with that first run in April. Bringing the mail to California in ten days." She hadn't exactly read the newspaper article herself—Papa didn't think perusing the paper a worthy pastime for women—but he'd read the news out loud to her and Flynn over dinner one evening.

Myles shook his head. "That wasn't done by one Express rider. We ride a hundred miles or more along our assigned routes. Then we return with the eastbound mail a few days later to our starting point and do it all over again."

He shrugged off her hold. "We carry mail, Miss Radford, not passengers. Besides, I've heard talk that Indian trouble has likely closed parts of the Pony Express between Utah and California—some of the mail might not even be getting through. What would you do once you reached Salt Lake City?"

"I am aware of the situation and the dangers, Mr. Patton." She'd heard plenty of talk—first on the stagecoach and later on the train after she'd left her aunt's home in Saint Louis. "But I'm willing to pay you."

He harrumphed. "I doubt you've got enough to make it worth—"

"How's five hundred dollars?" She patted the front of her valise.

His eyebrows rose and a flicker of emotion skimmed across his features. Was it interest?

"I recognize the absurdity of my request," Delsie admitted. He needed to know she hadn't worked out this solution with no thought to the consequences. "But I'm willing to pay you five hundred dollars, if you'll help me get to California by the twenty-first of this month."

With her request out in the open, she pressed her lips together and waited for his response. *Please, Lord*, she prayed through the ensuing silence. *I know this may be a foolhardy venture, but surely Lillian is that important to You, and to me, to make this work.*

Myles blew out his breath. Was he relenting? "What's so important you gotta get to California for?"

A flush heated Delsie's cheeks. "I'd rather keep the reason to myself."

"Look, miss." He readjusted his hat, pushing it up and pulling it back down again. "If I'm going to attempt this, even for five hundred dollars, I need to know what I'm getting myself into."

"So you'll do it, then?"

"Didn't say that. What's your reason for going all that way, Miss Radford?"

Delsie heaved her own sigh. "It's for my sister."

Myles frowned. "Is she dying or something?"

"No." But there were things that would die if she failed to reach California in time—like Delsie's promise to her mother on her deathbed and the chance to restore the close relationship she'd once shared with her sister.

A whisper of sadness swept through her at the reminder of their sweet and gentle mother. Lillian and their father, Owen Radford, were far more impetuous and stubborn, more prone to harbor a grudge. For this reason Delsie's mother had made her promise to look after the other two in Lydia Radford's absence.

Delsie had diligently done so, smoothing things as best she could between her father and sister for the past six years. At least until Lillian had refused to marry the man their father had chosen for her and instead followed her farmer beau to California ten months ago. Delsie hadn't known where her sister had been living or if Lillie was even all right until she'd found the letters her father had hidden from her. Now the only way to keep her pledge to her mother was to go after Lillie herself.

"I know it may sound silly." Delsie tilted her chin to meet Myles's stern look. "But it's imperative I be at my sister's wedding on June twenty-second. If I'm not there, I will never see her again. She and her husband are bound for Oregon the following day and I don't know where they'll be living once they reach their destination." Gripping her valise tighter, she added in a clear voice, "I'm willing to risk whatever this journey may bring to be there and fulfill a promise I made a long time ago. Surely helping family is something you can understand."

The lines around his dark eyes tightened. "I don't have any family."

Compassion filled her, but she schooled her tongue, certain he didn't want her pity. This loneliness must be what Lillie felt, without family there in California, thinking Delsie had no desire to contact her.

"Why me?" Myles asked, jerking Delsie from thoughts of her sister.

"That other gentleman said you were the fastest—"

"No. Why have *me* take you the whole way? Why not ask a different Express rider at each home station? Pay each one?"

"Because convincing one man to help me is proving to be most difficult," Delsie quipped. The barest hint of a smile twitched at his masculine lips before he suppressed it. "I also don't want to end up in the middle of Nebraska with no one willing to help me move forward or back."

He folded his arms, stretching his shirt tighter and hinting at the sinewy muscles beneath. Delsie glanced away. She watched the toe of his boot kick at a dirt clod and resisted the urge to do the same. Would he refuse to help her? If he did, there'd be no hope for reaching Lillie by the twenty-second—she'd be gone forever, assuming Delsie wanted nothing to do with her.

At last, Myles emitted a low growl and lowered his arms to his sides.

"Here's what I'll do, Miss Radford. I'll take you with me on my route today." A rush of gratitude prompted Delsie to step forward, with the intent of reaching for his arm again, but she stopped when Myles held up a hand. "I expect to be paid twenty-five dollars when we reach Guittard's tonight. I'll decide then if I think we can go the rest of the way to California."

She nodded. "Thank you, Mr.—"

"I wouldn't thank me just yet." He pulled off his hat and ran a hand through his thick, black hair. "We have a hundred and twenty-five miles to ride, changing horses every ten to twelve. I can't deliver the mail fast enough if we ride together, so you'll have to ride your own horse."

"I know how to ride."

A glimmer of amusement flashed in his eyes as he replaced his hat on his head. "We'll see. Since the station owners know me, I think we can get you a fresh mount each time I get one. But it'll cost you a few dollars for the extra horse and we don't waste time at any of the stations. We're in and out in two minutes or less. The moment you start to slow me down, I'll drop you off at the next station and collect you when I return to Saint Joseph. Is that clear?"

The reality of what she was about to do pressed down on her, momentarily bringing doubt and a panicked throbbing to her pulse. Could she really do this? A hundred and twenty-five miles in one day sounded suddenly daunting—and she had eighteen hundred to go to reach California.

The memory of Lillie's tear-stained face as she'd ridden away from the house rose into Delsie's mind. This same image still haunted her dreams. Surely she could endure anything to help her sister and keep her promise to their mother.

"I'll keep up," she said, infusing the words with haughty confidence, even if she didn't feel it.

The merriment returned to Myles's gaze, though she wasn't sure if it meant he, too, doubted her abilities or if he found her show of bravery humorous. No matter, he'd agreed, at least for today's ride.

"In that case, Miss Radford," he said, doffing his hat and giving her a mocking smile, "let me be the first to welcome you to the Pony Express."

Myles had plenty of reasons to suspect Delsie Radford, determined as she was, would falter in her resolve to travel to California—and soon. She was the epitome of a wealthy young lady, with her fine clothes, spotless gloves and a bag containing more money than he could make in six months working for the Pony Express.

*Just like Cynthia.* Myles ground his teeth against the thought.

Sure enough, the first crack in Delsie's confident facade came the moment he led the horses out of the stable.

"You…um…don't have a sidesaddle, do you?" She eyed the trimmed-down saddles on the two horses.

"Nope." Myles walked toward her, his spurs clinking, his scabbard and revolvers bumping the legs of his decorative trousers. The morning sun glittered off the silver decorations adorning his uniform and his horse. He plucked at his collar with one hand, counting down the minutes until he could change out of the fancy getup. "We use these lighter 'California tree' saddles with the shorter, broader saddle horn. Not a sidesaddle in sight." He stopped the horses beside her. "Change your mind?"

He saw her visibly swallow, then a grim smile graced her mouth. "If you'd be so kind as to help me up, Mr. Patton."

Myles cocked an eyebrow. Did the girl possess more gumption than she first appeared to? He quickly dismissed the idea—all these rich girls were alike. She'd be lucky if she made it the fifteen miles to the Troy station, let alone the hundred and twenty-five to Guittard's home station by tonight.

Once he'd helped her sit astride her horse, Myles swung up onto his own. Delsie did her best to pull down the hem of her dress, but she couldn't quite hide her button-up shoes or the section of her lower calves clad in stockings that peeked above them. Myles jerked his gaze away.

"We'll ride to the office at the Patee House to collect the mail, then we'll—"

The blast of a cannon from the direction of the hotel silenced the rest of his words. It was time to go. He nudged his horse in the direction of the Patee House.

Glancing back over his shoulder, he made sure Delsie guided her mount behind his. The only telltale sign of her embarrassment at straddling the mare could be seen in the pink blush that stained her cheeks. But she kept her ridiculously flowered hat tilted high, even as they rode down the street past the few people out and about at this hour.

"Wait here," he told her when they reached the office. He swung down and went inside to collect the mail. "Morning," he called to the man at the counter.

"Morning, Patton. Here's the mail from back East." The man handed over the leather *mochila* or knapsack, which fit over the horse's saddle and contained the mail inside four padlocked boxes.

Myles grunted in response. If he hurried out, maybe the other fellow wouldn't notice Delsie outside. He figured the less he had to explain about his tagalong passenger, the better. He exited the office, the *mochila* in hand, but the other man followed him outside.

"Looks like a nice day for a—" The man's friendly remark died the moment his eyes caught sight of Delsie. "Morning, ma'am." He removed his hat. "Are you in need of directions?"

The color in her face increased as she shook her head. "No. I'm waiting for Mr. Patton."

Myles felt the man's gaze boring into his back as he placed the knapsack over his horse's saddle.

"Didn't know you had yourself a new girl, Patton..."

Myles scowled and mounted his horse again. "I don't," he bit off the words. "Let's go, Miss Radford." He swung the animal around. "We ride full out down the hill to the river. The ferry will be waiting."

Not stopping to see if she followed or not, he charged his horse forward. They tore through the street at a full gallop. The *boom* of the cannon sounded behind him, signaling to the ferry that he was coming. He and his mount raced down the hill. The wind tore at his face and hat, and he had to keep a hand on the brim to keep from losing it. A few passersby cheered as he rode past and he lifted his chin in greeting.

At the river, he jerked his horse to a stop. The beast danced with energy from the spirited ride. Myles twisted in the saddle to see Delsie gallop toward him. Just when he thought her mare would ram into him, she yanked back on the reins and stopped the animal. Her hat had slipped off her hair to hang down her back by its ribbons, but her blue eyes, the color of deep twilight, glittered.

"Do you always ride this fast?" she asked, her voice breathless.

"No. Only when we're being pursued by Indians." Myles climbed out of the saddle. "It's mostly for show—like my outfit here."

He went to help her dismount. As he placed his hands on her trim waist and assisted her to the ground, Delsie frowned, her eyebrows dipping toward her pert nose. Did she look down on him and his lowly station in life as Cynthia had? Myles pulled his hands away and practically dropped her onto her feet.

"I know you're trying to scare me, Mr. Patton," she said, bracing herself against the saddle.

He tipped his hat up. "Come again?"

"With your remark about Indians." She righted her own hat and tucked a few strands of hair back into the elaborate coil at the back of her neck. "I told you I am aware of the dangers, but I'm still intent on reaching my sister for her wedding on the twenty-second."

She knew of the dangers? Myles resisted the impulse to laugh at her naïveté. "Can't say I didn't warn you." He took the reins of his horse and started toward the waiting boat. "Come on. It's time to board the ferry."

Once the mounts were situated on the boat and it had pulled away from the bank, Myles excused himself.

"Where are you going?" Delsie asked, a note of alarm in her voice.

"I'm not up and leaving. Like I said, this uniform is only for show. We always change on the boat."

Her face relaxed, though he noticed lines of worry still pinched her eyes.

"You ever been on a boat before?"

She shook her head. If a short ferry crossing made her this nervous, how in the world did she expect to survive the next eighteen days? Myles battled the urge to ask the captain to take Delsie back to the Saint Joseph shore. He'd given his word to accompany her all the way to Guittard's, though, and he'd do it. Not only because his stepfather had ingrained in him the importance of integrity, but Myles had also sworn an oath as a rider to conduct himself honestly.

He ducked into the room the Express riders used for changing and traded the fancy uniform and scabbard for a trail-worn shirt and a buckskin jacket and trousers, though he kept his Colt revolvers. Despite loving Cynthia, he'd always loathed the idea of having to dress up if they married. He much preferred the ease and comfort of his riding clothes, and the absence of stiff collars and scratchy fabrics.

When he emerged from the changing room, he was surprised to find Delsie standing at the railing. Her gloved hands held the metal rail in a vise-like grip, but she stood there nonetheless, her face turned toward the western horizon.

"Is trying new things a first for you?" he couldn't help asking.

She glanced at him, without loosening her hold on the railing. "Is it that obvious?" Her lips curved into a crooked smile. "Lillian, my sister, was the adventurous one. I was more content to stay near the house or our governess. But eventually she would coax me to join her in some harebrained scheme, in which one or both of us ended up dirty or in tears."

A feeling of loneliness cut through Myles at the familial picture she presented. His parents had both died of illness before he turned five. He'd been taken in by his stepfather after that. Charles Patton had lost his wife and new baby a few months earlier. The man soon became the only father Myles could remember— so much so that he'd taken on Charles's last name as his own. His stepfather had taught him everything he knew about horses and had encouraged Myles's dream of owning a horse ranch one day. Even five years after his death, Myles still mourned the man and the loss of the only family he'd ever known.

He cleared his throat to ward off the emotion collecting there. "Does your sister know you're coming to her wedding?"

Delsie shook herself as though she'd been caught up in memories, as well. "No...she doesn't. I considered writing, but when I heard the mail wasn't necessarily getting through out West, I decided to go in person instead. I didn't want to risk a letter not reaching her in time."

"Suppose that makes sense."

The ferry bumped against the shoreline. Myles led his horse down the gangplank, Delsie and her mare following behind. "Welcome to Kansas," he said drily.

"What do we do now?" Delsie asked as he assisted her into the saddle again.

"We ride."

Myles climbed onto his horse and urged it forward, whistling for his sparrow hawk, Elijah. He'd let the bird fly off earlier, as was his custom, to collect some breakfast of its own. A few seconds later, the brown-and-blue hawk swooped over the wharf and landed on Myles's shoulder. The bird would remain there most of the trip, except when Myles changed horses at the different swing stations or when it felt more inclined to fly ahead.

"Is that your bird?" Delsie nudged the mare closer and eyed the hawk with obvious fascination.

"I found him, out on the prairie, if that's what you mean." He rubbed the speckled breast of the hawk. "He was hurt, so I brought him home and fixed him up."

"Does the bird have a name?"

"Elijah," Myles muttered.

"Elijah? That's an unusual name for a pet."

He frowned at her remark, not wishing to get into the particulars. "Pick up the pace, Miss Radford. We've got mail to deliver."

Without waiting to see if she complied or not, Myles urged his horse to move faster. A few people called out in greeting to him as he made his way swiftly through town. Myles tipped his hat in response. If anyone thought it strange that a woman, and a well-dressed one at that, dogged his heels, no one said so. He'd have enough explaining to do at the stations along the route today.

Once the people and buildings gave way to open prairie, Myles pushed his horse into the usual slow gallop. The sunshine had burned away the coolness of the early-morning air and now it glistened off the dewdrops dotting the grass. The clean, fresh smell of wind and prairie filled Myles's nostrils and he sucked in a deep breath, filling his lungs completely. Only out here, charging across the plains, did he feel at home, with the sky, the earth and Elijah for companions.

Of course he couldn't entirely forget the woman riding several feet behind him. He shot a look over his shoulder to ensure Delsie was keeping up. Her hands seemed to grip the reins as tightly as she had the boat railing, but her wide-eyed stare appeared to hold more interest than fear.

"It's so big…and wide," she called to his back. A few moments later her horse drew alongside his. "I'm from Pennsylvania, you see. It's very different than this. Are you from Missouri originally, Mr. Patton?"

"Yes."

"Have you ever been back East?"

"No."

"What's the farthest west you've been?"

"Nebraska."

He eyed her with mounting irritation. Did she plan to talk the entire one hundred and twenty-five miles to Guittard's? He wasn't accustomed to hearing much but the thud of the horse's hooves beneath him and the occasional trill of birds in the distance. Elijah watched her, too, his head cocked to the side as though trying to figure out the strange creature tagging along with them today.

"How far is it to the first station?"

Was she already uncomfortable? He stifled a groan. She rode well enough, despite the absence of a side-saddle. "The Troy station is about fifteen miles from Saint Joseph," he answered. "It's at the Smith Hotel. We'll change horses there and head on to the hotel in Syracuse."

A smile quirked her lips, though she tried to hide it. Myles got the instinct impression she was laughing at him. "Something funny?"

She shook her head, but her deep blue eyes danced in a way that belied the gesture.

He raised his eyebrows in silent question.

"I was only thinking that was the longest speech I've heard from you since we started riding." She drew herself up in the saddle and glanced away at the distant trees. "I was beginning to think you couldn't sit a horse and talk at the same time."

Myles watched her shoulders rise with stifled laughter, bringing a low growl from his throat. This only added to her fit of merriment. He scowled at her hat. What had he gotten himself into by agreeing to bring her along?

"I'm sorry," she said, turning to face him again. "That was…unkind."

"Not at all." He feigned a forgiving smile. "If we could all talk a streak like you, Miss Radford, news would travel even faster than the Pony Express."

Her mouth fell slightly open and her eyes narrowed. Myles tried to maintain a deadpan expression, but he couldn't hold back his chuckle for long. If she could dish out the sarcasm, she could certainly learn to swallow some herself.

With another chuckle, he pulled his horse ahead, relishing the pounding of the hooves against the prairie sod and the blessed sound of quiet from behind.

# Chapter Two

The Smith Hotel, in Troy, Kansas, appeared ahead. Myles rode straight to its large barn and jumped to the ground. One man held the reins of his next horse, while another yanked the *mochila* from the saddle to throw it over the new one.

"I need a second horse," Myles explained as Delsie stopped her mare beside them. The two men gaped openly at her.

The man holding the new horse's reins recovered first. "What's wrong with this one, Patton?"

Myles hurried over to help Delsie dismount. "Nothing. But I need another horse—for the lady here." When the man shot Myles a bewildered look, he added, "I'll explain later, Rogers. Just get us another horse. She'll pay to ride it."

Thankfully, the man brooked no more complaint and raced into the barn to collect the second horse. Myles climbed into the saddle again, turning an expectant gaze on the hotel. Right on cue, a young lady exited the building and ran toward him. In each hand she held one of the fried pastries the Troy station was known for.

"Thank you," Myles said, accepting the treats. He immediately handed one down to Delsie, then bit off a bite of the chewy, sweet dough. "Delicious," he murmured.

Delsie sniffed at the pastry, then took a delicate bite. Myles rolled his eyes at her prim manners. Did she honestly think she could make it across half the country when she couldn't even— The unfinished question died within his mind as he watched the fried treat disappear between her lips in less than a minute.

A startled laugh escaped his mouth. If Delsie heard it, she didn't react. She simply stood there waiting for Rogers, looking as imperial and composed as a duchess, as if she hadn't just devoured her pastry in two bites.

*Well, I'll be*, Myles thought with a rueful shake of his head. She'd clearly been starving, though she hadn't let on one bit. He glanced at his own half-eaten pastry and extended it toward her.

"No, thank you," she responded politely, though she wouldn't quite meet his gaze as she sipped water from the canteen one of the riders had found for her.

At that moment, Rogers led her new horse out of the barn. Delsie handed him a few dollars before he helped her into the saddle. Myles kneed his horse forward and they were off again.

The next four relay stations brought more of the same routine, minus the pastries. He'd ride in first, tell the men he needed a second horse, then he'd wait while they gawked a few seconds at Delsie before scrambling to collect and saddle another mount. Delsie seemed to take it all in stride, paying for the horses and climbing back into the saddle each time without hesitation and even offering courteous smiles to the other Express workers.

When they reached their fifth station, though, Myles could see she was beginning to wilt like a flower in the height of summer. Once astride her new horse, she paused and squeezed her eyes shut. He knew from his first few Express runs the discomfort of being in a saddle for so long. But it couldn't be helped—not if he was to deliver the mail on time and not if she planned to ride this way from here to California.

Elijah left his shoulder to go hunt for a mouse or a smaller bird, reminding Myles of the hardtack he kept in his jacket. The Troy pastries and the promise of a full meal at Guittard's was sufficient food for himself, but he imagined Delsie wasn't used to such a long day with so little to eat.

With the ease of practice, he managed to remove the hardtack without slowing his horse. "Hungry?"

Delsie took a long moment to answer, her hand rubbing at the back of her neck. She'd been doing that more and more the past two hours. "Yes…thank you." She took the piece of hardtack he handed her, and without hesitation or inquiry as to what it was, she bit into it.

After she'd finished off that piece, he extended the other to her. "Aren't you hungry?" she asked, her gaze moving from his hand to his face. He couldn't recall ever seeing another woman with such dark blue eyes.

They were nearly black, like her hair, but still blue enough to add contrast.

"I don't usually eat much till I get to Guittard's. This is just for emergencies."

"If you're sure…"

When he nodded, she took the rest of the biscuit from him. Again, she lifted her hand to rub at her neck as she ate. She had to be sweating bullets in the thick fabric of her high-collared dress, and her silly hat barely shaded her eyes.

Myles reached for his canteen, an idea forming. "You got a handkerchief with you?"

Delsie reached into one sleeve and removed a white piece of cloth. "Yes, why?"

"Can I see it?"

She studied him quizzically, then handed him the handkerchief. Leaning slightly to the side, Myles poured a little water from the canteen onto the cloth and squeezed out some of the excess.

"Try putting this around your neck. It oughta help keep you cool." He pressed the damp cloth into her gloved hand.

Delsie obeyed, draping the wet handkerchief against the exposed skin at the base of her neck. An audible sigh of contentment reached his ears and her eyes fell shut. "That feels…wonderful."

Myles allowed himself a smile at her obvious relief, especially since she couldn't see him. "You're welcome."

She opened her eyes to look at him. "Thank you." The words were quiet and genuine, reminding him of the woman herself. At least when she wasn't talking a mile a minute. To her credit, though, she'd spoken very little the past few hours, only breaking the silence between them with an occasional question about the landscape or the next relay station.

"How far have we come?" she asked, looking around them at the rolling prairie. The sunshine had held and the blue sky arched bright and cloudless overhead.

"When we reach Seneca in a few more hours, we'll have come eighty miles from Saint Joseph."

"So we'll have forty-five more to go after that?"

He tipped his head in agreement, impressed with her quick figuring.

"Does that mean you aren't going to leave me behind, then?" Her words were coated with as much teasing as they were challenge.

Myles cut her a look before facing forward again with a grin. "We'll see, Miss Radford. We'll see."


"That's Guittard's Station there."

Myles's words took a moment to penetrate past the fog inside Delsie's mind caused by the endless riding and movement and pain. She lifted her chin from where it drooped nearly to her chest. Ahead of them in the evening sun, past the woods and creek, she spied a two-story wooden structure with a front porch and plenty of windows flanking its sides. A large barn was also visible. While the place might appear rustic standing beside the ornate hotels back East or her own brick house back in Pennsylvania, Delsie couldn't recall a more welcomed sight. Her first day on the trail was finally at an end.

They rode to the stable, where Myles dismounted first before coming to assist her. She was too exhausted in mind and body to pay much heed to the open stares from the other Express workers who'd come to collect the horses. She'd grown accustomed to the surprised looks or words exchanged at each station along the route when the men discovered her riding beside Myles and on a Pony Express horse, no less.

Myles lifted her to the ground, but when he released her waist, Delsie found her legs would no longer support her. Her knees crumbled beneath her riding habit, and she would have fallen onto the hard-packed dirt if Myles hadn't gripped her arm.

"Careful," he murmured, his voice surprisingly gentle. "You're likely a little stiff by now."

*Stiff?* She gave an unladylike snort. The single word didn't even begin to explain what she felt at the moment. Somewhere back on the trail, the throbbing ache in her back and legs had finally numbed, bringing temporary relief. But as she hazarded a step, with Myles still holding on to her elbow, sharp prickles of pain lanced through her lower body. She almost preferred the numbness.

Delsie bit her lip to keep from crying out as she hobbled next to Myles—she didn't want the triumph of the day marred by complaint. But, oh, how she longed for her bed at home, with its laundered sheets and feather-soft mattress.

"Myles!" An older man approached them from the direction of the house. A gray beard and a friendly smile graced his weather-beaten face. His blue-gray

eyes widened when he noticed Delsie limping alongside the Express rider. "Who's this young lady?"

Myles stopped walking, forcing Delsie to follow
suit. She didn't think she could manage a single step
on her own just yet. "Good to see you, Amos. This is
Delsie Radford." He motioned to the other man with
his free hand. "Miss Radford, meet Hank Amos. Express worker, avid explorer and accomplished harmonica player."

Hank Amos chuckled and extended his hand.
"Guilty as charged. Pleased to meet you, Miss Rad
ford."

Delsie shook his hand. "Nice to meet you, too, Mr.
Amos."

His laughter deepened. "Not to contradict a lady,
Miss Radford, but call me Amos. Everybody does."
He glanced at the sky. "Elijah off hunting?" he asked.

Myles nodded. "He flew off before we rode in."

Amos considered Delsie, his gaze lingering on the
spot where Myles still held her arm. "What brings you
West…with Mr. Patton?"

Myles released Delsie's elbow at once and took a
deliberate step to the side. She swayed a moment, but
her feet held firm. "I promised to escort her to Guittard's today."

Delsie threw him a questioning glance, but he
wasn't looking at her. He'd told her he would consider
tonight whether to take her the rest of the way to California. She hoped he hadn't already made up his mind.
While she felt nigh unto death, she'd certainly kept
up her end of the bargain by not slowing him down.

"Are you catching the stage from here, Miss Radford?"

"No. We're actually going—"

"To be late for dinner," Myles interjected. "Let's get you some real food, Miss Radford." With that, he clutched her elbow again and led her at a trot toward the house.

Delsie frowned up at him. Did he really care that much about her well-being? He had offered her his hardtack hours ago and helped her cool down with his wet-handkerchief trick. But something about his thoughtfulness right now struck her as false. Why hadn't he let her tell his friend about her plans? She opened her mouth to ask him, but the words were forgotten the instant she inhaled the tantalizing smell of cooked ham and rolls floating from the house.

Her stomach grumbled in response, resurrecting the gnawing sensation she'd felt for hours. She placed a hand over her middle to squelch it. "That smells absolutely scrumptious," she muttered, though not softly enough.

Amos gave another throaty chuckle. "Tastes even better."

"I think if shoe leather smelled that wonderful, I'd eat my fill and die perfectly happy."

There was a low rumbling that sounded in her right ear, not unlike distant thunder but more jovial. It took Delsie several seconds to realize the noise came from Myles—he was laughing at her remark.

Though she knew it shouldn't, the sound of his laughter and the knowledge she'd solicited it filled her with momentary pleasure. Her father would be displeased at her errant thought. She was supposed to be deciding if she loved Flynn Coppell, the man who managed her father's bank, not entertaining ideas of how to make some other man laugh once more. Of course what she was or wasn't thinking would likely be the least cause for worry, if Owen Radford could see her now. Alone in Kansas, having ridden one hundred and twenty-five miles with a man she'd never met before this morning.

Myles steered her toward the back entrance. Inside the kitchen, Delsie found herself seated at a large wooden table beside Myles and across from Amos. Her backside instantly protested the return to a seated position, especially on the uncushioned seat, but Delsie chose to be grateful that neither the chair nor the table would be moving any time soon.

They were served ham, eggs, rolls and coffee by the station owner's wife, who, upon discovering another woman in her kitchen, made a motherly fuss over Delsie. Uncertain why Myles wanted to keep quiet about her plans, she answered the woman's questions, and those from the other Express workers as they trailed in, with the simple explanation that she was going to visit her sister in California.

Delsie ate everything on her plate and even accepted seconds of the ham and eggs. Her father would have been horrified by her ferocious appetite, but he'd never ridden so far in a single day.

Though she longed to sequester herself in a room upstairs and wash away the dust from the day's ride, she lingered at the table, listening to the Express riders' stories. The tales they told of dodging Indian arrows, riding through thunderstorms or racing buffalo across the prairie sent tremors of fear and excitement up her spine. Would she encounter all these experiences herself? The conversation soon turned to the Indian troubles farther west and the speculation on how the other Express stations and riders were faring.

"Come, now, boys," the station owner's wife gently scolded in her slight French accent as she refilled the coffee mugs. "No more of that kind of talk." She tipped her head at Delsie. "Especially in the presence of a lady."

Delsie scooted her chair back and stood. "That's all right, Mrs. Guittard. I believe I shall retire for the night. Thank you for the delicious dinner. I can honestly say it was better than anything I've eaten back home in Pennsylvania."

The woman blushed at the compliment. "I'll show you to your room, Miss Radford."

Delsie glanced at Myles, as did everyone else in the room, but he was gazing into his coffee cup. "I just need to locate my valise first…"

Myles scraped back his chair. "I'll get it."

After bidding the rest of the workers good-night, she followed Mrs. Guittard up the stairs to a large and tidy bedroom. "I'll get you some water to wash up." She exited the room, pulling the door shut behind her.

Delsie unpinned her hat and set it on the bureau. The mirror revealed a stretch of pink across her nose and upper cheeks. She touched the sunburned flesh with a sigh. *Oh well.* She'd likely only get browner as the days went by.

*All for you, Lillie*, she thought ruefully as she went

to peer out the window. She pushed back the curtains and spied Myles talking with Amos near the barn. He shook his head at something the older man said, then removed his hat and ran a hand through his dark hair. His entire manner breathed agitation. Were they talking about her?

As if they sensed her watching, they both glanced at the house. She jumped back and let the curtain fall into place. A knock at the door alerted her that Mrs. Guittard had returned with the promised water. Delsie let her in and the woman emptied the pitcher she carried into the basin on the bureau.

"There you go, my dear. Let me know if you need anything else." She crossed to the door, where she paused. "Will you be leaving early?"

"I believe so…" Delsie wished Myles had been more forthcoming about what to expect for the second day of their journey, but either way, she imagined they would be departing as early as they had today.

Once Mrs. Guittard left her, Delsie unwound her hair and released the top button of her collar. The simple act brought instant relief to her tender head and flushed neck. With the aid of a small towel, she bathed her face and hairline.

She was so caught up in the luxurious feel of the cool water against her heated skin that she yelped in surprise when someone pounded on her door. After dropping the towel into the basin, she threw open the door and found Myles standing there, her valise in one hand and his hat in the other.

"I brought you your…" His gaze shifted from the floorboards to her face and his eyes rounded in shock.

Belatedly she remembered her unbound hair and loose collar.

Fresh heat burned her face as Delsie brought her hand up to cover her exposed throat. "Yes, my bag. Thank you." She plucked it from his grip, prepared to retreat in mortification, but he didn't make a move to leave. "Is there something else you needed, Mr. Patton?"

He shifted his weight from boot to boot. "Well, you see—"

"Oh, your money," she finished for him. She lowered her hand to open her valise. "I believe we agreed upon twenty-five dollars…"

His hand closed over hers before she could locate the cash. The gentle, almost caring, touch felt different than the times he'd helped her on and off the Express horses today and succeeded in derailing her thoughts. A strange flurry of sensation churned inside her, similar to what she'd felt on the ferry ride that morning.

"I don't want your money, Miss Radford."

"You don't?" The color of his eyes reminded her of warm, liquid chocolate, the kind she liked to sneak from the kitchen and drink in her room after her father was asleep. Myles released her hand, bringing clarity back to her muddled mind. "B-but I promised to pay you for today."

"Look." He ran a hand through his disheveled hair, mussing it more. "You did…pretty well today, Miss Radford."

*Pretty well?* She cocked an eyebrow at him in defense. How many women did he know who could keep up with an Express rider for a hundred and twenty-five miles?

His lips twitched when he caught her look. "All right. I can give credit where it's due." He blew out his breath. "You rode as well as…as well as a new Express rider might."

It was Delsie's turn to hide a smile. "Seeing as you are a man of few words, Mr. Patton, I'll take that remark as a compliment."

"As you should." The merriment in his dark eyes faded and his expression returned to one of complete somberness. "That being said, I think this is a fool's errand." She started to protest, but he held up his hand to stop her. "Let me finish. Whether it's plain crazy or admirable that you want to be at your sister's wedding on the twenty-second, it can't be done."

Spikes of alarm shot through her. "But what about today?"

"Today was different." He jammed his hat on his head and began to pace the hall in front of her door, his boots clomping against the floorboards. "I know these station owners. But that ends tomorrow. No one past Guittard's knows me. You'll have to pay—possibly double what you did today—to take a horse at every station. Two horses." He held up two fingers as if she didn't remember. "And another thing. Like I told you before, I've never been farther west than Nebraska. I don't know the terrain, the stations or the dangers beyond that."

Myles stopped pacing to face her directly. "The time it would take to learn all of that, to convince these station owners to lend you their Express horses…"

The dread that had tightened her stomach when he'd first begun his little speech grew worse, even before he half whispered his next words. "You won't make it to California when you need to."

"I… I have to." She clutched the valise to her chest, hoping to stop the panic rising into her throat and spilling over into tears. "There must be a way."

He shook his head, his look bordering on compassion. "Even if you rummaged up a guide and a couple of horses, the poor beasts wouldn't make it that far that fast. It's impossible. That's why we change out animals every ten to twelve miles. Besides, the supplies you'd need to strike out on your own would weigh the horses down too much."

The need to cry was growing stronger, the sting of tears forcing Delsie to blink. Had she left behind everything familiar, in order to reach Lillie, only to be turned back now?

"I'm sorry, Miss Radford." For once his voice held nothing but kindness. "If you'd like, we'll take it slow heading back to Saint Joe tomorrow."

"What I'd like is to go to California," she whispered, but she knew he heard her by the way he glanced at the floor again.

"Good night." He lifted his gaze to hers and held it for a moment. Though he didn't say it, Delsie sensed he, too, had experienced the bitter disappointment of having a dream ripped from one's grasp. "I'll see you at breakfast."

She gave a wordless nod and stepped back to shut the door. Alone once more, she sank onto the neatly made bed, her valise still crushed in her arms. She'd

never felt such fatigue, such despair. Every muscle in
her wearied body seemed to echo Myles's sentiment,
*It can't be done.* The first of her tears skidded down
her cheeks. In seventeen more days, her sister would
be lost to her forever and her promise to their mother
would be broken. There was nothing she could do to
change either one.

Unable to hold back the sobs any longer, Delsie
dropped onto the bed and buried her head in the pillow
to muffle the sound. She'd managed this first part of
her journey without crying once, despite the new and
somewhat terrifying things she'd experienced since
leaving her aunt's house.

Aunt Cissy had assumed Delsie was returning
straight to Pennsylvania, after her two-week stay in
Saint Louis, and Delsie hadn't bothered to correct
her. She'd been so full of optimism once she'd con-
cocted her plan to go to Lillie, just as she had today
when she'd convinced Myles to take her with him.
But now… The failure tasted worse than the hardtack
she'd stomached earlier.

Twisting onto her side, she stared at the room's nice
furnishings, not so different from the opulence she
was accustomed to at home. What sort of room did
Lillie live in? Did she enjoy being on her own as she'd
claimed to in the letters Delsie had discovered?

Her eyes narrowed in on the book lying on top of
the low table beside the bed. Delsie released her bag to
the floor and sat up. She pulled the book onto her lap.
Her own Bible would've weighed her luggage down
too much, so she hadn't brought it, but she was grateful to find one here.

She flipped aimlessly through the pages, wondering where to read, where to find solace. At her aunt's house, she'd been working her way through Hebrews. Delsie turned there now and located the last place she recalled reading. She began in chapter 10, but her mind was as much on her predicament as it was on the words before her. Until she reached verses thirty-five and thirty-six.

Cast not away therefore your confidence, which hath great recompence of reward. For ye have need of patience, that, after ye have done the will of God, ye might receive the promise.

A feeling of warmth began near her heart and spread all the way to her tired fingers and toes as she reread the two verses. She'd felt that confidence from the moment she'd decided to go to Lillie and at every step up to now. Why should she doubt, then? If God wanted her to be in California before the twenty-second—and everything inside her said He did—then she had to trust and be patient that He would make that possible. That she would receive the promise, the reward, of fulfilling their dying mother's wishes and reuniting with Lillie before it was too late.

Delsie set the Bible on the bed and stood to pace the room, her arms tucked tight against her. Myles thought it impossible to either procure horses at every station or to travel with their own for so long. But was there a third solution they'd overlooked? One obvious to the Lord?

"Please help me see it, too," she prayed in a soft voice.

Calculations appeared in her mind's eye like figures on a chalkboard, the way they always did—the number of miles they had to go, the number of miles a horse could reasonably trot before needing to rest. She dug through her valise to find a pencil and Lillie's last letter. Using the back of one of the pages, Delsie wrote down the numbers in her head. She began playing with them, organizing them, rearranging them.

And then she saw it—the answer—as plain as day and as clear as the sky had been earlier. So simple and yet so hidden until this moment. A ripple of excitement and gratitude ran through her. *Thank You, Lord.* One problem solved. Now she only needed a guide and three horses.

She left the paper on her bed and crossed to the window again. The yard sat empty, though light from the open doors of the stable attested to someone's presence. Weariness had certainly affected her mind when she and Myles had ridden up earlier, but Delsie thought she recalled seeing a number of filled stalls inside the barn. Would the Guittards allow her to purchase three of their horses?

A figure exited the stable. It was Amos. As Delsie watched, the man lifted his arm and whistled, his eyes toward the western sky. Elijah soon appeared and swooped down to settle onto Amos's arm. She hadn't seen the bird come to anyone else all day, except Myles. Clearly the creature saw something in both men that others might not.

What was it Myles had said about his friend? *Ex-*

*press worker, avid explorer and accomplished har-monica player.* Was it possible Amos knew the terrain beyond Nebraska?

Delsie studied the man's face as he gently ran his finger over the feathers on Elijah's head. Though she knew next to nothing about him, she instinctively sensed kindness within him, as the hawk obviously did. Just as she'd sensed integrity and honor within Myles, despite all his gruffness and sarcasm. Would the old man agree to join them? Would Myles be willing to split his money from her if Amos came along, too? There was only one way to find out.

Determination welled inside Delsie and she spun away from the window. She quickly did up her collar and arranged her hair in a hasty twist at the nape of her neck. There'd be enough time later on to finish washing and dressing for bed. Right now, she needed to corner Amos and present him with her new plan before Myles came to collect his bird.

She slipped into the hallway, down the stairs and out the front door without encountering anyone. As she stole around the side of the house, her eyes went to the streaks of pink and orange smearing the darkening sky overhead. The same sun was setting over Lillie. Delsie smiled at the thought. The assurance she'd felt earlier while reading once again filled her heart. Tomorrow she'd be back on her way to California and to her sister—she just knew it.

*Let the West do its worst*, she mused. She had Someone far greater on her side than all the Express riders and horses and hazards from here to the coast.

# Chapter Three

Myles pushed his eggs around his plate, his appetite not its usual hearty self. Sleep had eluded him for several hours last night, as it had after Cynthia's betrayal two months earlier. He kept thinking of Delsie's soulful eyes filled with disappointment and grief when he'd conveyed the impossibility of her plans. She was clearly disheartened, but she hadn't raged at him or laid blame at his feet as he might've been tempted to do.

Her quiet acceptance of defeat wasn't the only thing that had kept him awake. He'd had a difficult time erasing the image of her unbound hair and cream-colored skin from his memory, too.

*So she's pretty*, Myles thought, scowling at his half-eaten breakfast. *Any man would say the same.*

Not for the first time since meeting Delsie the day before, he felt some relief at the knowledge that they would be parting company very, very soon. She kept surprising him, acting in ways that contradicted his opinions about rich folk, and he didn't like it one bit.

He liked routine, consistency and taking risks only when he knew for certain what the outcome would be.

Funny that she'd all but admitted to being the same way on the boat yesterday. Except this harebrained scheme of hers clearly meant she'd thrown her normal caution out the window.

"Thank you for the breakfast, Mrs. Guittard." He stood, hoping she didn't take offense to him not finishing everything.

The woman smiled. "You're welcome, Mr. Patton."

Myles glanced at the kitchen doorway. "Should I let Miss Radford know it's time to eat?"

"She's already had her breakfast."

"Oh." He'd suspected she would sleep in, especially knowing how sore she'd be today.

"I believe she's in the stables," Mrs. Guittard added over her shoulder from where she was working over a pot of something at the stove.

Myles put on his hat and let himself out the back door. Apparently Delsie was as anxious to get back to Saint Joseph as he was. The thought erased some of his guilt over frustrating her plans, however unintentionally.

Good thing he hadn't let Amos in on her notion to reach California before the twenty-second—the man would have tried to make it work, no matter the foolhardiness of the venture. Amos hated to see a woman in distress. Myles suspected it was the fatherly nature in him, one he hadn't been able to practice on with his own children. Amos and his wife, who had passed away seven years earlier, had remained childless, despite a strong desire for a family.

The lightening sky overhead promised to be as clear and blue as the day before. The sight brought a whistle to Myles's lips, a tune he'd heard Amos play plenty of times on the harmonica. Elijah swooped down over the stable roof and landed on his shoulder.

"You get breakfast, boy?" He ran his hand over the bird's head, his gaze on the western horizon.

For one brief moment, he considered what it would've been like to travel farther than he'd ever been, all the way to California. His stepfather used to tell him a place like that, so far west, would have enough room for a horse ranch.

*Someday.*

Myles turned toward the stables. It was time to return to Saint Joseph and his current life. The longer he stayed with the Pony Express, the more money he'd make—money he could use to purchase that sprawling horse ranch in the future. Now that Cynthia no longer wanted to marry him, the ranch was his only dream and focus. It was the reason he'd considered Delsie's proposal to take her to California in the first place. But he'd just have to be content with earning the money slow and steady instead.

The whistle returned to his lips as he entered the nearest stable. Inside Delsie stood talking quietly to Amos, but she closed her mouth the moment Myles walked up. She had on a different dress than yesterday, her hair pinned up again beneath her ridiculous flowered hat. He looked past them and spied one, two... *three?*...saddled horses. His merry tune ended on a sour note. Something was afoot.

"You planning a trip to Saint Joe?" he asked Amos

with an attitude of nonchalance, despite the wariness churning inside him. Delsie avoided his gaze.

"Nope," Amos answered. The glitter in the man's blue-gray eyes only heightened Myles's suspicion.

"What's with the third horse, then?"

"Can't very well walk to California, can we?"

*We?* Myles scowled at Delsie's bent head. Sure enough she'd convinced Amos to go along with her wild scheme, just as he'd feared last night. Well, he'd put a stop to all this nonsense right now. "Miss Radford, we talked about this last night. It can't be done."

"But you said if we had our own horses—"

Myles tightened his jaw in exasperation. Had the woman heard the rest of his explanation? "I said even *if* we had our own horses, it still wouldn't work. They can't go fast enough."

"Not necessarily. I've figured out—"

"The supplies you'd need to travel that far will weigh them down. At that slow pace you wouldn't reach California until—"

"Myles?" Amos said, quietly but firmly.

"What?" he growled. Elijah ruffled his wings as if startled.

"Let the lady finish. She's come up with a plan that might work."

Myles took a moment to swallow back his irritation, then through ground teeth he managed to ask, "What do you propose, Miss Radford?"

Delsie glanced between him and Amos and back to him before her chin rose a notch. "I calculated everything out last night." She lifted her hand and showed him a piece of paper with numbers scrawled all over the back of it. "We can average a hundred miles a day, if we rest the horses for an hour about every fifteen miles. If we start at six in the morning, we could reach one of the Express stations, at that pace, by eight o'clock that evening."

"And supplies?" he countered, mostly in an attempt to hide how impressed he was with her calculations. Clearly Delsie Radford was more than a pretty face with a sudden penchant for adventure. She'd managed to come up with a fairly logical plan…so far.

"Instead of paying to use the stations' horses, I'll pay them for room and board and feed for the animals for the single night we stay there."

Myles scrubbed a hand over the stubble on his face. He hadn't bothered to trim his beard this morning in his anticipation of getting Delsie back to Missouri. "What about water or feed for the horses during breaks?"

Delsie slid a glance at Amos. "That's where Mr.…I mean, Amos comes in. He's familiar with the route. He knows most of the rivers and creeks along the way, as well as the Express stations."

A sardonic laugh nearly escaped Myles's lips. She'd clearly thought of everything, the little conspirator. While he'd lain in his bed awake last night, feeling guilty as he'd imagined her heartbroken and weeping in her room upstairs, Delsie had actually been scheming behind his back. And doing a decent job of it as evidenced by her clever equations and her solicitation of Amos's help as a guide.

"What do you need me for, then?" He crossed his arms over his chest as a feeling he couldn't quite name settled there, tight and uncomfortable. It reminded him of the taunts he'd experienced as a child at school, about being an orphan, about how Charles wasn't his real pa. He'd quit going at age ten.

"Because I promised to pay you first..." Myles frowned, ready to argue with her. While the money would be nice, even if he got less than she'd originally offered after she paid the station owners and Amos, he wouldn't be pitied. "And because you know the most about horses," she added before he could protest. "Amos told me you worked for years at a livery stable. You know better than either of us when to rest the animals, when to push them. So you see, I need you..."

An attractive blush stained her cheeks at her words. The image of her long hair and exposed collarbone from last night entered Myles's mind again. "What I mean is *we* need you. Me, Amos and my sister."

Myles blew out his breath and absently rubbed Elijah's feathers. Did he still want to help her? A good portion of him preferred climbing into the saddle and heading east, never to see Miss Delsie Radford again. But the other part of him, growing more insistent the longer the silence stretched between them, wanted to see if she—if they—could really do this.

Could they reach California in seventeen more days? The challenge, and the chance to earn more money for his future ranch, was as alluring as the woman watching him with those dark blue eyes. Eyes framed with long lashes, above a slightly pink nose. If anything the sunburn only added to her beauty.

*Careful, Myles*, he warned himself.

He'd fallen for a pretty face once before, only to

be spurned. Clever and attractive as Delsie might be, Myles knew all too well the impossibility of their two worlds ever coexisting. It had been that way with Cynthia and it would be no different with any other spoiled rich girl who came along.

"All right, Miss Radford. I'll send word to Saint Joe that I'll be gone for a few weeks. But mind you, if I lose my job over this, I'll hunt you down and demand more money." He regarded her with a level look. "Got it?"

A slight smile toyed with her mouth. "Yes, Mr. Patton."

He tugged his hat lower onto his head. "What do you want to do now?"

"Now," she said, smiling fully, "we ride."

If she'd thought she was sore after her first day of riding more than a hundred miles, Delsie knew better now. Nothing could compare to the pain and stiffness of a second day in the saddle. Her limbs felt as heavy as logs and as hard and unyielding as granite. Every rise and fall of the prairie ground seemed to radiate from her mare's hooves up through her back and all the way to her stiff neck. Sheer determination, coupled with the constant memory of her sister's tearstained face on the day Lillie had left, kept her from begging Myles and Amos to turn around.

Their pace nearly matched that of yesterday's, except for the rests that, according to Amos's fancy pocket watch and Myles's knowledge of horses, they were taking every hour and a half. Even Amos, riding behind her, didn't look the least bit uncomfortable, though he had to be in his early fifties. Perhaps by the time they reached her sister, Delsie would be just as seasoned on a horse.

She shifted in the saddle, hoping to find a position that didn't chafe her legs or add to her pain. Up ahead, Myles remained silent and alert as he had the day before, his bird perched on his shoulder. Delsie had fully expected him to refuse to accompany her any farther, despite her new and improved plan. But then he'd surprised her by agreeing.

*Why is he really here?* she wondered, not for the first time since they'd set out. Why hadn't Myles left her and Amos to fend for themselves?

Amos had told her his reasons for coming—the promise of adventure and a soft spot for helping women. She'd found herself telling him more about her sister, and why she had to reach her, than she'd confessed to Myles. Not that she trusted Amos more. But the older man seemed to grasp—and appreciate—her willingness to face whatever obstacles to help Lillie and her family by keeping her promise. It was something she sensed Myles didn't quite understand. Delsie could still visualize his hardened expression when he'd declared he had no family. The memory filled her with the same measure of sadness his words had on the boat.

Was it this pain and loneliness that made him hide behind a mask of curtness and annoyance? For it surely was a mask. She'd seen a glimpse here and there in the past twenty-four hours of a different man. One who possessed integrity and determination but also kindness and compassion. At other times, though, she could almost believe she'd imagined this different side to Myles. He hadn't spoken more than a handful of words to her since they'd begun riding. If he disliked her company so, why wasn't he headed straight back to Missouri?

With an amused sniff, she realized her questions had come full circle again.

"The horses need to stop soon," Myles called over his shoulder.

"Let's rest by those trees there," Amos answered.

In the distance Delsie spied a patch of trees alongside the river they'd been riding beside—according to Amos it was called the Little Blue. She sighed with relief at the thought of a rest. Perhaps some walking would ease the continued agony of riding.

Amos drew alongside her and examined his pocket watch. Shaking his head, he grinned. "Look at that. An hour and a half almost to the minute. The man's got a way with horses."

*Just not with people.* She instantly regretted the unkind thought. "How long have you known Mr. Patton, Amos?"

The older man squinted up at the blue sky. "Let's see, it's been about seven years now. Right after my wife died, God rest her soul."

"I'm sorry...about your wife. Did you have any children?"

"No." A wistful look passed over his weathered face. "Not for wanting, that's for sure. We hoped and prayed for a family, but we came to realize that God had other plans." His gaze traveled from her to Myles. "Myles is the closest thing I have to family now. He's the one who encouraged me to hire on with the Pony Express, despite my being up there in years—as he likes to remind me." His mouth curved up in a broad smile.

Delsie rubbed at the back of her neck. As soon as they stopped, she'd wet her handkerchief, as Myles had done yesterday, to help prevent a sunburn. The longer she rode, the more she realized the impracticality of her stylish riding hat. Maybe she could trade it some-where for a wide-brimmed one like the two men wore.

"Has he always been…um…" She searched for the right word.

"Hard-edged?" Amos supplied with a chuckle.

She bit back a smile and nodded.

"No, he hasn't." Amos wiped at his brow with his sleeve, then tugged his hat lower. "His folks died when he was real young, but he was raised by a good and godly man—his stepfather, Charles Patton. Myles took his stepfather's death pretty hard." He glanced at Del-sie. She'd told him last night about her mother dying when she was thirteen. "But things really turned bad for him two months ago when his girl, this rich young lady from Saint Joe, refused to marry him after string-ing him along for six years."

Delsie turned her attention to the man in front of them, riding tall and straight in his saddle. What had the man at the hotel in Saint Joseph said yesterday? *Didn't know you had yourself a new girl, Patton.* No wonder Myles had looked ready to pummel him.

Would Flynn feel the same, angry and bitter, if she returned home and told him she couldn't marry him? She couldn't picture him acting that way, but then again, did Flynn truly love her as it seemed Myles had this wealthy woman?

Flynn had told her she was the most beautiful woman in the world and would make him the happiest man alive she if agreed to marry him. But was it her that he truly looked forward to having or was it her inheritance? She'd been asking herself that question ever since she'd left Pennsylvania to visit Aunt Cissy in Saint Louis.

Now that Lillie had been struck from their father's will, Delsie stood to gain a great deal of money. Some she would inherit when she married, the rest she would receive upon her father's death, and Flynn knew the particulars. Despite her father's encouragement of the match, the thought that Flynn might be more interested in her wealth than in Delsie herself brought a mixture of unease and confusion to her stomach.

When they reached the trees Amos had indicated, the older man helped Delsie off her mare. She stumbled forward and braced herself against a nearby tree trunk as she waited for her legs to work properly again. Myles led the three horses to the riverbank and let them drink.

"Shall we eat the food Mrs. Guittard gave us?" Delsie asked. She didn't know if it was time for lunch, but the hunger in her middle could no longer be ignored.

"Fine by me," Amos said, taking a seat in the shade.

Myles gave a grunt of approval as he looped the horses' reins around several low-hanging branches. He removed the simple meal of bread, cheese and apples from one of the saddlebags.

Delsie eyed the ground, trying to decide if she preferred sitting or standing at the moment.

"You're going to get dirty, Miss Radford," Myles said with a shake of his head, "so you might as well start now."

"But I wasn't…" She pressed her lips over her defense and glared at his bent head as he set out the lunch things. The man could truly be insufferable, even if he had good reason to be.

Chin up, she stepped away from the tree and plopped right onto the dirt as unladylike as possible. A cry barreled up her throat as pain shot through her spine, but she swallowed it back when she saw Myles quirk an eyebrow at her. Was that amusement or admiration glittering in his dark eyes?

She accepted the food he handed her, then waited until he and Amos had their portions before she spoke up. "May I say grace?"

Myles leaned back against the tree trunk and scowled in response.

Maybe he needed an explanation. "I'd like to give thanks for the food…and for a safe journey so far."

"Let her pray, if she wants, Myles." Amos removed his hat and nodded at Delsie.

She looked at the younger man, waiting for him to take off his hat, as well. They locked glares for a moment before he removed his hat and dipped his head. Fighting a small smile of victory, she bowed her head, as well. "Thank You, Lord, for this good food. And thank You for keeping us in Thy watchful care. Please bless Lillie and help us reach her in time. Amen."

Amos echoed her amen. Myles remained silent as

he jammed his hat back on and started in on their meal. At least he hadn't put up too much protest about her praying. She bit into the homemade bread with relish. Quiet descended over their group, but it wasn't uncomfortable. A nice breeze gently swayed the trees and cooled her sunburned face.

Elijah, who'd flown off earlier, landed beside Myles. Something small and limp dropped onto the ground in front of him. As she watched, the bird began tearing into the rodent with its beak. Delsie's stomach twisted at the sight, robbing her of the rest of her appetite.

"I think I'll walk a bit." She stood and managed to get beyond the trees without limping.

Out of sight, though, Delsie slowed her steps to a faltering walk as she massaged the backs of her legs. She followed the river, enjoying the chance, however painful, to move on her own.

The blue sky and rolling prairie were so vast, so endless. Myles might scoff at her for thinking so, at least out loud, but she saw the hand of the Lord in the beauty of it. Something inside her stirred and responded to this new open world—something she didn't feel at home within the confines of her family's elaborate parlor or in the midst of a grand party.

Was it this restlessness that had come over Lillie, prompting her to leave her family and home behind and strike out after her beau, Clay Weeks? Delsie hadn't understood at the time why Lillie would defy their father's wishes or ignore his threats to disown her if she ran off to find *that farmer*. Her older sister had confessed she loved Clay, and if the rigidness of their society life and their father's disapproval wouldn't allow her to be with the man she loved, then she'd go West with him. And so she had.

Now looking over this wide country, Delsie felt for the first time a piece of what Lillie must have felt. Her life at home suddenly felt a bit stale and narrow when compared to what she'd seen and experienced in the past two days.

A low whistle sounded from behind. She turned to see Myles motioning for her. It was time to ride again. A loud sigh fell from her lips. Too bad she couldn't walk just as quickly to California. Even the thought of climbing back into that saddle sent tremors of fresh pain shooting through her legs and back.

"Only for you, Lillie," she murmured. "And for Mother."

When she reached the grove of trees where they'd stopped, she allowed Amos to assist her back onto her mare. Being the first to mount, she decided to move away from the trees to the open prairie, where she'd wait for the two men.

Delsie nudged the horse forward, dodging tree branches to keep from getting smacked in the face. One particularly long branch she pushed aside as far as she could while she passed by. But instead of swinging harmlessly through the air when she let go, the branch swung back and struck the rump of her horse with a loud *thwack*. The poor creature reared in fear. Delsie yelped and clung to the reins, her heart crashing hard against her ribs. The mare landed back onto all fours, then charged from the trees at a full run. From behind someone shouted, but she couldn't make out the words.

Squeezing her knees as tightly as she could, she

managed to stay in the saddle, despite the horse's wild dash across the grass. The skin on her inner thighs stung with the effort. She tried to slow the mare by pulling back on the reins, but the frightened beast would have none of it. If anything, their careening pace increased.

Delsie held on, her fingers and hands aching, her pulse pounding as hard and as fast as the hooves below her. Would the horse eventually slow down or would she be forced to jump off in order to save herself? She peeked at the ground rushing dizzyingly beneath her and gulped. If she broke a bone, or worse, how would she manage to keep riding for the next seventeen days?

*Oh please, Lord.*

It was the shortest prayer she'd ever prayed, but she figured God understood why and what she was asking.

Off to her right, huge brown masses began turning tail and running at the approach of the runaway mare. Buffalo! Delsie managed only a quick look at their giant wooly frames, dozens of them, before they fled over a rise in the prairie. At least she could say she'd seen them, before it was too late.

The buffalo interrupted the mare's path of retreat, causing it to angle back toward the river instead of the open plains. Ahead Delsie spied another thick grove of trees. If the horse made a dash through them, she'd surely be knocked off or struck in the head.

Time to jump, then. She eyed the ground again. The thought of striking the earth at this intense speed made her want to vomit with fear. But it couldn't be helped.

She pressed her eyes shut, hoping the temporary blindness might squelch her nausea and ignite some confidence. She took a deep breath and leaned to the side. If she lived through this, she planned to share a few choice words with Lillie, though she instinctively knew her predicament was no one's fault but her own.

Just as she was about to release the reins and leap to safety, or to her death, something jerked the mare hard to the right. Delsie scrambled to keep hold of the reins and opened her eyes. Myles rode next to her, his hand gripping her horse's bridle in a firm fist. He didn't let go, even as the mare tried to shake off his grasp. Eventually the scared creature was forced to slow its pace in order to follow Myles and his mount.

When her horse, at last, came to a shuttering halt, Delsie realized she was shaking.

"Are you all right?" Myles asked, still keeping a hand on the animal's bridle.

Her teeth were chattering too much to speak, so she settled for a quick nod. When had it gotten so cold? She shivered and forced her fingers to release the reins. They would hardly uncurl from their clawlike grasp.

"Let's get you down." Myles finally released the mare's bridle and dismounted. He talked soothingly to the horse, all the while rubbing its nose and patting the side of its head, before he circled around to help Delsie off.

For some unknown reason the sight of him calming the mare, instead of her, sparked anger inside her. His next words didn't help. "You're shaking, Miss Radford," he said as he set her on her feet.

The tiny flame of anger roared to life. She'd come so close to being maimed or nearly killed. Her legs and skin hurt horribly from hours and hours in the saddle, and her face and neck were tender from the hot sun. And now this man had the audacity to turn his nose up at a little shivering after all she'd been through?

"Yes, I am, Mr. Patton," she snapped. "Unlike you, I'm not accustomed to riding a hundred miles a day or dealing with frightened horses or having my skin clawed by that uncomfortable saddle." Her voice hitched with unshed tears and she swallowed hard.

"I didn't mean—"

"Please. I just need to…" She caught sight of Amos riding up. She didn't want to dissolve into tears before them both. "I think I need to walk…"

Without waiting for Myles's reply, she marched past them and the horses, heading west. At least if she was slowing them down, she was moving in the right direction. She walked as fast as she possibly could, in spite of the tremors that still shook her body. Folding her arms, she tried to ward off the cold inside her. A sob raced up her throat and she covered her mouth with her hand, willing the tears back. She was alive—no use wasting tears on what might have been.

Delsie spied a flat rock in the grass and sat down on it, her eyes on the western horizon. She'd only been on this portion of her journey for a day and a half, but already, it felt like months ago since she'd left Aunt Cissy's house or her own home in Pennsylvania.

Measured footsteps approached. Delsie cut a glance in their direction, surprised to see it was Myles walking toward her and not Amos. What did he wish to say now? Probably more comments about how unsuited she was for this trip.

She turned away from him and set her jaw. If she

didn't speak, maybe he'd take the hint and leave her in peace to finish working through her earlier fear and adrenaline.

Something warm and leatherlike in smell settled over her shoulders. She recognized the buckskin jacket Myles wore. "Thank you..." she admitted begrudgingly. Her shivers began to subside as she pulled the jacket tighter around her.

He circled the rock and stood watching her from beneath his hat. "It gets easier."

She tilted her head to give him a quizzical look.

"The riding, the soreness. You might want to get a pair of leather trousers, though." He kicked at a clump of grass. "That'll help with the chafing."

Her cheeks flushed at his words, but she didn't break eye contact. "I will not be wearing trousers, thank you."

One side of his mouth lifted. "I meant under your dress."

The heat on her face intensified. She ducked her chin and stared at the ground, hoping he would leave.

"Look, I didn't mean anything unkind back there." Myles removed his hat and ran a hand through his hair. She'd seen it mussed more times on their short journey than lying flat or slicked back like Flynn wore it.

Myles squatted down in front of her, his hat dangling between his knees. "I only mentioned the shakes because...well, because I wanted to be sure you really were all right. That horse was going mighty fast when I caught up."

"Yes, it was." Delsie toyed with the hem of his jacket, her anger deflating in the wake of his explanation. "Thank you…for coming to my aid. I was about to jump." She gave a nervous laugh, grateful again she hadn't been forced to fling herself from the mare.

His chocolate-colored eyes glinted with respect before he looked away. "You kept a level head, that's for sure."

"Is that another compliment, Mr. Patton?"

A deep chuckle erupted from him as he shook his head. "You are not what you seem, Miss Radford."

"And neither are you." She spoke the words so softly she wasn't sure he heard, especially when he made no reply. The question she'd been asking herself all day resurfaced in her mind. "I know what you think of me and my privileged upbringing, so why are you helping me?"

He fiddled with the brim of his hat. "I need the money. For the land I want to own someday. A lot of land, out West maybe, where there's fewer people." His face had softened with his answer, its usual hardness transforming into earnest vulnerability for a brief moment.

Did she have a dream? Delsie wondered. Something to work toward? Right now it was reaching Lillie, of course, and continuing to fulfill her promise to her mother, but what about beyond that? Did she want to return to the sameness of her life at home? The thought brought another shiver of cold sweeping through her.

"You ready?" Myles asked as he stood and offered her his hand.

With a nod, she placed her hand in his. He pulled her gently to her feet, which brought her nearly toe-to-toe with him. Delsie peered up at his shadowed face. His gaze had lost its guard, if only for a moment. She'd thought him quite handsome before, even with his scowl, but his nearness and the glimpse at this gentler side of his had her middle erupting into flutters.

He broke contact first, releasing her hand and stepping back. "Shall we get you to that sister of yours, Miss Radford?"

She took a deep breath to steady her emotions. Clearly the horse escapade had played with her head. She wouldn't follow in Lillie's footsteps by choosing a man her father would never approve of. Not only would it break his heart, but it would be going against her promise to look after her papa.

"Yes, Mr. Patton." She smiled and fell into step beside him. Only when they reached Amos and the waiting horses did she realize he hadn't asked for his jacket back.

## Chapter Four

When they arrived in Nebraska that evening, at the home station known as Liberty Farm, Myles discovered Delsie had fallen asleep in the saddle. And no wonder. For someone unaccustomed to riding more than a hundred miles in a single day, she had to be exhausted. She didn't even stir when her mare—Amos had traded her horses after her other one had gotten spooked—came to a stop outside the stable.

Amos glanced over at her and chuckled. "You want me to wake her?"

An unfamiliar twinge of protectiveness rippled through Myles, then faded. "No, I will." He released Elijah into the sky to hunt.

"I'll go explain our situation to the owners," Amos said, dismounting. "See how much they'll charge for room and board for the night."

Myles nodded and climbed off his horse. Taking the reins of both his and Amos's animals in hand, he approached Delsie. "Miss Radford," he called quietly so as not to startle her. "We're here, at Liberty Farm. You can get down now."

When she remained still, he crossed to her side and gave her arm a gentle shake. "Miss Radford?"

At his touch, her chin rose and her eyelids blinked open. She stared in confusion at the yard around them and the still-bright sky of the summer evening, then down at Myles. Her blue eyes lit with recognition and a smile angled one side of her lips. "Did I fall asleep?"

That smile, combined with the soft expression on her face and the way her hair had come loose in places beneath her hat, sent a jolt of feeling through him. *Watch it, Myles*, he warned himself. *Money and a pretty face only lead to trouble.*

"We need to get the horses in the stable," he replied in a slightly gruff tone. "I'll help you down."

She complied, swinging her skirt over the side of the mare and allowing Myles to help her to the ground. Once her feet struck the dirt, she peered up at him, her lips parted as if to speak, but instead she remained silent. The open, earnest look on her face matched the one she'd worn earlier on the prairie after he'd rescued her. Awareness of her, both then and now, along with their close proximity, quickened his pulse and dulled the warning still ringing in his mind.

A strange terror had seized him as he'd watched Delsie and her horse burst from the trees and go charging at reckless speed over the plains. He kept imagining her being thrown and injured. His heart had beaten with as much fear as adrenaline when he'd jumped on his own steed and gone after her. Thankfully, he'd reached her in time, especially after hearing how close she'd come to leaping off.

Why should he care that much for a complete stranger, though? He mentally shook his head. Maybe *stranger* wasn't the right word anymore—not after spending two full days together. He'd told himself he'd saved her today out of human decency and the money she'd promised to give him at their journey's end. And yet, his logical reasoning didn't explain the bizarre need growing inside him to look after her. Though truth be told, there were moments when he wondered if she needed his protection at all.

A smile curved his mouth at the thought. This tiny woman, regarding him solemnly, had the courage of a hundred trained soldiers. She hadn't let out a single scream as her mare had spirited her away or fallen into uncontrollable sobs afterward. Myles couldn't help but think if it had been Cynthia in that situation things would have gone much differently.

"What are you smiling about?"

Delsie's innocent question broke whatever trance he'd been under. Myles stepped away from her and added her horse's reins to the others in his grip.

"Nothin'," he said over his shoulder as he walked toward the stable. "Amos is inside the house. You can join him in there."

He didn't wait to see if she'd listen or not. Instead he entered the structure through the open doors. The smell of hay and horses greeted him with all the familiarity and comfort of a friend. Memories of working with his stepfather at the livery stable rushed over him, clearing his mind of a certain dark-haired beauty.

As a young child, he'd trailed Charles everywhere around the spacious barn, doing the small jobs he was given. Myles had loved looking at the horses, feeding them, riding them when he could, even mucking their stalls. His stepfather had taught him to respect the power inherent in such creatures but also their fear and stubbornness.

There were other lessons Charles had imparted to him, ones he'd largely ignored since his stepfather's death. Things like looking for God's hand in his life or keeping his heart open and receptive to God's will. His jaw hardened at the turn of his thoughts. God didn't care any more for him than Cynthia had.

"Howdy, stranger," a young man called out to him from the other end of the stable. He held a pitchfork in one hand.

"Evening." Myles stopped the horses and quickly explained they were passing through and would pay to have the horses cared for tonight.

The boy, for he couldn't be more than fourteen or fifteen, agreed to feed and groom the animals, if it was all right with the station owners. "For now, put them in those empty stalls."

Myles did so as Amos appeared. "Everything's taken care of," the older man said. "For us and the horses."

"Where's Delsie?" Myles kept his voice devoid of interest.

"Inside, starting on supper. You coming?"

He wasn't ready to be near her again, not until he had a stronghold on this growing attraction for her.

Eying the three horses, Myles shook his head. "No, go ahead. I'll help settle them in."

Amos studied him for a moment, while Myles fought to keep his expression impassive. Finally his friend shrugged. "We'll try to save you some." With that he left the barn.

The young stable hand offered to help, but Myles encouraged him to join the others inside. He wanted the comfortable solace of a quiet barn, with no one else around except the beasts in the stalls.

Once the boy showed him where the tack and feed were located, he started in on grooming Amos's horse. He ran the brush down its chestnut-colored sides, talking soothingly as he did so. When it gleamed as fresh and new as a colt, he brought the beast some hay, then started in on his horse next.

Soon his thoughts moved back to Delsie. That was the trouble with doing something so familiar—his hands stayed busy but his mind didn't.

He had to remind himself, hourly if needed, that this journey to California was nothing more than a business arrangement. Acting on any possible attraction he felt for Delsie would be entirely futile. Her father, like Cynthia's, wasn't likely to approve of any interest in someone as poor and unconnected as Myles. Besides, a life out here in the West, with him or any other horseman or farmer, would likely drain her of whatever vitality and beauty she currently possessed. His life was about survival and weathering hardship, not choosing whom to invite for tea or which social engagement to attend on the weekend.

"Business," he muttered to himself, causing the

steed's ears to flick backward. Myles reached out and ran a hand down its nose. "That's all it'll ever be." A measure of relief filled him now that he'd gotten his head in the right place. But the tiniest sliver of disappointment cut through him all the same.

Delsie slipped inside the stable. Though she was growing more accustomed to the smell, the trapped heat and scent of manure still had the power to make her wrinkle her nose in protest. Down the line of occupied stalls, she caught sight of Myles standing next to his horse.

"You missed supper," she said as she walked toward him.

He flinched as though struck, but he didn't glance at her. "I thought I'd see to the animals first."

Guilt trickled through her at his explanation. She'd been half-asleep when they'd arrived and had momentarily forgotten about the horses.

Delsie came to a stop beside the stall where he stood. Tentatively she lifted her hand to the steed and let it smell her.

"Where'd you learn to do that?" Myles asked, his voice bordering on sharpness.

She pulled her hand back. "Is that wrong?"

He'd removed his hat, giving her a full view of his face and beard. "No, that's exactly what you're supposed to do, but most people don't know that, especially…" He let the words trail off.

"Rich people," she supplied.

He frowned before picking up a brush and exiting the stall. Delsie stepped back to allow him room.

"I think it was Lillie's beau, Clay, who taught us that. He was a farmer."

"Your sister had a beau?"

"Still does. That's who she followed to California and who she's marrying on the twenty-second." And the next day, Lillie and Clay would head to Oregon. Never to see or contact the family again, according to Lillie's last letter, if she didn't receive some word by then that Delsie still cared.

Myles entered the stall where Delsie's mare stood. "Let me guess—your father didn't approve of him." His voice sounded flat, bitter. His manner was so different from when he'd woken her up in the saddle earlier.

Heat layered her face. "Papa had hoped she'd marry..." It was her turn to swallow back the rest of her words. She found she suddenly couldn't say someone rich or of the same social circle as her family. Someone like Flynn.

"I get it," Myles said, his tone no longer harsh but full of resignation. Silence descended between them as he began brushing the mare. Delsie watched him, mesmerized by the movement of his hands and the gentle murmurs falling from his mouth. Here he was in his element, like a duke in his castle.

"May I try?"

He jerked his head in her direction as if he'd forgotten her presence. "What? Brushing?"

She nodded. "I own them now, which means I ought to know how to care for them."

Myles looked from her to the brush in his hand as

if making a weightier decision than whether to teach her horse grooming or not. "All right."

Smiling, Delsie entered the stall. "What do I do?"

"Stand beside the horse," he said, moving behind her and pressing the brush into her hand, though he kept both in his grip. "Start up here on the animal's neck…" He lifted his arm, bringing her hand and the brush along with it, then he placed both against the mare. "Now you brush from front to back."

Together they moved the brush along the horse's side. "Then you repeat the motion," Myles said near her ear.

Gooseflesh rose along her arms, which thankfully, her long sleeves hid from view, at the low murmur of his voice and the warmth radiating from his solid chest behind her. When he leaned forward to help her again, his breath grazed the skin at the back of her neck. Delsie shivered, despite the temperate air inside the stable.

Myles stopped their motion, though their joined hands still held the brush to the horse's coat. Even the mare itself stood perfectly still. Delsie held her breath, anticipating something, though she didn't know what.

A soft touch skated her hair above her ear. Her heart drummed faster against her rib cage as she realized Myles was breathing in the scent of her hair.

"It smells like…" His nose skimmed her hair again.

"Lavender?" she whispered. After another full day of riding, she was surprised to learn she still smelled like her favorite soap and not just sweat and horse.

"Yes, lavender." His voice held a smile. "Smells better than gardenias."

*Gardenias?* Was that what his girl had worn, the

one who'd bludgeoned his heart? Intent on asking him just that, Delsie lowered her arm and twisted slowly. Myles still held her hand over the brush and stood so close she could see where the sun had lightened some of the hairs of his beard. What would those dark bristles feel like beneath her fingertips? She lifted her free hand to find out.

A throat cleared behind them, as loud as a gunshot in the quiet barn. Myles jerked his hand from hers so fast that she dropped the brush into the hay at their feet.

"Came to see if you needed help," Amos announced.

Delsie bent to retrieve the brush and hide her flushed face. Myles practically bolted from the stall. "I think you got the hang of it," he said when she straightened. He wouldn't look at her. "Amos can show you how to feed them. I'm gonna get me some supper."

Moving to the other side of her mare, she tried to ignore the sound of Myles's retreating steps and the searching glances Amos kept throwing her way. She ran the brush over and over across the horse's coat, fighting a sudden desire to cry.

Why should she waste a single tear on that ornery Express rider? They came from two completely different worlds, as Myles himself seemed to enjoy pointing out. Even if her heart should stray from what her father wanted for her, she'd witnessed firsthand what Lillie's choice had done to him. While Delsie didn't agree with his decision to disown her sister for going after Clay, deep down, she recognized he'd only wanted the best for Lillie. His wrath had masked his fear. She wouldn't follow the same path and tear apart what remained of their small family.

"You all right, Miss Radford?" Amos held a pitchfork in his hand.

"Of course." She kept her head tilted high, but she sensed the older man saw through the bluff.

Why did she have to feel this attraction toward Myles, one stronger than any she'd ever felt for Flynn, and after only two days? She needed to place all her energies and focus on reaching Lillie in time, and nothing more.

"Will you show me how to feed the horses?" she asked, infusing as much cheerfulness as she could into her tone.

Amos watched her, his blue-gray eyes keen. What did he see? Did he read the hurt on her face over Myles's rude behavior just now, how he'd acted as if nothing had happened between them? Could Amos see how hard she was trying not to care? Finally, the older man nodded and motioned for her to exit the stall.

The lesson proved to be the perfect distraction. Amos patiently taught her how to pitch the hay into the stall and how to feed some carrots to the mare. Perhaps she'd take more interest in the animals and in riding, when she returned home.

By the time they left the stable, Delsie had almost forgotten Myles and his shifting moods—until they met up with him on the front porch. He sat on the bottom step, feeding Elijah pieces of meat from his supper. Amos took a seat beside Myles and removed his harmonica from his pocket.

Delsie caught Myles glancing at her, but when she

turned his way, he busied himself with his bird. A wave of exhaustion engulfed her, restoring her earlier sleepiness. "I think I'll head inside."

"Good night, Miss Radford," Amos said. "We'll see you at breakfast."

"Please, call me Delsie." She cut a look at Myles. "Both of you."

"'Night, then, Delsie." Amos tipped his hat at her, a kind smile on his face.

"Good night, Amos. Mr. Patton." When the latter made no response, she blew out a sigh and entered the house. *I'm doing this for Lillie,* she told herself. *Just remember that, Delsie.*

She entered the room the station owners had told her to use and started to close the door behind her. Amos and Myles would bunk in one of the outbuildings.

"Delsie?"

Myles's voice drew her back to the doorway. "Yes?" She couldn't quell the sudden speeding of her pulse, no matter how much she wanted to.

"I…um…" Those dark eyes observed her in a way that reminded her of their close moment in the barn earlier. But she wouldn't let it go to her head—or her heart—this time.

"Do you need something, Myles?" She kept her tone nonchalant and businesslike.

A corner of his mouth lifted, ruining her attempt at being stoic. That lopsided smile made her insides flutter. "I'm not *Mr. Patton* anymore?"

Belatedly she realized she'd called him by his first name. "Would you rather I still call you that?"

He shook his head. "No, ma'am. Myles suits me fine. Just like Delsie...suits you."

"Very well," she said, trying to discount the pleasure his veiled compliment gave her, "what do you need, Myles?"

"Do you have a lock on your door?"

"A...lock?" She stared in confusion at him.

He motioned for her to move aside so he could examine the door. She saw that it did possess a latch. "Be sure to lock it tonight."

"Why?"

"Because there aren't any other women at this station."

"So?"

Myles ran a hand through his hair. "I don't...we don't...know the character of these men at this station or any other station from here to California. You need to be careful."

Understanding dawned, bringing warmth to her cheeks. "Oh. I see. Yes, I'll...lock it."

"Good." He turned to go, but she had a request of her own.

"Myles?"

He faced her again, his expression holding its usual guarded quality. Would anyone ever be able to help him shed his pain?

"I only wanted to thank you for rescuing me today... and for agreeing to come along." She fiddled with the dirty cuff of her riding dress. "While I understand everything about this arrangement is wholly unconventional... I would very much like it if you and Amos and I...could be friends."

She steeled herself for his refusal, and she couldn't blame him if he gave it. After all it was another woman, a wealthy one like herself, who had betrayed his friendship.

"I know it's silly," she added into the gaping silence. "But I don't know anyone out here, except for the two of you, and I just thought…"

He shifted his stance as if to walk away. Disappointment cut through her. She'd been silly to think they could, at the very least, be friends.

"You trust us, right?" he asked over his shoulder.

"Yes."

"So isn't that what friends do?"

He didn't wait for her answer. Instead he moved down the hall toward the front door. Delsie heard it click shut behind him. A few moments later she heard the soft, languid sounds of Amos's harmonica coming from the direction of the porch.

She closed the door to her room and locked it, her mind in disorder. Myles hadn't exactly accepted her offer of friendship, but he hadn't refused it, either. Certainly that was a good sign.

His actions earlier in the stable and his obvious desire to protect her were also proof he might be warming up to her. The thought filled her with a measure of hope as she readied for bed.

Despite the fatigue and aches that continued to plague her body, she found sleep wouldn't come easily. Instead she lay awake for some time listening to Amos play his harmonica and picturing a pair of haunting, chocolate-colored eyes.

\* \* \*

Myles returned to the porch and took his seat on the step again. Out of the corner of his eye, he caught sight of Elijah perched on a corner of the house's sloping roof. Amos continued to play his instrument, performing one melancholy ballad after another. Myles gritted his teeth in annoyance. The music didn't help erase the memory of Delsie standing close as they'd brushed the horse together or the teasing scent of her hair.

He ran a hand over his face and released a frustrated breath. What had come over him that he'd given in to smelling her hair or testing the silkiness of it against the tip of his nose? And then she'd gone and asked to be his friend. Myles didn't want to be friends with her—that path would only lead to further regret and pain. Better to keep his distance, although he hadn't actually denied her request, either. He'd wanted to, but the honesty and innocence shining in those big blue eyes of hers had killed whatever refusal he might have made.

"Can you play something else?" he snapped, rising to his feet. "A livelier song, maybe?"

Amos lowered the instrument from his mouth. "I can. But first, you wanna tell me what's got you wound up tighter than a noose?"

Myles stepped away from the porch into the empty yard. He didn't want to talk. Doing so would only mean admitting he'd let his feelings get the better of him where a woman was concerned—and here he'd sworn them off only eight weeks before.

"This likely doesn't need to be said..." Amos stood and joined Myles in the yard, slapping his harmonica against the palm of his hand. "But you need to remember Delsie isn't Cynthia."

"I know." Myles glanced at the stars above.

"Do you?" Amos countered.

Myles shifted to give his friend a level look. Amos never could leave well enough alone. "All right, old man. What have you got to say?"

Amos gave an innocent shrug. "Not much tonight." Myles crossed his arms and waited—he sensed a lecture. "I'll only say this. I know you got reasons for not liking the kind of people Delsie comes from, and that's fine."

"But…" Myles prompted.

"But go easy on her. She isn't some simpering female like Cynthia."

Myles uncrossed his arms as irritation sliced through him. If Amos had harbored reservations about Cynthia Grover, all these years, the man should've voiced them long before now. "You mean to tell me, you—"

"Yes, I didn't care for her." Amos pocketed his harmonica and turned his attention to the starry sky.

"Why didn't you say something sooner?"

The older man shrugged again. "I probably should have." Silence filled the space between them for a minute or two before Amos continued, "About Delsie, though."

That twinge of protectiveness, the one that had prompted Myles to have her lock her door, rose inside him again. Did Amos sense it? Myles had never felt a driving need to be sure Cynthia was all right. "What about her?"

Amos chuckled. "There you go, being surly again. I only wanted to say she's proven her strength these last two days."

Myles grunted in agreement. He never would have guessed she'd make it this far when he'd first seen her standing outside the Express stables in all her finery.

"She needs a friend."

The words so closely echoed Delsie's that Myles threw Amos a sharp look. Had the older man overheard their conversation and Myles's noncommittal response? He swept his hand through his hair—he'd left his hat in the stable in his hurry to leave earlier. Being friends with Delsie Radford sounded dangerous and difficult—not unlike this journey they were taking now. Could he do it, though? Could he put a portion of his heart on the line to be her friend?

Amos rested a hand on Myles's shoulder, much like Charles used to. A lump lodged in his throat at the recollection. The man standing next to him was the closest thing in the world he had to a father or a family anymore.

"Just think on it," Amos urged. "That's all I'm asking."

Myles hesitated only a second or two, then nodded.

His friend strolled back to his earlier seat on the porch. The harmonica came out again, but this time, Amos played a rousing tune. As he listened, Myles's thoughts drifted through the events of the day, settling on Delsie's passing mention of her chafed skin. With only that fancy dress between her and the saddle, it was no wonder she was in pain.

A sudden idea filled his mind. "What's the next place we come to where we can buy a few supplies?"

Amos paused in his playing. "We'll pass Dobytown tomorrow. Why? What do you need?"

He gave a lazy shrug that belied the spark of enthusiasm growing inside him. "Nothing much." Amos let the noncommittal answer go unprotested and returned instead to playing another lively tune on his instrument.

Crossing back to the porch, Myles sat down once more. He might not be ready to fully embrace a friendship with Delsie, but he could try to look out for her and ease her discomfort a little. And now he knew how.

# Chapter Five

"I don't understand. Why can't we stop?" Delsie twisted in the saddle to watch the adobe buildings of Dobytown receding behind them. They'd charged right past Fort Kearney two miles back, as well. "It's time to the rest the horses anyway."

She turned back around in time to catch Myles's scowl. "I told you earlier. Dobytown is no place for a lady."

"But it isn't like I'd be alone. I have the two of—"

"No."

Delsie glared at him, irritation making her skin as hot and itchy as the sun did. Who did he think he was, ordering her around like a servant? She opened her mouth to argue further when Amos joined the heated conversation.

"What Myles is trying to say…" The older man shot Myles a pointed look, which solicited a momentary expression of contrition. Delsie needed to master such a look if it put him in his place. "Is that it might not be safe. Like I mentioned last night, Dobytown is usually rampant with drunks and harlots. We'd rather keep you outside its borders, than risk anything by entering them."

She tipped her chin upward in her best imitation of a haughty matron. "I suppose when you put it that way." But annoyance still simmered under her choking collar. She'd only wanted to take a peek at the fort or the city, not move in.

The conversation ended in strained silence as they followed the line of the Platte River. After another mile or two Myles announced it was time to stop.

Amos helped her dismount, and though she welcomed the feel of solid ground beneath her shoes, walking around only intensified the chafing of her dress against her legs. Would her skin ever feel normal again? She'd tried scratching her thighs, discreetly, during their last stop, but that had only made matters worse. Now her legs felt raw and prickly as if a thousand pine needles had taken up residence inside her skirt.

After they'd eaten the small lunch she'd paid the last station owners to provide them, Amos spread out in the shade to take a nap. His snores filled the air almost immediately. Delsie was considering how to pass the time herself when she noticed Myles climbing back into his saddle.

"Where are you going?" she asked.

Without looking at her, he wheeled his steed around. "There's something I need to buy back in Dobytown. I shouldn't be long."

"Buy? Why didn't you just get it when we…" She bit her lip as a sudden thought penetrated her confusion. An awful, shocking thought. Anger followed quickly on its heels. "Myles Patton, you took an oath as an Express rider. And I will not be party to—to riotous behavior on your part. I won't pay you a dime, so help me, if you're planning to go—"

"Good grief, woman." His exasperated tone cut off the rest of her indignant speech. "I'm buying a few supplies. That's all."

"Oh." Her face felt twice as sunburned. "What about the horse? Isn't he going to lag if you don't rest him?"

"I'll ride slowly." He nudged the mount forward.

"But I didn't think we needed anything else." Why was he being so mysterious? She was paying him, after all, to get her to California quickly, not take in the sights. Not unless he planned to take her along, too, which he clearly wasn't. "What do you need that's so important?"

"I'll be back soon," he called over his shoulder. "Stay near Amos while I'm gone. I don't want you walking around by yourself out here. Not this close to the city."

Delsie's jaw tightened as she glowered at his back. She wasn't a child. Had he so easily forgotten how well she'd held her own the past three days?

"Oooo, that man," she muttered as she whirled around, her hands balled into fists. One moment he had her feeling weak in the knees over his kindness and handsome face, and the very next he had her so mad she wanted to throw something at him.

She eyed her mare, debating whether to follow after

him or not. He'd likely just drag her back the moment he noticed her coming up behind him.

Her gaze wandered to the river. The cool liquid looked so inviting she couldn't resist the idea of wading into it. What if she took a quick swim instead? Amos would still be napping for a while longer—the man could sleep heavily anywhere, anytime. She could hike up the river a short ways, take a dip in her chemise and return before anyone was the wiser.

Myles's warning repeated in her mind, but Delsie brushed it aside. She wouldn't be too far away.

The thought of ridding herself of the grime and sweat of three days was too appealing. Surely it would help her chafed skin, too. Her mind made up, Delsie gathered her skirt in one hand and stole softly into the brush.

Myles fought to breathe through his mouth, instead of his nose, to avoid smelling the foul odor emitting from the trapper standing behind him. He was used to strong scents, having worked for years in the livery stable, but this man's aroma surpassed anything he'd known before. The man was tall, too. His coonskin cap and long, greasy hair hovered a good six inches above the top of Myles's hat. And the profanity spewing from the man's chapped lips was as foul as his aroma.

Not for the first time since entering the confines of Dobytown, he felt relieved he'd convinced Delsie to stay behind. Though he'd nearly had to tell her his secret because of it. The woman could be downright determined when she wanted.

Raucous laughter filled the trading post. Myles's lips curved upward, but not at the drunken joviality. The horrified look on Delsie's face, when she'd suspected him of wanting to participate in one of the unseemly businesses offered in Dobytown, resurfaced in his mind. Wouldn't she be surprised, and a little humbled, when she learned his real reason for coming back had to do with her?

When his turn came, he made his request to the clerk. "I need a pair of leather trousers and a good hat. Both in the smallest size you've got."

The man moved away to collect the items. Myles let his gaze wander over the crammed shelves of the trading post. Was there anything else they needed or that Delsie might like? He thought of the lavender scent on her hair. Would she appreciate more soap?

"Anything else for you?" the man asked, after naming the price of the items he'd slapped onto the counter.

Myles leaned forward. "Do you have any soap? Maybe lavender scented?"

"Lavender soap?" the man repeated in a loud voice, his bushy brows nearly reaching his hairline. "What do you think I'm running here, a mercantile?"

The trapper behind Myles hooted. "Hear that, fellows. The Express rider here is gonna show us up with the ladies by buying one of 'em some soap."

Myles ignored the ribbing, letting the man's sarcastic tone roll off him. "Any nice soap will do."

"I might have something in the back." The clerk walked away, grumbling under his breath and shaking his head.

Would Delsie be pleased or angry with him for coming here to purchase things for her? Myles hoped the former. While he enjoyed seeing her dark blue eyes spark with determination, he liked her smile best of all. Or maybe hearing her laughter. Or taking in the sweet scent of her hair.

Myles frowned. He was acting like the friend she wanted, nothing more. Even the soap could be considered a friendly, kind gesture—if the clerk had any. He shifted his weight in impatience at the same moment a thought nudged him hard. *Delsie's in trouble.*

Myles shook his head, dismissing the notion. She'd been fine when he left. There was no sense conjuring up false concern.

But try as he might, he couldn't completely rid his mind of the thought. Then a sense of urgency seized him with a vicelike grip. He needed to leave—now. Something wasn't right.

Jerking his money from his pocket, he hollered for the clerk. The man lumbered back into the room, a scowl on his face. "Here's what I owe you for the trousers and hat." Myles plunked the money onto the counter and grabbed up his purchases.

"What about the soap?"

"Maybe next time."

After elbowing his way out of the crowded trading post, he untied his horse. He swung into the saddle and set off at a gallop down the street, his purchases clutched under one arm. He had no idea what awaited him—only that his need to reach Delsie, to ensure she was all right, intensified with every passing minute. He only hoped he wasn't too late.

\* \* \*

Delsie lay on her back in the water, not caring that she'd soaked her chemise from neck to knee. Her toes kept her anchored in the sandy river bottom. With her face turned toward the warm rays of the sun, she shut her eyes and focused on the gentle rush of the water as it flowed past her head and ears. She spread her arms out and let the river slide over and through her fingers. A feeling of freedom, of complete contentment, spilled out of her in the form of a soft laugh. Perhaps she'd have to make this a habit when they stopped.

Sitting up, she wrung out her unbound hair. She might have washed it properly, if she'd remembered to grab her soap. But she'd been so focused on the thought of being clean and cool after so many dusty hours in the saddle that she had slipped away without bringing anything with her.

*Oh well, next time.* Delsie scooped up some water in her hand and let it dribble back to its source. She didn't want to leave yet, but she needed to wrestle back into her riding dress, wet as she was, and return to Amos before he woke up. Or worse, before Myles discovered she'd gone off on her own. Even if it was just a short distance. With a sigh, she started to climb to her feet.

"Well, howdy there, girlie," a gravelly voice intoned.

She whirled around, a startled gasp rising toward her mouth. The sound tangled in her throat when she saw three men watching her from the other side of the river. They appeared to be trappers, rifles hung loose over their shoulders, their beards unkempt, their eyes keen. Eyes that stared with undisguised interest at her.

"Out for a little dip?" the tallest continued. "A little far from town, aren't you?"

Myles's warning rang like a bell through Delsie's mind and sent her heart crashing in panic against her rib cage. She shouldn't have wandered off, at least not without telling Amos where she'd gone.

"Not a real talker, are you?"

Delsie glanced over her shoulder at the nearby bank. It didn't seem so close now. Could she make it to the trees and back to Amos before the men overtook her? Perhaps the trappers were merely being friendly, though their attentive stares suggested otherwise.

Eyes trained on the men, Delsie tried to slow her pounding heart as she scooted a few inches across the river bottom toward the bank. Hopefully, her movements would go unnoticed until the last moment when she would have to jump up and sprint. To her horror, though, the tall trapper set down his rifle and stepped into the river.

"Why don't you come on over here, girlie? We're not so bad, once you get to know us." One of his companions snickered and jostled the other in the ribs.

Fear prickled across Delsie's skin, turning the pleasant water to ice. How could she have been so foolish? She scrambled backward, no longer caring if they saw. The trapper continued his deliberate advance toward her, his smile large and leering.

Delsie eyed the bank again. She might not be able to outrun the man, especially in her wet chemise, but she had to try. The sand beneath her hands registered in her fear-clouded mind. Scooping up a handful, to hurl at the man if needed, she bolted out of the water and pushed through the meandering current at a clumsy run.

"Hey," he cried from behind, "what's your hurry? Come on back here."

Her toes at last sunk into the mud at the bank's edge and she scrambled from the water, her breath coming so fast and hard she could hardly breathe. Her feet caught in the hem of her chemise and she tripped. *No, no, no.*

"You can't hide for long, girlie."

Delsie threw a quick glance at her pursuer as she struggled to free her feet. He was halfway across the river by now, his large boots eating up her lead.

"There's no one else out here—"

The sudden cocking of a gun preceded Myles's loud command, "Leave her alone."

Relief washed over Delsie with such intensity she nearly cried out. The sight of Myles standing above her on the bank, his gun aimed at the trapper, stilled her frantic movements. Shivering, she dropped the sand and wrapped her arms around her sodden gown and knees.

The trapper had stopped, his arms lifted halfway. "You know you ain't the only one with a gun here." Sure enough, his friends had drawn their weapons, which were now pointed at Myles.

The hard look on his face didn't waver for a second. "True. But you'll be a dead man before you ever find out if your friends succeeded in shooting me, too."

Delsie held her breath as the two men glared at one another, as frozen as stone. At last, the trapper backed up, his hands reaching higher. "She's all yours then. Not worth the trouble."

Myles didn't lower the gun or look her way until the trapper had joined his companions on the other side of the river and the three of them headed back the way they'd come. By then, Delsie's shivers had grown worse. Her teeth had begun to chatter behind her tightly pressed lips.

"Get your dress and shoes," Myles ordered, his tone sharp with barely concealed fury.

Was he angrier at the trappers or at her for not listening? Too exhausted and chilled to ask, she collected her riding dress, took the hand he offered her and climbed onto her trembling legs.

Once Delsie stood erect, Myles turned his back to her. "Go ahead and get them on."

After several false starts at getting the dress over her wet chemise, she finally had the gown on. Her fingers shook so hard she could hardly do up the buttons. The relief she'd felt at Myles's appearance was fast fading in the wake of the shock coursing through her at what might have happened if he hadn't come along. As she pulled on her shoes, tears blurred her vision and she hurried to brush them away before he noticed.

"Done?" he asked after several minutes.

"Yes." She wasn't sure he heard her whispered reply as she started past him.

Myles's hand seized her arm in a firm grip, turning her toward him. His eyes blazed dark beneath his hat. "What were you thinking?" The edge had returned to his voice. "I told you not to wander off. Do you know what they could have done?" He released her to run his hand over the stubble covering his jaw and chin. Only then did Delsie notice his own fingers weren't as sure and steady as normal.

"I—I didn't think anything would happen—"

"That's the problem. You didn't think."

"I wasn't trying to court trouble, Myles." She folded her arms against another bout of tears rising fast toward her throat and eyes. "I just wanted to…to wash up. I didn't mean—"

"Why did I even bother warning you?" He yanked off his hat and plunged his shaking hand through his hair. "You're clearly going to do whatever you please. Including walking right into a group of trappers, dressed in just your…" He waved a hand at her, his face momentarily flushing before his expression hardened again. "Might as well have ridden into the fort and announced you were taking callers."

An angry spark lit inside Delsie, stoked by Myles's stubborn refusal to listen. It wasn't as if she'd chosen to swim with an audience of onlookers. "I admit I was wrong to go off alone, and for that I apologize. But I refuse to stand here and let you reprimand me another minute."

"Reprimand? I'm trying to talk sense into you. Something I'm beginning to think you left back in Pennsylvania."

Hands on her hips, she glowered up at him. "I'm sorry if my lack of sense requires you to keep rescuing me, but you agreed to come along. Not the other way around. Need I remind you that I'm not used to this way of life?"

He reared back as if slapped. "You're right," he said slowly. "Which is why… I'm trying to protect you."

Her anger, and her strength, ebbed at his admission. "You may also recall—" her voice wobbled a bit "—I was nearly kidnapped and accosted back there and I don't know that my knees can hold me much longer. I'm going to find Amos…"

Delsie moved away from him but not before a sob leaked from her lips. Covering her mouth, she stumbled forward. The luxury of being clean no longer held any appeal—she felt only wet and cold, her feelings brittle. The magnitude of her journey weighted her footsteps and dragged at her head and heart. Would she continue to skirt danger, in the nick of time, to reach Lillie alive and well? Or was this truly a fool's errand?

She tripped, unseeing, over something, but before she landed on the dirt, Myles caught her elbow. This time his touch exuded only gentleness.

"I left my horse right over there, Delsie. You can ride back."

She tried to find the animal, but she couldn't see much through her tears. Then Myles's strong arms were around her, holding her in a comforting embrace. Delsie pressed her cheek to his jacket, breathing in the familiar scent of leather, and let her sobs flow unchecked.

"It's all right," he soothed, as if she were one of his horses, "you're all right. No one's going to hurt you."

"I'm sorry. I'm so sorry. If you hadn't come right then…" She shuddered in horror.

He tightened his hold and ran his hand down her

wet hair. "Shh. Don't think about it. You're safe with me and Amos."

After another minute, her tears were spent and she stepped back. Myles offered her a bandanna to wipe her damp face.

"Thank you."

He nodded, seeming to understand she was expressing gratitude for more than just his gentlemanly gesture.

Delsie followed him to his horse. There on the ground sat a hastily dropped pile of clothes. Myles picked them up and thrust them at her. "These are for you. From the trading post. They oughta help."

She accepted the hat and trousers, too surprised to form an immediate response. Myles had gone back to buy her more appropriate riding gear? Surely that meant he believed in her and her attempt to reach her sister. She glanced up at him, but he wasn't looking at her. He was staring in the direction of the river.

"I would have got you soap, too, but…"

She shook her head, pressing the things to her wet bodice. "No, no. This is wonderful. Thank you, again."

"I knew you were in trouble." His voice was low and tinged with wonder. "Knew it as sure as if someone had said it out loud. Riding back across the prairie, I couldn't seem to go fast enough. I had no idea what was wrong, but I knew…" He finally returned his gaze to hers. "I knew I had to reach you."

He lifted his hand and ran his thumb over the drying tears on her cheek. "Just promise not to wander off like that again." Something warm spread through

Delsie, burning away the last remnants of cold, both inside and out.

"I won't," she whispered back.

The earnest look on his chiseled face, the warmth of his touch on her cheek, the gift of the new clothing told a different story from the one Myles wanted people to believe—he cared. In spite of his occasional brusqueness, he cared about her. The realization rocked her nearly as much as her harrowing experience earlier.

*He cares as a friend*, she told herself. For that was all they could ever be—especially after their journey was over. Myles would never be content to live in her world, and her father would never allow her to live in his. But it was enough to know he was her friend.

Even when he lowered his hand and the guarded look returned to his dark eyes, even when he hastily lifted her onto his horse, she told herself it was enough to know he cared. As long as she stuck with Myles, she would be fine.

## Chapter Six

Myles cast a glance at Delsie over his shoulder—the fourth or fifth time in the past hour of riding. After the events at the river yesterday, he was simply making sure she was still behind him and holding up. He told himself it had nothing to do with how charming she looked in her new hat or with her trousers sticking out the bottom of her skirt.

She caught his eye and smiled, though the gesture lacked her usual spark. At least her face had lost its paleness and her shoulders had returned to their normal upright posture. If he hadn't heeded that thought of warning…

Facing forward again, he stared grimly at the open prairie before them. He and Delsie had agreed to keep the details vague when they'd explained their absence to Amos the day before—Delsie had gone swimming and Myles happened by at the same moment some trappers wandered up on the opposite side of the river. If the older man had known the truth, Myles didn't doubt Amos would wrestle the men's descriptions from him and hunt them down. He was still of a mind to do the same. The lurid look in the one trapper's eyes still had the ability to turn his gut to ice and his hands to fists—ready for revenge, even in memory.

One thing he knew for certain. God might not remember him, but He was watching over Delsie. That was the only explanation that made sense to him when he thought back on his earlier intuition about Delsie being in trouble.

The responsibility to protect her settled like a heavy saddle blanket over Myles's shoulders. Would he and Amos be able to keep her safe over the next fifteen days? What if something happened to one or both of them, and she were left on her own? The possibility filled him with enough horror to constrict his breath for a moment.

No, he wouldn't let that happen. He rubbed at Elijah's feathers as the bird playfully pecked at his hat. No matter what lay ahead, Myles vowed to get Delsie to her destination, well and whole. To do that, though, he would need to teach her how to handle herself in this unfamiliar world. His world. Could she do it? he wondered. Cynthia never would have.

He set his mouth in a hard line. Delsie had to. Any other thought or plan was unacceptable. He would best keep her safe by helping her help herself. Starting today.

At their first resting spot, Myles slid from his horse and removed one of his Colt revolvers from the saddle holsters. He waited for Amos to help Delsie down before he announced, "You need to learn how to shoot a gun."

"Now?" Delsie's eyebrows rose in surprise as she removed the wide-brimmed hat he'd bought her and hung it on the saddle horn.

"If you ever need to shoot something or someone—" he gave her meaningful look "—you'll know how."

She visibly swallowed. "But I don't own a gun."

"You're never far from one. I've got two revolvers, and Amos has one, too."

The older man nodded and pulled back his jacket to reveal the gun stuck into the waistband of his trousers.

"It's more than shooting, too." Myles motioned to the horses. "You need to know how to saddle and unsaddle your mare, and how to climb on and off without assistance."

Her blue eyes appeared troubled. "All right, I'll learn. However, I don't see the reason. If you and Amos are right here..."

Myles let his gaze flit past her to the western horizon, a rare feeling of uncertainty eating at him. "We most likely will be," he said, not wishing to scare her. "But if something should happen to either of us, or both of us, you can still make it on time yourself."

From the corner of his eye, he saw her studying him, as if trying to put a name, or a reason, to his insistence. But he couldn't explain it himself. All he knew was that he felt a responsibility to help her reach her sister, no matter what lay ahead, that went deeper than the promised money or adventure.

"I agree with Myles," Amos interjected as he gathered the horses' reins to lead them to the river. "I'll tie up the animals, but be sure you're shooting that revolver a ways off."

Myles nodded and started in the opposite direction. When Delsie didn't immediately follow, he turned back. "Coming?"

Her brow pinched in a determined way. "Very well."

He led her north toward a distant stand of trees. A tin can or two would've been nice for target practice, but Myles figured he could improvise. When they reached the trees, he went to the thickest and pointed to a particularly large knot in the wood. "This is your target."

Moving closer, she scrutinized the marking, then nodded.

He paced off ten steps. "Stand back here." Delsie threw another glance at the knot before coming to stand next to him. "Here's the gun." He set it in her hand.

Her gaze went wide like a spooked animal. "But I don't know what to do."

He released a soft chuckle. "Right now, I just want you to hold it. Get used to the weight of it."

Something more than determination etched her pretty face. Myles realized with a start it was trust. She trusted him, through and through. How long had it been since he'd inspired that sort of confidence? Since someone had relied on him? Not since Charles's death.

A soft exhale of breath pulled his attention back to Delsie. "I think I'm ready to try shooting it."

"Then face the tree." When she did so, he stepped directly behind her. "First thing you want to do is cock the hammer. You'll do that each time you shoot." He indicated the hammer on the gun and waited while she clicked it back. "Next you want to bring the gun to shoulder level and line up the notch on top of the hammer with the bead on the end of the gun."

Delsie lifted the gun and aimed at the tree.

"Now, when you're ready, you squeeze the trigger. But remember the gun will kick—"

The sudden explosion of the revolver ended his warning. Delsie slammed back against him with a cry. Instinctively, Myles gripped her waist to steady her. A whisper of lavender still scented her hair, reminding him of the moment they'd shared while brushing her mare two nights before. Had it only been two days ago? The more time he spent in her company, the harder it was to believe he hadn't always known her.

"Are you all right?" So much for his warning about the gun kicking back.

She twisted to look at him, her eyes as large as wagon wheels. "I think so. Did I hit the tree?"

Releasing her from his grip, Myles walked over to the tree and examined the trunk. A couple feet above the knot, he found the dent from the bullet. "You hit it here," he called back to her, indicating the spot on the tree.

Delsie's expression lit up. "Really? I didn't think I hit it at all."

"Let's have you try again." She swung the gun up to shoulder level, causing Myles to leap out of the way. "Wait a minute, woman. Don't shoot until I'm behind you."

"Sorry." Her cheeks flushed, but she threw him an impish smile.

The action coaxed a smile from him, as well. Learning to shoot might be serious business, but that didn't mean he couldn't enjoy it.

"Don't forget to cock it, either," he reminded as he positioned himself behind her.

Delsie cocked the hammer, lifted the gun again and took aim. This time, when she fired, she rocked back only a few inches.

"I think you were closer." Myles moved to the tree, Delsie trailing him. Sure enough the mark of the bullet stood only four inches above the knot.

"Again," she declared. Myles bit back a chuckle at this sudden desire to best herself.

They resumed their places and she pulled the trigger for a third time. Myles started to step past her to see where she'd struck the tree this time, but she motioned him back with her free hand. "I think that one was a little closer, but still to the left. Let me try once more."

She fired the revolver again, then joined him at the tree. The bullet had hit the outer edge of the knot. "Look at that." Her entire face lit up with pleasure as she fingered the dent in the trunk. "How many bullets do I have left?"

"Two."

"Then I want to see if I can be consistent."

Myles nodded in appreciation—Delsie didn't do things by half. It was another trait to add to the growing list of her redeeming qualities. Too bad he wouldn't get more than two weeks to discover all of them. She made for an intriguing puzzle of contrasts. Rich but humble, pretty but strong, unskilled but determined to learn.

Delsie waited a moment after he'd moved to stand behind her before she cocked and fired the revolver in rapid succession, twice. When she'd finished, she lowered the weapon and rushed to the tree as fast as her long skirt would allow.

"I did it," she declared over her shoulder.

Sure enough two bullet holes marred the knot, one almost dead center and the other slightly to the right. Myles ran a finger over both, disbelief and pride weaving through him. He'd expected to take the whole hour to teach her to shoot. Instead she'd mastered the skill in less than half that time and with a consistency that rivaled some of the Express riders he'd observed doing target practice.

"You sure you've never shot a gun before?" he asked, taking off his hat and brushing at his forehead with his sleeve.

She shook her head. "Does that I mean did all right?"

"All right?" Myles plopped his hat back on and chuckled. "You shoot nearly as good as Amos and me. And that's after one lesson. I don't think any nefarious characters stand a chance against you."

"Really?" A brilliant smile lifted her lips and turned her eyes as stunningly blue as the sky overhead.

Locks of her hair had escaped their pins, several curling against the creaminess of her cheeks. Myles fought the urge to feel one and lost. Lifting his hand, he fingered one long black curl.

"My hair must look a sight." Her voice sounded breathless. He swallowed a grin at the idea that he might be the cause. Perhaps there were a few things in this world that unsettled Miss Delsie Radford just a bit.

"I like it this way." The words were no more than a murmur, but he knew she'd heard him when the hand she'd self-consciously lifted to touch her hair fell to her side and a pretty blush stained her cheeks.

She gave a delicate cough. "Thank you for the lesson."

Whether she meant to or not, her gratitude had the power to jerk him back to the present and the task at hand. He needed to prepare her, not stand here ogling.

"That's just the first one." He let go of her soft curl and stepped back, ignoring the feeling of emptiness that settled in his gut. "Now you need to know how to saddle your mare."

With that he took his gun back and clomped toward the horses. There were a couple of lessons he needed to get through his own head, too. Like how to avoid falling for another pretty face with a full purse. That path only meant further pain. Because all he had to offer a rich young lady was a hard life and little money.

If he let his feelings for Delsie run deeper than his promise to see her safely to California, he would simply be reliving his experience with Cynthia. And that was something he wouldn't allow.

After saddling and unsaddling her mare and climbing on the mount unassisted at every stop along the trail, Delsie's arms ached. Now that it was evening, she could hardly hold the reins. But at least Myles seemed satisfied with her efforts. Or so she hoped.

His face had hardened into familiar lines and the

camaraderie they'd shared during her shooting lesson that morning had given way to determined quiet. She tried to coax another smile or laugh from him, but he remained solely intent on her instruction. While she was grateful for his help, even touched that he'd thought to teach her, she wished for the affable Myles to return.

Thank goodness there was only one more rest period before they stopped for the night, at a place known as O'Fallon's Bluff. She didn't know if her sore arms could last any longer. Her legs, on the other hand, were rapidly adapting to so much time in the saddle. The trousers Myles had given her helped, too, relieving her from the horrible chafing. She rather liked her wide-brimmed hat, as well. It certainly kept her face shaded from the beating sun.

Amos soon announced their stop, and Delsie gratefully slid to the ground. She stretched her arms above her head and behind her back to work out the soreness.

"I have a lesson for you, too," Amos said.

"What? No more saddling or unsaddling my horse?" She shot a rueful look at Myles, who was feeding Elijah pieces of jerky.

Amos chuckled. "I think you've got the hang of it now. Doesn't she, Myles?"

Myles grunted in agreement.

"All right. What's the lesson?" Delsie walked over to Amos, but she froze when he lifted a dead rabbit into the air.

"How to cook your supper."

She tried not to look at the lifeless eyes. "Where did you get that?"

Amos shrugged. "Two stops back, while you were working on saddling your mare." He motioned for her to follow him away from the copse of trees back onto the prairie. "First thing, you want to do is to clear a patch of grass, then you need to collect some dry wood for a fire."

Swallowing her revulsion for the dead animal, Delsie set her jaw. She could do this.

She tore up handfuls of grass until she had a circular plot of earth. Then she searched back near the trees for twigs and branches. Once she had an armful, she returned to Amos's side. He produced some flint and steel and patiently taught her how to use them to produce a spark. The tiny flame she finally manufactured filled her with immense pride. If only her father and sister could see her now.

Following Amos's instructions, Delsie fed the small fire with prairie grass and sticks until it doubled in size. "Now you've got to skin the animal," the older man explained.

"Skin it?" A clammy feeling crept over her, making her shiver despite the summer heat.

He simply nodded and handed her the knife he'd pulled from his boot. "You'll need to skin and gut it so you can get to the meat."

Delsie bit her lip. *No different than our cook at home would be doing,* she tried telling herself. But the sickish feeling grew worse as she accepted the knife and knelt beside the rabbit. She momentarily shut her eyes to gather her resolve, then opening them, she pushed the blade into the limp creature.

The sight of the crimson trail trickling from the

punctured fur made her turn and retch in the grass beside her. A kind hand settled onto her shoulder, bringing comfort even as she continued to spill her previous meal. At least it was Amos, and not Myles, who had witnessed her humiliating reaction.

When there was nothing left in her stomach, she shakily wiped at her mouth with the back of her hand. A part of her longed to flee and forget this whole wretched task, but another part wanted to prove she wasn't the spoiled, rich young lady Myles still saw her as. Resolute, she picked up the knife she'd dropped in her queasiness and squared her shoulders.

"You want to continue?" Amos asked gently.

Delsie bobbed her head once, her jaw clenched so hard it hurt. With his quiet voice filling her ears with instructions, she set about skinning the rabbit. Another wave of nausea washed over her as she proceeded to gut the creature, but Delsie clamped her teeth against it. She was too close to finishing to quit now.

At last the small hunk of rabbit meat lay ready for cooking. She stuck the blade into it and lifted it for Amos to see. "Done." She threw him a triumphant smile, which made him chuckle. Her dress and hands might be spotted with dirt and blood, but she'd skinned and gutted her first animal.

"Good work." His blue-gray eyes were warm with approval. When was the last time her father had looked at her that way?

The sense of true accomplishment coursing through her nearly made her dizzy. "What do I do next?"

"Now we cook it." Amos showed her how to make a spit over the fire to roast the meat. While she sat beside it, he graciously removed the rabbit's remains. He returned with a water canteen and Delsie used it to rinse her mouth and wash her hands and skirt hem.

"You've done real well today." Amos took a seat on the ground next to her.

Myles's curtness during the saddling lessons came back. She plucked at a long piece of grass and twisted it around her finger. "I'm glad you think so."

Amos shot a look toward the trees, where Delsie could barely see Myles dozing, his hat over his face. "He thinks so, too, for all his gruffness. My guess is you surprised him, and he doesn't like surprises."

"I did?" She laughed. Annoyed him was probably more accurate. Although he did occasionally act as though he wanted to be her friend and protector.

"You don't fit his prejudice against rich folks, and it's unsettling to him."

Delsie eyed the fire and the meat. Did she really unsettle Myles? A small smile curved her mouth at the thought of keeping him on his toes, instead of the other way around.

"Don't give up on him." Amos's entreaty was low and heartfelt. "He needs your friendship. Maybe even more than you need his."

She shot a look at the older man's weathered face. "How can I possibly help *him*? I only learned how to cook my first meal today." She tossed her piece of grass into the fire with a smirk.

Amos rubbed at his bristled chin. "Maybe," he mused. "But I got a feeling God has the two of you here together for more than just reaching your sister."

The surprising thought seeped into her heart, but

before she could respond, Amos examined the meat and pronounced it was done. Removing the rabbit from its spit, he used a nearby flat rock to cut off a few sections. He popped one in his mouth, murmuring, "Tastes delicious."

Delsie accepted the piece he offered her on the end of his knife and took a bite. The meat, while not as seasoned as what she was used to at home, didn't taste as gamey as she'd thought it might. "Not bad."

"Why don't you see if Myles wants a piece, while I douse the fire? It's about time to ride again."

With a nod, she picked up the remaining meat and walked toward the trees. Myles was still dozing. Though his hat covered most of his face, she could see enough of it to notice the relaxed quality of his jaw and the way his handsome features were slack with sleep. He looked so peaceful. And she likely looked a fright. Her hair hung as limp as the rabbit had earlier, her dress still soiled in places from her cooking lesson. But she'd accomplished something she'd never done before today—three things, actually. The reminder renewed her confidence as she used her shoe to tap Myles's boot.

Immediately he scrambled up, wildly looking around. "What's wrong?"

She couldn't help a laugh. "Nothing. I have something for you to eat." She held out one of the pieces of meat.

Myles glanced at it, then up to her face. "Is it going to kill me?"

She shook her head. "If so, Amos and I will be joining you soon. Come on, try it."

"It's good," Amos said, approaching them.

Myles took the piece and tossed it into his mouth. Delsie watched him as he chewed. A flicker of surprise filled his dark eyes before he schooled his expression. "Not too shabby for rabbit," he conceded.

"Not too shabby for her first cooking lesson on an open fire, either," Amos added.

"Did you skin and gut the thing for her?"

Delsie placed one hand on her hip and glowered down at Myles. "He most certainly did not. I did it completely on my own."

"Is that so?" he studied her, his lips tweaking at the corners of his mouth. "In that case, my hat's off to the cook."

The caution had fled his gaze, replaced by blatant admiration that darkened the color of his eyes. Delsie's stomach quivered in response and her face felt suddenly warm. It was the same reaction she'd had earlier when he'd touched her hair and told her he liked it down.

"Thank you," she murmured quickly before turning her attention to Elijah and offering the bird the last morsel of meat. Had Amos been correct—did she unsettle Myles as much as he did her? Did he really need her friendship?

She glanced at him from the corner of her eye and caught him doing the same, his respect still evident on his face. Though he might not say it exactly, he was proud of what she'd accomplished. The realization set her heart thumping a little faster and couldn't erase her smile as they climbed onto the horses and struck out again.

Come what may, she wouldn't give up on Myles, just as Amos had admonished. Friendship, at least, was one thing that came easily to her. Even with a gruff Express rider.

## Chapter Seven

Dark clouds bunched together in the western sky, bringing steady unease to Myles. They were in for a storm, and reading the charged tension in the air, it wouldn't be a mild summer one, either. From the corner of his eye, he saw Amos watching the clouds, too, his mouth a hard line.

Slowing his steed, whom Myles had jokingly named Moses for taking him into the wilderness, he motioned for Amos to join him in front. "What do you think?"

Amos glanced back at Delsie, who was moving at a steady clip several paces behind them. "It might be best to wait it out, but…"

"We won't be able to make up the difference tomorrow," Myles finished for him.

"Better ask Delsie." The older man twisted in the saddle and called back to her. "Come on up here, Delsie."

She guided her mare next to Myles, looking for all the world like a horsewoman through and through, except for her fancy dress. But even that was showing signs of wear after five days of long travel. Still, Delsie hadn't lost one ounce of beauty.

"What's wrong?" She gazed at him, then at Amos, a slight frown on her lips.

Myles pointed at the sky ahead. "There's a storm coming. A good one, by the looks of it. We can wait it out, but that'll mean covering fewer miles today. It's your call."

As the men had done, Delsie scanned the darkening sky before them. A flicker of hesitation entered her eyes before her expression tightened with resolve. "I think we ought to keep going."

"Let's pick up our pace, then. The sooner we're through it, the better." Myles dug his heels into Moses's flanks and spurred the steed faster. Amos and Delsie followed suit.

A short time later the first drops of rain began to fall. The sudden rumble of thunder overhead made both Myles and his horse flinch. Elijah swooped down and took refuge on Myles's shoulder, hunkering down like a feather ball beneath his hat.

Gripping the reins tighter, Myles kept Moses moving at a steady gallop. The rain soon dampened his jacket and trousers, but thankfully, his hat kept his face—and Elijah—mostly free from the moisture. He'd ridden through storms before during his short time as an Express rider, and yet, the black clouds crowding each other like boulders overhead stirred unfamiliar uneasiness in him.

The rain had become a blustery drizzle, causing cold drops to slide down Myles's collar, when Amos announced it was time to stop. The three of them sought shelter in a small stand of trees, but even those didn't block the water completely. One look at Delsie told him she was beginning to feel as miserable as he was. She folded her arms tight against her soaked dress. Strands of wet hair lay down her back and shoulders.

"Here." Myles removed his jacket and draped it around her shoulders.

She shot him a look of gratitude and gripped the leather garment between both hands. "Th-thank you," she said, her teeth chattering. "Do you think it'll get any worse?"

Myles hated to lie. "Most likely."

"We shouldn't linger," Amos interjected, his gaze on the sky. "We can slow the horses to make up for not resting the full hour."

Delsie passed around some jerky they'd acquired at the home station that morning. No one spoke—Myles guessed the other two were paying as much attention to the driving rain and churning sky as him.

Once the dried meat was gone, he led the horses to a nearby creek. Though small, the rain had swelled the stream beyond its banks. He let them drink their fill, then led them back to the group. A nod from Amos signaled the brief rest period had come to an end. It was time to brave the weather again.

He saw some of the determination fade from Delsie's face as he helped her back into the saddle. She made a move to return his jacket to him, but he shook his head. "You keep it for now."

She rewarded him with a tiny smile before turning her mare around. Back in the saddle, Myles let

Amos take the lead this time. The rain soon had him
and Moses lowering their heads in a vain attempt to
avoid the sheets of water. The only parts of him not
wet were the patch of hair beneath his hat and the spot
on his shirt where Elijah roosted.

They plodded on, alternating the horses between
a walk and a trot. A shiver cut through Myles. He
couldn't remember the last time he'd been this
drenched. He looked beside him at Delsie, but she
wasn't there. Twisting in the saddle, he saw she'd fallen
behind. In the driving rain, he hadn't noticed. A prick
of alarm raced through Myles as he turned Moses
around.

"Delsie," he called as another crack of thunder filled
the air. She jerked in the saddle, making her mare
dance to the side. Her hands were pale where they
held the reins. "What happened? Are you all right?"

Her chin dipped, but Myles could see it was quivering from her chattering teeth. She had no color to
her face, either. "J-just c-cold. But I'll b-be all right."

Myles couldn't argue about the cold. "Can you keep
up?"

She gave another wordless nod. But he couldn't
shake his concern that she wasn't all right. He coaxed
Moses to quicken the pace and was relieved when Delsie did the same with her mare.

After that Myles lost count of how far they'd gone
or how much time had passed. The rain was the only
constant across the waterlogged prairie. Amos didn't
signal for them to stop again, so Myles kept Moses
moving, although he let the animal set its own pace
now and then.

Sometime later a sudden sting against his hand had him lifting his gaze to the sky. The rain was fast becoming pea-sized hail. Moses whinnied in protest and Myles fought the urge to do the same. No wonder the sky had looked ominous before. He hunched his shoulders, bringing Elijah to rest against his neck, to avoid some of the hailstones. Ahead Amos was doing the same, though he kept right on setting a steady pace for all three of them.

Myles glanced to his left, expecting to see Delsie there as she'd been the past while. All he saw, though, was open prairie and leaping icy stones as they struck the ground. She'd fallen behind him again.

He craned his head to see her. Her horse plodded along at least a hundred yards back. But it was the unnatural bounce of its rider that resurrected Myles's earlier fear.

Jerking Moses around, he hollered at Amos, then galloped back to Delsie. She appeared to be dozing, despite the hail, her arms no longer holding the reins but folded inside his jacket. Her entire body appeared to shake with the cold. He reached for her reins and stopped her mare. Only then did Delsie startle awake.

"Ar-are we there?" she rasped out from lips Myles thought looked more blue than white now.

"No. But you're riding with me." He passed the reins to Amos, who'd ridden up beside them. "I think she's too cold," he told the older man in a low voice. "I don't want her freezing to death."

The raw concern in Amos's blue-gray eyes mirrored the emotion tightening his own lungs. "I'll tie her horse to mine," Amos offered.

Myles passed him the reins, then he scooped Delsie off her saddle and onto his own. After removing his jacket from around her shoulders, he draped it around them both, cocooning her as best he could within its warmth. She settled back against his chest, her entire body trembling with cold, as Elijah readjusted his perch on Myles's shoulder. He wrapped his arm around her waist, gripping the reins with his free hand.

"Let's go, Moses," he urged, prodding the animal forward.

By now the hail had ceased, replaced by the steady rain once more. At least that was something to be grateful for, Myles thought wryly. He glanced down at Delsie, but all he could see was the top of her hat.

*Please help her be all right*, he found himself thinking, almost like a prayer. The idea of no longer having her in his life cut deeper than he'd ever thought possible five days earlier. *Because she's become as good a friend as Amos*, his mind argued. But his heart, thrumming fast within his chest, told a different story. It had been weeks since he'd last held a woman in his arms, and yet, the experience of embracing Cynthia had never inspired this sort of contentment, despite the precarious situation.

"Delsie?" he said, bending to speak near her ear.

Several long seconds passed before she answered, "Hmm?" Sleepiness laced her voice, provoking fresh anxiety within him.

"You've got to stay awake, sleeping beauty." The endearment rolled without effort off his tongue, though he wondered if she even noticed it in her dozing state.

"At least until we can get you out of the rain and get you warm."

"But I'm just…so tired… Myles."

He pressed her tighter to him, hoping his own warmth would add to hers. "I know, but I need you to stay awake for me. All right?"

She murmured something inaudible, then seemed to shake herself. "You could tell me a story."

"A story, huh?" He searched his memories for one. There were plenty of sad tales, but could he think of a happy one? "I remember the first time I got bucked off a horse. Landed so hard on my backside, I couldn't sit at the table for two days." He thought he heard her chuckle. "I told Charles, my stepfather, I would never ride again. But he said, 'Son, life's all about getting bucked off. You can't let it make you wallow in the dust, though. You gotta get yourself back up there and show it you ain't afraid.'"

Myles paused, the recollection filling him with a trace of happiness he hadn't felt in a long time. While he missed Charles, perhaps he'd been mistaken in not remembering the man more often in an effort to avoid the continued grief of his passing. Yes, there was pain in recalling some parts of the past, but there were plenty of joyful moments, too, like the one he'd just shared.

"So did you?" Delsie prompted, her voice still faint but no longer sounding so sleepy. "Did you get back up on the horse?"

"I did, and he never bucked me off again."

He could sense the smile on her face when she said, "Good for you, Myles. Do you have another story?"

"Plenty."

"Then I want to hear them."

The conviction in her tone warmed him through and through.

Delsie tried to focus on Myles's tales, some funny, some thought provoking, but the lure of sleep tugged at her again and again. She'd never felt so cold in her life. Even with the heat of Myles's jacket and his solid, warm chest behind her, she could hardly keep her body from shivering and her teeth from rattling. At least she was mostly protected from the rain.

Biting her frozen lip, she shifted in the saddle, hoping to keep herself awake. She knew she ought to be mortified about riding with a man like this. But she couldn't muster up any real emotion except a strange glimmer of satisfaction. What was it Myles had called her minutes or hours ago? *Sleeping beauty.* Did he really think her beautiful? She exhaled a soft sigh. Within the shelter of his arms, she felt safe, protected, comforted. If she weren't so chilled, she might be content to ride in this fashion all the way to California.

"Delsie?"

Myles's voice pierced her thoughts. "Yes?"

"Just making sure you're awake."

His concern brought a limp smile to her mouth. "Trying, truly."

"Good," he murmured, tightening his grip around her waist. She leaned back. A feeling of contentment drifted over her. She was powerless to keep her eyes open.

Sometime later she sensed a change in Myles's

voice. He was no longer telling her a story but talking urgently to Amos. "Are those lights up there? We've got to get her out of this weather. I can't keep her awake."

*But I can hear you*, she wanted to say. And yet, to speak the words out loud would take more energy and effort than she could muster.

"That's Julesburg," Amos was saying, "but we can't stop there."

"Why not?" Myles demanded.

Amos continued in his calm, unflustered way, "There's been talk of trouble, outlaw trouble. We can't afford to have the horses stolen."

A breath of resignation washed over her, heavy with defeat and fear. "Fine. But we've got to pick up the pace, Amos, even in the rain. I don't know how much longer she'll last out here."

*I'll be fine*, she wanted to reply. No harm would come to her when she had someone as good and decent as Myles around. Before she could attempt to voice her thoughts, though, the blanket of sleepiness descended once more.

The next thing she knew she was being jostled awake by the sudden stopping of the horse and the absence of Myles behind her. Delsie pried her eyelids open wide enough to see a lantern cutting through the wet darkness.

"We need one of your dugouts," Myles called to someone before he gently pulled Delsie from the saddle and settled her in his arms. Still cold and sleepy, she shut her eyes once more and rested her head against the crook of his neck. The bristles of his chin tickled her forehead as he carried her.

"Meat and coffee are needed, too." The other person made a reply that was lost to Delsie, but she didn't miss Myles's thunderous answer. "I don't care. The lady is sick, and we'll pay you double for whatever you can rummage up."

A grumbled murmur she took for consent drifted to her ears as Myles continued walking. A few moments later the battering rain disappeared, and she sensed she was no longer outside. With great effort, she opened her eyes. They were inside what she presumed must be a dugout. One wall butted up against a hillside and was comprised of solid dirt. The other three had been papered over entirely with newspaper.

"I'm going to set you down on the bed." Myles eased her onto the lumpy tick mattress, then stepped back, his face full of concern in the lamplight. A stove in the middle of the room gave off some heat, but she still shivered. "You need to change out of those wet clothes."

She nodded. "W-will you get m-my bag?"

"I'll be right back with it. Stay put."

Delsie nearly smiled. How would she possibly go anywhere on her shaky limbs? Besides, the fire, though weak, had begun to melt the frigid cold from her bones. There wasn't anywhere else she wanted to be. Except maybe in Myles's strong arms again. Her face flushed at the thought. Thank goodness he couldn't read her mind.

Myles returned sooner than she'd expected and thrust the bag at her. Delsie forced her frozen fingers to close over it. "There's no woman here to...to help you."

"I—I can do it."

He looked skeptical, but finally he gave her a curt nod and moved toward the door again. "I'll be right outside."

"Th-thank you, Myles."

The moment the door was closed, Delsie scooted to the edge of the bed. She removed her other traveling dress from her bag, grateful to find it was still dry, and began the laborious process of peeling off her wet clothes. Her fingers shook so badly she could hardly make them work, but after several starts and stops, she had the dry gown on and the wet one laid over one of the boxes serving as a chair to the nearby table.

"Delsie?" A knock followed Myles's call from the other side of the door.

"You can c-come back in." Her teeth were chattering less and less, though she still felt chilled to the core despite the dry clothes.

Myles and Amos both ducked inside, their hands full. Elijah flew from Myles's shoulder and alighted on the back of the only chair in the dugout. "We got the station owner to give us some coffee and some biscuits," Myles explained as he and Amos set the food on the table.

"Sounds good." When was the last time she'd eaten? Not since the jerky they'd shared when the rain had first started. She moved toward the table, but Myles shook his head, his mouth a fierce line.

"You need to be in bed. You can eat there."

Delsie wanted to argue, and yet, her knees had

begun to tremble again. With a sigh, she woodenly moved to the bed and sat down. Myles dropped a large buffalo robe onto her lap and legs. Immediately the warmth began to thaw her.

"Here's a biscuit and some coffee." Amos handed her the food and cup. Then he and Myles took their seats on the boxes around the table.

Delsie lowered her chin and silently blessed the food before thanking the Lord for their safe arrival. She was too exhausted to insist both men join her in prayer tonight. When she opened her eyes, she found Myles watching her, a slightly amused spark in his dark eyes.

"You gonna say one for all of us?"

A jolt of surprise ran through her. He was inviting her to pray? "Of course." She bent her head a second time and quietly repeated the words she'd just said. "Father, bless this food. Thank you for our safe arrival and for Your watchful hand over our journey. Bless us this night. In Thy Son's name. Amen."

The repeated amens, especially from Myles, filled her throat with a lump of gratitude that the coffee couldn't quite wash down. She likely owed her life tonight to these two men.

She managed to drain her cup and finish off her biscuit before her energy began to wane once more. Lying down on her side, Delsie pulled the buffalo robe nearly to her chin. The fur smelled stale, but she wouldn't begrudge its warmth.

At any minute, she expected Myles and Amos to head off to their own dugouts. A measure of loneliness filled her at the thought. The cold had eased considerably within her, but she still felt weak and vulnerable. Instead of leaving, though, once the food had been eaten and the lamp turned low, both men pulled more buffalo robes from the corner and spread them out on the dirt floor. Each one removed his boots and hat before lying down on his respective fur. Amos immediately shut his eyes.

"What are you doing?" Delsie asked Myles in a whisper. He'd taken the spot nearest the bed.

"Someone needs to keep the fire going all night." He placed his hands behind his head, his gaze toward the ceiling. "My turn is first."

Surprise, and tear-filled relief, washed over her. She tried to blink back the moisture, but a few droplets escaped her efforts and slid down her warm cheeks. Myles and Amos were going to keep the fire going all night for her.

Her father would be furious if he could see her now, sharing this small space with two men who'd been complete strangers to her less than a week ago. But Delsie couldn't muster up any amount of embarrassment, only weariness and more tears.

"I'm sorry I've been such a burden," she admitted in a soft voice that wobbled with emotion. She'd been so determined to reach Lillie that she hadn't stopped to think about what trouble a city girl such as herself might cause two seasoned riders.

"Delsie." Her name sounded as much a chastisement as a gentle touch. Though the shadows hid his face, she still sensed that intense gaze leveled on her. "There aren't many women who could've survived a single day of this kind of travel. Let alone five." She watched him twist onto his side to face her. "Some Express riders haven't even gone through half of what you have."

The honest praise warmed her more successfully than either the fire or the heavy buffalo robe. "Maybe I'll work for the Pony Express, then, after we've reached California," she teased.

"I hope not."

Delsie frowned. "But you just said—"

"I know." His low chuckle made her pulse quicken. "I figure the rest of us will be out of a job if they hire you."

She joined in his quiet laughter, smiling to herself at the implied compliment. "What would you do instead? If you weren't an Express rider?"

Myles shifted onto his back again. "I'd be a horse rancher." Delsie recalled his words from the other day about needing money to buy property. "Someday I'm going to own a big spread of land." His earnest tone reached out and held her captive, painting images in her mind as he spoke. "I'll build a nice big house on it with stables large enough to hold dozens of horses. Horses I'll breed and sell. I've even got the name of the ranch."

"What is it?"

"The B and P."

Delsie pulled the robe higher. "I imagine the *P* stands for Patton. But what does the *B* stand for?"

"Brown. It was my parents' last name."

"But you took Charles's name?"

Myles murmured agreement.

"He must a have been a wonderful father."

"He was." Both pride and pain colored his answer.

A strong urge to reach out and hold his hand swept through her. She understood the intense grief of losing a parent, and yet, Myles had lost three. Afraid he might not welcome her touch, though, she kept her hands buried beneath the robe and instead infused her next question with an empathetic tone. "What was he like?"

"Happy," Myles said with another chuckle. "Always an optimist, no matter how bad things seemed. He was honest and kind, too." He paused as if weighing whether to add something else to the list. "He was also God-fearing. Like you."

She sensed what he didn't add—Myles had been the same, at one time. It was easy to tell how much he admired Charles Patton. But did he see that he, too, was as trustworthy and caring as his stepfather had obviously been?

Before Delsie could give voice to her thoughts, a loud snore from Amos filled the dugout. She and Myles both laughed. With a grunt, Amos rolled onto his side. Quiet descended over the room once more.

"Tell me another story," she prompted. She wasn't ready to have their conversation over yet—Myles had talked more to her today than he had the past five days combined.

"About what?"

She thought a moment. "About Charles. What are your favorite memories of him?"

When Myles didn't respond for a moment, she feared he would retreat back behind his typical gruffness. Then he cleared his throat. "All right. I can still remember the first time I met him…"

Delsie burrowed deeper beneath the buffalo robe

as she listened. His deep voice soothed her exhaustion. She no longer felt bone-tired or cold but perfectly comfortable.

Sometime later the creak of the stove door startled her awake. She hadn't realized she'd fallen asleep. "What time is it?"

Myles lay back down on his makeshift bed. "Late."

"I didn't mean to fall—"

"Delsie," he said cutting her off.

"Yes?" Was he upset that she hadn't stayed awake?

"Go to sleep," he said in a firm but kind tone.

"I can?" Even as she asked it, her eyelids refused to remain open.

"Yes, sleeping beauty." His unseen smile permeated each word. "You'll be fine now."

*You'll be fine.* Peace blanketed her at the heartfelt reassurance, as effectively as the heat from the stove. How long had it been since she'd felt such peace?

*Rather ironic*, she thought with a smile, as she snuggled deeper into the lumpy mattress. That peace would find her in a dirt house in the middle of Nebraska.

## *Chapter Eight*

To Myles's keen eye, his horse's steady gallop had begun to lag. Time for another rest. "Amos?" he called. The older man, acting as lead today, twisted in the saddle to look at Myles. "Know where you want to rest?"

Amos pointed at the rock formation that had been in their sights the past thirty miles or so. "I heard there's a spring near Chimney Rock. We can stop and water the horses there."

Myles eyed the rock, which had grown increasingly taller the closer they came to it. It wasn't the first unusual formation they'd seen today—they'd passed by two others that Amos had informed them were called Courthouse Rock and Jail Rock.

Judging by the surrounding terrain, Myles knew the flatness of the plains would soon be a distant memory. Not that he minded. The thought of the mountainous landscape Amos had explained lay ahead filled him with as much excitement as it did trepidation. There was so much of the West, and this country, he hadn't expected to see. But now that he had a taste of what lay beyond his own Express run and Saint Joe, he couldn't help wanting to experience more and more. In a way, traveling farther than he ever had before made his dream of a horse ranch feel a little more within reach.

"Are we stopping?" Delsie rode up beside him.

Myles nodded and pointed at Chimney Rock. "Amos says there's a spring near the rock."

"Oh good," she said, turning to gaze at the formation. "I was hoping we might get close to it."

Myles studied her profile, analyzing those beautiful features for any signs of fatigue. After their ordeal in the rain the night before, he had purposely slowed the pace of the horses on the first two stretches of their ride today to ensure she wouldn't tire too easily. Once she figured out what he was doing, though, she'd insisted on returning to their normal speed.

If anything she looked more radiant this afternoon, her blue eyes bright as she took in the passing scenery, her lips curved in a slight smile. Or perhaps riding close with her last night and telling her stories from his life had addled his brain. Myles could almost believe it. Some of those stories he'd never told anyone, not even Cynthia, whom he'd known for years. But it was more than that. Despite his best efforts, Delsie was slowly picking her way through his defenses.

The fear he'd suffered last night when he thought she might not make it had felt as frigid and paralyzing as a snowstorm on the prairie. He would have done anything to help her. The last time he'd felt that way was when he'd watched Charles's life slip away. Thankfully, Delsie had survived. The relief he'd experienced, knowing she would be all right, had been every bit as sweet as his anxiety had been bitter.

There was no doubt in his mind Delsie was a fighter. If he could find a woman like that, strong and determined, then perhaps he wouldn't mind sharing his name and his dream of a ranch with someone else.

The thought brought a ripple of surprise running through him. Did he really want to meet and court another woman after experiencing Cynthia's treachery? Of its own volition, his mind filled with the memories of the last time he'd seen her.

*Myles waited in the moonlight by the gardenia bush. The heady scent of the flowers always reminded him of Cynthia's perfume. Music and laughter floated on the warm evening air from the nearby three-story house. The Grovers' party was in full swing. Would Cynthia be able to sneak away as her note had promised?*

*The swish of full skirts preceded her. Myles smiled and stepped forward. He'd always thought Cynthia looked like a porcelain doll with her white face, red lips and blond hair.*

*"Myles," she said, her voice breathless as if she'd raced across the lawn. As eager to see him as he was to see her, he hoped.*

*He took both her gloved hands in his. "Hello, darling."*

*She turned her cheek to allow him to press a quick kiss to her smooth skin. "I couldn't get away from the captain a moment sooner. Have you been waiting long?"*

*"Not long." The thought of that army gentleman*

*dancing with Cynthia made Myles frown. It should be him whirling her around the Grovers' fancy parlor. But try as he might he couldn't quite picture himself there—dressed in something nicer than his church clothes, talking with Cynthia's father about politics and the state of the world.*

"I only have a few minutes." She heaved a sigh, then brightened just as rapidly. "Do you like my new ball gown?"

He twirled her around. "You look as pretty as ever. Did you speak with your mother and father?"

Cynthia shifted her weight, throwing a glance at the house behind them. "I did."

"And?" Some of his impatience leaked into his tone, making it sharper than Myles had intended. But he'd waited six long years for this day—the day Cynthia would finally be twenty-one. Old enough to decide for herself whom she wanted to marry.

"Myles, I love you. You know that."

Why did the words set off a loud clang of warning inside his head? He gave her hands a gentle squeeze. "I love you, too, Cindy, and that's why I want to marry you."

"I—I know. It's just... Mother and Father..."

Myles ground his teeth as irritation washed over him. "They still don't approve of me, do they?"

Cynthia dipped her head in a nod, sending her blond curls bobbing. "I don't think they've forgiven you for turning down the position of livery stable overseer this winter. I told them that your job with the Pony Express is a good one, but my father said the venture's *too new to know for certain. He says you can't pro-vide for me."*

*"I can—I will." Myles rubbed his thumb over the fine fabric of her gloves. "I can make good money as an Express rider, but I don't plan on doing that for-ever. You know I want to have a horse ranch some-day."*

*"I told my parents as much."*

*Myles pushed out his breath. "You're old enough to decide for yourself, Cynthia." He tugged her closer. "I may not be able to give you ball gowns or servants, but I promise to be a loving and honorable husband."*

*She broke free from his hold to cover her face with her hands. A quiet sob escaped her fingers. "Oh, Myles." He drew her head to his shoulder. "I don't want this to end... I don't want to say goodbye."*

*Goodbye? He released her, his gut twisting into a knot. "What are you saying?"*

*"I can't marry you. Father forbade it."*

*"But...but we love each other. We could go right now and wake the pastor. Start our life together like we've always wanted. Even without your parents' per-mission."*

*Cynthia brushed at her cheeks. "I want to, I do. But I can't defy my mother and father. I'm the only child they have and they want me to marry well."*

*"To someone like the captain?" Myles didn't bother to hide his bitterness.*

*"Oh, see. You do understand. I knew you would."*

*His jaw went slack. Did Cynthia care for him at all? Had their courtship only been a way for her to rebel against her parents' demands? He'd waited all this time for her to choose and now she had, but it wasn't him she'd chosen.*

As he stared into her half-smiling face, something hardened inside Myles. She was like every other debutante he'd seen come into the livery stable—spoiled, frightened of poverty and in love with wealth. At least he'd discovered the truth now, rather than several years into their marriage.

"Goodbye, Cynthia." The words tasted ripe with rejection.

"Will I see you again?" All traces of her earlier distress had disappeared.

Myles shook his head. "Give your mother and father my best."

"Myles, are you angry?"

He didn't respond. Instead he spun around and marched down the street, toward the river. He'd been a fool, thinking he—an orphan and Express rider—could woo and marry one of the town's most eligible young ladies.

Moses suddenly danced to the side and halted, jerking Myles from his thoughts. He looked up to see he'd nearly plowed them into Amos's horse. "Sorry," he grumbled as he and the older man dismounted. They'd reached Chimney Rock and the spring while Myles had been lost in his memories.

Amos shot him an amused look but kept blessedly silent.

"Want to explore the rock?" Delsie asked, her face etched with wonder.

Myles glanced at Amos, but the man was already

leading the horses toward the water. "You two go on. I'll see to the animals."

Delsie led out, holding her skirt in one hand as she picked her way across the grass. The pant legs of her trousers showed beneath her hem, calling to mind Myles's brief glimpse at her shapely calf that first day. A smile worked his mouth at the memory of how proper she'd tried to be, even without a sidesaddle.

*Now look at her*, he thought with a wry shake of his head, *traipsing through the brush without a care for her dress and wearing that hat like a real rider.* He could hardly believe they'd only met less than a week ago. It seemed more like a month after all they'd been through.

At the base of the rock spire, Delsie stopped. Myles came up beside her. Instead of the lofty height of the formation, her attention seemed riveted on the names and initials carved into the soft rock. There were dozens and dozens of them, some fresh, others growing faint from the effects of the sun, rain and wind.

"Just think how many people have passed by this very spot." She reached out and traced a name with her finger. "All looking for a new life out West." Her voice held the same wistfulness it did whenever she spoke of her sister. Did Delsie hold out hope of possibly carving a new life out here, too?

Myles reached into his boot and withdrew his knife. "I say we add our names to theirs."

She looked from the knife to him, then smiled fully. "All right." She accepted the blade then began chiseling her name into the stone. He let his gaze wander up the towering rock. Had God made it this way? As a beacon for those coming West?

"There." Delsie brushed dust from the letters with her hand and passed him the knife. She'd carved only her first name.

Myles went to work, scoring his full name—Myles Brown Patton—into the rock. When he'd finished, he stepped back in satisfaction. Let all the world know he'd come this way, and the next time he passed by this rock, he'd see how well his name had weathered the elements.

Delsie had walked a short distance away as he'd been carving. He found her staring east, her arms clasped tight, her expression pensive. The reason she hadn't chiseled her full name into the rock suddenly hit him.

"Your father doesn't know you're doing this, does he?"

Pressing her lips together, she shook her head.

"Don't you think he's sick with worry?" He might not be a parent himself, but he couldn't imagine a father being anything less than panicked over the disappearance of his daughter.

Delsie kicked at a clump of grass. "No…he thinks I'm still at my aunt Cissy's in Saint Louis. At least for another few weeks."

"Where does your aunt think you are?"

A half-rueful smile appeared on her lips. "Heading back home, by way of a friend's."

Myles followed her gaze across the prairie to the eastern horizon. What would Mr. Radford do if he found out his daughter was not in Missouri as he'd supposed but halfway across the country? "Why not just tell him what you were doing?"

"He would have refused to let me come." Her voice held such melancholy that it twisted Myles's heart. "Papa told Lillie if she went after Clay that he would never contact her again. It would be as if she no longer existed." She blew out a breath as if repeating the words caused her fresh pain. "He wasn't trying to be cruel—he may be stern and rigid sometimes but never cruel. I think he honestly thought such an ultimatum would make Lillie change her mind. But she's as stubborn as him." An embittered laugh escaped her mouth.

"Then why risk his anger yourself?"

Delsie turned to look at him, her gaze full of the same raw resolution he'd seen time and again these past six days. "Because I made a promise to my mother, when she was dying. She pleaded with me to keep my family together. When Lillie left, I thought I'd failed."

She removed her hat and brushed a lock of dark hair from her forehead. "Then I found the letters she'd written me—letters Papa had hidden. In her last one Lillie told me if she didn't hear from me by the time she married, she would not attempt to contact me again. Our family..." Delsie visibly swallowed as if gathering courage to finish. "Our family would be dead to her, as she'd been to our father this last year."

Admiration burned warm inside Myles. For the first time since agreeing to come along, he could see what this journey could cost Delsie, especially if she didn't make it to her sister in time. She was willing to sacrifice physical discomfort, her father's potential wrath and possibly her own life in an effort to hold her small family together. That was something Charles had understood and lived, up until the day he'd died.

A sudden longing for a noble cause, for a family of his own, filled Myles to distraction. He'd told himself he was content living alone with only Elijah for company and visiting with Amos during his Express runs. But maybe it wasn't enough.

He reached out his hand, motioning her toward him. She hesitated only a moment before she moved into his arms. "We'll get you there, Delsie," he murmured. "Don't you worry. We'll help you keep your promise."

She nodded against his shoulder, while he stroked her hair as if she were a frightened child or the sister he'd never had. Nothing could be further from the truth, though. The same perfection he'd felt riding with her on Moses and carrying her into the dugout yesterday rose up within him as he held her.

Too bad the one girl he could easily picture being at his side forever would never be free to choose him. She'd witnessed the pain her sister's choice in beaus had inflicted on their father—and Myles knew as sure as she was standing here that Delsie would never do the same.

The beginning notes of a fiddle drew Delsie from the station porch where she'd been sitting with Amos and Myles. They'd left Chimney Rock behind hours ago.

"Do you hear that?" she asked, her toe tapping beneath her skirt.

A short distance to the west a large wagon train had

encamped for the night. It was the first wagon company Delsie had seen. She'd wanted to wander over and talk to the emigrants, but her dusty, dirt-covered traveling dress made her hesitate. Not that the wagon occupants would be faring significantly better. Now the lure of the music called at her to abandon her embarrassment.

While she appreciated Amos's occasional harmonica concert, Delsie still missed the music she'd experienced nearly every day back at home. Playing music on the piano, listening to it at the opera and especially, dancing to it.

"Do you think they're going to have a dance?"

Myles shrugged at her question, even as the song changed from a lively ditty to a polka.

Delsie returned to the porch and motioned for the two men to stand. "Come on, gentlemen. I need a partner."

Amos laughed but shook his head. "Don't know if these old bones can handle dancing after another hard day's ride." Delsie couldn't help thinking his words contradicted his usual agility, which sometimes seemed to rival even hers and Myles's. The older man cut a glance at Myles—one that looked rather calculated to Delsie. "Why don't you go on, Myles?"

"Me?" Myles removed his hat and wiped at his brow with his sleeve. "You know I'm not much of a dancer, Amos."

"I'll teach you," Deslie volunteered. Even if Amos was scheming to give her and Myles more time to themselves, she didn't care. Right now she only wanted to dance and forget for a few blissful moments the hard task ahead of her and her father's irate response when he eventually found out about it. "Please, Myles."

He eyed her sternly, but she gave him a sweet smile in return. Finally he pushed out a sigh and climbed to his feet. "Fine."

"Thank you." She resisted the urge to kiss his bearded cheek in gratitude. Instead she clasped her hands together and fell into step beside him as they headed toward the wagon train. The music grew louder the closer they came. Delsie did a little skip at the thought of dancing.

Myles's low rumble of a laugh sounded beside her. "I don't think I've seen you this excited since I told you I'd take you on my run that first day."

Her cheeks warmed with a blush, but she ignored it. "I love dancing nearly as much as I do my sister." He rewarded her joke with a full smile, making her heart skip right along with her feet.

At the edge of the circled wagons, he stopped her. "Why don't you teach me here?"

Between two of the wagons, she could see a group, young and old, dancing to the fiddle's lively music. Their energy begged her to come closer, but she feared she'd lose her partner if she insisted. At least they were close enough to easily follow along to the tune.

"All right." She turned to face Myles and lifted her right hand in the air. "You'll hold this hand here and your other will go on my waist."

He complied, taking her hand in his. He placed his right hand on her waist as she rested her left one on his shoulder. Flurries erupted in Delsie's middle at his touch and the way he gazed intently at her. Being in his arms, in this way, felt different than when he'd comforted her earlier that afternoon.

"You…uh…might want to take off your hat," she said, the words sticking in her dry throat.

Without breaking eye contact, Myles pulled off his hat and tossed it onto the grass nearby. Delsie couldn't help chuckling.

"You're going to do fine. Just follow my lead."

"Sounds like business as usual." His lips worked up into a teasing smile, drawing her attention to them. What would it be like to kiss those masculine lips? Flynn had given her several chaste pecks on the cheek, though he hadn't attempted to kiss her mouth yet. She'd harbored a slight disappointment over that fact, but now she felt secretly glad. Perhaps Flynn wasn't the man she wanted to share her first real kiss with after all. "So what do we do?"

Myles's inquiry broke through her thoughts, eliciting another blush. She'd be mortified if he could guess at what she'd been thinking.

Lifting her chin, she did her best to school her chaotic feelings. "The polka is quite simple. It's basically a skip step and a turn." She demonstrated with her feet, tugging Myles with her. "One and two, one and two."

After a few steps, he caught the gist. They whirled around across the ground, in time with the music.

"You're doing good," Delsie declared with a smile. "Now that you have those steps, we can try to add something fancier—"

Myles interrupted her by spinning her out and back to him, all the while keeping time with the polka beat.

Delsie stared at him in astonishment. "I thought you said you didn't dance."

"No. I said I wasn't much of a dancer." He spun her out again as he added, "Charles taught me more than how to work with horses. It's just been a few years since I made use of his lessons."

"Did you never dance with your girl back in Missouri?"

It was the wrong thing to say. Myles slowed to a stop, his expression one of hardened pain. "Not in her fancy parlor. I was never invited to those parties."

Delsie sensed he didn't want her pity, so she kept silent. But that didn't stop memories marching through her mind of parties at home in Pennsylvania, parties Lillie's beau had never been invited to. "Well, I think that's a real shame." She tipped her head up to look him in the eye. "Because you're quite adept on your feet."

The guarded quality faded from his dark eyes, replaced by an appreciative gleam. "I've had two good teachers."

She laughed as he led her through another of the fiddler's polka numbers. They moved in perfect time with each other, his hand holding her waist with gentle pressure. The longer they danced the more his normal gruff exterior dropped away. Without his hat, she was able to peruse his face unencumbered. She could easily imagine him turning many female heads back at home with his bristled jaw, strong shoulders and unfathomable dark eyes.

Those eyes studied her with equal abandon, setting Delsie's pulse galloping along with their feet and re-

newing the flurry of sensations in her stomach. Wasn't
this how Lillie had described her feelings for Clay
when Delsie asked if her sister loved the poor farmer?

*I love him very much*, Lillie had answered.

*But how do you know it's love?* she'd countered.

Lillie had smiled. *You know it in the way your heart
pounds every time you see him. Or how butterflies
alight in your stomach when he touches your hand.*
She had drawn her knees up to her chin and wrapped
her arms around them. *But most of all, you know it
when he fills your thoughts. When your heart wells
up with peace and joy at the idea of being with him
forever.*

Delsie had never felt anything even remotely similar when it came to Flynn. Myles on the other hand…
Her breath caught in her throat. Could she possibly be
feeling more than friendship for this Express rider? It
seemed ridiculous, having only known him a mere six
days, and yet, she'd experienced many of those same
emotions in regard to Myles that Lillie felt for Clay.

"Are you all right?" he asked.

Delsie realized she'd slowed and was no longer following his lead. "I'm sorry. I think I just need to…to
sit down." He didn't look convinced until she added
in a light tone, "All that twirling around."

Myles finally released her. Taking a seat on the
ground, she took in deep breaths of the summer air to
slow her rapidly beating heart. He dropped down beside her. They listened in silence to the dance music.

When the song ended, the fiddler struck up a different sort of number. Instead of dancing, the emigrants

began to sing. She couldn't decipher the words, but the melody rang with conviction and hope.

"My father has a man at home he wants me to marry." The admission was out before she even considered why she was saying it. Something about Myles's comforting presence and the music pulled it from her. "His name is Flynn Coppell. He manages my father's bank."

Myles didn't respond right away. Instead he leaned back on his elbows, his gaze on the emigrants. "Do you care for him?"

"I don't know. He's Papa's choice." She ripped up a piece of prairie grass and twisted it around her finger. "Did you care for…?"

"Cynthia?" he supplied.

"Yes, Cynthia." She knew she was being overly bold by asking, but she couldn't dismiss her curiosity about this woman who'd clearly captured Myles's attention.

Myles sat up and rested his arms on his knees. "I did care for her. Thought she felt the same, too. But she didn't."

"What happened?" she asked quietly, fearing he wouldn't answer.

A heavy sigh drifted toward her before he spoke again. "I guess you could say she was a lot like your sister. Except instead of choosing me, she chose the man her parents wanted."

Sadness filled Delsie at his story along with a measure of irony at the similarities to Lillie's. "How long had you known her?"

"Six years." Picking up his hat off the grass, he fingered the brim. "She came into the livery stable three times in a matter of days. Charles finally told me it wasn't because she had a real need of a horse. We saw each other at least twice a week after that."

"Did her parents know?"

"Not for a few years." His regretful tone wasn't lost on Delsie. "Maybe if they had, things might have gone differently." He shrugged. "Then again, I don't know that she and I would have been happy together. Cynthia would have hated all this."

She felt relief to hear his voice no longer held bitterness but resignation. "You mean the dirt and the weather and the scanty food?" She swept her arm in an arc to take in the Express station, the distant bluffs and the wagons. "Why, this is a palatial palace, Myles Patton."

He chuckled, as she'd hoped. "Then that makes you the queen, Delsie Radford."

Rather than teasing, the words sounded more like an endearment. One that filled her heart with warm pleasure. She busied herself with the grass she'd plucked up.

"We'd better head back," he said, disrupting the quiet between them. "Early start again tomorrow."

She dipped her head in a nod. Before she could climb to her feet, though, he offered her his hand. Delsie allowed him to help her up, though it meant she stood rather close to him again.

"Thank you for the dance lesson." He brushed an errant hair from her face, her hand still gently gripped in his.

"You're welcome," she managed to get out over the

pounding of her heartbeat in her throat. "Thank you for dancing with me."

He smiled and released her hand. But even as they started back across the grass toward the home station, Delsie couldn't quell her racing pulse. Why in the world had she let herself develop feelings for a man her father would never condone as a suitable husband? A man who, if she chose, would only further divide her splintered family?

# Chapter Nine

After witnessing the distant bustle of Fort Laramie, Wyoming, as they'd ridden past, Delsie found the present hills almost too quiet, devoid of people or movement. She shifted in the saddle, tugging her hat farther down on her head against the incessant sun. Though she hadn't wanted to stop at the fort after her last encounter near Fort Kearney, she couldn't entirely squelch her curiosity at seeing a place that teemed with more life than she'd seen in several days. They'd been riding for a solid week now.

"Which means today is Sunday." She'd forgotten until this moment. At home she would have been attending church with her father, but out here, there was no house of worship. That didn't mean she couldn't hold her own little service, though. Amos would certainly join her, but Delsie wasn't sure about Myles. "No harm in asking."

At the next stop, Delsie broached the subject as soon as she'd dismounted. "Gentlemen, I've realized it's the Sabbath and I would like to hold a little service."

She caught the sudden rigidness of Myles's shoulders even before she'd finished. "If you don't wish to take part, that's perfectly fine. I'll be…" She motioned to a spot along the banks of the North Platte. "Over there."

"I'll join you." Amos removed his hat. "It's been far too long since I've had someone else to worship with."

Delsie smiled her pleasure. "Wonderful. And you, Myles?" A strong hope stirred within her, but it was dashed the moment he spoke.

"I'll tend to the horses," he muttered.

"We'll be over there should you change your mind," she said with forced cheerfulness. She kept her chin up as she walked to the spot she'd indicated, Amos trailing her. But inside she felt like crying. Why should she care if Myles didn't want to participate? Why couldn't she be content with him asking her to bless their meal the other night and not hope for more?

*Because I like him—very much*, her heart admitted.

She pushed the thought aside. No good would come from exploring it. Her father would never approve of her choice, just as he hadn't Lillie's.

Once she was settled on the grass, Delsie watched the flow of the river for a moment. Too bad she didn't have a Bible. "What shall we do first?" she asked Amos when he sat down next to her. She wasn't entirely sure the best way to proceed.

He rubbed at his gray beard. "How about we start with prayer?"

"Yes." She managed another smile. "That would be lovely. Would you say it, Amos?"

With a nod, he bowed his head and verbalized their gratitude for a safe journey and for God's blessings in their lives. He prayed for her family, for her and Myles, and for continued protection and guidance. By the time he murmured "Amen," there were tears swimming in Delsie's eyes.

No matter her worries or unconventional situation, she felt certain she would be all right. God was looking out for her. *And Myles, too*, something whispered inside her. *Don't give up on him*. The words echoed those Amos had said to her.

Brushing at her wet eyes, she smiled at the older man. "Thank you. Now how about we share our favorite Bible verses?"

The sound of singing reached Myles's ears, even though he was trying hard to ignore the two figures seated by the river's edge. Amos's tenor mixed perfectly with Delsie's sweet soprano. Against his better judgment, Myles found himself listening.

For the beauty of the earth,
For the glory of the skies,
For the love which from our birth
Over and around us lies:
Lord of all, to Thee we raise
This our hymn of grateful praise.

For the beauty of each hour,
Of the day and of the night,
Hill and vale, and tree and flower,
Sun and moon, and stars of light:
Lord of all, to Thee we raise
This our hymn of grateful praise.

Could there be more perfect words to describe their journey West this past week? Try as he might he couldn't resist the pull and harmony of the music, even if he didn't know the words. He began to hum baritone, quietly, as he walked toward them. On the now-familiar chorus, Myles finally joined his voice full force with theirs.

Delsie whirled around, her eyes wide with unconcealed surprise. She kept right on singing to the end of the chorus, though, as Myles lowered himself to the ground at her left.

The final harmonious notes floated crystal clear across the river. "That," Delsie said, clearing her throat, "was lovely. Thank you, both."

He couldn't quite work up the nerve to look at her fully—not after refusing to join them earlier. But he was spared having to do so when Amos suggested they end with another prayer. Delsie offered it.

He'd grown accustomed to her simple, heartfelt prayers, ones that sounded more like a conversation than a list of blessings or needs. *Perhaps if I could talk to God that way.* The thought startled Myles enough that he opened his eyes. When had he started thinking he needed the Lord in his life again?

Probably about the time this dark-haired female sitting next to him had showed up at the Express stables, with her double measure of determination and faith.

After Delsie's prayer, Amos volunteered to check on the horses. Myles let the not-so-subtle excuse go; he found he wasn't ready yet to disrupt the peace he felt sitting here beside the river with Delsie. Though he might have to corner the older man later and ask what Amos was doing by constantly trying to give them time together. Nothing would come of it. They were both aware of that. Amos was wasting his time trying to create something that would never be.

"Did you like that hymn?" Delsie asked. Her tone sounded innocent enough, but he guessed what she was really asking. Why had he decided to join them at the end?

"It sounded like a good one." He bit back a smile when his noncommittal answer brought a frown to her lips.

She started to rise. "Yes, well, I suppose it's time to go."

"I haven't sung a hymn in years," Myles admitted, keeping his gaze on the river. From the corner of his eye, he saw her slowly sit back down. "Haven't been in a church, either." He fingered his hat. "Not since before Charles died."

Delsie drew her knees up to her chest and rested her chin there. "The death of a parent is very difficult, at any age."

"I didn't think I fit in after that," Myles added. A part of him wanted to stop talking, to rebury the hurt, but a greater part of him wanted to share the burden weighing him down. "I had no family, no wife. What use did God have for me? He started to feel about as unobtainable and distant as Cynthia and her rich society life."

Momentary silence met his words. Myles stared at his hat, embarrassment creeping over him. He'd gone and said too much. Delsie was likely to pity or condemn him, and he had no use for either.

"Why did you name your bird Elijah?"

The question caught him off guard. "What?"

"Elijah? Where did his name come from?"

Myles glanced up to see that determined glint in her dark blue eyes. He'd underestimated her—again. She wasn't going to heap judgment on him; she was going to root around until she found even a single seed of faith still sprouting inside him.

"His name comes from the Bible," Myles answered over a rueful smile. "But you knew that, didn't you?"

She shrugged, but not without smiling herself. "I suspected as much. Which story inspired you to pick Elijah?"

He couldn't help a grin. "The one when he and the pagan priests square off to call down fire from above. I always liked how he teases them to cry louder because he says maybe their god is sleeping." He chuckled, remembering the animated way Charles would tell the story. "But my favorite part is how he douses the entire altar with water before praying. And then the fire comes, lots of it."

Delsie remained silent, listening. Resting his hat on his knee, Myles found a pebble among the grass. "Elijah had no doubts God would hear him. Only faith and confidence." He lobbed the small rock into the river. "Of course, I also like the story about the ravens feeding him. I guess both of those influenced the bird's name."

"Maybe influenced you, too." She didn't pose it as a question, but Myles nodded just the same. "I think those are excellent reasons for naming him Elijah. Especially since it looks like God sent you a little fire, too. In the form of the bird, I mean."

Myles frowned in confusion. "Come again?"

Delsie twisted on the grass to face him. "When did you find Elijah?"

"About four months ago."

"Before everything ended with Cynthia, right?"

He rubbed at his chin, trying to figure out her line of reasoning. "Well, yes."

"See?" She sounded as if she'd just presented him with his horse ranch. "God knew you'd need someone. Someone who needed you, too." Her face radiated confidence in a way that enhanced her natural beauty.

Myles turned to stare at the river again. Uncertainty clouded his mind. What did Delsie know of real hardship or real faith? She'd never been challenged before this week, living in her fancy house with every possible need provided for.

*But she did lose her mother, a quiet voice inside reminded. Along with her sister. And now she's caught in a tug-o-war with her father over her family, with very little freedom to choose her own life.*

Tasting regret at his harsh judgment, he honestly considered her theory. Had God really sent Elijah to him, knowing Myles might need something in his life to care for if things didn't work out with Cynthia? The idea seemed far-fetched, and yet, something deep within him stirred at the possibility. Were there other evidences that God hadn't abandoned him like Cynthia had?

He catalogued his friendship with Amos and how the older man had stepped in after Charles's death to be as much a father figure as a friend. Then there was the freedom Myles enjoyed, being able to give up the livery stable for the Pony Express without the worry of having to support a family yet.

A glance at Delsie plucking up grass beside him brought another revolutionary thought. Maybe their paths had crossed for more reasons than him helping her reach California on time. Maybe she was here to help him, as well.

Myles had no doubt God was watching over her— the experience near Fort Kearney had solidified that. And if He cared enough for Delsie to help her keep her family together, then perhaps He cared enough for Myles to bring her into his life.

"Time to go, you two," Amos called from behind.

Myles plunked on his hat and stood, offering Delsie his hand and helping her to her feet. "Thank you for joining us, even if it was at the end." The sincerity in her gaze and her feminine nearness brought a familiar jolt to his heart.

"You're welcome." He rubbed his thumb over the smooth skin on the back of her palm. She'd abandoned her gloves somewhere along the trail. "Thanks for your words."

He led her back to the horses, her hand firmly gripped in his, though he knew he probably ought to let go. There was no sense meddling in things that weren't meant to be. Still, he ignored the argument. Only when Delsie reached her mare did Myles finally release her.

But long afterward, he could still feel the coolness of her fingers against his and the heat of her faith in his heart.

\* \* \*

Delsie dismounted in the shadow of Fort Bridger's adobe wall. This fort and the other landmarks they'd passed in the past four days—Devil's Gate, Independence Rock, Pacific Springs—were no longer mere names told to her by Amos. Each one now held a mental picture inside her mind.

"Why are we resting here?" A frisson of concern ran up her spine at being so near another fort. She wouldn't soon forget the terror she'd experienced outside Fort Kearney—and she hadn't even been close to the structure itself.

"Moses slipped a shoe," Myles replied evenly as he gathered his horse's reins.

Delsie pushed up her hat. "Moses?" *Another Bible name*, she thought with a smile. She'd sensed Myles's faith during their impromptu church service, even if he'd insisted it was weak.

"Didn't you name your horse?" he countered, his black eyes showing more mirth than irritation.

"Yes. It's Horse."

He barked a laugh. "Not very creative. What do you call your horse back home?"

"Gabriel," she said, blushing. Lillie had teased her about the name, but Delsie refused to change it. The young foal had been given to her shortly after their mother's death, and to Delsie, the horse was a comfort.

Myles's teasing expression softened. "That's a good one. I'll have to keep it in mind." He started for the fort entrance, calling over his shoulder, "Do you want to come?"

She pressed her lips together in indecision. She

wanted to see the inside of a real fort, but what if something happened again?

"You'll be fine," Amos reassured as though he could read her mind. Perhaps the old man could. "This fort is quite safe. Just stick with Myles. I'll watch out for the horses."

On impulse, Delsie went up on tiptoe and pressed a quick kiss to the man's whiskered cheek. "Thank you, Amos. For everything." He would have made some boy or girl a wonderful father.

Amos shrugged and turned away, but not before she caught sight of his happy grin and tear-filled eyes. She would miss him when she reached Lillie—he and Myles both. Picking up her skirt in one hand, she hurried after Myles.

The fort teemed with noise and people. Trappers, Indians, horses and pioneers created a moving sea of color and conversation. Delsie paused to take it in, her gaze sweeping from the wooden and adobe structures of the fort to the different occupants. A dark-haired Indian dressed in leather leggings and shirt stared intently back at her with eyes as dark as coal. He wore round earrings and a number of beaded necklaces draped his neck.

Delsie turned to ask Myles about the Indian, but he was no longer nearby. A worm of alarm uncurled inside her. Where had he gone? She pushed through the crowd, searching frantically. At last she spied him heading toward the stables, leading Moses behind him.

Pushing out a breath of relief, she rushed after them. She wanted no reoccurrence of what had happened the last time she'd ventured off on her own near a fort.

"There you are," Myles said before leading Moses into the stable. "Wasn't sure if you preferred looking over the things to buy."

Delsie shook her head. "I don't mind waiting here with you…" She blushed as she realized how her words might sound to him. "And Moses, too, of course," she added with a forced laugh.

Myles, thankfully, made no comment. Instead he spoke to the smithy about Moses's shoe.

She glanced around and found a barrel to sit on. Taking off her hat, she fanned herself with it, relishing even a moment to sit without moving.

Riding wasn't as trying anymore, but she would be glad when her days no longer consisted of hours and hours in a saddle. Or would she? She allowed her gaze to sweep the fort beyond the stable's overhang. While she didn't have much taste for fort life, she'd grown so used to the open sky and the endless miles to think, to pray and to simply breathe. Her beloved home back in Pennsylvania had grown increasingly more confining in memory—a place to be seen and conform.

She couldn't go back and expect things to be the same because she was no longer the same. Learning new skills, besting the elements and pushing herself through one difficulty after another had succeeded in peeling away nearly all of her former shyness and uncertainty. She was stronger than she'd imagined and longed for greater freedom than she'd once thought. But she had no other choice. Home was where she was needed, where she'd promised to be.

For the first time in years, that promise felt as weighty as a buffalo robe upon her shoulders instead of a tenuous thread of connection to her mother. "Is this truly what you had in mind, Mother?" she whispered, her lips barely moving, as her eyes sought the blue sky above. "To find Lillie and return home to life unchanged? To someone like Flynn?"

A sudden hard pinch to her arm made her yelp as much from pain as surprise. She twisted on the barrel to find the Indian she'd seen earlier towering over her. Delsie's heart pounded with panic as the man released her arm and fingered her hair.

"Myles," she managed to squeak out of her dry throat as she plunked her hat back on her head.

The Indian proceeded to pull at her lower lip and examine her teeth as if she were a horse on display. Delsie lifted a trembling hand and firmly pushed his away. "Myles?" she called, louder.

"What?" he grumbled. From the corner of her eye, she caught sight of him moving toward her, but he froze when he saw the Indian standing there.

"Squaw very beautiful," the Indian said, his tone languid and deep.

"Yes, she is." Myles stepped closer, not taking his gaze off the man. He might stand several inches taller than her companion, but the fierce protection in Myles's black eyes eased Delsie's panicked pulse a little.

"You need new horse?" The Indian gestured to Moses behind them.

"Not new horse, just new horseshoe," Myles answered evenly.

The Indian sized up Moses as he had Delsie earlier. "Horse look old and tired. Ride too hard. I have new horse. Young and full of energy." He waved his hand toward the fort entrance.

Myles darted a glance in that direction, then back at the Indian. "What do you want for your young horse?"

Delsie held her breath as she waited for the Indian's reply. Something in his unemotional face made her shiver.

"I give you horse," he answered matter-of-factly. "You give me squaw."

A soft gasp escaped her and she started to rise, intent on refusing the man. But Myles pressed a firm hand onto her shoulder, indicating she stay seated.

When he seemed satisfied she wouldn't move, he let go and rubbed at his chin as if actually contemplating the offer. Delsie gripped the sides of the barrel with both hands, irritation replacing some of her fear. Would Myles really consider trading her for a horse? After all they'd gone through? She tightened her fists. He wouldn't get one cent from her if he handed her over to this Indian now. Not one single...

Myles slowly shook his head, his expression almost apologetic. "It's a good trade—for me. But not for you." He motioned to Delsie. "Squaw is trouble."

She gave a squeal of protest, then pressed her lips together when he shot her a warning look.

"This squaw doesn't cook and she can't sit a horse too well." She felt her whole body tremble at his words, but it wasn't with fright this time. Now it was anger coursing through her. "She knows nothing about skinning an animal, either, or how to tan a hide. And she never, never stops talking."

The Indian glanced with obvious skepticism at the silent Delsie.

"She's quiet now," Myles explained, "but the moment you're out of earshot, I can guarantee you that I'll get an earful."

"But you keep squaw?" Confusion clouded the man's bronzed features.

Myles lifted his shoulders in a lazy shrug. "Her father owns a very accurate shotgun."

The Indian sniffed with dismissiveness. "I keep horse, then, and you keep troubling squaw."

"Only if you're sure."

Spinning on his heel, the Indian marched away, his back erect.

Delsie scrambled off the barrel, her hands clenched at her sides. Anger made her skin itch and her collar too tight. "Why would you—"

Myles clapped his hand over her mouth, his face mere inches from her own. "Shh," he hissed, throwing a glance at the retreating Indian. "I had to be convincing. Otherwise he and his friends might have followed us once we left here and simply taken you. We might not have stood a chance if he found you…" He visibly swallowed as he lowered his hand. "If he found you pleasing."

He'd said all those things to protect her—once again. Delsie reached out and touched his arm, the firm muscle almost familiar beneath her fingers. "Thank you." She folded her arms as a sudden shiver ran through her. "For a moment there, I thought you might actually give in. Of course your arguments to the contrary were very believable, as well."

Myles grinned. "There was only one thing on that list that was true."

"Yes, I can't tan a hide," she said with a laugh.

But he shook his head. "Not that one. I've no doubt you could do it if you had a mind to." He started back toward Moses and the smithy.

Delsie stepped quickly after him. "Then what?"

He paused long enough to throw her a look over his shoulder. A look that held a mixture of amusement, appreciation and regret—all rolled into one. "The part about being trouble," he murmured in a voice that sent a tingle racing down her spine. Not one of anger but wild hope.

She ducked out of the way as he paid the smithy and gathered Moses's reins. But even as they wound their way back toward the fort entrance, Delsie knew she wouldn't soon forget the husky tone of Myles's voice as he'd said those words or the caring in his dark eyes. One day, soon, when she was no longer riding at his side day in and day out, she would pull out this memory to savor again and again.

## Chapter Ten

Myles pushed his empty plate aside and rested his elbows on the smooth wood table as he leaned forward to better hear the Express rider seated across from him and Amos. The dining room at Porter Rockwell's Hot Springs Brewery Hotel, south of Salt Lake City, remained full of people and conversation, despite the late evening hour.

"You'll probably fare all right," the rider named Tucker stated matter-of-factly as he lifted his mug to his mouth and took a drink. "It's the stations what's in real trouble."

"How many have been attacked?" Amos asked, his voice tight with seriousness. Myles sensed the older man was every bit on edge as himself tonight. As of tomorrow, they were riding straight into the lion's den, so to speak, with little knowledge on how bad things might be.

Tucker set his mug down. "Can't say for certain. My run's been fairly quiet, except for a scrimmage between one station owner and the Indians. But I have heard of other stations being burned, stock driven off and owners killed."

Amos shot Myles a look. It was the same dire rumblings they'd heard before leaving Nebraska behind. Would the rumors prove true? Would they be able to find sufficient food or shelter in the middle of a warpath?

"I'd get new horses, if I was you," Tucker said. "Especially since you've been riding the same ones for nearly two weeks. Those Indian ponies have a harder time outrunning Express horses. That might be your greatest weapon."

Myles ran a hand over his beard. He hated the idea of parting with Moses—the horse had been as faithful a companion as Elijah. But if acquiring new mounts might save their lives, he would let Moses go. That was if Delsie was in agreement about funding the purchase of three new horses.

Looking past Amos, he found her seat at their table was empty. At some point during the conversation with Tucker, she must have slipped away. A tremor of unease flitted through Myles. While there were a number of women here tonight, the male occupants of the hotel far outnumbered the female ones.

"Where'd Delsie go?" he asked Amos quietly.

Amos shrugged. "Not sure. She said she needed some air."

His agitation increased, especially given the popularity of the nearby brewery. "I'm going to look for her. Tell her what we found out." He nodded at Tucker, snagged some meat to give to Elijah and stood. "Excuse me, gentlemen."

He made his way out of the dining room. Outside Myles paused in the dying light. Delsie wasn't milling about the hotel like several of the other guests. Should he knock on her door? His gaze settled on the adobe barn near the hotel, and an inner nudge guided his feet in that direction.

Horse-scented air filled his nostrils as he stepped through the open doors of the large building. Sure enough he spied Delsie beside one of the stalls, stroking Moses's nose. The anxiety churning in his gut dissipated at the sight. Elijah swooped down from a rafter to land on Myles's shoulder. The bird had obviously followed Delsie. The thought pleased him, though he knew it shouldn't matter if the sparrow hawk had taken a liking to her, as well.

She turned as he approached, her smile less vibrant than normal. "Hello."

He came to a stop beside her. "Didn't see you slip out."

"I couldn't listen to that sort of talk anymore." She stated the words simply, but Myles didn't miss the melancholy that seeped into her tone.

"We'll make it, Delsie."

He placed his hand over hers where it rested on the stall door. Without a word, she entwined her fingers with his. They stood that way for at least a minute, neither one speaking. The solace of the barn and her presence eased some of the tension from Myles's shoulders. He meant what he'd told her—somehow, some way, he would get her to her sister.

"You're a good horse, aren't you?" Delsie rubbed the animal's nose again.

"He's been more than willing to do what we've asked him to." He released her hand to pull some hay from a nearby bale and feed it to Moses. "I've only known a couple of horses like that, even after twenty years of working with them."

Elijah hopped onto the stall door and ruffled his feathers in indignation when Moses blew air in the bird's direction. Myles smiled. Too bad he couldn't keep the beast. "That man Tucker suggested we buy new horses."

Delsie sighed and let her hand fall to her side. "Is that what you think we should do?"

He leaned against the stall post and offered Elijah some of the meat from his pocket. "I do, given what might lie ahead. And the sooner the better. I hate to part with a perfectly decent horse, but we need ones that haven't been ridden hard for eleven days straight."

Her mouth pressed into a hesitant line.

"If it's about the money…"

She shook her head. "It isn't that. I've got enough to buy new horses and still pay you and Amos what I promised."

"You just hate to say goodbye," he murmured, his eyes fastened on her profile. Would he ever meet another woman as beautiful, strong and compassionate as Delsie Radford? He was beginning to have his doubts.

She twisted to face him. "Yes, I don't want to say goodbye." Myles had the sudden impression she, too, was talking about more than the horse. Then the hesitancy in her expression transformed into familiar determination. "I want you to have him, Myles."

"What?" he said, laughing quietly.

"I'm serious." She took a step toward him, filling his senses with the momentary scent of lavender. "You said he was a good animal. The best."

"Well, yes, but…"

Her dark blue eyes pleaded with him. "I don't want him left behind. Not after all he's done for me…for us. Please. I'll pay to have him boarded here until you and Amos return. Then he's yours. You can sell your new horse, too, on your return trip." She laid her hand against his arm. "Consider both an investment in your future ranch."

Myles stared at her, hardly daring to believe she meant it. He'd never owned his own horse. Charles had, but Myles had left the aging Jedidiah behind when he quit the livery stable. Could he afford to keep a mount on what he was paid for Express riding? The logistics paled in comparison, though, to the sight of Delsie's expectant face and the possibility of being one step closer to his dreams for the future.

"Why?" He couldn't help the question. Other than Amos, no one else had taken an interest in what he did or where he went in a very long time.

She lowered her gaze and fingered his sleeve. The gentle touch sent shoots of feeling up his arm. "Because Amos…and you…have come to mean a great deal to me."

And yet she wasn't giving Amos a horse. Was it possible that she'd come to care for him as much as he did for her? He decided to test his theory, despite the voice of reason in his head telling him he was foolish to give his heart to another rich female. One who wasn't free to give her heart in return.

With his finger, he tipped her chin upward. Unshed tears glistened in her eyes as they met his. "Then I accept," he replied huskily.

"I'm glad," she whispered with a faint trace of a smile, pulling his attention to her lips. It wasn't the first time he'd contemplated kissing her—he had the night they'd danced by the wagon train and the day the Indian had tried bartering for her. But those moments had felt too public, unlike this one.

"Thank you, Delsie," he murmured.

He didn't know which of them moved first or if they moved in tandem. But one moment he was staring into those beautiful eyes and the next he felt her lips beneath his own. The kiss was featherlight. Her hand came to rest alongside his bearded jaw as Myles poured his hopes—however blighted—for a future together into this one kiss.

When Delsie stepped back, several long heartbeats later, there were tears on her cheeks. "I'd better go."

She hesitated a moment, then reached out once more and trailed her fingers down the side of his face, as if memorizing the lines and features. Pain filled her eyes—a pain Myles couldn't erase this time no matter how badly he wanted to.

"Good night, Myles."

She lowered her hand and moved slowly past him. The words hit him with all the force of a hoof to his gut. She wasn't simply bidding him good-night. She was saying an early goodbye. Myles watched, with irritating helplessness, as she exited the barn.

When he could no longer see her, he rammed a fist against the stall post, disrupting Elijah and sending the bird flying to an overhead rafter. The ache inside him felt too reminiscent of what he'd felt as a four-year-old boy when he'd lost both his parents to illness within two days of each other. His grief at losing Charles, too, nearly paled to the pain lancing through him now.

Why had he allowed himself to fall for Delsie? A woman he couldn't have, no matter how much she clearly cared for him in return. She wouldn't divide her family further by accepting a life with him, and Myles could no longer blame her. Riding with her and Amos day after day had given him the closest thing to family that he'd had in years. He wouldn't want to give that up, no matter how attractive another avenue. Delsie had come too far and endured too much to break her father's heart a second time.

So it would be Myles's heart that took the beating. But if it meant Delsie was happy, if it meant she got what she ultimately wanted, he would do it again—a thousand times over.

He hung his head at the realization, and a weight as heavy as cast iron settled over his shoulders. The unknowns before them faded in consequence to the thought of her slipping out of his life for good in seven short days. The woman he'd spent nearly every minute of every day with for the past two weeks, the woman he'd enjoyed kissing a hundred times more than he'd ever liked kissing Cynthia, the woman who'd bolstered his faith and given him a reason to smile would be gone—and he was powerless to stop that final goodbye.

"Please, God," he found himself whispering, his hands gripping the ledge of the stall in earnestness.

He hadn't really prayed in years, but he couldn't face this last portion of their journey on his own. "Help me endure the next week and see her, safely, to the end."

Delsie bit her lip as she eyed the mountains from beneath her hat. The sunbaked land they'd ridden through today boasted little in color or leafy vegetation. A patch of light rain earlier had turned the desert into a watery beauty and filled the air with the smell of damp earth and sagebrush. But now, the unrelenting sun had burned away the last of the moisture.

A deep feeling of melancholy welled within her, bringing the threat of tears. She sniffed hard to will them back. She'd never been prone to tears like Lillie was, and yet, she'd been moved to crying twice in no time at all. First in the barn with Myles, and now at the barrenness surrounding her, in a place so unlike home she felt as if she were moving through a dream world.

The memory of kissing Myles filled her thoughts as it had countless times since last night. She'd never felt so cherished as she had in that moment. Her first kiss had proven to be more wonderful than she'd imagined it would be. And yet, she'd also felt a strong measure of heartbreak intermingled with the joy. It had taken every ounce of her will to walk away from Myles and not beg him to stay with her—always. Was this what Lillie had experienced at the thought of being parted forever from Clay?

Instead of compassion, though, an ember of anger filled her heart. Why should Lillie have her greatest desire, a life as the wife of the man she adored, and Delsie must uproot her wishes for the sake of their family? Immediate shame accompanied the angry question. Lillie had followed her heart, but it hadn't come without a heavy price. And no matter how Delsie ached to remain at the side of the man riding stoically in front of her, she wouldn't exact such a price from her father a second time.

Myles had clearly drawn the same conclusion. While he'd remained solicitous as they'd purchased new horses at Camp Floyd and along the ride since, she'd sensed the partial return of the reticence he'd worn like a shield in the beginning. His gaze no longer lingered in her direction as it once had, and his gentle grip fell from her elbow quicker than before.

Delsie hated knowing she was the cause of his hidden grief, but she felt incapable of changing any of it. Better to concentrate on reaching Lillie, as she had so many times on this journey, than to dwell on the painful reminders of what might have been between her and Myles.

That didn't stop the single tear from dripping down her cheek, though. She hastily brushed it away, hoping Amos hadn't noticed it from his spot to her right. The older man had been quieter than usual today, casting troubled looks between her and Myles more than once. She didn't have the heart to explain the source of the unspoken tension radiating among the three of them.

"I think we ought to rest on the other side of that riverbed," Amos called to Myles. The announcement sounded loud in Delsie's ears after a long stretch of relative silence.

Myles twisted in the saddle. "Will do. The horses are starting to slow."

Delsie searched the opposite bank of the river for something that might provide shade and was relieved to see several short trees. The temperature felt much hotter here than it had on the prairies or among the mountains. Hopefully, she'd be able to fill her nearly empty canteen at the river, as well.

They reached the bank and she peered down at the trickle of water running along the riverbed. Not much of a river, but enough water for them and the horses to drink. She followed Myles and his mount down the sloping incline and held her breath until her horse's hooves struck the bottom. Her mare dropped her nose and began to drink from the gurgling brook.

"When they're done drinking," Myles directed, "let's get them up on the opposite bank. It looks like there's a little grass near those trees."

Delsie nodded. Once her mare lifted its head again, she dug her heels into its flanks and guided the horse up the other bank. At the top, she slipped from the saddle and led the animal to the trees she'd seen earlier. She looped the reins around a nearby branch and turned to see Amos and Myles coming toward her.

"I need to fill my canteen," she said over her shoulder as she removed the object from around the saddle horn.

"Me, too." Myles tied up his mount and grabbed his canteen.

"What about you, Amos?" she asked. "Can I fill yours?"

Amos shook his head from where he'd spread out in the shade. "Mine's nearly full. But thank you."

Delsie didn't know how he did it, drinking so little

but never getting overly thirsty as far as she could tell. "All right. Enjoy your nap, then." She coaxed a smile from him, as she'd hoped, and trailed Myles back down the bank to the river bottom.

Kneeling, she scooped up a handful of the cool liquid and drank. Droplets escaped her grip and slid down her chin and dress front, but she didn't mind. She wet her hand again and rubbed it across the back of her neck and forehead.

"It's hot, isn't it?" she mused as Myles filled his canteen.

He eyed the sun from under his hat and gave a wordless nod.

Strained quiet filled the air between them, depressing her further. She wanted to go back to the banter and friendliness. Perhaps kissing him had been a mistake—though Delsie couldn't wish away the moment altogether.

"About last night..." She stared at the water flowing into her canteen instead of at Myles's dark eyes. "I didn't mean for us to..." She licked her dry lips, the words clogging in her throat. "If I offended you, Myles..."

The sudden pressure of his finger beneath her chin made her heart sputter, both with happiness and trepidation. What would he say in response to her bumbling apology?

"Delsie."

She lifted her gaze to his handsome face.

"Don't be sorry." His intense look held her captive. Emotions shifted across his features—hope, regret, acceptance. He moved his finger from her chin to her lower lip. Her pulse beat harder, filling her ears with the sound of rushing wind. "But we can't change…"

Myles lowered his hand and cocked his head, as if listening. "Do you hear that?"

Could he hear the pounding of her heartbeat? "No," she said, shaking her head.

"It sounds like wind, but nothing's moving."

*Wind?* Wasn't that her pulse? Delsie took a deep breath to steady her drumming heart rate, but even as she calmed, the sound grew louder. "Wait. I do hear it."

Myles tossed his canteen on the bank above them, then stood and jerked her to her feet. "Come on."

"But my canteen…"

"Leave it." With his hand still gripping her arm, he rushed her toward the bank at a jog.

"Myles? What's going on? What's that sound?" A movement to her right pulled her attention in that direction. To her horror, she saw a wall of churning water at least ten feet high racing along the river bottom straight toward them. "Myles!" she screamed.

He glanced over her head at the flood and his face hardened. With quick, strong movements, he yanked her to his side and tried to help her scramble up the bank. The dirt slid beneath their shoes, slowing their progress.

Delsie froze with fear. She could hardly breathe through the terror engulfing her as she watched the water coming closer and closer. If it hit them, she knew instinctively that they'd be swept away and drowned.

"Come on," Myles yelled, pulling on her arm again. "We can make it, Delsie."

His confidence snapped her out of her horrified

trance. She clawed at the river bank with both hands. The roar of the water filled her ears, as loud and awful as any nightmare creature. The first droplets of angry spray smacked her face just as Amos appeared above them and hauled them both onto safe ground.

Delsie dropped onto her back, knocking her hat from her head and breathing heavily. If they hadn't moved when they did, if Amos hadn't come to their rescue… She squeezed her eyes shut against the thought.

"Delsie? Are you all right?"

She opened her eyes to find Myles leaning over her, his expression haggard. "I'm…" She swallowed hard, trying to push back the sob racing up her throat. But it leaked out in a strangled cry.

He lifted her carefully from the ground and cradled her against his chest. "It's all right," he murmured. "You're all right."

"B-but I lost my canteen," she said in between shaking, sobbing breaths.

His soft laughter eased the trembling in her body. "Is that what you're most upset about?"

She shrugged, inciting another chuckle from him, right before he pressed a tender kiss to her forehead. Flutters of delight filled her stomach and eased any lingering dread.

"You darling, little soldier."

Delsie tipped her chin upward to find him smiling down at her. His earlier reserve had disappeared, replaced by amused adoration. She wiped at her wet cheeks, her gaze shifting from his dark eyes to his mouth. As if Myles sensed her longing, he rubbed his thumb against her lips once more, then placed another kiss to her hairline. Slowly he helped her onto her feet.

"Let's get you some water and a little food."

Even when Amos passed her his own canteen, his eyes full of questions, she didn't feel embarrassed at Myles's show of affection. No matter what happened between them now, she knew from the top of her head to the toes of her shoes that he cared for her—perhaps even loved her. And that was enough. At least she prayed it would be.

# Chapter Eleven

"Another empty station," Myles announced as he ducked out the door to where Delsie and Amos sat in their saddles waiting.

Her somber expression matched the gravity stirring within him and mirrored the lines of concern pinching Amos's weathered face. Myles eyed the nearby corrals. "No stock, either."

The horses and cattle had likely been run off by the same Indians who'd driven the workers from the station. He moved to his horse and scanned the surrounding clumps of brush for any sign of movement, though he guessed the station had been emptied several days ago.

A feeling in his gut last night had told him yesterday's ride through the desert—and their near drowning in the flash flood—might be considered easy. At least when compared with what lay ahead of them now.

Several of the stations they'd passed by today weren't simply empty like this one—they'd been burned to the ground. The little food they'd procured from one diligent owner had been eaten, and from the looks of things, they weren't likely to find a home station to eat or board at tonight.

The sun was already dropping toward the western horizon. Both he and Amos had agreed to ride longer than normal, in hopes of finding a post that hadn't been on the receiving end of an Indian ambush.

"What you do think?" he asked Amos.

Amos's sharp gaze swept across the desert, his mouth a thin line. "I say we water the horses at the well there, then ride south a few miles. We can camp under the open for the night."

If Delsie feared the departure from their typical evening routine, she didn't say. Instead she simply slid off the saddle and led her mare toward the well. Amos followed suit, pulling his gun from his waistband. Myles located a broken bucket—one of the few things that hadn't been taken from inside the station. While Amos stood guard, he managed to get enough water in the bucket for all three horses to drink. After that, he filled his and Amos's canteens. Who knew when they'd find another water source?

Amos kept his gun at the ready as they saddled up and turned their mounts south, to skirt the nearby canyon. They picked their way among the sagebrush for several miles before the older man stopped them beside a clump of trees he called pinyon pines.

"I'll see what I can hunt up in the way of food," he said, dismounting. "Start the fire now, so we can be through with it before dark. Don't need anyone else knowing we're here."

Myles tied up the horses as Delsie began gathering sticks. "I suppose it's a good thing I learned how to cook when I did," she said with a trace of amusement. "Do you think it will be like this the rest of the way to California?"

"It might be," Myles answered honestly, taking the sticks from her. He set about starting the small fire, while she settled onto the ground nearby.

"Is Elijah off hunting, too?" She glanced up at the sky.

Myles nodded and coaxed the tiny flames to life with some dry grass and more twigs. "I suppose if Amos can't find anything, we could share whatever rodent Elijah catches." He meant the comment to be humorous, but Delsie didn't laugh.

"Thank you, again, for doing this, Myles. You didn't have to." She drew a circle in the dirt with her finger. "And now I've landed us in the middle of the desert with marauding Indians and little food. Just to reach Lillie." She lifted her chin to reveal raw anguish in her deep blue eyes. "If anything happened to you... or Amos..."

"We chose to come." It was as simple as that. Or maybe, it wasn't them who'd chosen, but rather Someone else choosing *them* instead. Either way he no longer had any doubts about the validity of their journey. He might have agreed in the beginning for the sake of his future, but he'd stumbled onto two things far more precious than even his dreams of a horse ranch—his friendship with Delsie and a renewed seed of faith. Charles would be proud.

"Besides," he continued, "this isn't just about reaching your sister. It's about your family, Delsie."

"And that's something you can understand?" Her words were nearly identical to something she'd said that first day in Saint Joseph. Something he'd thought of over and over since.

He dipped his head in a nod, his eyes locked on hers. "That's something I can understand—now."

The smile she rewarded him with brought the distinct memory of kissing her to Myles's mind. Not the chaste kiss of yesterday after they'd been rescued from near drowning, but the kiss they'd shared in the quiet barn. But giving in to his wish now would only increase the inevitable pain of goodbye later—for both of them. So he busied himself with the fire and with talking over what details Delsie knew about Lillie's whereabouts until Amos came back.

"He's a bit scrawny," Amos said, hoisting the jackrabbit in his hand, "but he'll do."

Delsie insisted on skinning the creature herself, even when Myles volunteered to do it for her. He couldn't help admiring her all the more as she set about the gruesome task without complaint or outward show of disgust. She'd changed a lot in the past two weeks. Or had she always possessed these qualities but hadn't been given opportunity to cultivate them? He couldn't help wondering if she would be content to return to her rich house and easy life after all she'd been through.

Once he'd thought her too pampered to survive in his world, but he'd been forced to reassess his opinion somewhere along the trail. Delsie would make any horse rider or rancher a fine wife. But it wouldn't be him. The hard truth cut deep as Myles focused on making a spit from sticks to cook the rabbit.

Elijah returned soon afterward with a mouse and settled outside their little circle to eat. The horses picked at the few patches of grass nearby. For tonight, at least, they would all have something to eat, despite the less-than-optimal situation—Myles felt gratitude for that.

When the rabbit had been thoroughly cooked, Amos divided up the meat between the three of them. Myles noticed the older man took a slightly smaller portion for himself than what he handed Myles or Delsie. The feeling of thankfulness inside Myles grew larger at the gesture. Amos was not only a good man but a true friend. Myles vowed he wouldn't take the man's companionship for granted anymore.

After all the meat had been consumed, Myles doused the fire. The sun had set minutes before, taking the heat of the day with it. Delsie visibly shivered at the drop in temperature.

"It'll be cold tonight," Amos told them. "Better use the saddle blankets."

Myles gathered the blankets and passed one to Delsie and to Amos. His own he spread out on the ground on the other side of Delsie. Amos quietly regaled them with a few stories from his youth and answered Delsie's questions about his wife. Though he tried hard to listen, sleepiness stole over Myles and he drifted off.

Sometime later he jerked awake at the sound of something rustling nearby. He sat up, his hand on the revolver at his side, but it was only one of the horses shifting beside the trees. Taking a deep breath to calm his thudding heartbeat, he shot a look at Delsie. She'd curled into a ball beneath her blanket, and yet, Myles could see she was still shivering. Amos slept soundly on her other side, oblivious to her cold or the horse's movements.

Myles hated the thought of her freezing and getting little sleep because of it. If he gave her his blanket, though, he'd end up just as cold and sleepless. He rubbed a hand over his jaw, considering what to do. In the moonlight he spied the sturdy trunk of the closest pinyon pine. The branches began high enough on the tree that it formed an easy shelter to climb under.

Removing his blanket, he set it over Delsie and gathered her into his arms. She startled awake and blinked up at him.

"You're quaking like an aspen tree, sleeping beauty," he murmured, "but I've got an idea to keep you warm."

He carried her to the pine and ducked beneath its branches. Resting his back against the trunk, he settled Delsie at his side and draped his blanket over them both.

"What will my father think?" Delsie said sleepily, even as she nestled beneath his arm. Warmth spread through him, as much from her nearness as from the contentment that filled him at holding her again.

Myles smoothed her hair and tucked her tighter against him. "Just tell him I promised to get you back in one piece, and that's what I'm doing."

"Thank...you... Myles."

Shutting his eyes, Myles let his breathing even out and his body relax. Sleeping sitting up would likely mean a less than restful night and a kink in his neck by morning. But he didn't care. If he couldn't embrace

Delsie forever—and he couldn't—then he'd simply be grateful for this moment. This moment watching over the woman he'd come to care for more than Elijah or horse ranching or himself. A moment he would cherish for the rest of his life.

Delsie kept her eyes shut, even as she slowly began to wake. She'd never felt so content or comfortable— even more so than in that dugout, with its thick buffalo robes. Her hand loosely gripped soft fabric and warm air fanned her hair. A steady heartbeat thrummed in her ears. She pressed her cheek more snugly into the solid warmth beneath it. Until she heard a deep rumbling chuckle that vibrated through her chest.

"Would've thought you'd be warmed up by now."

Reality doused Delsie with all the shock of ice water. She was dozing beside Myles and had been all night. She scrambled up, her face hot. What would her father do if he could see her? Any amount of freedom she'd enjoyed would be gone. She would likely be foisted off on Flynn to save her reputation.

"I— I'm sorry. I didn't mean…" She let her apology fade out when he chuckled again. "It's not funny, Myles. If my father…"

He shook out his blanket. "Like I told you last night, I intend for you to reach your father in one piece, Delsie. And that means not letting you lie on the cold ground all night and catching sick." He bent forward to peer directly into her eyes. "Besides, nothing untoward happened. I promise."

"Well, that's good to know." Amos watched them from beneath the branches.

Myles stiffened beside her, red creeping up his neck. "Amos. Morning." He ran a hand over the bristles of his jaw without looking at Delsie. "Delsie was shivering something fierce. I wasn't sure what else... to do."

It was her turn to laugh softly. "Apparently Myles was being gentlemanly."

A smile worked at Amos's mouth as though he, too, was trying not to chuckle. "Good to hear. I'm going to see if I can't rummage up some breakfast."

Delsie maneuvered out from under the pinyon pine and brushed bits of dirt and twigs from her dress. Myles offered her some water from his canteen. The water tasted good, but her stomach still rumbled with hunger.

While he saw to the horses, Delsie started making a fire. By the time she had some good-sized flames built up, Amos returned. "What's on the menu for this morning?" she asked teasingly.

"Snake." Amos held the long reptile aloft. Delsie fought a cringe by reminding herself it was food, and possibly the only meal they'd get until tonight.

Amos helped her prepare the snake, then the three of them ate the meat. She certainly wouldn't put it down as a delicacy or even something she wished to have on a regular basis, but she had to admit it wasn't all bad.

After washing down the snake meat with a little more water, each of them climbed back into their saddles. Amos led the way through the sagebrush to the main trail, where they headed due west again. The sun had fully risen in the east, and with it, the temperature. Delsie could hardly believe she'd been shivering violently with cold last night, when the day felt warm and pleasant now.

The memory of being cold sparked the recollection of waking with her cheek pressed to Myles's shirt and his arm resting loosely against her shoulders. She ought to be mortified, but he'd done nothing improper. He'd just been concerned for her.

Not for the first time, she offered a silent prayer of gratitude for Myles's presence in her life and for his and Amos's help. God had truly been looking out for her to lead her to two such competent and kind men. She wished there was more she could do to repay them, beyond the money she'd promised them at the end of their journey and the horse waiting for Myles. If undying thankfulness could be converted into wealth, these two men riding silently ahead and beside her would live like kings the rest of their lives.

Delsie smiled at the thought of either Amos or Myles sporting a crown and strutting around a palace. While they had both insisted they'd chosen to come on this journey and would see it through fully, she was still grateful they had all made it so far unscathed. In light of all she'd experienced—a runaway horse, nearly freezing to death, an unwelcome marriage proposal, a flash flood and a night out in the open with only rabbit and snake to eat—Delsie couldn't imagine anything worse ahead. A seed of optimism sprang up inside her and she fueled it with thoughts of Lillie and the rapidly narrowing distance between her and her sister. Lillie would be married in five days, and Delsie had every intention and belief she would be at the blessed event.

The first station they came upon that morning stood as empty as the one they'd encountered the night before. Thankfully, this one also had a well. Amos suggested taking a rest earlier than normal to water the horses and let them feed on the surrounding grass, and Myles agreed.

Delsie dismounted and accepted another drink from Myles's canteen. Wiping her mouth, she eyed the nearby cabin. Could there possibly be any food left inside? Something they might take with them? She left the men and moved with purposeful steps to the door, which had been left ajar. A quick peek through the gap showed the place was devoid of its former occupants. She pushed through and smiled when she spotted the cupboard across the room. Perhaps there was a little flour inside it.

She started forward but stumbled over something on the floor. Righting herself, Delsie glanced down to see the offending object. It was a boot and not an empty one, either. Her gaze shifted from the boot, to the pant leg, to the dead man's vacant eyes and finally to his bloodied forehead. A panicked scream fled her mouth as she stumbled blindly back out the door.

"Delsie?" Myles rushed toward her, Amos right behind him, his gun in his hand.

"Th-that man in there. He's been…" The horror washed over her anew, sickening her stomach. She clamped a hand over her lips and fled to the nearby corral, where she dropped to her knees beside the fence. In a matter of minutes, she'd emptied her meager breakfast into the dust. Her body trembled with shock as if cold, though a clammy feeling made her sweaty, too. She sank against one of the fence posts and wrapped her arms around her knees.

"It's all right," she whispered to herself. "It's all right."

From the corner of her eye, she watched Myles slowly approach her as if she were a skittish colt. "Delsie? You all right, darling?"

She shook her head and rocked her body back and forth.

"You've had a shock, but you're going to be fine. Do you hear me?" He squatted next to her and placed his hand on her shoulder. The human contact released some of the numbness inside her.

"I wish I hadn't seen… I'll never forget…" She stifled a cry with her hand to her mouth.

"Amos is burying the man now." Sure enough she heard the scrape of a shovel against the dirt. Where Amos had procured a shovel, she didn't know.

"Do you want to sit some more or do you think you can stand?"

"I… I'll stand."

Myles gently helped her onto her feet, then pulled her to his chest. Delsie wrapped her arms around his waist and allowed the steady beat of his heart to soothe her shock.

"What have I done, Myles?"

He rested his chin on top of her hair—she'd hung her hat on the saddle horn before going into the cabin. "You didn't do anything. That man was dead long before we came along."

"No. I mean having us come all this way, in the middle of a warpath." She bit her lip to keep from sobbing. "I knew we might encounter things, but I foolishly let my desire to reach Lillie outweigh the dangers."

Myles eased back and tipped her face upward. "It wasn't foolish. God knew you'd be here—now—on this very trail, fighting to restore your family."

"Do you really believe that?"

A faint smile creased his mouth. "Do you?" he countered.

Delsie thought back to the night Myles had told her the journey wouldn't work, at least not in the way she'd planned in the beginning. She'd been full of doubt and despair until she'd read that verse of scripture. *Cast not away therefore your confidence.* She'd tossed aside some of her confidence since then, but she still had some remaining. This was what God wanted her to do and He'd provided everything she'd needed to make it happen.

"Whatever comes, Delsie, He's with us." His words so closely mirrored the ones in her own head that she wondered if he could somehow read her thoughts. "Isn't that what He wanted Elijah and those priests to understand?"

She nodded, grateful for the reminder.

"Don't give up on Him or Lillie. Not yet. Not when we're so close."

His assurances restored some of her own, but doubts still loomed large in her mind. "But the worst might lie ahead. We could end up like that..." She swallowed the taste of bile in her throat. "Like that man."

His expression hardened with resolve, deepening

the black of his eyes. "Then we'll do so, knowing we followed God's will and didn't let fear rule our lives."

Embracing him, she cleared her throat enough to say, "You're a good man, Myles Patton."

"And you're a strong woman, Delsie Radford. Don't let anyone tell you otherwise."

She let his courage and compliment seep into her troubled heart and thoughts.

"You ready to keep on?"

She took a deep breath and stepped back to see his face—this handsome face she'd come to know nearly as well as her own. "As long as you're keeping on with me."

He tucked a curl behind her ear and smiled, though the gesture held a trace of sadness. "Until the last inch of the trail."

# Chapter Twelve

*Where* had those faith-filled words come from? Myles thought ruefully. Fifteen days ago he would have scoffed at the idea of spouting off religious sentiments, especially to a beautiful woman. He and God had parted ways after Charles's death and both of them had seemed fine with it. Today, though, he'd known exactly what needed to be said to bolster Delsie's shattered confidence. But more than that, he believed every word he'd spoken, too.

Whether it was God working through him or Myles's own desire to be the man Delsie clearly saw in him or perhaps both, he wasn't sure. All he knew for certain in this moment was that this journey was no longer some foolhardy venture.

God was aware of him—even as lonely and embittered as Myles had been—and He'd placed something directly into his path that he couldn't ignore or run from. A little soldier with eyes of deep blue, a smile that brought him pure delight and a faith as large as the prairie sky. He'd been dodging God, but God hadn't let that bother Him. Instead He'd dropped Delsie right in front of Myles and let her work her charm and kindness, a compassion Myles guessed had held her family together for so long after her mother's death.

However deep her strength and confidence ran, though, he still wished she hadn't been the one to discover the scalped station owner earlier. If only he could have protected her from such a gruesome sight. He darted a glance to his left. She rode with her back erect, her face trained forward, but he sensed the sadness lingering around her.

*A few more days*, he reassured himself. *Then the worst will be over.*

At least in terms of the trail dangers. His biggest obstacle still lay ahead—saying goodbye, indefinitely, to Delsie. He didn't want to think about not seeing her lovely face every day or hearing her laughter or feeling her gentle touch that had a far greater effect on him than all the hazards they'd faced so far.

He drove such depressing thoughts from his mind by studying the surrounding desert, looking for signs of possible ambush. Sometime later he spotted buildings and movement up ahead that had him reining in his horse and placing a hand on one of his guns.

Amos and Delsie drew to a stop beside him. "What is it?" she asked quietly, her hands clenching her mare's reins tighter than normal.

Myles shook his head. "Not sure. Looks like a bunch of horses and people."

Amos squinted. "I don't think they're foes. But let's ride in slow just the same."

"Suits me." Myles nudged his mount forward, but

he removed one of his revolvers and set it across his lap, just in case.

He led the way, slowly, toward the station and the group ahead. The closer he came, though, the more the details came into focus. It wasn't Indians. A group of what appeared to be Express riders and workers milled about the station. Myles hadn't seen this many men in one spot for several days.

"Howdy," he called out as he, Amos and Delsie stopped at the edge of the station yard.

"Howdy back," a man with sandy blond hair answered. He and a few other riders strode over to the trio.

Myles dismounted before helping Delsie to the ground. He knew full well she could get off her mare unassisted, but he didn't particularly like the wide-eyed looks from the men watching her. "Got some sort of rendezvous going on?"

The sandy-haired man chuckled. "Not by choice." He turned his attention to Delsie. "What brings you to this fair desert, miss?"

She glanced at Myles, then smiled at the man. "We're traveling to California as quickly as we can. For my sister's wedding." She removed her hat and studied the group of men. "We'd be very much obliged if we could purchase some food from you, gentlemen. We didn't have a home station to lodge in last night, which meant little to eat for dinner or breakfast."

"Sorry to say but you won't find any posts open from here to Carson Valley, Nevada," a short man replied. "Indians have attacked them all and driven off the livestock."

The sandy-haired rider spoke up again. "That's why we riders and station keepers met here. We're waiting for soldiers to come and help us reopen them."

Myles looked at Delsie. The color had drained from her face, but she held her chin aloft.

"We can certainly feed you," the same rider added. "Come on."

Myles trailed Delsie and Amos to the nearby cabin. They were introduced to the owner, then invited to sit for a meal of flapjacks. Myles and Amos ate three helpings each, and even Delsie had seconds.

Once they'd eaten their fill, the owner explained the current situation with the Indians. Myles grew more and more discouraged as he talked. Without home stations, or any stations at all, they'd be forced to find their own food and water again. Then there was the very real possibility of meeting up with some of the Indians themselves. Their safest option was to wait for the soldiers, too, but that would mean Delsie would miss her sister's wedding.

Delsie excused herself when the talk turned to those who'd been killed, though Myles remained behind. If they were to continue, and everything in him told him they would, he wanted to know exactly what sort of fight they were riding into.

After a time the conversation turned to geography and landmarks. Myles left Amos to find Delsie. She'd been outside, alone, for at least a half an hour. Was she safe? Had any of the riders tried taking advantage of his absence?

Relief coursed through him when he found her, standing alone, feeding grass to several of the station horses on the other side of the corral fence. She turned at his approach and threw him a tight smile.

"Sounds rather...dire...doesn't it?" She fed the last bits of grass to one of the animals, then brushed off her hands.

"Yes." He couldn't deny it. "But you knew it might be. *We* knew it might be."

Resting her hands on the highest rung of the fence, she stared at something across the corral. "It all sounded so simple two weeks ago. Ride as far and as long as we can, purchase food, sleep, do it again the next day."

"And it has been." Myles placed his hand atop hers. "Apparently now is where it gets more complicated, but it's not impossible. Do you want to keep going?"

She twisted to face him, her back to the fence. Her gaze was full of equal parts uncertainty and determination. "I have to try, Myles. But I understand if you and Amos don't want to..."

"I'm not leaving," he practically growled.

He planted himself in front of her, encroaching on her space. She tipped her chin up to look at him. The undisguised trust shining in her blue eyes, the warmth of her breath against his jaw and the nearness of this beautiful woman stole his words.

He loved her. The realization washed over him as soft as a whisper and as brash as a thunderstorm. And because he loved her he would accompany her through one danger after another before letting her go at the end of the trail. Her happiness and desire for a complete family meant more to him than a thousand horse ranches.

With great effort, he stepped back. A hint of what might have been disappointment flitted across her somber expression, making him wonder if she might love him back. Myles pushed aside the hope such a thought inspired. It didn't matter.

"So what will it be, Miss Radford?" His voice sounded husky with emotion, even to his own ears. "Are you ready to finish this, no matter what lies in our path?"

She glanced past him in the direction of the station, her shoulders rising and falling with a soft sigh. He wanted to reassure her, as he'd done earlier after the incident with the dead man. But this time, with the knowledge of the new perils they might face, she needed to make the decision herself, whether to go or stay.

When she met his level look straight on a few moments later, every lovely feature was etched with resolve. "I'm ready."

Delsie shifted in the saddle and licked her dry lips. *Don't think about food or water,* she chided herself for surely the hundredth time, even as visions of roasted lamb, mashed potatoes, meringues and pitchers of ice-cold lemonade rose into her mind.

What she wouldn't give to feel the same burning tenacity she had two days earlier when she'd told Myles she was ready to keep going. That determination, while still smoldering deep within her, had cooled considerably after forty-eight hours of little to eat or drink.

That Express rider had been right—none of the sta-

tions they'd passed were occupied. Out of sheer ne-
cessity they'd lingered at those with working wells or
nearby springs, but both Amos and Myles were reluctant to stay in one place for long.

The lack of real sustenance for them and their
horses was beginning to show in their slower pace.
They'd been forced to ride until well after dark the
night before to cover the needed distance. That also
meant no fire, so they'd divided the small amount of
jerky they'd procured at the rendezvous Express station among the three of them. Delsie was grateful for
even that little bit, but she'd still gone to bed more
hungry than not. Amos had managed to kill another
snake this morning, which meant some breakfast. But
that had been hours ago.

She pressed a hand to her grumbling stomach and
tried to focus on something else. Like the way Myles
had looked at her beside the corral—his intense gaze
capturing hers. Their shared kiss in the barn seemed
like months ago now and the start of her journey back
in Missouri felt like another lifetime.

What if she didn't make it to Lillie's wedding in
two days? What if she expired from thirst or hunger
instead? Her sister would never know what Delsie had
endured to reach her. Or their father, either.

"You all right?" Myles nudged his horse closer to
hers. He'd asked the same question nearly every hour
or whenever her pace started to lag behind his and
Amos's.

She nodded, too tired and thirsty to form a reply.

As if sensing her need, which Delsie was starting

to think he could, he passed her his canteen. "Here. Drink."

"But..." She swallowed to bring moisture to her parched mouth. "We aren't supposed to drink until we rest."

Myles continued to hold the canteen out to her, his mouth a grim line.

With a sigh of acceptance, she took the canteen. The tepid liquid still felt glorious sliding down her throat. She allowed herself one more swallow, then passed the container back. Instead of taking a drink himself, Myles put the water away. The sight brought the sting of tears to Delsie's eyes. Never in her wildest dreams would she have imagined she'd find a man so loyal and good-hearted and so far from home to be her dearest friend.

*He's more than a friend*, her heart argued. The press of tears increased. Yes, she cared for Myles—loved him, even—in a way that went well beyond mere friendship.

*I love him.*

The truth hit her with such force that Delsie sucked in a sharp breath, the moisture in her eyes gone as quickly as it had come.

"Something wrong?" Myles asked, peering closely at her.

She gulped and shook her head. She loved him, this ornery, wonderful, handsome Express rider sticking close to her side. The pure joy and giddiness of her realization was short-lived, though. Loving Myles didn't change the fact that she had to return to her father after Lillie's wedding. The only way she knew to fully mend the rift in her family was to return home. But when she did, she couldn't marry Flynn—not anymore. Not when she knew what it felt like to love a man. She glanced at Myles and saw him watching her. *And be loved in return.*

Perhaps she would find someone else back in Pennsylvania. But she guessed it would be a very long time before she had any room in her heart for anyone but Myles.

Wiping sweat from her forehead with her sleeve, she set her jaw, determined to think of something other than food or Myles. Two things she couldn't have. A soft prick of claws near her collarbone alerted her to Elijah's sudden perch on her shoulder. Stunned, she twisted to face Myles.

"Well, I'll be," he said with a chuckle. "He's never done that before. Not even with Amos."

A ripple of pride wound through Delsie. A few short weeks ago she hadn't ridden anything but sidesaddle or known how to cook or even understood her own strength. Now she easily sat on her horse with a sparrow hawk on her shoulder.

She released one hand from the reins to brush her finger over Elijah's soft feathers. No wonder Myles loved the bird so much. The cloud of despair she'd been riding beneath for almost two straight days evaporated under the hawk's calming presence. She could do this—they could do this.

Myles eyed the distant station with relief. Even the missing roof and charred adobe were a somewhat welcome sight, a chance to rest and hopefully find some food and water. He hadn't liked the weariness lining Delsie's face earlier. She'd been wilting before his eyes the past two days and it scared him. On occasion he still saw that spark of life and optimism flare in her expression, as it had when Elijah chose to ride on her shoulder, but it faded all too quickly. The burden of riding so far without regular meals and water was taking its toll on her and the horses. He'd had to slow their pace to compensate.

When they reached the burned station, Myles cautiously slid from his saddle. He moved slowly, a revolver in each hand, to the cabin and pushed the door in with his boot. There was no one, alive or otherwise, inside. He blew out the breath he'd been holding. While there didn't appear to be anything in the way of food, either, Amos had told them of a nearby spring.

"It's empty," he announced as he stepped back outside.

Amos nodded. "Figured as much. The spring's back that way."

Delsie dropped to the dirt beside her mare, while Elijah flew off to hunt. "I can taste the water already."

The spring sat several hundred yards from the station. The horses eagerly drank, then Myles, Amos and Delsie knelt down to scoop up water for themselves. Myles removed his hat and dumped handfuls of the cool water onto his head and warm face. Delsie followed suit, laughing as tiny rivers ran down her hair and cheeks.

"How much farther will we go tonight?" she asked Amos.

Amos rubbed at his bristled chin. "I figure another

twenty miles will put us just sixty more from Placer-ville, where your sister lives."

Delsie's face lit brighter than Myles had seen it in hours. "We're that close?"

The older man nodded, a pleased smile on his face. Myles guessed the reason had more to do with Delsie's enthusiasm than being so close to the end of their journey. "We can try and hunt up something to eat around here, then keep going before we stop for the ni—"

A bloodcurdling yell pierced the air, cutting off Amos's explanation and sending ice-cold shivers up Myles's spine. The horses shifted nervously, their eyes wide. Myles jumped to his feet, but he couldn't see the source of the war cry.

"Take one of the guns and get into the brush," he hollered at Delsie. "We'll get the horses in the corral."

Her face devoid of color, she accepted the gun he thrust into her hand and scrambled into the bushes to lie down on her stomach. Satisfied, Myles grabbed the reins of her mount and his and sprinted toward the corral. He sensed more than saw Amos and the other horse coming right behind him.

He pushed open the gate, grateful the fence had survived the earlier attack on the station, and led the horses inside. The moment Amos had the gate closed, Myles released the reins. "You guard the horses," he told the older man. "I'll take a position by the cabin."

Amos gave a quick nod, his expression grim.

After vaulting the corral fence, Myles moved half-hunched-over until he reached the cabin. His heart beat double time within his chest and his mouth felt full of sand, as though he hadn't just drunk his fill at the spring.

The Indians still hadn't shown themselves, but he wouldn't be fooled into thinking they'd left. He crept forward along the cabin wall until he reached the front corner. Five Indians on ponies were riding hard toward the station from the east, bows drawn. Had they been trailing them for some time, waiting for them to stop? Either way, they would have to ride past Myles before they reached the corral at his back.

Taking aim at the lead rider, he offered a quick prayer of forgiveness. He'd never shot a man before, but he wouldn't let harm come to Delsie or Amos. He cocked the gun and squeezed the trigger. The blast was nearly as loud as his own heartbeat in his ears. He watched as the Indian fell to the ground.

The other men jerked away from the dead man and continued forward. Myles fired the gun again, hitting one rider in the leg. The man screamed in pain and wheeled his horse to the side, but the other three didn't slow. Sweat dripped into Myles's eyes, obscuring his view for a moment. He shot at one rider attempting to go around the cabin the opposite way from where he crouched, knocking the man off his pony.

Myles emptied his gun on the remaining two Indians, but they weaved out of range each time. Shots from the corral confirmed Amos, too, was trying to stop their advance.

It was time to load the extra cylinder he'd grabbed. He tried to hurry, but his hands fumbled through the task as if it was his first time. Memories of teaching Delsie to shoot filled his thoughts, but he gritted his teeth and pushed them aside. If he focused on her or his fear of something happening to her, he wouldn't be able to protect her.

He'd just finished with the cylinder when a sudden thought filled his mind. *Look up.* Jerking his head up, Myles saw the Indian he'd shot to the ground earlier was back on his feet. Even worse, he had a bow and arrow trained at Myles's heart. Myles cocked the hammer, took quick aim and fired his gun, but the Indian had done the same with his weapon. He'd released his arrow with deadly precision, straight at Myles.

Within a single heartbeat, Myles fired a second time, then twisted to shelter his chest. He heard the Indian's death cry right before a searing pain below his shoulder tore a similar cry from his own mouth.

Red-and-white dots covered his vision as he slumped to the ground. Where were the other three Indians? He couldn't see them.

"Myles!" Delsie screamed.

"Stay back," he cried, his voice hardly more than a whisper. "Don't come out."

He crawled forward, intent on reaching her, the sounds around him growing more and more distant. He thought he heard Amos call his name from behind, thought he caught sight of the other two Indians leading the injured one away. But he couldn't be sure over the roar of the pain in his head, his back, his lungs. He only knew he had to reach Delsie, had to be sure she wasn't hurt. But he only managed to drag himself another few feet before the agony reared up to claim him and he pitched forward into darkness.

# Chapter Thirteen

"Myles!"

The scream left Delsie's throat raw. She'd watched in horror as the Indian had released his arrow toward the spot where she knew Myles was crouched, then the man had fallen, unmoving, to the ground. But she couldn't see or hear Myles. Fear pulsed icy in her veins at the thought of him hurt, or worse… She bit her lip against her rising panic. Branches scratched at her face and dress, but she waited, her eyes trained on the cabin. *Please be safe. Please be safe.*

Movement to her left pulled her attention in that direction. The other Indians were leaving. Relief coursed through her, but it was fleeting. She heard Amos yell Myles's name as well, but there was no response. Where was he? She climbed slowly to her knees, her body trembling with worry. Not even the sight of their pursuers had inspired as much fear in her as the thought of losing Myles did.

Then suddenly he was there, crawling in front of the cabin. Delsie rushed to her feet, a smile working the corners of her mouth. Until she saw the arrow sticking out of his back, below his shoulder. Fresh terror washed over her as she stumbled from the shelter of the brush, the revolver still gripped in her hand.

"Myles," she screamed again, but he slumped to the ground, his eyes shut. "No, no, no, no." She rushed across the station yard, doing her best to ignore the dead Indian still lying there. This couldn't be happening.

Amos reached his side right before her. Delsie dropped herself and the gun to the ground, her hands hovering over Myles's still body. Blood wet his shirt around the arrow.

"He's not..." She couldn't even voice the word.

Bending down, Amos glanced at her and shook his head. "He's not dead—just unconscious from the pain. That arrow's gonna need to come out. Go see what they've got in that cabin by way of supplies."

She willed back the tears pressing hard against her eyes and nodded. Climbing to her feet, she hurried into the cabin. What would help Myles? She turned in a helpless circle, her mind too cloudy with fear to think. "Come on, Delsie," she chided herself.

She found a blanket under the bed that had been singed but still had plenty of workable material left to it. There was also a tin cup and a chipped china bowl. She added them both to the blanket in her arms. Her search of the rest of the cabin produced nothing else of value, so she ran back outside.

Amos glanced up as she came near him. "What have you got?"

"A blanket we could use as bandage material and a cup and bowl for carrying some of the spring water."

"That's all?"

"Yes," she said, nodding.

The gravity of the situation had etched itself onto every line of Amos's face. Still, he set his jaw and turned to face Myles again. "Will you go get some water from the spring?"

Setting the blanket next to him, Delsie obeyed. She filled the cup and bowl with as much water as they could hold, then she moved carefully but quickly back to Amos and Myles.

Amos took the filled dishes from her and placed them on the ground. "Now I need you to go over by the horses, Delsie."

"What for?" She didn't want to leave Myles.

The older man released a breath of resignation. "I've got to pull this arrow out, and I know he wouldn't want you around when I do it."

Delsie gazed down at Myles. His handsome face blurred with renewed tears. "All right."

"Good girl."

She set her sights on the corral and forced her feet to move in that direction, away from Myles's prone figure. When she reached the horses, she walked the fence line until the cabin obscured her view of the two men. What would happen when Amos pulled out the arrow? She didn't have to wait long to find out.

A cry so loud and full of pain it made her gasp shattered the quiet evening air. The horses even skittered at the sound. No longer checking the tears coursing down her cheeks, she wrapped her arms around the nearest fence post and hung on. Another agonized shout filled her ears. "Please don't let him die, Lord. Please don't let him die."

After several long minutes, she heard Amos call for her. Delsie rushed back. The arrow no longer protruded from Myles's back, but he was no longer unconscious, either. Hard lines of pain creased his face, and his chest rose and fell with labored breaths. Amos had tied a portion of the blanket over his wound, though the blood still seeped through.

"We need to get him inside but moving him is going to hurt something fierce." Amos knelt in front of Myles's head. "I'll take his upper body, but I need you to get his legs."

Delsie pressed her mouth over a fresh sob. "I can do that." She positioned herself below Myles's boots, praying she would have the strength to carry him and not injure him further.

"All right," Amos said. "On the count of three, we'll lift him together. Ready?"

She managed a nod, even as her heart beat faster against her ribs.

"One…two…three!"

She lifted Myles's legs as Amos raised his head and shoulders. Myles cried out in agony as they slowly turned him toward the cabin. The cry tore at her heart, but she made herself focus on walking one step after the other. Once inside she helped Amos lay him, stomach down, on the tick mattress.

When she stepped back, she saw that he'd passed out again. Perhaps that was better, for now. "I'll get more water," she volunteered. At least it was something she could do.

She collected the bowl and cup, which had both been emptied of nearly all their liquid, and returned to the spring. Had it only been a short time ago when they'd all been sitting here happy? Delsie filled the vessels and carried them back to the cabin. Amos had pulled a chair up to the bed and was once again examining Myles's wound.

"Is it very bad?" She hated not knowing, but at the same time, she feared his answer.

"It's not good," Amos replied honestly. "But we would have lost him for sure if it had struck his chest or stomach." He stood and headed for the door. "Since it looks like we'll be here for some time, I'm going to see what I can find for supper and get to work burying those two men outside."

Delsie sat in the chair next to Myles. A minute or two later, Amos ducked back inside, both of Myles's guns in hand.

"You keep one of these with you," he said, handing her one of the guns. "I doubt those Indians are coming back tonight, but you know how to use this if they do."

She gave a wooden nod, her eyes trained on Myles.

"Delsie?"

She turned toward Amos, standing in the doorway. "Yes?"

"I'm praying for him, too."

His words infused her with renewed hope.

"I'll be back." He shut the door behind him.

She set the gun on the floor, within easy reach, beside her chair, then she took Myles's hand in hers.

How many times had these strong, masculine hands provided comfort to her over the past few weeks? She gave his fingers a gentle squeeze, willing all her strength and hope and love to reach him through her touch.

Shutting her watery eyes, she bent her head and began her silent prayers for help.

Bright light and immense pain registered simultaneously in Myles's mind. He jerked awake, opening his eyes, and regretted the movement at once. The back of his shoulder roared in agony. Sucking his breath in through clenched teeth, he did his best to relax his body.

"Myles? Are you awake?" The scent of lavender wafted over him as Delsie leaned near. Carefully he turned his head to look at her. She sat on a chair at his bedside, her eyes wide with concern, her hands twisting and untwisting a handkerchief in her lap. The sight of her alive and unharmed brought him a moment of peace.

"Where's Amos? Is he all right?"

A sheen of tears graced her long lashes, but she managed a tentative smile. "Amos is fine. He went to find some breakfast. Are you hungry? You didn't want anything last night."

"Last night?" Myles ran a hand over his tried eyes, trying to recall the last thing he remembered. Amos had pulled the arrow from his back—that was something he wouldn't soon forget—then he'd been carried into the cabin. After that, he could vaguely recall

Amos rebandaging his wound once or twice. "What time is it?"

Delsie glanced at the roofless ceiling of the cabin. "Probably nearing eight o'clock or so."

"Eight o'clock?" he echoed. Normally they would have been two hours or more into their journey by now. Delsie couldn't afford a late start—not when her sister was getting married tomorrow. "Can you help me sit up?"

"I don't think that's such a good—"

"Please, Delsie. Help me up." He'd vowed to get her to the end of the trail, no matter what, and he wouldn't go back on his word.

She hesitated a moment longer, then set her jaw and sat forward. "It's probably best if you roll onto your good side first."

He nodded. Gently he moved his left arm under his body and rolled onto that side. Pain screamed at him to keep still, but he fought it by gritting his teeth. "All right. Now help me sit up."

Biting her lip, she reached out and gingerly took hold of his right arm. Even the reluctant tug she gave his arm aggravated his injury. He clenched his jaw over the ache and sat up. Immediately the cabin began to spin and tilt. Myles lowered his head, nearly to his chest, and gripped his knees until the dizziness subsided.

Would he be able to sit on his horse? Anxiety churned his empty stomach at the thought of not being able to continue on for Delsie. He loved her and he'd promised to protect her—he had to keep going.

When he could see straight again, he tipped his chin

up, his left hand curling into a tight fist against his thigh. "All right. Now I want you to help me stand."

"What?" Delsie shook her head. "Myles, you were shot with an arrow last night. You've either been passed out or restless with the pain since then."

He met her determined gaze with one of his own. "We were supposed to go another twenty miles last night before we stopped. That would've put us only sixty miles from your sister. She gets married tomorrow, Delsie."

She visibly swallowed, but the firmness in her expression didn't waver. "I'll just have to miss it. Because I'm not leaving you behind."

She'd give up her chance to reconcile with her family, for him? He studied her beautiful face, an unfamiliar lump filling his throat. He coughed it away. "You don't know what you're saying. I'm not going to let you quit."

"And you can't ride today."

"Stubborn woman," he muttered, shaking his head.

The tiniest smile lifted her lips. "Pigheaded man."

Her fortitude would be the death of them both, he thought wryly. How could he convince her that he would do anything for her, even if that meant they had to tie him to the saddle? But already, the room was beginning to tip again and he felt as if he might vomit from sitting up even this long. With a groan of defeat, he dropped to his side.

"Are you all right? Can I get you anything?"

"I'll take some water," he said, more to give her something to do while he took the few minutes to himself to think. Or try to think. The pain messed with his normally clearheaded mind. That, and the concern and sacrifice of the woman he loved.

"I'll be right back." She picked up a cup and exited the cabin.

Myles forced a few deep breaths, though his chest protested it as much as his shoulder did. If he couldn't ride, then what? He would not lie here and watch Delsie miss the very event she'd come nearly eighteen hundred miles to be at.

Could Amos go with her? Possibly. But without the older man's help, Myles might not survive long enough to climb back into a saddle. As much as he hated to admit it, he needed someone here to help him get food, water and fresh bandages.

That left only one solution, and the more Myles pondered it, the more he felt the rightness of it deep down. Delsie could go on. The lessons he'd given her on the trail hadn't been just happenstance. Surely God had seen what might happen, and He'd inspired Myles to help her learn to fend for herself.

Did he dare let her go, though? He hated the idea of not being at her side, protecting her, as she ventured on her own in an unfamiliar desert.

*But she's not alone.*

The thought reminded him of the one he'd had right before the Indian had shot him. The recollection filled him with awe, temporarily numbing his pain. If he hadn't looked up when he did, he wouldn't have turned away from the arrow. It would have struck him in the chest or abdomen, and that would have meant a sure and agonizing death.

God wasn't just aware of Delsie. He was looking

out for Myles, too. The man who'd bitterly told himself he'd been abandoned, that God had no need of him and his lowly station in life, had been wrong. If anything, God had stepped up His efforts to help Myles since Charles's death, giving him a friend in Cynthia, and Elijah and Amos. And now Delsie.

The lump returned to his throat and this time tears pricked his eyes as a feeling of warmth and peace settled like a blanket over his entire body. His shoulder still throbbed with pain, but he would be all right.

And so would Delsie.

She stepped back into the cabin, carefully carrying the full cup. "Here you go."

Myles willed back the moisture in his eyes and lifted his head as she brought the cup to his mouth. "Thank you."

She smiled, a real smile. "You're welcome. Amos should be back soon, and then you can have a little meat."

He reached out and took her free hand in his. She threw him a questioning glance. "After he comes back, I want you to have him saddle up your mare."

"Myles, we went over this." She glanced away. "I'm not leaving—"

"Delsie?" He waited for her to face him again. "I need you to do this. Your sister needs you to do this." He turned her hand over and ran his thumb over the hardened blisters of her palm. "I think God needs you to do this, too."

Her brow knit in disbelief. "I don't know when to stop or what to feed my horse."

Was she relenting? "Amos can give you his watch

or you can simply stop at every other station and pay them to feed you and the mare."

"What about the Indians?"

"We're close enough to Carson Valley that there shouldn't be any more trouble like that. The Express stations should be open from this point on." He motioned to the gun on the table. "Just in case, you can take one of my revolvers with you. You'll be fine. Your horse can outrun those ponies we saw yesterday."

She pressed her lips together. "I don't know."

"You can do this, darling." The endearment rolled effortlessly off his tongue. Would he say it as easily again, to some other woman, someday? "We practiced how to saddle and unsaddle your mare, if you need to do that. You also know how to shoot and how to cook. It's only eighty miles. Slightly less than a typical day for us on the trail."

Delsie released a heavy sigh and dropped her chin. A single tear rolled down her face.

"It wasn't just coincidence that we met," Myles said, using his other hand, despite the pain it caused, to brush the tear from her skin. Skin that was no longer creamy white but slightly brown and freckled. And he loved it. "God put you and me there together by the stables that day. And He helped me teach you everything you need to finish this, Delsie. You can set everything right with your family. You can keep your promise."

When she lifted her head, her chin was trembling. "But I don't want to say goodbye." Her words were perfect echoes of those she'd voiced right before their kiss in the barn all those days ago.

Was that the real reason for her reluctance? He

didn't want to say goodbye, either, especially not now, like this. "It was coming eventually," Myles replied, if only to mask the ache near his heart at the thought of not seeing her again.

She frowned. Was she hoping he'd say more? The words pushed toward his mouth and made his heart pound in his chest. He wanted to tell her how much she meant to him, that he loved her more than he'd ever loved anyone. But he couldn't. It wasn't fair to her, to claim her heart when neither of them could make good on such a claim. She had to return to her father and her life in Pennsylvania and he had to return to his job and his tiny room back in Saint Joe.

"I'll never ever forget you, Myles." She clasped his hand between both of hers. "You have become..." Her voice hitched with a sob. "My dearest, dearest friend."

"And you mine," he murmured so low he wasn't sure if she heard him. "Does this mean you're going?" he asked more loudly.

She laughed, in spite of her tears. "I suppose it does."

"Then I'll say farewell, Miss Delsie Radford..." Foolish or not, he lifted one of her hands and kissed her knuckles, enjoying the feel of her skin beneath his lips for the last time.

"Goodbye, Myles Patton." That steely spark had returned to her dark blue eyes. "Promise me you will get better?"

"I promise."

With a decisive nod, she stood and went to the table where her valise sat beside his gun. "Here's the money for you and Amos." She set the stacks of bills on the chair beside his bed.

"That's too much," Myles protested. "We didn't get you all the way there."

She glared down at him. "It's my money and I'll do with it as I want."

Amos appeared in the doorway, a limp coyote hanging from one hand. "Myles, you're awake." He took in Delsie and the money and cocked his head. "What's going on?"

She shot Myles a look, then raised her chin. Her bravery was better medicine than anything he could think of. "I'm going on, alone."

"You certain?" Amos asked.

This time she didn't hesitate. "Yes."

Amos shot her a sad smile, reminding Myles that he wasn't the only one regretting Delsie's approaching absence. "Then we'd best draw you up a map."

## Chapter Fourteen

Delsie hadn't felt this weary since her first full day of riding, almost three weeks ago. Or this lonely since Lillie had left. While Amos and Myles hadn't been real conversationalists most of the time, she'd realized after only a few miles on her own that she missed their steady company.

After adjusting her grip on the reins, she checked the pocket watch Amos had insisted she take with her. *A gift,* he told her, *for a woman I would have been proud to have as a daughter.* The face of the clock became distorted from her tears, but she sniffed them back. Another thirty minutes or so before she needed to rest the mare.

She released the watch to dangle from where she'd pinned it to her waistband and gazed at the landscape around her. Unlike the desolate desert landscape, now there were trees and green hills. But even the lovely scenery couldn't keep her thoughts from returning— once again—to Myles.

Saying goodbye to him had left her feeling more

hollow inside than seeing her sister leave. At least she would be reunited with Lillie tonight. She was likely to never see Myles again.

She pressed a hand to her heart, wishing she could relieve the pain throbbing there. No wonder people talked about dying of a broken heart. Would time eventually ease the ache or would she carry this soreness for the rest of her life?

She'd wanted so much to tell Myles that she loved him and couldn't bear to have him gone from her life, and for him to say the same. But she knew it would've only made leaving him that much harder.

"What am I to do, girl?" she murmured to the mare. The mount flicked her ears back as though listening. "I don't know that I can ever truly forget him."

Memories of Myles were tightly, and wonderfully, woven through every part of her journey West. And though her pain was acute at separating from him, she wouldn't trade the experience of knowing him. A traitorous tear slid down her cheek, but she quickly swiped it away. She'd cried enough the past few days. Recalling Myles's words of confidence, that she could make this last stretch alone, renewed her usual optimism and faith.

Lowering her chin, she shut her eyes. "Bless me to make it to Lillie," she quietly prayed aloud. "And bless Myles that he'll fully recover. Help him get the horse ranch he desires. Bless Amos, too. They are both good men. The best I've ever met." Her voice wobbled with emotion, but she swallowed it back. "I'll be forever grateful for the chance to know them."

When she opened her eyes, Delsie lifted her head

and nudged her horse to move a little faster. She had nearly eighty miles to go before she could once again embrace her sister. And nothing would stop her from getting there.

Fire streaked the western sky as the sun disappeared. Delsie removed her hat and allowed the nice evening breeze to ruffle her sweat-dampened hair. Her muscles felt unusually sore tonight, especially considering she'd been riding every day for weeks. But she'd had to perform all their daily tasks alone these past fifty-five miles or so. Getting in and out of the saddle, talking to the Express station owners, watering her horse, procuring food for both of them. She hadn't realized how much Amos and Myles had helped, or the company they'd provided, until they were no longer with her.

Blowing out a tired sigh, she plopped her hat back on and patted her mare's neck. "We're so close, girl. Only twenty-five miles to go."

She'd already decided to keep riding, even after dark. Stopping now was unthinkable when she was so close to reaching Lillie. Thankfully, she and her horse had been well fed at the last station where they'd rested. With a full belly, she figured she could easily keep going, especially if the moon were bright enough to see by.

With no one to talk to, she began to hum a song. It was the one she and Amos had sung before Myles had finally joined in. A smile lifted her lips at the recollection. She'd had her suspicions early on that Myles's faith had only been shaken and not completely erased.

And that had proven true. She hoped he would continue to nourish it, though she couldn't help thinking a handsome, God-fearing man like him would surely be snatched up sooner than later by some young lady.

The possibility made her smile slip, so she hurried to replace it with thoughts of Lillie. What would her sister say when Delsie knocked on her door at the boardinghouse in a few more hours? She couldn't wait to see the surprise in her sister's green eyes and to throw her arms around her. Why, she'd even be able to help her dress for the wedding tomorrow.

Sunset soon gave way to dusk, lengthening the shadows around her. She checked her watch. It was about time to stop and rest the mare, but she'd wait until she found some water.

The light was fast fading from the sky. Delsie peered up at the crescent-shaped moon. It wasn't nearly as bright as she'd hoped, though it would surely provide enough visibility to keep riding.

The sound of water reached her ears before she found the stream. She slid from the saddle and took a moment to let her legs adjust to being on the ground again. Then she led the mare toward the water.

Darkness shrouded the brush and trees along the stream's bank. A shiver of concern slid up her spine, but Delsie squelched it with the knowledge that she had Myles's gun in its holster on her saddle.

"Everything's going to be fine," she murmured as she let the mare drink its fill from the stream. Once the horse had finished, she looped the reins, more by feel than sight, around a nearby branch. Thirsty, too, she knelt beside the gurgling water and scooped some into her hand to drink. When her immediate thirst had been satisfied, she set the canteen Myles had given her into the water to fill it.

The stirring of the horse in the brush caused her to jump, then laugh at her own foolishness. "Hang on," she called out to it. "I'm almost done."

Sticking her finger into the canteen, she determined she had enough water. Delsie climbed to her feet. The shadows had deepened even in the few minutes she'd been by the stream. Which tree had she tied the mare to?

"Here, girl. Where are you?" A knot of worry began to tighten her stomach and made her pulse trip faster in concern.

Hearing a noise ahead, she moved in that direction. Branches scraped at her face and arms until she finally stepped out from under their shelter. Where was her horse? The worry churned to full panic as Delsie scanned the trail. A movement jerked her attention to her right. In the faint light of the moon, she finally caught sight of the mare, moving at a trot in the opposite direction.

"Wait. Come back." She dropped the canteen to the ground and hiked up her skirt in order to run. Her rapid footfalls matched her heartbeat as she raced after the horse. "Come back."

The animal continued to move at a steady clip, indifferent to Delsie's repeated cries and frantic sprint. Before long she could no longer see the mare in front of her. She tripped over something in the semidarkness and stumbled to the ground. Her breath came in great heaves, made worse by the sobs she tried to hold back.

Anger, at the horse and herself, had her pounding her fist against the dirt with a choked cry. The loss of her mare was unthinkable. How would she ever reach Lillie now? She couldn't purchase another animal. All her remaining money had been stowed in a knapsack on the saddle, along with Myles's gun. Everything she'd owned and needed had just disappeared into the night.

Her frustration soon gave way to hopelessness and fear. She pulled herself into a sitting position and shivered. What was she to do now? She still had more than twenty miles to go to reach Lillie in Placerville and nothing but her own two feet to get her there. Had she come so far, and endured so much, only to be thwarted in this moment, nearly within sight of her goal?

*You're a strong woman, Delsie Radford. Don't let anyone tell you otherwise.*

Myles's voice filled her head and heart and warmed her trembling body. He had never given up on her, not once. And neither had God.

Rising to her feet, she moved purposely back the way she'd come. While she no longer had her map, either, she knew they'd been heading more or less in a westerly direction all day. And that was the way she'd keep going.

Her foot struck something hard. Kneeling down, she realized she'd kicked the canteen. Not only would it give her needed water but it also oriented her in the darkness. This was where she'd veered off the trail to reach the stream. She whispered a prayer of gratitude and a petition for protection, then continued forward.

Once she located the trail, Delsie turned west and

began walking as quickly as she could. It didn't take her long to realize how cumbersome her long skirt was to moving on the ground instead of on a horse. Stopping, she sat down and tore several inches from the hem. The fabric, trail-worn as it was, ripped easily. Delsie tossed the strip of cloth away, hoisted her canteen again and took a few steps.

*Much better.*

She picked up her pace to make up for the few stolen minutes. The creaking of branches and the whoosh of wings overhead sounded louder than normal, making her clutch the canteen tightly to her chest like a shield. But she didn't let the nocturnal noises slow her down.

Thankfully, she still had Amos's pocket watch. Every ten minutes, she allowed herself a drink to help keep her strength up. Soon she was taking sips every five minutes, though, to keep herself awake. Her feet ached in her shoes, and her tired eyelids longed to fall shut.

Biting her lip against the sleepiness, Delsie forged ahead. She passed the time by doing calculations in her head. If she averaged a walking speed of twelve minutes per mile, she could walk five miles in an hour. At that rate, she would be to Lillie's in…five hours. Plenty of time before the wedding, though she wasn't sure if the boardinghouse proprietress would admit her inside in the middle of the night.

She would figure something out—

"Oomph." She suddenly found herself sprawled on hands and knees. What had she stumbled over this time? Feeling along the dirt with her hands, Delsie discovered a hole, most likely a burrow of some sort, that she must have stepped into. "No harm done," she muttered to herself as she rose to her feet, but a sharp pain in her left ankle had her crying out in protest.

Fighting panic, she straightened to her full height and gingerly set her left foot down. "All right. Let's try this again." She tried to take a step forward, but painful shoots of feeling radiated from her injured ankle.

"No!"

She hobbled forward, determined to keep going, but the throbbing made walking painfully slow. How was she supposed to reach Lillie on a sprained ankle? Was it time to admit defeat? She didn't have a horse, and now she couldn't walk…

Despair, every bit as raw and stabbing as her ankle, drove her to the ground, where she sat, clutching her injured foot. There was no way she would make Lillie's wedding now. The thought of breaking her promise to their mother and never seeing her sister again had her hanging her head in defeat.

And what of Myles…? Were he and Amos safe or had the Indians come back? She wasn't likely to see either of her companions ever again. The thought filled her throat with the bitter taste of pain and regret.

"What do I do now?" she whispered through the heartache tightening her lungs.

After allowing herself another moment or two of self-pity, Delsie lifted her head and set her jaw. The next station had to be close by, given the miles she'd ridden before stopping the mare at the stream. If she could reach the Express station, she might just find a way to make it to Lillie after all. Rising to her feet, she began a painful shuffle forward. She had a wedding to get to.

The light spilling from the window up ahead infused Delsie with needed energy. Had she ever seen anything more beautiful? She quickened her limping pace. Crossing the empty yard, she hobbled up onto the porch and knocked at the door. A tall man, probably in his midthirties, answered.

"Can I help you, miss?" He glanced past her into the shadowed yard.

"Yes," she gasped out over the pain of her ankle. "I've lost my horse, you see. And then I sprained my ankle. But I need to be at my sister's wedding tomorrow…" The room behind him had begun to shift and Delsie felt herself falling forward.

"Whoa there." He reached out and grasped her elbow. "Let's you get off that foot and then you can tell me where you're from and where you're going."

Delsie allowed him to lead her into a tidy parlor, where she sank into one of the armchairs.

"Now, which ankle is hurt?"

She pointed to her left. The man nodded, then gently lifted her foot and placed it on a cushioned footrest. Clearly she'd arrived at a place much nicer than a simple remounting station for Express riders.

"Let me go get my wife. I'm sure she'll want to help." He gave her a friendly smile.

"Thank you."

The man slipped from the room, leaving Delsie alone again. She took off her hat, rested her head against the back of the chair and shut her eyes. When was the last time she'd felt this tired?

"What do we have here?"

Delsie opened her eyes and sat up. A blond-haired woman, pulling a shawl over her nightgown, was coming down the stairs.

"I'm sorry to disturb you," she started to say, but the woman shook her head.

"We're rather used to strangers coming here at all hours of the night. What with the stagecoaches and teamsters stopping all the time." She came to stand next to Delsie's chair and smiled. "Never had a woman here on her own, though. What's your name?"

Her kind manner was nearly Delsie's undoing. Willing back useless tears, she gave the woman a tentative smile. "My name is Delsie Radford. I lost my horse about five miles back and then twisted my ankle walking in the dark."

The woman took a seat on the nearby settee. "And what were you doing riding alone, Miss Radford?"

Delsie swallowed. "My companions were waylaid about sixty miles back when one of them was injured by Indians."

The woman's green eyes widened and she gave a startled laugh. "I think you'd best start at the beginning of your tale. But first, if you'll follow me into the kitchen, we'll see what we can do for you in the way of food and something for that ankle."

"Thank you…" Delsie waited for the woman to supply her name.

"Please, call me Edith."

With Edith's help, she stood and limped down the

hall to the kitchen at the back of the house. She took a seat at the table, her left leg propped up on the bench next to her. Edith sliced some bread and brought it to the table for Delsie to eat before sitting down in a nearby chair. While she nibbled on the bread and jam, she told Edith her entire story—from finding the letters from Lillie in her father's desk to leaving Myles and Amos this morning.

"And that is how I ended up here," Delsie finished, "and why I must be at Lillie's wedding tomorrow."

"What time is the wedding?"

Delsie shook her head. "I don't know. Morning, I assume."

"Placerville is a good twenty miles from here," Edith said, drumming her fingers on the chair arm, "but I'm sure one of the teamsters headed in that direction could drive you."

A flicker of hope filled Delsie until she remembered she had nothing with which to pay for a ride. "I'm afraid I can't pay someone to take me or afford lodging tonight. But if I could sleep in your stable…" That solved one problem, though it didn't solve how she would get to Placerville on a sprained ankle.

"Nonsense." Edith reached out and patted Delsie's hand. "You will stay in one of our rooms tonight and I'll talk with the teamsters in the morning at breakfast. Ol' Ike is a regular here and a man to be trusted. He could probably drive you."

Delsie's chin wobbled with emotion. Edith's genuine compassion reminded her so much of her own mother that a keen sense of loss swept through her.

"I don't even know what to say." Myles would laugh at that.

Edith chuckled and stood. "Then don't worry about saying anything. Now let's get that ankle wrapped up."

In no time at all her ankle had been securely wrapped with a bandage and Edith was helping her up the stairs to a vacant room. After dressing in a borrowed nightgown, Delsie slipped into bed. She would allow herself to sleep for a few hours, then she'd be up before the sun and back on her way to Lillie.

## Chapter Fifteen

Warm rays of sunshine nudged Delsie awake. She blinked at the unfamiliar surroundings and sat up, trying to orient herself. Her torn dress and Amos's pocket watch brought instant remembering. Throwing off her blankets, she limped across the room to pick up the watch. It was already seven o'clock. Had the teamsters left? Her heart beat wildly at the thought. But no, Edith would have come to wake her.

Pacified, she quickly changed out of the nightgown and back into her dress. Dirt marred the material and the once vibrant color had faded after days in the sun. Not the most proper thing to wear to a wedding, but it couldn't be helped.

Delsie raked her fingers through her hair and settled for a simple braid. Her gaze fell onto her hat and trousers. Did she dare part with them? The trousers she didn't mind leaving behind. But as uncomely as the wide-brimmed hat might be on her, she couldn't part with it. It represented her only token, beyond memories, from her time with Myles.

Placing the hat on her head, she shuffled out of the room and down the stairs. Edith met her at the bottom.

"I was just coming up to see if you were awake. How did you sleep?"

"Very well." Delsie steadied herself against the wall. "Did Ike agree to drive me?"

Edith nodded, smiling. "He's leaving now, though. So you'll have to take these biscuits with you." She handed Delsie several biscuits wrapped in a napkin. "I would have had you join us for breakfast earlier, but I figured you needed the rest."

"Thank you, Edith." On impulse she gave the woman a quick hug.

"You are more than welcome, Delsie. I wish you all the best." She helped Delsie out the door and down the porch steps, where a large wagon sat waiting. "I'll be praying you make it."

Delsie thanked her again, then allowed Ike, a wiry man with gentle eyes, to help her onto the seat. As the wagon rolled forward, she waved goodbye to Edith.

Ike spoke little, reminding Delsie a bit of Myles, but he wasn't unfriendly. She even coaxed a smile from him after offering him one of the biscuits. The sky overhead was a perfect arc of blue, bringing recollections of the prairie to her mind. She could hardly believe she'd come almost eighteen hundred miles in nineteen days.

The creak of the wagon and the thud of the team's hooves filled the quiet between her and Ike. He kept the horses moving at a steady pace, but it still felt slow compared to what Delsie was used to. She checked the pocket watch again. It was eight o'clock now. Would she make it on time?

She shifted on the hard seat, almost wishing for her saddle. How strange it felt not to be on the back of a horse as she'd been every day these past few weeks.

Each turn of the wheels brought her closer to Lillie, but Delsie willed them to spin faster. She couldn't miss her sister, not when she was so very close.

*I'm coming, Lillie*, she thought, her foot tapping out a rhythm of its own. *I'm coming.*

If Ike sensed her fretting energy, he didn't comment. Instead he kept his gaze ahead and the reins gripped securely in his sun-spotted hands. Delsie wished her own hands were as occupied. Instead she rubbed at the watch face with her thumb, fiddled with her dress cuffs, and adjusted and readjusted her hat.

At the moment she thought she would either scream with nerves or throw up her hastily eaten breakfast, she spied buildings in the distance.

"Is that Placerville?"

"Yep," Ike intoned in a calm voice.

Her heart began to thud double time. Her journey's end was in sight. She only prayed she wasn't too late.

"Where do you need to go, miss?"

She told him the name of the boardinghouse.

"I know it. I'll take you there, but I can't stay. Got to keep on schedule."

"I understand. Thank you, Ike."

He nodded in acknowledgment. Delsie gripped her hands in her lap as he slowed the horses at the edge of the town. Once they reached what she guessed must be Main Street, Ike turned the huge wagon onto a side street and stopped. "This is it."

Her hands shook so badly, she could hardly climb down. "Thank you again, Ike," she called over her shoulder as she hurried at a painful hop to the door. She tried the handle, but it was locked. Behind her she could hear Ike and the wagon driving away. Delsie knocked once, twice.

"Coming," a voice hollered from inside. At last the door opened and a short woman with a severe bun glowered down at her. "You need a room?"

"No. I need to see Miss Lillian Radford."

"Miss Lillie?" the woman echoed. "She's up and gone. Left first thing this morning."

*Gone?* Deep regret pulsed through Delsie's veins and she sagged against the door in despair. Lillie wasn't supposed to leave for Oregon until tomorrow. "Thank you." She turned away and stared unseeing down the street. Where was she to go now?

"If you need to speak to her, she's likely still at the church. Gettin' herself hitched to that handsome Clay Weeks." The woman gave a low whistle and chuckled. "I would've been there myself but couldn't find no one to watch the place..."

Delsie whirled around, hope burning strong in her throat and eyes. "She's still at the church?"

"I reckon so."

"Which church?"

The woman pointed down the street. "Right there. On the other side of Main."

She took off at a shuffling run. Her ankle ached with the effort, but she ignored it. When she reached

Main Street, she hurried across, dodging several wagons. There was the church, a white clapboard building with a bell tower and spire. She hobbled down the dusty street to the bottom of the steps. There she paused to catch her breath. She couldn't hear anything from inside, but several wagons were still sitting out front.

Gripping the banister, she hopped up the stairs to the front door. She gripped the handle and pulled it open. Cooler air greeted her as she limped inside and stopped. There at the front of the church, before the preacher, stood Lillie dressed in a simple ivory gown and veil. She held hands with Clay, who was looking tall and handsome in a nice brown suit.

The sight of her sister after so many months apart ripped a sudden cry of longing from Delsie's mouth. The sound echoed in the quiet church. Delsie pressed her hand to her lips as the few people in the congregation turned around. Lillie and Clay twisted to face her, too. Delsie's eyes met her sister's beneath the lacy veil.

"Delsie?" Her name came out as a gasp.

"Yes, Lillie." She took a step forward. "It's me."

Within seconds, Lillie was hurrying up the aisle, Clay right behind her. Delsie met them halfway and threw her arms around Lillie. She held her sister for a long moment, her tears wetting the shoulder of Lillie's gown.

When Lillie drew back, she was smiling, in spite of the tears on her own cheeks. "I can't believe you're here." She took in the sight of Delsie's hat and disheveled dress. "What happened to you?"

Delsie clasped her sister's hand and squeezed it. "That, dear Lillie, is a very long story."

"Perhaps it can wait until after your sister and I are married," Clay said, his smile teasing.

"Yes, of course." Embarrassment washed over her anew as Delsie glanced at the preacher and the guests, all staring with curiosity at her and her sister.

Lillie tugged her toward the front of the church. "Now that you're here, you must sit right in front."

She started to protest given her unsightly attire, but Clay murmured good-naturedly, "I wouldn't cross her if I were you."

Delsie chuckled. "A fact I know all too well. All right." She took a seat on the front pew.

"Are we ready now?" the preacher asked, his gaze inquisitive but not unkind.

Lillie and Clay nodded as one and turned to face each other once more. The love emanating from their glowing faces brought another surge of joy to Delsie's heart.

"Dearly beloved," the preacher began.

*I made it, Myles.* Delsie wished so badly she could tell him. She glanced in the direction of the window, but instead of buildings, she saw the handsome face and dark eyes of the man she loved watching her from astride his horse. *I made it.*

"Do you think Delsie made it, to her sister?" Myles said as he rotated his shoulder, trying to stretch the stiff muscles from lying on his side or stomach, despite the aggravated pain. He and Amos had just finished supper. It had only been a day and a half since

Delsie had left them to continue on alone, but it felt twice that long to him. "I guess we'll never know," he murmured more to himself than to Amos.

The older man sat at the table, cleaning his gun. Myles owed his healing, however slow, to Amos. Even without a doctor or proper medical supplies, his friend had so far kept Myles's wound from festering and becoming worse. He had God to thank for that, too.

"I think she made it," Amos said quietly.

"What if something happened, though?"

He felt the familiar apprehension churning inside him, souring the food in his belly. Typically he fought the worry with reassurances that he'd done the right thing. But every now and then, especially since they'd had no word and probably wouldn't, the doubts crept in and robbed his peace of mind over Delsie.

He lifted his head to find Amos watching him intently. "I think she made it," he repeated, "because something deep in here says she did." He tapped his chest. "Something that goes beyond sight and knowledge to tell me everything will be all right. With Delsie." He raised his graying eyebrows at Myles. "And with you."

The words hit Myles with as much force as the Indian's arrow. If he searched his heart, really and truly searched, he sensed a calmness there, confirming what Amos said. Delsie would be all right, and so would they. Though Myles still couldn't help wishing he'd been able to see her reach her sister, been able to kiss her once more, been able to tell her that she was the best thing to come into his life in a long time.

"Think we'll have our jobs waiting for us?" he

asked, changing the subject. He let his gaze move from Amos to where Elijah sat on the nearby cupboard eating some of the leftover supper meat.

"Sure hope so," Amos said with a chuckle. "The Pony Express hasn't been going long enough to get kicked out yet."

Myles cracked a smile. "Do you like working at the station?"

"I like working with the stock and visiting with the riders." He glanced up from his gun. "What about you? You thinkin' of being an Express rider for much longer?"

Myles's answer came easy. "Just long enough to make a little money."

"And start your ranch?" He'd told Amos more than once about his dream.

Myles nodded and propped his good shoulder against the headboard. "I reckon another six months, a year maybe, of Express riding and I should have enough to buy a little land. I've already got me a horse."

Amos shot him a surprised look. "Have you, now?"

"Delsie gave me Moses."

"Moses?" Amos laughed.

Myles feigned a scowl. "Don't you start on the name, too."

"So she gave you a horse, huh?" Something in the other man's tone had Myles on edge.

"And?" Myles pressed, though he wasn't sure he wanted to hear the rest.

Amos gave a nonchalant shrug, his hands still working over his gun. "That's a rather generous gift." He paused to throw a meaningful glance at Myles. "Don't know that I'd let a horse-giving lady with a spine of iron slip away from me that easily."

Myles sniffed. Delsie wasn't here anymore, and Amos was still playing matchmaker. "I shouldn't have to spell out why that's impossible."

"No," Amos said, giving a thoughtful shake of his head. "But you might get closer to having what you want if you start pondering over ways to make it possible."

With a noncommittal grunt, Myles rested his head back and looked up toward the absent ceiling. Thank goodness it hadn't rained yet. It wasn't as if he hadn't thought through the scenarios over and over since Delsie had left. But she wouldn't leave her father to marry a lowly Express rider and Myles didn't have any way to make more money unless he kept riding.

His chances of winning her, and her father, over were likely to decrease with every passing month, too. Even if he did eventually acquire his horse ranch and made it successful, there was no guarantee she wouldn't already be married to someone else by then. And he wouldn't ask her to wait, months or years, for him. It wouldn't be fair to someone as lovely and remarkable as Delsie.

"Nope." He dropped his chin and glared at Amos. "Still doesn't change things. She has to return to her father, who already has someone picked out for her, I might add. And Delsie would sooner be hung than split her family a second time by running off with a poor horse rider."

Amos's continued calm in the face of Myles's impassioned speech irked him. But Myles could at least appreciate his friend's efforts to see him and Delsie happy and together, however unlikely.

"You ever heard the verse about the Lord working in mysterious ways?"

The question surprised Myles. "I reckon so, yes."

The older man lifted his gaze to Myles's, those blue-gray eyes filled with quiet confidence. "I suggest you remember that verse from time to time, Myles Patton. And instead of ruminating about it in your finite way, why not turn the matter over to the Lord?"

Myles twisted his head to peer out the window. Charles would have likely said something similar. And while every part of him balked at the impossibility of he and Delsie finding their way back to each other, he wouldn't give over to the bitterness and mistrust that had filled his old life. His life before meeting her.

Hope had been awakened inside him, and whatever his fear at believing too much, he couldn't wrestle the idea from his mind. *All right, Lord*, he finally prayed in silence. *You know I love her. And whether it's meant to be between us or not...* Myles swallowed and brushed at his eyes with his thumb. *I turn the outcome over to You.*

"Oh, Delsie. I'm going to miss you so much." Lillie hugged her once again, crushing the small hat she'd given Delsie to keep. Along with the dress she wore, a nightgown, an extra change of clothes and enough money to travel home. Lillie and Clay wouldn't hear of her taking anything less. "I wish you could stay longer."

Delsie eased back and squeezed her sister's hands. While they'd enjoyed several hours talking after the wedding yesterday, their time together still felt too brief. "I do, too. But you and Clay are pulling out in a few hours," she gently reminded. "And I need to return home. To Papa."

Lillie nodded, though tears still shone in her eyes. "You will write, won't you?"

"Of course. Once a week, at least."

"Maybe someday you could even come visit us in Oregon." She glanced up at Clay with an adoring smile. "It's going to be beautiful there. Lots of trees, just like back home. But with almost no winter."

"I will try."

"Try?" Lillie laughed and kissed Delsie's cheek. "That doesn't sound like the girl who stumbled into my wedding yesterday with a sprained ankle and eighteen hundred miles worth of dust and dirt on her clothes."

Delsie chuckled. How she'd missed Lillie. And now she had to say goodbye all over again. This time, though, she told herself, she would be able to write her sister and receive letters in return. She would make certain their father understood that.

"Time to go, miss," the stagecoach driver said. "Where's your luggage?"

She lifted the borrowed valise from Lillie. "This is it."

The driver's eyes widened and he shook his head. "Never seen a lady come through with something so small."

Delsie wanted to tell him she'd learned to travel

quite light, and if needed, could skin and cook a rabbit for supper, as well. But she held her tongue.

"Goodbye, Delsie." Lillie crushed her in another tight hug. "Tell Papa... I love him."

Surprised, she drew back to search her sister's face. "Do you mean that, Lillie? Have you forgiven him?"

Her sister released her to clasp Clay's hand. "It's me I hope he's forgiven. I was angry and stubborn. But I understand now the lengths we'll go to keep those we love safe and happy. Look at what you did, Delsie, for us."

It was Delsie's turn to pull Lillie close for one last embrace. She'd been right, all along, in coming. "I love you, Lillie."

"I love you, too."

Delsie went up on tiptoe and gave Clay a quick kiss on the cheek. "Welcome to the family."

"Thank you." He looked down at her sister and beamed. They would be happy together. A tremor of melancholy passed through her at the thought of not finding that herself.

"Let's go, miss." She heeded the driver's call this time and allowed him to help her into the stagecoach. An older woman and her husband sat on the cushioned seat opposite hers. Delsie leaned out the open window and waved to Lillie and Clay as the stagecoach jerked forward.

"Oh dear, close that window, child," the woman protested, waving a handkerchief at her. "That dreadful dust will come in."

Delsie bit back a smile at the thought of how harmless dust truly was and shut the window. She kept the curtain up, though. Now that she was inside the stage-coach, she felt suddenly confined. She longed for the open sky and sun overhead and the chance to ride side by side with Myles again.

Shutting her eyes, she let herself drift through the memories of the past several weeks—meeting Myles that first day, how he'd saved her from the runaway horse and later from the trappers, his care when she'd taken sick with cold, his kiss in the barn, his strong embrace. Each recollection brought vivid sweetness for their time together. Until she recalled the moment she'd told him goodbye. Bitter sadness swept through her then. This time the roll of the wheels was taking her farther and farther from the one she loved.

"Do you think we'll be set upon by highwaymen or Indians, my dear?" the woman asked her husband in a loud whisper. "I can't think of anything more horrid."

Delsie opened her eyes and stared at the passing scenery. Indians or highwayman no longer elicited the same fear in her that they once had. She'd experienced the former and lived to tell the tale. Besides, there were more horrible things to encounter in life than dust or an attack on the stage. Leaving behind the man she loved, forever, now ranked highest in Delsie's mind.

## Chapter Sixteen

"Lookee there. Patton's back!" someone yelled as Myles climbed from his saddle and took Moses by the reins. He glanced up at the sign hung over the Pony Express Stables. Had it really been seven weeks since he'd last stood here, talking to Delsie? It felt more like seven months.

He passed his horse off to one of the stock hands. "Take care of him for a bit, will you? I'll be back." Hopefully, with his job still intact.

"Nice-looking horse. Is he yours?" the man asked.

"He is." The first smile he'd felt in days worked at Myles's mouth. This was the first of what he hoped would be many of his own horses.

Thinking of Delsie's gift didn't come without a price, though. It brought to mind the giver, too. As if Myles needed any more reason to remember her. She might have been physically absent on his and Amos's long trek home, but every inch of the trail held some tender recollection of her.

He'd come to accept, long before he'd sold his other

mount and collected Moses near Salt Lake City, that he missed Delsie, intensely. He missed her smile, her determination, her strength, her beauty, her goodness. The trail held none of the same excitement or interest for him without her alongside him to talk to, or tease or watch over.

While he went through the motions of rising, riding, eating and sleeping every day, deep down Myles felt a dull ache that couldn't be completely ignored. Only in his nightly prayers, a habit he'd taken up on their way back East, did he find some relief from the gnawing inside him.

Setting his jaw, Myles walked to the Express office at the hotel. Express riding had lost some of its luster, too, but he still needed this job. His absence had been twice as long as he'd originally thought. Had they given his job to another eager rider by now?

His gaze wandered over the familiar streets and buildings of Saint Joseph. But Myles no longer found them as appealing as he once had. He missed the wide-openness of the West and the lure of its new possibilities.

*As soon as I have the money I need*, he vowed, *I'm heading back to California.*

It would mean being even farther away from Delsie, but maybe then he could find the peace that had eluded him since she'd ridden off the day before her sister's wedding. Besides, he'd turned all of that over to the Lord, as Amos had suggested. It was in His hands now.

After a rather short stop at the Express office, Myles had to admit his unrealistic hopes for him and Delsie weren't the only things God was looking out for. His fears over his employment had been unfounded. He still had a job as an Express rider, though his superior did admit to considering giving the job to someone else if Myles hadn't shown up by the following week.

He offered a silent prayer of gratitude as he retraced his steps back to the stables. He needed to see about boarding Moses for a while, using some of the money he'd got from selling the other horse.

Grateful to find Moses had been brushed and fed, Myles led him on foot to the livery stable. Memories of working with Charles filled his thoughts as the welcome scent of hay and horses permeated his nose. He hadn't been here in months.

"Myles," the new owner said, smiling. "What can I do for you?"

"I need to board my horse for at least a month." He rubbed a hand down Moses's nose. "Maybe longer."

The livery owner nodded. "This isn't an Express horse, is it?"

"No, sir. This horse is mine."

"Well, we would be more than happy to board him for you."

After settling the arrangements and paying the man, Myles returned to the stables. Elijah was waiting for him on a corner of the roofline. The bird alighted onto his shoulder as Myles strode up. He wanted to see if any of the other riders had a hankering for something other than boardinghouse fare for dinner. Not that he relished the idea of company, but he'd realized after parting ways with Amos a day and a half earlier that he was tired of living so isolated.

"There's a lady here to see you," another rider announced when Myles entered the stables. "Just outside, near the corral."

"A lady?" Myles threw a glance over his shoulder, though he knew he couldn't see whoever was waiting for him from here. "Did she give you a name?"

"Nope."

"All right." Myles headed back outside, his heart beating faster in his chest. It couldn't be Delsie, but telling himself so didn't stop the wild hope from taking root inside him nonetheless. She was likely still traveling back to Pennsylvania. But had she decided to stop and see him? The possibility had him moving faster with anticipation.

He forced a slower pace as he neared the corral, not wanting to appear too eager to whoever waited. Sure enough a woman stood with her back to him, but right away, Myles noticed the coil of hair at her neck wasn't dark. It was blond. Bitter disappointment scalded his tongue as he swallowed. Whoever the woman might be, he wasn't going to transport someone else across the country. Delsie would remain his first and only human parcel.

"Can I help you?" he asked as he came to a stop several feet away from the lady. Elijah flew off, leaving him alone.

The woman turned and smiled, but her friendly reaction did nothing to ease the sudden wariness roiling in Myles's gut.

"Cynthia? What are you doing here?"

"Myles." She moved with purpose toward him, though her whole demeanor radiated nervousness instead of her usual carefree manner.

He folded his arms and regarded her silently. What did she possibly have to say?

"You look...well."

"As do you," he replied evenly. She was still a beauty, but he'd found someone else who exhibited beauty both inside and out. Even if he couldn't be with Delsie, he would seek someone like her—at least someday.

Cynthia glanced at the ground, her lips pulled into a frown. "I don't blame you for still being angry, Myles. I've had a lot of time to ponder over that night."

"I'm not angry, not anymore." Myles lowered his arms to his sides. The words seemed to echo through him and he recognized their truth. When had he forgiven Cynthia? *Somewhere along the trail with Delsie*, he thought wryly.

Hope lit Cynthia's green eyes. "Oh, good. Because things haven't been the same without you." She sidled up next to him and put her gloved hand on his arm. "I've missed you. The captain has become such a bore."

Her touch did nothing to him. He felt no regret or bitterness but no thrilling joy, either. "That's too bad, Cynthia." He gently extracted his arm from her clutch. "I hope you find someone who truly makes you happy, someone who you'll make happy, too."

Her brow knit together in a familiar look of confusion. "Whatever do you mean, Myles? I came here today to tell you that I'm sorry for the way things ended. I want you back."

He couldn't help a laugh. "And don't I get a say in this?"

"Well, yes, of course. But I assumed you'd be a little happier to see me, to know I've missed you..." Her voice trailed off and her eyes widened. "You've met someone else, haven't you?"

He wouldn't tell her all about Delsie or how his feelings for the woman before him had paled to mere infatuation when compared to what he felt for Delsie. "There is someone," he stated simply.

Cynthia drew herself up as though truly offended. "Aha. I knew it. Does she care for you as much as I do? Can she give you a sizable fortune, like I can?"

Her mouth curved up into another smile, but this one struck Myles as more calculating than anything else. "Father and I reached a little negotiation a few weeks back. Because I'm of age now, he agreed to give me a share of my inheritance. A large portion, to use for whatever, or whomever, I wish. You wouldn't have to ride these smelly horses anymore. You could have your ranch, Myles. Right now."

So that was how she thought she could ensnare him. She was cleverer than he may have given her credit for in the past. But while the thought of having his ranch much sooner than he'd planned sounded attractive, it wasn't worth a lifetime as Cynthia's husband. Accepting her offer wouldn't be fair, to either of them.

"Look, Cynthia, I'll always appreciate your friendship." And he meant it. Her presence in his life had stoked within him the desire to push himself, to achieve more than he might have thought possible. "But there isn't anything more between us. I'm sorry."

She looked momentarily stunned, as if she couldn't fathom anyone refusing her—and maybe she couldn't.

Her reaction was short-lived, though. With a lift of her chin, she shot him a haughty look. "I suppose it is your loss, then. Goodbye, Myles. This time it's final."

"Goodbye, Cynthia. I wish you all the best." He clasped her hand between his, hoping she sensed his sincerity.

"I intend to have the best," she said with an over-confident laugh as she pulled her hand back. "Adieu." She sauntered away, a handkerchief pressed to her nose.

He blew out his breath, then whistled for Elijah. The bird appeared a few moments later and landed on his shoulder. "What'd you fly off for?"

Elijah cocked his head.

"It's safe now," Myles said, chuckling. Ironically his earlier melancholy had faded during his encounter with Cynthia.

What if he hadn't met Delsie all those weeks ago? He likely would have accepted Cynthia's offer today. A shudder ran through him at the thought. Neither of them would have been truly happy.

It was one more thing to be grateful for regarding his time with Delsie. Being with her had changed him and what he'd once thought he wanted. If nothing else, he'd try to be content with that.

Taking a deep breath, Delsie entered the house. "Papa? I'm home." She unpinned her traveling hat and hung it on the hall tree, her gaze sweeping the beautifully carved banister and gas-lit chandelier overhead. She was home. And yet, standing here among the opulence, she felt as if she were a guest herself. Nothing around her had changed, but she had.

"Delsie!" Her father strode forward and embraced her tightly, bringing a rush of happiness to her. Whatever his faults, she'd missed him. "You are home at last. How was the journey?"

She stepped back, hoping he wouldn't yet notice her fading brown skin or the healing blisters beneath her gloves. "Long," she answered truthfully. Riding on the back of the horse at express speed had felt infinitely faster than the tiring ride in a jostling stagecoach that she'd endured the past several weeks.

"I received your telegram from Missouri. Who is this friend you detoured to visit?"

Delsie tucked an errant curl back into her chignon in a casual manner that belied the rapid thumping of her heart. "I'll tell you all about it later. But first, I want to hear all the news of home." She linked her arm through his.

"Not much in the way of news, but I do have a surprise." He led her into the parlor, where a tall figure with dark hair stood with his back to the doorway. Backlit by the bright evening light, Delsie couldn't tell who waited for her. Could it be Myles? Her pulse tripped faster and faster with hope. Had he learned her address from Amos and beaten her home?

Then the person turned and her hope shattered like glass.

"Flynn," she said more brightly than she felt.

"Welcome home, Delsie." He crossed the room to place a quick kiss on her cheek. She waited for the smattering of flurries in her middle or for some reaction at all. But she felt nothing. Worse, Flynn's kiss succeeded in stirring memories in her mind of kissing Myles. "We've missed you," he said, smiling fully at her.

"Have you?"

He chuckled as if she'd said something truly clever. "Of course. Two months is a long time to be away."

*Yes*, she thought, *it is*. Long enough that she no longer felt at ease in her old life.

"Let us adjourn to the dining room for dinner," Mr. Radford announced, patting her hand where it still held his arm.

Delsie nodded and woodenly followed him into the next room, where she took a seat beside him at the table, across from Flynn. She'd hoped her first evening back would include time alone with her father, to tell him everything simmering in her conscience. But it appeared she would have to wait until their guest left for the night.

The food tasted delicious. After weeks of stagecoach fare, the roast mutton and greens were better than anything she'd eaten since that first home station in Nebraska. Delsie ate every bite, including two helpings of Mrs. Kipling's custard. Her appearance wasn't the only thing to change during her journey West; her appetite had increased, too.

"You seem rather famished, my dear," Mr. Radford remarked with a touch of censure and teasing. "Don't they feed you on those coaches?"

Delsie blushed. "Yes, of course. It's just that… I've missed Mrs. Kipling's food." Which was largely true. She would never take food, whatever its source, for granted again. "Did any correspondence come while I was away?"

He dabbed his mouth with his napkin. "Actually, there is. One from your aunt, though I can't imagine what she'd have to say when you only just saw her. And another from someone named… Allan?" He shook his head. "No…it was… Amos."

"Amos?" Delsie scrambled up from her chair and went to the buffet table, where the letters were kept on a silver platter. A letter from Amos lay on top of the stack. She picked it up and pressed it to her heart, suddenly able to breathe for the first time since entering the house. "If you'll excuse me, I'll read it in my room."

"Now?" Mr. Radford frowned. "Can't it wait, Delsie? Flynn is here. And who's this Amos person anyway?"

She placed a kiss on his cheek. "Don't worry, Papa. I'll explain everything soon. But I must read this letter. Please excuse me, Flynn."

Flynn gave an obviously forced smile, but he dipped his head in acquiescence.

"Good night." With that she hurried from the room and up the stairs, anxious for news of her friends. Once inside her bedroom, she flopped onto her stomach across the waist-high bed and tore open the letter.

The date was from a week earlier, from Guittard's Station in Kansas.

Dearest Delsie,
I hope this letter finds you well and safely back home, after seeing your sister. Myles and I made

the return trip a bit more slowly than the three of us did West. His injury has healed well, though he will likely bear a scar for the rest of his life. We both hope the reunion with your sister was all you'd hoped it would be.

I can't say we didn't miss your presence riding east. Moses was anxiously waiting for Myles when we returned to Rockwell's. You'll be pleased to know, too, that Myles and I still had our jobs with the Pony Express awaiting our return. I hope you'll write when you're able. Your faithful servant,
Hank Amos

Delsie had forgotten his first name—to her, he would always be simply Amos. She read the letter through again, relieved to hear Myles was healthy once more and that she hadn't cost either of them their jobs.

Taking a seat at her desk, she pulled out a clean stack of paper and began writing a letter back to Amos. She detailed her experiences that last day and night before finally reaching Lillie, the long travel back to Pennsylvania and how much she dearly missed her friends.

When she finished, she set the letter aside and stared at the next blank page. Should she write Myles? Amos hadn't said that Myles wanted to correspond, as well. She picked up her pen, then set it down once more. Better to leave what had passed between them behind. No good could come from trying to continue something that would never come to fruition, as long as her father held to his stubborn opinions. But there was one thing she was determined to change his mind about—her marrying Flynn.

An hour or so later, Delsie waited unseen at the top of the stairs while her father walked Flynn to the door. Once the man had departed and her father had retired to the parlor, she finally descended. Cheery lamplight lit the parlor and reflected off the beveled glass of her father's book cupboard. He glanced up from his reading as she entered the room and took a seat in the armchair opposite his.

"Flynn departed." He stuck his finger in his book. "I think you may have disappointed him by scurrying off to your room so quickly after dinner."

Delsie leaned back against the familiar softness of the chair. "If I offended him in any way, I am truly sorry."

Mr. Radford nodded and opened his book again. "I'll invite him for dinner tomorrow night and you can apologize to him then."

"Actually…" Delsie licked her lips, her heart racing. It was her moment to be strong. "I'd rather you didn't invite him."

The book closed with a sudden *clap*. "Why ever not?"

She straightened in her chair. "Because I don't love Flynn. And I will never love him." She tucked her shaking hands demurely in her lap. "I know that now."

"But it's an excellent match," he protested. "With your beauty and inheritance and his business sense, he can take over the bank for me. You would be set up very comfortably for life, Delsie."

"That may be true, but I won't trade my happiness for it. I can't marry where I feel no love."

His brows lowered in consternation. "Is that what all these weeks at your aunt's has done? Turned you as rebellious as…" He visibly swallowed and glanced away, unwilling or unable to say Lillie's name.

"I will not defy you as Lillie did," Delsie said in a gentle tone. "But I will not marry Flynn, either."

"Aren't they one in the same?" he countered, his voice more weary than angry.

She shook her head. "No, because I won't leave you, either." She reached forward and rested her hand against his where it gripped his knee. "We will simply have to find another suitor who can provide for me, but one whom I love, too."

He blew out his breath in a resigned sigh. "Very well. You know I've never been good at refusing you anything or staying angry at you for long."

A lump of emotion filled her throat. Her father was a good man, even if he and Lillie had both reacted badly to her choice to follow Clay. "I'm glad to hear I still have some sway." She threw him a teasing smile that made him laugh lightly. "Because I have something else to confess."

He chuckled once more and ran a hand over his eyes. "I don't know that I can take any more revelations tonight, dear daughter."

"Just one more." Though it was likely to upset him far more than her announcement about Flynn.

He finally nodded for her to continue.

Delsie's heart resumed its harried pace as she sat

back and clasped her hands together. "I've been to see Lillie, Papa."

"Lillie?" He smirked with disbelief. "That's impossible. Your sister is, who knows where, in California."

"I know where she is. I found her letters. In your desk."

The startled merriment drained from his face, leaving it looking haggard. "When did you find them?"

Delsie kept her chin up. "Right before I went to Aunt Cissy's." Stony silence met her words. "Please don't be angry at me for discovering them. I've been so anxious to hear from her, to know she's all right."

Mr. Radford glanced away, staring into the light of the lamp. "I probably shouldn't have kept them from you. But I worried that you…you might wish to leave, too, if your sister put it into your head to follow after her." She could tell the words cost him to say.

Delsie waited for him to look at her again. "I am not like Lillie, or you," she added tenderly. "I told you I would never leave you to go live far away, and I intend to keep my word. But it isn't right to keep Lillie from me. Or from us. She is sorry for the way she handled things. She loves you, and I'm sure she would welcome your blessing on her marriage to Clay."

"So she finally up and married that farmer, did she?" He sniffed. "Did she write and tell you that? About her and the Weeks boy and about being sorry?"

"No." Delsie shook her head. "She told me in person about her being sorry and that she loves you. And as far as the wedding…" She swallowed her dry throat and plunged on. "I was there. That's what I meant when I said I'd been to see Lillie."

His jaw went slack as he gaped at her, his expression one of confusion. "That's where you've been all these weeks?"

"Actually, no." She gave a nervous laugh. "I stayed with Aunt Cissy for two weeks, then traveled to California over the course of nineteen days, where I witnessed Lillie and Clay's wedding. Then the next day I boarded the stage to return here. So theoretically, I was only with Lillie for a day."

He bent forward, frowning, his forearms on his knees. "I don't understand."

She released a shaky breath. "I should probably start at the beginning."

"That would be preferred."

In a voice that became stronger the more she confided, Delsie shared the details of Lillie's last letter and about her plan to reach her sister in time by using the Pony Express as escort.

"Alone?" Mr. Radford bellowed. "Without a chaperone? Were you out of your mind, Delsie?"

She calmly shook her head—she'd known there would be many parts to this story he would not like. "I was in my right mind. Only anxious to get to Lillie and let her know I cared before she left for Oregon." She gave him a patient smile. "And I was not alone. I was in the company of two gentlemen. An Express rider and a guide."

He muttered something inaudible beneath his breath and lumbered to his feet.

"Please, Papa. Sit down. There's more to tell."

"I prefer to stand, thank you." He began pacing the rug in front of her. "Or rather...walk. Especially if all your exposés prove to be as distressing as this first one."

Doing her best to ignore his agitation, Delsie explained the necessary changes to her plan in order to arrive in California on time. She told him about soliciting Amos's help and Myles's agreement to continue on, as well. She shared the things she'd seen on her way Westward, the daily routine, the purchasing of the new horses and the change in landscape from prairies to mountains to desert.

There were things she left off mentioning, though, especially her feelings for Myles. When she got to the part about needing to continue on alone, she simply shared that an injury to one of her party meant she had to ride the rest of the way to Lillie's by herself. She did tell her father about losing her horse and spraining her ankle, but how in spite of such challenges, she was still able to make it on time to the wedding.

"Lillie looked so beautiful and happy. I wish you could have seen her." Delsie blinked back the sheen of tears the memories brought to her tired eyes. "Clay will take care of her, I can promise you that, and she will care for him. It was wonderful to see them both."

He'd quit his pacing to come stand beside her chair, his hands clasped behind his back. "Thank you for detailing your experience. However…"

Delsie lifted her chin to look at him. "However?"

"You mean to tell me you traveled across the entire country without incident, beyond losing a horse and twisting your ankle?" He narrowed his gaze. "You suffered no other risk to life or limb?"

"No." The word came out no louder than a whisper,

but it carried the weight of all the incidences when she might have been killed. Delsie glanced away.

"Ah, I see. So I am right." Mr. Radford marched away from her chair again. "I need to know everything, Delsie. Please."

She studied her hands. Most of the blisters had long since faded, as had the freckles on her skin from days in the sun, but they looked different from the way they had before she'd left all those weeks ago. They were hands capable of hard work and comfort. Hands that had held those of the man she loved, hands that had been protected by him, as well.

"I nearly fell to my death on a runaway horse," she said, her voice low. "And later, was almost assaulted by a group of trappers. Myles… Mr. Patton…came to my aid both times."

"Is that all?" His tone, though firm, couldn't hide the heartbreak she sensed in him at hearing she'd come so close to being hurt.

Delsie shook her head and gave a humorless laugh. "I took very ill riding through a storm one night and we barely escaped a flash flood in the desert." Telling these accounts, independent of the overall story of her journey, brought home their seriousness in a way she hadn't felt quite as keenly when going through them. "We were also attacked by Indians."

"What?" he barked. "Is that what happened to the rider?"

Memories of that day raced through her mind and Delsie shivered. "Mr. Patton held them off, but he was struck with an arrow in his shoulder."

"And did he…"

Delsie blew out a breath, sharp relief coursing through her once again. "No, he's recovered. Amos told me so in the letter I read tonight."

He returned to his seat, his hands draped loosely between his knees. "Anything else?"

"That's all." Except for her realization that she loved Myles, but there was little point in sharing such news. "And I'm here now—safe and well."

Silence accompanied her words for nearly a minute. Finally her father stirred from his statue-like position to run a hand over his face. Delsie hadn't seen him look so full of despair since the death of her mother.

"What is it?" she asked, kneeling beside him.

He lifted his hands in a helpless gesture. "I had no idea my stubbornness would drive you to do something…so…so dangerous. You might have been killed, Delsie."

She rested her arm on his knee. "But I wasn't. I wouldn't have gone, especially without your permission, if I hadn't felt it was right and that I would somehow make it."

"There's that rock-solid faith again," he murmured, shooting her a patronizing smile.

"Yes, but not just in God. I have faith in you and Lillie, too."

He took her hand inside his and squeezed it. "I was wrong about Lillie. I shouldn't have driven her away like that. But I…" He pressed his mouth into a tight line before continuing, "I feared what might happen to her. If she stayed close by, and married who I thought she should, then I could protect her, keep her safe. Unlike your mother."

"Oh, Papa." She gave his hand a squeeze in return. "You can't keep anything and everything bad from happening, even to those you love. But we can pray and trust in the Lord that He will make all things right in the end. Just as things have been made right this time."

"Have they all been made right?" His searching gaze made Delsie wonder if he could read what she hadn't shared.

She pulled her hand back and turned to rest her back against the settee. "I'm not sure what you mean."

"What happened to those two men?" he asked as he sat back.

"They…um…returned to their jobs at the different Express stations. The one in Kansas and the other in Missouri." She didn't dare look at him, afraid he'd see the longing on her face at the thought of Myles.

"And will you be writing to them?"

The conversation had taken a disastrous turn. Delsie couldn't bear the idea of hearing him say out loud that he didn't approve of Myles, that a marriage to an Express rider from Missouri would mean leaving him without any family nearby.

"I believe I shall correspond with Amos," she said brightly. "He's rather lonely with his wife gone and no children." She stood and shook out her skirt. "I believe I'll retire now. It's been a long day."

Pretending she didn't see his questioning look, she bent and placed a kiss on his cheek. "Good night, Papa. It's wonderful to be home."

"Good night, Delsie." He picked up his neglected book and rubbed at the cover. "Thank you for telling me your story. And for doing what you felt you must to keep the family together."

"You're welcome." She moved toward the door, but she turned when he called her back, her heart jolting with sudden dread.

His attention had returned to the open page. "With all that traveling, are you sure you're content to be home now?" The question sounded innocent enough, though Delsie couldn't help feeling as if he were really asking something else. Something she wasn't ready to voice—perhaps she never would be.

She dipped her head in a decisive nod. "I am here to stay."

# *Chapter Seventeen*

The hot, sticky days of July melted into August and still Delsie couldn't find relief from the incessant heat. She often took to spending time beneath the giant shade tree in the yard, hoping for a breeze, as she helped their gardener with weeding and planting.

She longed for the dry warmth of the West and for more to fill her time than gardening and social calls. A feeling of uselessness permeated nearly every hour of her day. The only bright spots since returning home were exchanging letters with Amos and with Lillie. Her father had even penned a postscript in Delsie's last letter to her sister. A full reconciliation between them not only appeared to be inevitable but likely to happen much sooner than Delsie had thought possible.

Dabbing at her damp forehead with her handkerchief, she stepped into her father's study, where he sat working at his desk. "Here are the household accounts." She'd been keeping them since the death of her mother, when her father had discovered her skill for numbers.

She set the ledgers on his desk, then dropped into one of the chairs opposite his. "I'm so ready for this heat to be over."

He glanced up from writing, his brow furrowed. "You've never been bothered by the summers before."

"No, you're right. But it somehow feels more humid this year."

She glanced out the nearest window at the flowers resting against the glass. The blossoms she'd seen heading West weren't so manicured, but they were no less beautiful. She felt a bit like a wildflower herself these days—transplanted from the open prairie to the confines of a stately garden.

"Is something wrong, Delsie?"

"Hmm?" She turned to look at him.

He sat back in his chair and studied her. "You seem a bit restless, my dear."

She forced a reassuring smile to her lips. "I'll be fine. Truly." Her gaze dropped to the account books. "Though it might be nice to have more to occupy my time than household numbers and gardening and paying visits to our friends."

To her surprise she heard him chuckle. "I thought as much. You've been wandering through the house for weeks like a seaman banished to land."

"I'm sorry." She twisted her handkerchief around her finger, afraid to say more.

"Or maybe," Mr. Radford continued, "like a woman who's lost her heart?"

Delsie jerked her head up. "Whatever do you mean?"

He gave another chuckle and waved away her shock.

"Never mind that now. I have something I'd like you to help me with. A project to occupy your time."

Interest thrummed through Delsie as she scooted her chair closer to his desk. "What sort of project?"

"I would like to open another bank." He shifted some papers on his desk, and thankfully, didn't see the expression of disappointment she felt creep onto her face. "With Flynn doing such an excellent job managing the one here, I'll admit I, too, have felt a bit like a horse put out to pasture."

"Where would you open a new one?" she asked, more out of politeness than genuine curiosity now.

He grinned as he placed a map before her. Delsie studied it, surprised to see the town didn't look exceedingly large. Then she read the name scrawled in the top left corner of the map—Stockton, California. A soft gasp escaped her lips, prompting more laughter from her father.

"You want to build a bank in California? But whatever for?"

"Because I can," he stated simply. "And because my dear, youngest daughter seems to have left her vitality for life somewhere out West." He lifted his hands in mock surrender. "I figured it might be worth discovering what some of the appeal is out there."

Delsie looked at the map again and shook her head in disbelief. "But how would you oversee a bank in California from here?"

Mr. Radford nodded thoughtfully. "An excellent question, one I considered quite a bit when I first conceived the idea. Then I started to think there was nothing still holding you and me here, now that you and Flynn are no longer a possibility."

Her heart began to race as Delsie anticipated what he meant to say next.

"While we have this lovely home and all its memories of your wonderful mother, it doesn't seem to make much sense to remain so far from the rest of our family." He glanced around the study, his expression wistful. "I have carved out a good life here, but perhaps, it's time for both of us to carve a new life somewhere else."

"Do you really mean that, Papa?" Hope beat so wildly inside her it almost hurt. The thought of being closer to Lillie and Clay in a new and exciting place, a place that meant being in closer proximity to the memories Delsie had made with Myles, brought a lump to her throat. While she might not be able to be with him, she could bravely take the path her time with him had opened up for her.

"Of course I mean to go through with this—and quite soon. I'd like the bank built and functional by October. And that's where I need your help, dear daughter." He picked up another large paper. This one appeared to be a drawing of a building instead of a map. "I would like you to oversee the expenditures and plans…of our new home in California."

Twilight filled the sky as Myles dismounted near the stables at Guittard's Station. After passing off the mail to the next rider, he entered the familiar kitchen, but his appetite hadn't been the same since Amos had taken sick. "Evening, Mrs. Guittard," he said to the woman working at the stove.

She turned and smiled at him. "Bonjour, Myles. Supper is almost ready."

"How is he?"

Her face immediately changed from welcome to worry. "He is worse since last week." She stepped closer as she added in a hushed tone, "I don't know that you would have seen him, to say goodbye, if you had come even a day later."

Though he'd suspected as much, the news still hit Myles hard like a punch to the gut. He'd hated seeing Amos waste away these past few weeks. The alert guide who'd traveled with him and Delsie months ago had been reduced to a shell of a man, confined solely to bed.

"Can I see him, before supper?"

"Of course, of course."

Myles nodded his appreciation and slipped back out the door. Elijah had been waiting for him and dropped to his shoulder as Myles walked past the stable to a lone, small cabin. Knocking softly, he didn't wait for Amos's reply but simply entered. A good fire burned in the fireplace, blocking out the October chill that sharpened the air outside.

Myles placed the single chair next to the bed where Amos slept. Elijah alighted on a peg near the door. The similarities between this moment and Myles's time in the desert after being shot with the arrow struck him sharply with its irony. Only this time it was him keeping a vigil at Amos's bedside, instead of the other way around.

Raspy breathing filled the quiet cabin. Myles studied his friend's face. Gray whiskers covered the thinning lines. "Amos?" he called softly.

Amos slowly opened his eyes and blinked. "Myles," he said in a hoarse voice. "You're here. I was just thinking about you."

"You were?" Tears burned his eyelids. He wasn't ready to say goodbye to someone else he cared about.

"Lots to tell you." Amos lifted a trembling hand and pointed at the table behind Myles.

He turned to see the supper tray there. "Are you hungry?"

Amos gave a slight shake of his head. "No, the letter."

An envelope sat near the tray. Myles picked it up and handed it to Amos.

"No," Amos rasped out. "Look who it's from and where."

Myles glanced at the name and address and felt his heart stop for a brief moment. The letter was from Delsie, which wasn't surprising. He'd known she and Amos were corresponding. But the address penned beneath her name wasn't from Pennsylvania. It was from California.

A scraping noise came from Amos. It took Myles a second to realize it was a laugh. "She and her father moved...to California."

"When?"

"End of last month."

Questions fired through Myles's mind, too many to burden Amos with. "Whatever for?" he managed to get out.

"Her father opened a bank there. Wanted to be closer to Delsie's sister in Oregon."

Delsie was no longer in Pennsylvania? She was living out West—where Myles had longed to live for months now. Was it possible this renewed his chances to be with her? He mentally shook his head—he was still a lowly Express rider with limited means to provide for a wife.

"Well, good for her." Myles set the letter back on the table. While shocking, the news still didn't change their impossible situation.

Amos studied him, his gaze more alert than Myles had seen it in weeks. "You need to go there, too, and start your ranch." He started to cough, but he shook off Myles's offer of a drink from the cup on the tray. When he'd finished, he continued, "You go find her and marry her. She loves you still, Myles. And I know you love her."

He ran a hand over his jaw. If only things could be that easy. "That's all well and good, Amos, but I don't have the kind of money I need to build a ranch right now." Boarding Moses at the livery stable all summer and into autumn had eaten into his savings.

"There's something else." Amos coughed again, his face contorting with the pain. Myles looked away. He hated the feeling of helplessness stirring within him. "I know I'm not your pa." The words brought Myles's head back around and renewed the watering in his eyes. "But you, and Delsie, have been the closest thing to a family for me."

Myles reached out and clasped Amos's pale hand. "You've been like a father to me." It was the first time he'd admitted out loud how much Amos's friendship had meant in his life. Myles was better because of knowing this honest, hardworking man of faith for the past seven years.

Amos's mouth curved up into a slight smile. "That's good. 'Cause I got something to give you."

"What is it?" Probably his gun. The older man had already given Delsie his prized pocket watch.

"It's under the floorboards, beneath the bed."

Myles bent and peered under the bed. The space looked rather small. "All right." Lowering himself onto his stomach, he felt around until his fingers touched a hole in the wood. Myles pulled up on the board and it lifted.

"Inside is a knapsack," Amos said.

Moving more by feel than sight, Myles managed to wrestle the sack from the space beneath the floor. He crawled back out from under the bed, brushing dust from his hair and shirt.

Amos caught his eye and nodded. "Open it."

He sat back down and lifted the flap of the sack. Bundles of cash filled the entire satchel. He released a startled laugh. "You rob a bank or something, Amos?"

Another raspy chuckle came from the ailing man. "No. That was earned, from honest work, over the last twenty-something years."

"I don't understand." Myles had assumed Amos was paid as much as the rest of the Pony Express workers, but there had to be at least five or six hundred dollars sitting inside this bag.

"Me and the missus lived simply and we saved."

Amos gestured to the bag. "I want you to have it, Myles. All one thousand and ten dollars of it."

Myles gaped at the money, hardly daring to believe. "But…"

Amos shook his head. "It's for your ranch. Yours and Delsie's."

The words sunk deep into Myles's heart, setting hope to burn anew inside him. "Is this what you meant back in that burned-down cabin in the desert? About the Lord working in mysterious ways?"

Some of the old spark returned to Amos's gaunt countenance. "Maybe it was. Can't think of much more mysterious ways than the Lord blessing you through the riches from one old station worker."

The tears were getting harder and harder to resist. "I can't thank you enough, Amos. But why now?"

"It's time," Amos murmured, his look full of double meaning.

Myles set down the bag and reached for his friend's hand again. "What do you mean, old man? You're tough and stubborn. You'll weather this."

"Not this time." Amos patted Myles's hand in a gesture to comfort him. "You are a credit to your father, Myles. And I'm proud to call you my friend."

Amos's words sounded similar to the ones Delsie had told him four months earlier. Did she really still love him? Could he win her hand once he had his horse ranch running? Everything about his future was changing—again—and it both thrilled and terrified him.

"If you hurry back to Saint Joe," Amos continued in a voice growing weaker by the minute, "you can get Moses and head West in time to avoid most of the snow."

"I will, but not tonight." He wouldn't leave Amos yet.

Amos closed his eyes. "You don't have to stay."

Myles squeezed the man's hand once, then released it. "Yes, I do."

He let Amos sleep, his mind awhirl with plans and thoughts for how quickly he could find land and horses and start building stables, corrals and a house. When Amos woke again, he asked for a little water, but nothing more, insisting Myles eat the food. Myles obliged, though he couldn't stomach much. What he didn't eat, he shared with Elijah.

Sometime later, he jerked away, aware of the sudden silence and cold. He jumped up and stoked the fire, then moved back to his chair. "Amos?" he said, leaning forward.

The older man's rattling breaths had ceased. His chest no longer rose and fell, and his face appeared relaxed as if in peaceful slumber.

"Amos." Myles's voice broke as the tears he'd held back so long broke free of his restraint. "Goodbye, old man." He gripped Amos's lined hand one last time. "You will be missed."

He knew he ought to go tell Mrs. Guittard the news and see what needed to be done to bury Amos properly. But instead of moving he simply sat, staring at the wall for some time, remembering. Memories of Charles, Amos and Delsie filled his thoughts. He'd had to say goodbye to the three people he cared for most in the world. But one of them might still be waiting for him.

Fresh energy coursed through Myles. He shouldered the sack of money Amos had gifted him and climbed to his feet. "Come on, Elijah. We've got things to take care of." The bird flew to his shoulder as he stepped out of the cabin.

The darkness outside had begun to recede, which meant morning was fast approaching. His future, one made possible by God and the generosity of Hank Amos, awaited him. And with a great amount of work, and even greater faith, perhaps a beautiful dark-haired woman waited for him, too.

*California, June 1861*

"Morning, Miss Radford." The general-store owner, a Mr. Jasper, smiled at Delsie from behind the long counter. "Here for your weekly letter?"

Delsie nodded. "I have one to post to Lillie, as well."

True to their word, she and Lillie had faithfully written each other, almost every week, since last year. Delsie expected the news any day now that she was an aunt. Had Lillie given birth to her and Clay's first child this week?

She paid to mail her letter and accepted the one Mr. Jasper handed her in return. Before she could tear it open, though, the man spoke again. "That hat you ordered last month came in today." He lifted a hatbox onto the counter and opened the lid.

Peeking inside, Delsie smiled. Her father had insisted she order a new hat from back East for her birthday the month before. Twenty years old now. She could hardly believe it still. While she might have felt ancient at such an age, and unmarried, back in the parlors of Pennsylvania, out West she felt as young as ever. With her whole life ahead of her.

She was content and happy with her life here in California, save for one thing. Her smile faltered a little at the thought. There had been something—or rather someone—she'd really wanted to see for her birthday, silly as it was.

Delsie closed her mind to the foolish hope of once more seeing a certain dark-eyed, dark-haired horseman. Instead she focused her attention on the blue hat before her.

Lifting the creation out of the box, she admired the stacked folds of velvet and the gorgeous white feathers. It was the loveliest creation she'd seen in ages. Although she'd heard from her father, one of the town's most successful bankers, they were to get a milliner here soon, so perhaps fashionable hats would be much easier to come by in the future.

"It's beautiful," she said with sincerity.

Mr. Jasper beamed as if he himself had fashioned the hat. The idea of the white-haired man with spectacles constructing a delicate lady's hat made Delsie choke back a laugh.

"Thank you, Mr. Jasper. I'll see you next week." Looping the string of the hatbox around her wrist, she let herself out the door. She paused on the wooden walkaway outside to tear open her letter from Lillie. Her eyes quickly took in the first few lines until she found what she'd been hoping to read for days.

"I'm an aunt," she whispered to herself, "to a healthy baby boy."

Her earlier bright smile returned to her face. She would hurry to the bank to tell her father that he had a grandson. Delsie kept reading as she walked down the sidewalk, completely absorbed in Lillie's words.

So intent was her gaze and concentration on the paper in her hand that she didn't see the person in front of her until she bumped into a solid shoulder. "I'm so sorry," she murmured, without lifting her eyes. "Please excuse me." She moved a step or two past the stranger.

"I'm guessing that fancy getup you're wearing means you can read," a deep voice intoned.

Delsie froze, her chin snapping up in surprise. That voice; those words. She lowered the letter to her side and pivoted slowly. Her pulse pounded rapidly even before she caught sight of the man's bearded face beneath the shadow of his hat.

"Myles?" The name sounded more like a breathless squeak than anything else.

He removed his hat and smiled at her. That slow, full smile that had the power to weaken her legs beneath her, even after all this time. "Hello, Delsie."

"Wh-what are you doing here?" She glanced around at the other people, who were filing past them as though this were any ordinary day. But it wasn't. The man she'd loved and missed for nearly a year now stood close enough that she could smell soap and sun and leather on him.

"That's a rather long story. But if you'd care to take a buggy ride with me, I'd be more than happy to tell it." He pointed with his hat to where a shiny black rig and a horse—*could that be Moses?*—stood waiting half a block down the street.

Delsie stared at him in silence, her mind trying to keep up with the reality that Myles was here, asking to take her on a buggy ride.

"If you'd rather not…" He threw her a concerned look and put his hat back on.

"No, no." She shook herself from her stunned stupor. "I would love to, very much. Although, I need to ask my father first. If it's all right…to go."

Myles smiled again, this time in obvious relief. "Fine by me."

"He owns one of the banks. It's not far from here."

"Lead the way."

Delsie began walking, but she kept shooting glances at Myles every few steps. He was really here—alive, well and still incredibly handsome.

Myles laughed. "You're looking at me like you did when I told you I didn't have any sidesaddles for your Express horse."

"Am I?" A blush warmed her cheeks, but she laughed at the memory. Had it really been an entire year since their journey West together? Back in Myles's presence again, the time had shrunk to almost nothing. "I heard about Amos. Mrs. Guittard was kind enough to write and tell me."

"I was with him, at the end," Myles said quietly. "He was the best of men."

"There are still days I think of writing him, only to remember he's no longer with us."

"I've done the same." He placed his hand on her elbow to steer her around a group of women talking in the center of the sidewalk. The touch sent immediate warmth cascading from Delsie's arm to her toes. Oh, how she'd missed him.

When they reached the bank, Myles held the door open for her. Delsie thanked him and slipped inside. What would her father say about Myles? Would he approve of him? Seeing him again had only confirmed the feelings she'd tucked away, but she wasn't sure if Owen Radford would still harbor objections of having an Express rider as a potential son-in-law. Her heart renewed its pounding.

"I'm here to see my father," she told the clerk, then she knocked lightly on the door of his personal office.

"Come in," Mr. Radford called from inside.

Delsie smiled over her shoulder at Myles, with more reassurance than she felt, and entered. "Morning, Papa."

"Done at the general store already?" He stood and came around his desk. "I see the new hat you ordered came in."

"Yes. Thank you." She'd forgotten all about the hatbox. She set it on one of the chairs drawn up to the desk. "I have something to ask and someone to—"

Mr. Radford approached Myles and held out his hand. "Mr. Patton, a pleasure to see you again."

Delsie's mouth fell open as she watched the two men shake hands and exchange pleasantries. "But... how do you...?" She glanced from one man to the other, completely baffled. "Myles is the Express rider, Papa, who helped me..."

"Ah. I suspected as much." A spark of amusement lit his green eyes. "Mr. Patton is also the owner of The

B and P Ranch, located about an hour north of here. I've been helping him with his banking needs for a few months now."

"Y-you have your ranch now?" Delsie sank into the empty chair, her mind so full of confusion she could hardly formulate her words. "And my father… You've known him…for…for several months?"

Myles shot her a contrite look. "I promise to explain everything, Delsie. But first…" He turned back to her father. "Do I have your permission, sir, to take your daughter for a buggy ride? I'd like to show her my ranch."

Grinning, Mr. Radford nodded. "Certainly." He bent and kissed Delsie on the cheek. "Have a nice time. I myself have been hoping to see Mr. Patton's spread one of these days."

Woodenly Delsie stood. Her gaze fell to the letter still clutched in her hand. "I almost forgot. You're a grandfather, Papa. Lillie had her baby. A boy."

His grin spread even wider. "Wonderful news. I will write her my congratulations right away." He returned to his desk as Delsie stepped to the door. She looked expectantly at Myles, but he made no move to follow.

"There's something else I'd like to ask your father, before we go. If that's all right?"

She lifted her shoulders in a most unladylike shrug, but she could hardly keep up with all the revelations this morning. Waving absently to her father, she exited the office and shut the door behind her. A nearby chair provided another welcome refuge for her unsteady feet.

How had she not seen Myles around town before now? More important, why had he waited so long before coming to see her? She tamped down her bewilderment, and the accompanying flicker of disappointment, with the reminder that he'd promised to tell her everything. Hopefully, that meant today, during their ride.

*At least Papa seems to approve of him*, Delsie thought with an astonished laugh. First the news she was an aunt, then seeing Myles again after so long and now learning Owen Radford knew him. It was almost too much to take in.

The door to her father's office opened and Myles walked out. "Ready?"

"Yes. Very much." Delsie rose to her feet. Myles once again took her elbow in hand, re-creating the warm tingly feeling inside her, and gently directed her out of the bank and to his waiting buggy.

"Remember Moses?" he asked as he handed her onto the seat.

Delsie settled onto the pristine leather. "Of course. I thought I recognized him."

Myles gathered the reins and clucked to Moses. Within minutes they were moving down the street, heading for the edge of town. Myles's arm rested firmly against Delsie's, but she made no effort to scoot away. The feeling of comfort and safety she'd so often felt in his presence wrapped itself around her now, and she couldn't bear to shatter it by moving.

"I'm guessing you have a few questions," he said once they'd left the town's buildings behind.

"Just a few," she teased.

He shot her a smile, which resurrected the rapid thrumming of her pulse.

Delsie leaned back against the seat. When was the last time she'd felt this content? Probably not since she'd left Myles, wounded, in the desert. "Why don't you tell me everything that's happened since last summer and I'll throw in the questions as needed?"

"Fair enough." He turned to look at her. "I suppose Amos already told you about my recovering from that arrow and making our way back East?"

Delsie nodded.

Myles faced forward again. "I wasn't sure if I still had a job waiting or not."

"But you did?" She already knew the answer, but she wanted to be sure she hadn't caused him any trouble.

"Yes. That wasn't the only thing waiting for me, though." He cast a sideways glance at her and grinned. "Cynthia came to see me the day I got back to Saint Joe."

The wealthy woman he'd cared about for years? A worm of fear uncurled inside Delsie. "What did she want?"

Myles chuckled. "She actually wanted me back. Told me she was bored with her captain and would use some of her inheritance to help fund my ranch."

The fear grew a little more. "What did you say?"

His eyebrows rose as if he found her question as ludicrous as he did amusing. "I told her no, in the kindest way possible. I knew I didn't care for her in that way and I never would."

Delsie released the breath she'd been holding. Her stomach relaxed, too. "Still, the promise of all that money…"

"Not worth it," Myles said in a firm tone. "After that I continued riding for a few months, until Amos took sick." He licked his lips as if the memory was still a bit raw. Delsie could relate. "It was the night he passed that he gave me something. Something that changed everything for me."

"What?"

Myles shifted the reins to his left hand and reached over to take her hand in his right. The memory of his strong but gentle grip filled her thoughts and her fingers. She hadn't believed she would ever feel his hand in hers again.

"Apparently Amos had saved a considerable amount of money through the years, in addition to the money you gave us." His low voice was tinged with deferential awe. "And since he had no other family, he gave it all…to me." He twisted to face her. "He had over a thousand dollars stuffed inside a knapsack, Delsie."

"A thousand dollars?" She gasped. "Is that what you used for your ranch?"

Nodding, he lifted her hand and kissed her gloved knuckles. "He told me to come West and set up the ranch. Then I was to find you."

Delsie swallowed the lump forming in her throat. Even without her voicing it aloud, Amos had known she hadn't stopped loving Myles. "But how long have you been here? Why you didn't come—" she blushed again "—sooner?"

He rested their joined hands on his knee and gave a self-deprecating laugh. "Believe me, I wanted to. Dozens of times. Especially when I first arrived last October." A reassuring squeeze of her fingers seemed to attest to his sincerity. "But I wanted to have the land and some of the horses purchased and the stables and house begun before I sought you out. I wanted to prove to you that I could get a ranch established."

"I never doubted you, Myles." She placed her other hand on top of his. "So when did you meet my father?" She still couldn't believe he and Myles had not only met one another but seemed to have a good rapport, too.

"I first visited his bank back in February. Though I had to make certain his daughter wasn't in the vicinity beforehand." He threw her a sheepish grin. "I would have waited to meet him until I saw you again, but I figured I could use the financial advice. And I didn't think it would hurt to let him warm up to the idea of me, either."

Delsie laughed. "Yes, that was probably wise. What did he say when you told him you were the Express rider who conveyed me to California?"

"I only told him last week," Myles admitted. "But you know, he didn't seem as surprised as I thought he might after I confessed to knowing you already."

Smiling, Delsie brushed hair from her eyes and studied the scenery around them. She'd come to love this valley surrounded by hills and so different from what she'd known in Pennsylvania, though gorgeous in its own right, too.

So her father had guessed at her feelings for Myles. She'd thought herself clever for keeping them a secret, but he knew her better than she suspected. A sudden thought had her turning to Myles again. "What was it you asked him, before we left? Did it have to do with your ranch?"

"Sort of." His dark eyes reflected hidden amusement. "All in good time, darling."

It was the same endearment he'd called her the last time she'd seen him. Too happy to press him further, at least for the moment, she rested her head on his shoulder.

A few minutes later, he tugged her arm. "There's the ranch, Delsie."

She lifted her head as he drove the buggy between two large corrals, one on either side of the road. A few horses grazed in the left, while a number of foals and their mothers watched them from the one on the right. Straight ahead sat a white two-story house with a wide veranda that ran along the front and sides. Behind it Delsie could just make out a good-sized barn. A carved sign above the porch indicated the property's name in scrolled letters—The B and P Ranch.

"Oh, Myles, it's beautiful," she said as he helped her from the buggy.

He smiled, his expression full of pride. "Finished it last week. We'll start on a bunkhouse soon, though it might be some time before we fill it."

"We?" She followed him toward the house, her hand still tucked inside his, and up the porch steps.

"I hired a young fellow, Joe Cunningham, to help me build the house. He's real good with woodworking and has a knack for horses, too."

Delsie glanced at the two rocking chairs that faced the yard from one side of the veranda. "Did he make those?" She started toward the chairs to examine the handiwork, but Myles gently pulled her toward the front door.

"We'll look at those in a minute. I want to show you the house first."

The inside was sparsely furnished, except for the kitchen and an upstairs bedroom, but Delsie could easily see the potential in each of the rooms. Windows let in plenty of natural light and allowed views of the surrounding valley and hills from nearly every angle.

After the tour, Myles showed her the large barn. There were plenty of stalls to accommodate the many horses.

"I already sold several of the foals to folks in town," he said as they walked back to the front yard.

Delsie took in the beauty once more, shaking her head in wonderment. "It's all so lovely, Myles. You've done a fine job."

He grinned, then tipped his head in the direction of the porch. "I've one last thing for you to see." Still holding her hand, he steered her up the steps again and over to the rocking chairs. "I had Joe carve these. They're identical except for one thing."

Delsie released his hand to run her fingers along the smooth wooden arms and up the intricately carved spindles at the back. "They're gorgeous."

"Try it out," Myles prompted.

With a laugh, she complied. The seat, though elaborate in decoration, was still comfortable. She leaned her head back and shut her eyes. Rocking the chair with the toe of her boot, she let the gentle morning breeze caress her cheeks as she released a sigh of peace. "I don't think I want to leave."

"I don't want you to, either."

The huskiness of his tone made her open her eyes. He watched her intently, making her heart stutter faster.

"Did you figure out the difference between the two chairs?"

The question took her by surprise. "Oh. Let's see." She studied both rocking chairs, but she couldn't identify any dissimilarities. "I can't see anything."

Myles pointed to the back of the other chair. There in the wood an *M* had been carved, in the same delicate scroll style as the ranch sign.

Delsie twisted to look at the back of the chair she sat in. Instead of an *M*, this chair had a *D* carved into it. One tiny letter, but she knew its significance at once.

Her gaze met Myles's and she did her best to suppress the smile attempting to break through. "I'd say you're rather confident of yourself, aren't you, Myles Patton?"

He knelt in front of her and reclaimed her hand. "I thought I'd take a chance," he murmured. He placed another kiss on her knuckles. "Kind of like you did all those months ago with an ornery Express rider."

"Is that all you remember?" She couldn't contain her smile any longer. "I remember meeting a good, honest, handsome Express rider. Who—" she waved her free hand "—on occasion might have been…a little grumpy."

Myles laughed, the sound deep and happy and sweeter than anything Delsie could remember hearing in a long time. "All I can say is I'm glad I didn't turn you down that day. And I'm hoping—" he lifted her other hand in his and gently tugged her to her feet "—that you won't turn me down, either. Because I have something to ask you, Miss Delsie Radford."

Delsie's pulse began galloping again. "Yes?"

"With your father's permission and blessing..."

Her eyes widened as she suddenly realized what he'd asked her father earlier. And what his answer had been.

"Will you do me the honor of becoming my wife?" Myles turned her hands over and placed a kiss against each palm of her gloves. "There's no one else in this world I would rather have riding and working and raising a family right alongside me. I love you, Delsie. I think I've loved you since that first time I watched you straddle that horse, with that determined look in those beautiful eyes."

Tears of happiness blurred Myles's rugged face for a moment. These were the words she'd waited more than a year to hear, words she'd long given up hope of ever hearing from this man. "I love you, too."

"So what do you say?" He bent forward, touching his forehead to hers. "Will you marry me?"

There was no hesitation; no need to consider. Delsie knew exactly what she wanted. "Yes, Myles," she said with a full smile. "A hundred times over, yes."

The grin he offered her, right before tucking her hands around his neck, made her stomach pitch with pleasure. Then his lips met hers in a kiss that filled her head to toe with happiness.

In that moment, Delsie recognized she'd at last reached the end of the trail she'd embarked on a year ago with Myles. Only it wasn't really an ending. This was just the beginning and this time her journey would not be as the Express rider's lady—this time it would be as his wife.

\* \* \* \* \*

## WE HOPE YOU ENJOYED
## THIS BOOK FROM

# LOVE INSPIRED
### INSPIRATIONAL ROMANCE

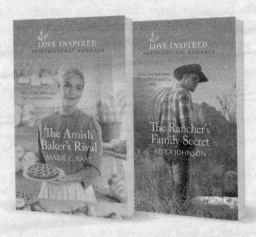

*Uplifting stories of faith, forgiveness and hope.*

Fall in love with stories where faith helps
guide you through life's challenges, and discover
the promise of a new beginning.

**6 NEW BOOKS AVAILABLE EVERY MONTH!**

LIHALO2021

## SPECIAL EXCERPT FROM

❧

# LOVE INSPIRED
### INSPIRATIONAL ROMANCE

*After a traumatic brain injury, military vet
Behr Delgado refuses the one thing that could help
him—a service dog. But charity head Ellery Watson
knows the dog she selected will improve his quality of
life and vows to work with him one-on-one. When their
personal lives entwine with their professional lives, can
they trust each other long enough to both heal?*

*Read on for a sneak peek at*
The Veteran's Vow *by Jill Lynn!*

Ellery approached and held out Margo's leash for him. She was so excited he was doing better. The thought of disappointing her cut Behr like a combat knife.

Margo stood by Ellery's side, her chocolate face toggling back and forth between them, questioning what she was supposed to do next. Waiting for his lead.

Behr reached out and took the leash. If Ellery noticed his shaking hand, she didn't say anything.

"I want to teach her to stand by your left side. That's it. She's just going to be there. We're going to take it slow." Ellery moved to Behr's left, leaving enough room for Margo to stand between them.

A tremble echoed through him, and Behr tensed his muscles in an effort to curb it.

Margo, on the other hand, would be the first image if someone searched the internet for the definition of the word *calm*.

"Heel." When he gave Margo the command and she obeyed, taking that spot, Behr's heart just about ricocheted out of his chest.

This effort was worth it. Was it, though? He could get through life off-kilter, running into things, tripping, leaving items on the floor when they fell, willing his poor coordination to work instead of using Margo to create balance for him or grasp or retrieve things for him, couldn't he?

Ellery didn't say anything about his audible inhales or exhales, but she had to know what he was up to. The weakness that plagued Behr rose up to ridicule him. It was hard to reveal this side of himself to Ellery, not that she hadn't seen it already. Hard to know that he couldn't just snap his fingers and make his body right again. Hard to remember that he needed this dog and that was why his mom and sisters had signed him up for one.

"You're doing great." Ellery's focus was on Behr, but Margo's tail wagged as if the compliment had been directed at her.

They both laughed, and the tension dissipated like a deployment care package.

"You, too, girl." Ellery offered Margo a treat. "Do you want me to put the balance harness on her so you can feel what it's like?" she asked Behr.

He gave one determined nod.

Ellery strode over to the storage cabinets that lined the back wall. She returned with the harness and knelt to slide it on Margo and adjust it. Behr should probably be watching how to do the same, but right now he was concentrating on standing next to Margo and not having his knees liquefy.

Ellery stood. "See what you think."

Behr gripped the handle, his knuckles turning white. The handle was the right height, and it did make him feel sturdy. Supported.

Like the woman beaming at him from the other side of the dog.

*Don't miss*
The Veteran's Vow *by Jill Lynn,*
*available March 2022 wherever*
*Love Inspired books and ebooks are sold.*

LoveInspired.com

Copyright © 2022 by Jill Buteyn

LIEXP0122B

**IF YOU ENJOYED THIS BOOK, DON'T MISS NEW EXTENDED-LENGTH NOVELS FROM LOVE INSPIRED!**

**In addition to the Love Inspired books you know and love, we're excited to introduce even more uplifting stories in a longer format, with more inspiring fresh starts and page-turning thrills!**

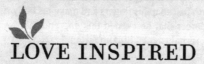

# LOVE INSPIRED

*Stories to uplift and inspire.*

Fall in love with Love Inspired—inspirational and uplifting stories of faith and hope. Find strength and comfort in the bonds of friendship and community. Revel in the warmth of possibility, and the promise of new beginnings.

**LOOK FOR THESE LOVE INSPIRED TITLES ONLINE AND IN THE BOOK DEPARTMENT OF YOUR FAVORITE RETAILER!**

LITRADE1221

# LOVE INSPIRED

*Stories to uplift and inspire*

Fall in love with Love Inspired—
inspirational and uplifting stories of faith
and hope. Find strength and comfort in
the bonds of friendship and community.
Revel in the warmth of possibility and the
promise of new beginnings.

Sign up for the Love Inspired newsletter
at **LoveInspired.com** to be the first
to find out about upcoming titles,
special promotions and exclusive content.

## CONNECT WITH US AT:

Facebook.com/LoveInspiredBooks

Twitter.com/LoveInspiredBks

LISOCIAL2021

# Get 4 FREE REWARDS!

## We'll send you 2 FREE Books plus 2 FREE Mystery Gifts.

**Love Inspired** books feature uplifting stories where faith helps guide you through life's challenges and discover the promise of a new beginning.

FREE Value Over $20

**YES!** Please send me 2 FREE Love Inspired Romance novels and my 2 FREE mystery gifts (gifts are worth about $10 retail). After receiving them, if I don't wish to receive any more books, I can return the shipping statement marked "cancel." If I don't cancel, I will receive 6 brand-new novels every month and be billed just $5.24 each for the regular-print edition or $5.99 each for the larger-print edition in the U.S., or $5.74 each for the regular-print edition or $6.24 each for the larger-print edition in Canada. That's a savings of at least 13% off the cover price. It's quite a bargain! Shipping and handling is just 50¢ per book in the U.S. and $1.25 per book in Canada.* I understand that accepting the 2 free books and gifts places me under no obligation to buy anything. I can always return a shipment and cancel at any time. The free books and gifts are mine to keep no matter what I decide.

Choose one:  ☐ Love Inspired Romance Regular-Print (105/305 IDN GNWC)  ☐ Love Inspired Romance Larger-Print (122/322 IDN GNWC)

Name (please print)

Address                                                                                          Apt. #

City                                      State/Province                          Zip/Postal Code

Email: Please check this box ☐ if you would like to receive newsletters and promotional emails from Harlequin Enterprises ULC and its affiliates. You can unsubscribe anytime.

### Mail to the Harlequin Reader Service:
**IN U.S.A.:** P.O. Box 1341, Buffalo, NY 14240-8531
**IN CANADA:** P.O. Box 603, Fort Erie, Ontario L2A 5X3

Want to try 2 free books from another series! Call 1-800-873-8635 or visit www.ReaderService.com.

*Terms and prices subject to change without notice. Prices do not include sales taxes, which will be charged (if applicable) based on your state or country of residence. Canadian residents will be charged applicable taxes. Offer not valid in Quebec. This offer is limited to one order per household. Books received may not be as shown. Not valid for current subscribers to Love Inspired Romance books. All orders subject to approval. Credit or debit balances in a customer's account(s) may be offset by any other outstanding balance owed by or to the customer. Please allow 4 to 6 weeks for delivery. Offer available while quantities last.

**Your Privacy**—Your information is being collected by Harlequin Enterprises ULC, operating as Harlequin Reader Service. For a complete summary of the information we collect, how we use this information and to whom it is disclosed, please visit our privacy notice located at corporate.harlequin.com/privacy-notice. From time to time we may also exchange your personal information with reputable third parties. If you wish to opt out of this sharing of your personal information, please visit readerservice.com/consumerschoice or call 1-800-873-8635. **Notice to California Residents**—Under California law, you have specific rights to control and access your data. For more information on these rights and how to exercise them, visit corporate.harlequin.com/california-privacy.

LIR21R2